Totally Bound Publishing books by C.J. Burright

Music, Love and Other Miseries
Every Kiss
Every Minute
Every Breath

I0526279

Music, Love and Other Miseries

EVERY BREATH

C.J. BURRIGHT

Every Breath
ISBN # 978-1-83943-856-1
©Copyright C.J. Burright 2020
Cover Art by Erin Dameron-Hill ©Copyright February 2020
Interior text design by Claire Siemaszkiewicz
Totally Bound Publishing

EVERY BREATH

Dedication

To Jack, my own personal Garret…minus the music skills and with a whole heap of ninja clown talent.

Chapter One

Weddings suck. Gia Hellman trailed her finger around the rim of her second-round wine glass and tried not to feel jealous or sorry for herself.

Endless strings of twinkling white lights peppered the country club's vaulted ceiling with imitation starlight. Soft, sublime, romantic music performed by professional musicians, all friends of the groom, blended perfectly with the sweet scent of roses lacing the summer air. The food made her wish she had an appetite instead of the twisting pit in her stomach.

In the center of the dance floor, her best friend Adara melted into her new husband. She'd never seen Dar so happy. The fact that anti-romance Dar had followed through with a formal wedding ceremony and until-death vows should've made Gia all weepy in a good way.

It should be me.

She slouched in the cushioned chair and rested her chin in her hand. It wasn't that she wanted Dar's husband, Garret. It was the 'happily ever after' fantasy she wanted, would have had by now if fate hadn't been an unfeeling witch. But her 'happily ever after' had vanished a little over two years before, when the love of her life had been ripped from the world too soon.

Joey. He was irreplaceable.

"Dance with me, Ms. Hellman." The smooth, low voice brushed her ear and sent tendrils of warmth through her, more intoxicating than the wine in her bloodstream.

Gia twisted in her seat and lifted her gaze to the ridiculously sexy man standing behind her, his hand out, waiting with annoying confidence. He knew she wouldn't say no, even though she absolutely should. Ian O'Connor was her co-worker and the off-limits man of her darkest fantasies — breaker of hearts, hater of love, lawyer for the right price. And the groom's oldest friend. Avoiding him was impossible, resisting him a full-time pursuit.

"Have you already made your way through the throngs of willing women?" She batted her eyelashes. "Must be a new record."

"I strive for perfection." Ian's cool, blue eyes gleamed, his hand still out, expectant. The lights danced in his dark hair and gave his every line a magical edge. He always looked good, but in a tuxedo, the tie loosened at a rakish angle? *Devastating.* "You can't blame me, Princess. I had to do something to make the time pass while you made your own, more elegant way through the ranks of men slavering on your heels, waiting their turn to cop a feel."

"Classy." She set her glass on the table and stood, facing him. "All my dance partners tonight have been nothing but respectful." Gia planted a hand on her cocked hip and lifted an eyebrow. "Not all guys are like you, Sugarpop."

His smile was pure wolf. "No wonder you look bored out of your mind."

She sighed and slipped her hand into his, ignoring the tingles that ran up her arm at the contact. Dwelling on them would only bring trouble, and she'd had enough man trouble for a lifetime. "One dance. That's it."

"One is perfect," he murmured, pulling her close to his side as he led her onto the dance floor.

One. She repeated the word in her head instead of dragging in a full breath of Ian's spicy cologne. One was his rule. One night, no more. One night of fun, then on to the next woman who wanted nothing more than casual. There seemed to be an endless supply of women who'd settle for a single hookup with Ian O'Connor.

But she wasn't fling material, not anymore. Still, as he slid his arms around her and pulled her tight against his solid heat, it was hard to remember why.

"Nice dress." His breath caressed her earlobe as he skimmed his fingers over her bare shoulders, drifting all the way to the base of her spine. "At least Adara and I agree on one thing—this dress, on *you*. Off would be even better."

The responsive shiver was impossible to hide, so she narrowed her eyes at him. "Careful, O'Connor. She hasn't officially lifted the ban on you."

Nearly a year and a half before, Gia had drunk one too many margaritas at the annual law firm Christmas party, and in her state of missing-Joey inebriation, she'd been too weak to resist Ian's charms. Adara had come to her rescue, ripped Ian a new one, reminded Gia why she should stop at two margaritas and the Ian Threat Act had been established.

"It's a risk I'm willing to take." His focus flicked to where Adara slow-danced with Garret, oblivious to the outside world.

Gia kept her gaze on the dancing couple, the pit in her stomach expanding. The last thing she'd expected was Adara dealing with Joey's death before her, let alone finding her true love and getting hitched. When Joey had fallen sick, he'd made Gia promise to drag Adara out of solitude — a brother's desperate way of looking out for his introverted older sister when he would no longer be around to do it. Now her vow to Joey and her obligation to Adara were finished, and instead of being happy, a longing for what used to be rose from the deep, unstoppable.

That was why she couldn't keep up the fling routine. She wanted what she'd had with Joey again — more than a mere physical connection, to be someone else's favorite person. She wanted to find someone who made her sun shine brighter, even in the rain, to give her heart to the man who deserved it, a man who had enough sense to notice her excellent taste in shoes.

Basically, the full-price fairy tale, with no discounts.

She slid her hand from Ian's sculpted shoulder to the hard curve of his biceps, a last, torturous hurrah. She was tired of falling for halfway. She wanted it all, and no matter how he made her neurons sing, surrendering to Ian's charms was another dead-end. She had to escape before his melody became an orchestra her body couldn't deny.

"Thanks for the dance." She tried to twirl free of his hold, but he tightened his arms around her. Planting her palms on his firm chest, her push was weak, ineffective. "Gotta go."

"That was only an eighth of a dance, at best." His fingers were spread over her bare back, warm skin on skin, holding her gently captive. "Don't short-change me, Princess."

"Oh look, it's Karen from accounting." She pointed over his shoulder at some random wedding guest who definitely wasn't Karen. "She's asking for you."

"Karen can wait." Not falling for it, he brought his mouth closer, close enough that his breath mingled with hers. "You pressed against me is all that matters for the next two minutes."

She couldn't resist a smile. "Two minutes? That's it?"

"Two minutes is all I need to convince you that the next twenty-four hours should be spent with me...in bed. On the couch, the stairs, the counter..." He brought his lips dangerously close to her jaw. "I promise my hands are slow, my tongue enchanting and, as for the rest of me" — he brushed her earlobe with his nose — "the best things are only definable through experience."

She let her eyelids droop as tingles swirled in the emptiness inside. It would be so easy to surrender just for one night, let Ian work his magic, make her forget. Her gaze drifted to the happily married couple. Adara smiled at something Garret whispered in her ear, her smile so much like Joey's that Gia's throat closed. She ripped from Ian's hold.

"Have to pee." Without looking at him, she escaped the wedding party before she exploded, nabbing her wine glass along the way. She swept through the open double doors and into the hallway, her sparkly silver stilettos clicking a quick cadence on the tile, the raven skirts of her taffeta dress swishing against her legs, while the corseted bodice made it hard for her to breathe. *Leave it to Dar to choose black as one of her wedding colors — Gothic matrimony at its finest.*

She smiled politely at a wedding guest coming the other way and propelled her feet into the banquet room, where vows had been said and lives forever joined. Red rose petals still flanked the black runner leading to the podium, sweetly infusing the air. She flounced onto a front-row chair and drained her wine.

Joey's picture stared back at her from where it still sat on the stand from the ceremony, Adara's way of including her absent brother in her wedding.

"Don't look at me like that." She waved her empty glass at him. "It's only my second." But if someone happened to overhear her talking to the picture of her dead boyfriend, she'd totally blame it on the wine.

His fierce gray eyes stared back at her, holding a secret smile.

"I know, right? Adara...married. It's a miracle." Tears blurred the lines of his handsome face. "I think miracles maybe only happen once in a lifetime. The one we had together turned out to be a complete bust." Aching emotions clogged her throat. "I miss you, Joey...so much."

As if a small part of him were there with her, a sense of comfort curled around her and she smiled through the tears. "Don't worry. Adara reminded me who I am, so you can cross haunting her off your 'unfinished business' list. You were right that I'd forget, but when you're not here to remind me every day how loved I am, it's hard." She released a shaky sigh and pointed at his picture. "So, I'm waiting for another you. I get that he won't be you—no one ever could be—but you promised me he was out there. And I know love slams into you when you're not looking for it, because that's what you did to me. So I'm checking out of the dating game. While I'm waiting for my fairy tale, I'll figure out how to make an impact on the world, like you would have."

She blew out a long breath, feeling like she'd made a sacred vow of her own. And if she was making vows, she might as well get back up. She lifted her gaze to the rafters. "If I'm on the right track, give me a sign—a clap of thunder or flickering lights. *Something*. Throw me a bone or even a fingernail. I'm not picky."

Joey's picture clattered to the floor, so fast that she didn't see it, landing face-up.

"Get. Out." Gia pressed her palm to her hammering heart. "Joey?" She searched for a shimmering phantom or fluttering orb, maybe a ghostly whisper, but only the distant strains of *Death of a Bachelor* softened the silence. If Joey was there, he didn't reveal himself.

On wobbling legs, she climbed the two steps to the podium and picked up his picture. "I can take a hint. Let the quest begin."

* * * *

Ian took another swig of beer and attempted not to look surly. He propped an elbow against the improvised bar counter and pasted on a bored expression instead.

"Another one bites the dust." Roman slid up beside him and clinked Ian's bottle with his. The tuxedo couldn't completely disguise his cop edge. Even without the weapons and badge, he exuded watchfulness, his gaze always alert and cutting, his relaxed pose a ruse. At the first sign of danger, he'd go off like a gun. "At least Garret picked a woman who can defend herself. Ethan's still talking about her unconventional usage of an umbrella against Garret's stalker. He's tossing around the idea of a women's self-defense class focused on making a weapon out of whatever happens to be lying around."

Ian curled his lip rather than respond verbally and focused on the delusional duo still clinging to each other, even after the music had ended, as if no one else in the world existed. He didn't care that Adara had been grieving for her brother, that Garret had forgiven her for pushing him away or that she'd apparently made it up to him by committing the rest of her life to their mutual happiness. She'd bruised his best friend's heart, and that, he'd never forget.

Even if she basically thought he'd done the same to *her* best friend.

But his situation with Gia was completely different. Speaking of, Gia hadn't returned to the reception. An uncomfortable twist sparked against his steel heart, trying to get in. So she'd ditched him on the dance floor. That was nothing his ego couldn't bounce back from.

"Hey, guys." Barak, the guitarist Garret had befriended overseas and who Ian had instantly filed into the 'don't-like' category, joined them at the bar. He ordered a beer and mimicked Ian, elbows on the counter, gazing out at the crowd. "Have you seen Gia? She promised me a dance and I wheedled my way out of playing guitar in the next song." He grinned, all musician suave, charismatic in his black tux. His English was clipped and perfect and the exotic accent had already won him a few hearts at the wedding rehearsal. Gia was undoubtedly too keen to join the ranks of his initial victims—just another reason Ian found her so captivating. "I am surely not allowing her to avoid her vow."

Ian turned a dismissive look on him. "Take a tip from someone who knows her. You're not her type."

Barak's black eyes glinted a challenge. "From what I saw, neither are you. But she danced with you anyway, and I am not one to surrender." He took a casual sip of beer. "I heard she's into musicians."

"Not since Joey died," Ian drawled. That corkscrew against his heart became a drill, a reminder of every non-musical bone in his body. *Joey.* Magical violinist, Gia's lost love and the main obstruction to his unfinished business with the one woman he couldn't get out of his head. He'd tried to exorcise her by dedicating himself to other women, sports and work, but no matter the attempted distraction, the failure had been complete. One night with Gia was all he needed. One night to get her out of his system and move on.

One night.

"I sense a wager opportunity." Roman's teeth flashed, a small smile that was all sorts of evil. "Guitar or not, bet a Ben that she lets Barak down easy and slides away so smoothly that he doesn't even realize he's been dismissed until she's gone."

Ian's approval of Roman rose another peg. Maybe it was the wedding indignities he'd endured, the buzz of dark beer or the bruised dance-floor ego, but he added, "Bet you two she goes home with me instead."

Roman arched his death-black eyebrows and widened his smile. "Easiest two hundred I've ever made, Boy Wonder."

"Your lack of faith wounds me, Baconbits."

Barak glanced between them, his drink halfway to his mouth, clearly wondering what he'd missed. Maybe men didn't happily disparage each other across the sea. Garret should have brought him up better before extending an invitation to his wedding.

Ian plopped his bottle down and pushed away from the counter. "Later, Roman."

Roman jerked his chin in farewell and tipped his beer back as Ian turned to leave.

"Was it something I said?" Drifting on the heels of Ian's impending departure, Barak's tone hinted at humor, a reflection of Garret's effortless charm. Ian liked him even less for it.

"Probably," Roman said, a shrug in his voice. "Are you in on the bet or not?"

Ian smirked and entered the empty hallway. Roman always had his back. Straightening his tie, he strolled away from all the things that reflected exactly what he didn't want—long-term commitment, sharing life and scars with someone else, love and devotion and soulmates. For Garret, believer in all things fanciful and serendipitous, he had no doubt it would work. For him? Never.

As he passed the doors leading to the banquet room, a gleam of gold caught his eye and he backtracked. Her back to him, Gia sat among the abandoned decorations like a lost queen, black-and-silver ribbons lining the aisle, surrounded by red roses. Stuffing his hands into his pockets, he leaned a shoulder against the doorjamb and waited for her to notice him.

Glitter Girl. He'd overheard one of their coworkers call Gia that and it fit. No matter the day, whether it was at the office, social gatherings or her best friend's wedding, Gia always looked the part. Today, though, she was dressed in shimmering black, her blonde hair up to expose the lickable length of her delicate neck, and he was sharply reminded of their delicious backroom encounter at the holiday party going on two years now. Pleasure interrupted.

He'd intended to scorch Gia out of his system that night. Instead, she'd left a permanent burn in his lungs. His smirk faded. That burn had been there before Joey's demise, when she'd been out of his reach. Now, it aggravated him with every breath.

He absently adjusted his straight tie again. There was only one way to alleviate an itch, and now that Adara was occupied with Garret, he had direct access to the cure. Keeping his steps light, he strolled between the decorated chairs and made it all the way to the second row without any sign from Gia that she knew he was there. Ian slipped into the chair behind her and leaned over her shoulder, close enough that her sweet perfume drifted into his lungs, reminding him of blue skies and spring days.

She held Joey's picture in her lap.

That annoying twist in his chest reappeared. Joey, always blocking him, even from the grave. He narrowed his eyes on the image of his constant competition. Joey had been an unconventional violinist like Garret, adored by everyone. Musicians always got the girls.

Not this time.

He scanned Gia's bare shoulders and had a strong urge to follow up with his finger. Until Adara had barged in on them, Gia hadn't protested his touch. A year or so surely wouldn't change her that much, no matter that they'd hardly talked since. According to Garret, she wasn't dating anyone seriously, and despite the dance and ditch, there was no reason he could fathom that she wouldn't want to pick up where they'd left off.

Lightly, he caressed her shoulder blade.

Gia yelped, jumped and spun in her seat. Her eyes wide and wild, she clutched Joey's picture tight, hiding her lovely breasts. *A shame.* "Ian" — she sucked in a breath — "you jerk."

Smirking again, he relaxed in the chair and spread his arms along the backrests. "Sorry."

"Liar." She plopped back down and pushed a loose wave of hair from her face. "Is the 'true love' and 'forever' mush too much for you?"

"Something like that." He angled his chin at Joey's picture still clutched to her chest. "Pining over lost love?"

She bit her delectable, pink-glossed lower lip. "Something like that."

Damn. He *was* a jerk. Ian scrambled for the perfect words to smooth her feathers. "Garret makes it all look easy, doesn't he?"

A tiny smile intruded on her sadness, and the knot in his gut eased. "Garret and Adara remind me that love happens when you least expect it."

"I see they got to you too." Ian unleashed his shark smile. "Weddings are a virus, Gia. They infect suckers with the promise of happily ever after, but no one ever celebrates when the infection spreads and cripples the dream with real life."

"Ian O'Connor" — she said his name like a curse — "do *not* speak that poison to the universe on Garret and Adara's wedding day. It's like wishing them bad luck or something."

He rolled his eyes. "Have you met Garret Ambrose? The universe conspires to fulfill his every happiness. He's immune to bad luck."

Her gaze sharp and knowing, she studied him long enough to make him want to squirm, but he never buckled under pressure — not anymore. "Jealous, Mr. O'Connor?"

"Hardly." He hated it when she called him 'Mr. O'Connor'. It reminded him too much of his father, and he could do without thinking of that bastard ever again. "Garret can have Miss Crabapple, if that's what he wants. Only he has the power to pry the princess of the north from her tower. I would've been content to leave her there."

Gia twisted in the chair and laid her elbow on the backrest, watching him even closer. "You can't stand it, can you? That fate and serendipity and true love actually exist, that love can overcome anyone's secrets or darkness… Garret and Adara are in-your-face proof of it, and you can't deal."

"I don't have to deal." He put on his bored face. "If people want to delude themselves into believing marriage is the key to happiness, that's their choice. No one's going to force me to drink the Kool-Aid."

Lifting her empty wine glass, Gia grinned. "I prefer wine, anyway."

"I thought it was margaritas." Blood pumped hard to all of his best places. Her lips had tasted of tequila and lime that night, and he'd had far too many fantasies about them. That was a drink he'd savor, always.

She shrugged her slender shoulders. "People change."

"No, they don't." He leaned forward, holding her gaze. "They pretend to change, hope to change, but true nature only bends before bouncing back."

"You're such a cynic," she said softly, not moving as he inched ever closer to the mouth that had haunted him for years, the mouth he had to get out of his head, one way or another. "People evolve all the time. If we didn't, we'd never survive."

"I've survived just fine." He trailed a fingertip along her bare arm, reveling in the softness of her skin, the tremor that rolled through her. He hadn't forgotten how she'd responded the same way to his touch before. He was even less likely to forget now.

"Not all of us are as stuck in their ways as you." She dipped her eyelashes, hiding her summer-sky eyes.

A few inches from her mouth, he paused. "Adara will be gone on her honeymoon in a few hours." His voice was husky with growing need, the memories of his brief and not nearly long enough encounter with Gia an urgent tug. "She won't be around to interrupt." On a whim, he turned her hand over and pressed a lingering kiss to the inside of her wrist. The rapid thrum of her pulse danced against his lips. "I haven't forgotten that night."

Her eyes closed, Gia exhaled, but before he swooped in for contact with her lush, pink mouth, she pulled her arm gently free of his grasp and leaned back. "Tempting as that is, I have to decline."

"Actually, you don't." He made his tone a smooth, coaxing caress. "We'll see them off as the admirable and dutiful maid of honor and best man we are. Then we can pick up where we left off at my place. No declining necessary. No one else has to know, if that's what you want."

"What I want..." She bit her lower lip again, and everything from his scalp to his toes throbbed in anticipation. After a lingering pause, she shook her head. "You were right about the Kool-Aid. I drank it, and it gave me an epiphany." She dropped her gaze to Joey's picture on the seat beside her. "I temporarily forgot who I am, but I'm not going back to that girl who seeks solace with men who believe my purpose lies mainly in the bedroom."

"That's not how I think of you." And, surprisingly, he meant it, for the most part—no matter that his relationships never spanned more than one night. True, he wanted Gia, but unlike the other women he pursued or let pursue him, he didn't mind talking to her, which was why he generally avoided her at the office and chose to admire her from afar. Talking to a woman without ulterior motives would ruin his reputation and might make him want something more.

That was a danger he could never allow.

Enjoyable conversation or not, he still needed to burn Gia out of his system.

"Whatever." She gave him a look that said she didn't believe him, even a little. "I've moved on to the next chapter in Gia's book of trials and errors. No more casual, no more flings, no more online dating, no more margaritas. I'm going to figure out how to impact the world in my own way while waiting for my personal Prince Charming to show up and sweep me off my feet, because me looking for him hasn't turned out so great." She patted his cheek — affectionately, not in the sex-kitten way he preferred. "And I know for a fact that Ian O'Connor ain't him."

"I'll file a formal protest. I have a family suit of armor and various weaponry at my house. I'd be happy to show you all my swords, too." He wriggled his eyebrows so she'd know exactly what sword he wanted to show her most. He dropped his voice to a purr, one women didn't resist. "Invitation still stands — my house, a bottle of wine or two, the rest of the weekend to demonstrate the merits of no armor or clothing of any kind." So it was one more day than he'd agreed. He suspected he'd need it with Gia.

She blinked, and it didn't take his persuasion skills to decipher that she was imagining them together, with or without armor, absolutely with a sword. Her gaze refocused and she shook her head. "Good lord, you're a terror, in and out of the courtroom." She stood and stepped beyond his reach, a golden angel wrapped in sinful black. "Go use your silver tongue on someone else. This princess has downed a sleeping potion and refuses to wake up for anything but the right kiss."

"It's been over a year. Memories fade." A strange sense of urgency rose, as if he were a dying man in need of an organ and the donor had bailed at the last second. He'd been banking on this moment to get her out of his system, out of his thoughts for good. "Maybe you've forgotten how right I am."

Gia laughed.

It was his turn to blink. She *laughed*, as if he'd made a cute joke, not asked her to spend the weekend with him exploring every pleasure they'd missed out on earlier. He hid a scowl behind calm composure. Nothing about him was *cute*.

"I already know how wrong you are for me, Ian, but don't worry. There are at least five lovely ladies at the singles table sighing over you." She winked. "You'll be fine without me."

He'd never claimed he wasn't wrong for her long term, just not wrong for this particular moment, and random wedding guests weren't the ones edging into his thoughts at every inconvenient turn. He crossed his arms and gave her his best cut-throat stare while he slid through possible ways of keeping her close enough to change her mind. He smiled benignly. "Want to help me put lewd and suggestive decorations on Garret's car?"

"You're so far behind the game." She flicked her fingers in a dismissive gesture as she floated by, heading for the door. "I did that over an hour ago."

He smirked at her back, watching the seductive sway of her hips until she slipped out of sight. Laughing softly, he faced the stage again, needing time to cool off before returning to the reception. Scandalizing old ladies wouldn't help him reach his goal of rising to partner at the firm of Hamilton & Associates. His smirk widened. *Rising. Firm.* He was on fire.

"Just passed Gia on her way out. Alone." Roman's smug voice came from the doorway. "Pay up, Boy Wonder."

Digging in his pocket for his wallet, Ian rose and strolled toward his friend. He ignored Roman's self-satisfied smile and slapped two one-hundred-dollar bills into his waiting palm. "The best cases can't be stopped by frivolous motions…only delayed."

Roman scrutinized the money as if checking to make sure it wasn't counterfeit, then stuffed it into his shirt pocket. "Someone has to steer the wheels of justice. It might as well be us." He slung an arm around Ian's shoulders as they walked out together. "I'll buy you a drink when this is over. I'm suddenly feeling generous."

"Someplace they won't spit in our cups, Baconbits." Since the offer Ian wanted had been tabled for now, he might as well get some of his lost winnings back. "And wings."

"Sure." Roman gave him a sly look. "Since the legs are out."

Ian let Roman have his laugh. They both knew that if he didn't want to go home alone tonight, he wouldn't. But no one else could erase the lingering taste Gia had left behind in his mouth.

Maybe it's time to switch trial tactics.

Chapter Two

On Monday morning, Ian followed Mr. Hamilton's receptionist into his office, returning her smile, not missing the sparkle in her eyes. She was attractive enough, but he'd never make the mistake of messing with his boss' personal circle. He wasn't an idiot.

"O'Connor..." Mr. Hamilton, always immaculate in the appropriately expensive suit, equally impressive tie and shoes that would pay for enough groceries to feed an entire village in Africa for a month, handed him a cup of coffee—black with a touch of Bailey's, just like he preferred.

A bad sign.

"Have a seat." Hamilton waved at one of the leather chairs in a half-circle before his desk as the door shut with a decisive prison-gate click.

Ian refused the sudden chill in his blood a foothold. He'd known Mr. Hamilton ever since the stubborn goat had battled his way into Ian's personal teenage hell and dragged him out by the scruff of his scarred and scrawny neck. He owed everything to the old codger.

He sipped his coffee and waited for the warmth to take hold.

Mr. Hamilton retreated to the leather chair behind his desk, which was a few inches higher than the other chairs, a ploy Ian used in his own office to give an extra sense of power. He steepled his hands at his mouth, his bushy white eyebrows drawn down.

Ian managed not to choke on his coffee or look away. Whatever bomb Mr. Hamilton was about to drop was more than bad. There'd been no office rumors about partnerships or potential firings, and he'd be the first to know. Women loved to talk, and he loved women. He ran through every possible scenario, every underhanded courtroom move he'd ever used, every nuance of his private life that might backfire—and nothing especially damaging came up.

Except his signed-and-sealed abandoned past.

The chill deepened. Mr. Hamilton surely wouldn't dig up old bones now, not after his spotless trial record, the negotiations he never lost, the huge settlements he'd earned for the firm.

"O'Connor, you've been an asset to Hamilton & Associates and you've never made me regret hiring you."

"Thank you, sir." *Been.* Not the most comforting word.

Hamilton lightly tapped the desktop, his green eyes narrowed and eagle-sharp, skewering Ian in the chair with his offering of laced coffee. The old man paused for so long, staring, that the unnerving urge to confess something simply to be excused nearly drove Ian to fidget.

Instead, Ian turned the sensation into gasoline for his veins and held Hamilton's stare with icy calm. No one would ever break him again — not in an office, not in the courtroom, not in any dark corner of life.

"A delicate situation has been brought to my attention," Hamilton said at last.

Ian sipped his coffee, willing the hot liquid to dissolve the knot in his throat. A delicate situation could be anything.

"I'm reassigning all your cases."

The boulder in Ian's throat doubled.

Mr. Hamilton somehow assumed an even sterner expression. "What I'm about to tell you does not leave this room, O'Connor. If even a whisper of it gets back to me, you're done here, and I'll make sure you never practice in this state again. Got it?"

"Of course. Confidentiality is a tenet I never break." That was absolute truth. He might twist the truth or manipulate the facts to his own benefit, but he kept his secrets close. Curiosity burned out the initial unease. Maybe this was it, the big case that would land him his lifetime goal of partner. He'd make sure the outcome was superior, no matter the method.

Mr. Hamilton leaned forward, his unblinking gaze fixed on Ian, as if they were co-conspirators plotting a prison breakout. "I'm sure you're familiar with the Clancy family in Greenville."

Ian nodded. His hometown of Graywood wasn't reclusive enough to avoid news of Greenville, thirty miles away. Mayor Clancy was a pillar of the conservative community — advocate for families, responsible for all manner of city improvements and humanitarian outreach…the perfect politician. Everyone respected him, and those who didn't rarely stayed around long — or so he'd heard.

"Joann Clancy, wife to the mayor, is a long-time family friend of mine," Hamilton continued in a spider-soft voice. "She keeps a happy, friendly face in public, but in private, things are bad." His eyes glinted. "Extremely so."

Ian sipped his coffee. Hamilton & Associates dealt with enough high-profile clients from neighboring cities, clients who felt more comfortable hiring an out-of-town attorney with a high-ranking reputation. Small town rates didn't apply. It wasn't especially surprising that a politician's wife would turn to them.

"The delicate situation needs a surgeon's hands, O'Connor. She wants out, and if Clancy suspects anything, he'll do whatever is necessary to protect his image."

Whatever is necessary. A shudder tiptoed down Ian's back. A man with a secret he'd do anything to protect was a dangerous, unpredictable beast, a fact he understood to the core.

"She's watched every minute. All electronic activity is, of course, monitored. She can't communicate freely. He's effectively separated her from any hope of allies."

Ian unleashed an evil smile. "Except us."

"And he must not discover our involvement," Hamilton added gravely. "This case will require...*unconventional* tactics, and I know unconventional won't be a problem for you."

Bowing his head in a semblance of humble acquiescence, a thrill coursed through Ian's nerves. He could almost taste the partner title headed his way. The promise made to his mother and to himself would be fulfilled at last. "I won't disappoint you."

"I know you won't," Hamilton growled, his white eyebrows taking on lives of their own. "If you do, I'll hang your balls beside my Harvard diploma."

"That would be a tragedy in more ways than one, sir."

Hamilton sat back in his chair with a huff. "Joann's only true escape is the stables she operates outside of Greenville. Clancy has the place monitored, of course, but there's a better chance of avoiding surveillance there. That's where you'll go to meet with her and dig up whatever information she's able to give you without being detected. You'll have to let her take the lead, to talk when she feels it's safe."

Ian kept his expression neutral. "If I may ask, how did she manage to contact you without detection?"

"A political fund raiser. I hadn't seen or talked to her since high school, so when she spilled wine on my sleeve and slipped the Gaelic word for *help* in mid-apology, of course I was curious."

"Why would she use Gaelic?"

"Our Irish grandmothers were friends, and they both decided their grandchildren needed to keep the old language alive." Clancy sighed, his gaze distant. "One summer, instead of swimming at the lake or causing the usual, out-of-school trouble, Joann and I were assigned Gaelic lessons. It was miserable. Our teacher was a tyrant. But we learned some words, and when school started up again, to keep practiced, we created our own secret language. We'd scatter Gaelic in with the English, like a code to figure out." His eyes sharpened again, back to the present. "Frankly, I'd forgotten all about it until she asked for help."

Ian wasn't about to comment on Mr. Hamilton's memory.

"Clancy never let her out of his sight the whole evening," Hamilton continued, "but she managed to convey the gist of her situation among bits of conversation spread throughout the night. We were never alone and never talked apart for more than a few seconds at a time." He folded his hands over his lean stomach. "I should get an award for keeping the act of blasé acquaintance while one of my dearest childhood friends divulged the nightmare of abuse."

"She's being abused?" His voice was calm, hiding the storm stirring to life in his chest. Memories flashed to life, dark and violent, and Ian pushed them back.

"Mentally and emotionally, for certain. He's very careful with the physical abuse. From what I gathered, it's never in places where the public might catch a glimpse."

Ian's stomach clenched.

"That's your job to detail, O'Connor." Hamilton swiveled in his chair and opened a drawer behind him. "Do you trust your legal assistant explicitly?"

He raised his eyebrows at the change of subject, hiding his surprise by the time his employer faced him again. "I wouldn't go that far, since she quit on Friday."

Hamilton's mouth tightened, the first sign of censure. "Expectations should be liquid, O'Connor, dependent on who you're dealing with. The local secretary supply will eventually run out."

"I have high expectations, and they are made fully aware of that before being hired." He shrugged. "I don't settle for mediocre."

"Projecting your own need for perfection on others doesn't work." Hamilton made an impatient noise. "Alexander's out on vacation this month. His assistant will help you on this project. She's sharp and trustworthy. After working with her, you might even want to end your assistant troubles and steal her for yourself."

Alexander's assistant was...*Gia*. Heat rushed through him. Working with Gia would be a disaster. He'd have to spend time with her, talk to her, undoubtedly learn things about her that would only further fire his intrigue. He wanted to get her out of his system, not submerge himself deeper.

"I'd prefer to work with a more" — *ugly, unstimulating, unfashionable* — "experienced assistant."

"If you kept your assistants around longer than three weeks, you'd already have one at your disposal." Hamilton handed him a company credit card. "Everyone instantly likes Gia. No one at the stables will suspect her of anything. She'll balance out your confrontational nature."

"I have no idea what you're referring to, sir." He hid his smirk with some effort.

Hamilton snorted even as his gaze sharpened. "I hope you aren't implying that my assistant recommendation isn't qualified to meet your needs. Gia has worked here three years with no complaints or problems."

"Of course not." He smiled benignly. "I didn't realize she'd been here so long." A lie. He'd noticed her the moment she'd walked through the front doors of Hamilton & Associates, all perfect curves in pink heels and a smile that made the lobby chandelier dim. Her unswerving devotion to her musician boyfriend had been a great misfortune.

But now her boyfriend was gone, and maybe he should feel guilty for even thinking it, but he couldn't deny a sense of serendipity.

Serendipity. Garret's favorite word, a word that usually made his lip curl. He straightened his already-straight tie, needing to do something. Joey's young death was regrettable, not his own personal serendipity.

"I'll discuss the situation with Gia privately," Hamilton continued, regaining his full attention. "I want you at the stables by this afternoon. Ask for Joann directly, and if she isn't there, find a way to see her without giving anything away. You'll have to be smooth, O'Connor." He flashed his shark smile, the one Ian had practiced from example and perfected. "I'm confident you can handle it."

Ian stood and lifted his coffee cup in a smooth salute. Handling the case to a satisfactory conclusion didn't worry him. He'd do whatever it took to have his name added on as partner. However, working closely with Gia for an unknown length of time would test his dedication to justice. He'd have to establish his own set of laws if he wanted to skate free of any penalties.

* * * *

Gia barely resisted pressing her nose against the car window for a closer view as Ian pulled into the parking lot of an impossibly posh farm. If horses hadn't been wandering in the surrounding green and a long, three-story building sprawled beyond the neat fence line, she would've guessed the grounds were used as an arboretum.

A landscaped lawn highlighting a natural brook and rocks rolled out beside the paved drive leading to the stables, ending at a pond. Elegant iron lampposts acted as twin guardians to another world. Maple and birch trees circled the grounds on three sides while numerous fenced fields stretched on the other to a distant tree line. The barn itself resembled a mansion more than a stable.

"This is the best special assignment ever." She lightly backhanded Ian's arm without looking away from her new heaven on Earth. "Even if I do have to work with you."

"It's a privilege, Ms. Hellman." Ian's honeyed voice slid over her.

She ignored the responsive sparks in her gut. Gia's Quest Rule Number One—physical chemistry alone did not a full knight make and had nothing to do with finding her niche in the world. "Ms. Hellman?" She turned from the window, her eyebrow arched. "What's with the formality?"

"Just establishing the ground rules for our temporary situation." His ice-blue eyes gleamed, all cool and professional, the same way he always looked at her in the office—with one scorching exception. Months ago, when Garret had returned to town and met Adara, he'd wanted more information on her. Ian had obliged his friend by calling Gia into his office and interrogating her. She bit her lip at the memory, of Ian leaning over her, the picture of control and dominance. *Who knew interrogations can be so stimulating?* And not helpful to her quest.

"As you wish, Mr. O'Connor." She gave him her sweetest smile. Most games were made for two or more players and she didn't mind taking her turn. "We'll go with professional."

His gaze dipped to her mouth, and the ice in his eyes vanished beneath banked heat. "I'm thrilled you understand."

The arrogance in his tone rankled her, as if he knew she'd never challenge him. He didn't know her very well, no matter the few stolen kisses in a back room at the annual holiday party. Hot kisses, mind-blowing kisses, but a kiss only revealed one sliver of a person, and she was so much more than what she allowed him to see.

"I understand perfectly." She licked her lips, the flare in his eyes shooting a thrill through all of her girly parts. Maybe playing along was more detrimental to her battlements than his. "I thought we were here to find Mrs. Clancy, not sit around in your obnoxious car discussing formalities and rules."

He smirked. "You like my Porsche."

"So?" She opened the door and slid free of the butter-smooth leather seat. "It's still obnoxious." As she shut the door, she didn't miss his low chuckle.

Closing her eyes, Gia drew in a long breath of fresh summer air tinged with the sweet blend of hay, horses and countryside. Monday had started out with the same routine of dragging herself out of dreams, putting on her happy face, happy clothes, happy shoes and grabbing a chai tea to go. Now, of all things, she was at a horse farm with Ian O'Connor, the one man who made the formal name of 'Ms. Hellman' sound like an indecent proposal.

"With all that bling on your jeans, I'm not sure you'll fit in with the equestrian crowd, Ms. Hellman." Ian paused beside her.

She mock-gasped and widened her eyes. "Were you checking out my ass, Mr. O'Connor?"

"Hard not to with all the pocket glitter."

"Poor excuse, city slicker." She gave him a purposeful once-over, from the tips of his glossy black boots to the seriously sexy designer jeans and up the impeccable gray button-down shirt. "Careful not to step in any special brown pies. Wouldn't want to muck up your 'purdy' boots."

"I'll let you go first." His smirk widened. "Darlin'."

"I knew it." She snorted and moved up the paved drive toward the stables. "Chivalry's dead and buried."

"Ages ago," he muttered, following a step behind.

The door to the stables looked like any other fancy entrance leading into a home of the rich and famous, heavy oak and meticulously gleaming. *No doorbell.* Gia pushed inside and paused. Clancy Stables was truly a luxury horse resort—vaulted ceilings, glossy oak paneling, black-tile floor. Beyond two open doors that likely led into people rooms, stalls with split wood-and-iron doors lined the long corridor. Soothing classical music drifted through hidden speakers. *These horses have it good.*

"Wow." Gia trailed her finger over the emblem affixed to the door, a red shield with an iron horse rearing, one foreleg striking out at an unseen enemy. "If Garret ever decides to give up concerts and teaching, I bet they'd hire him to serenade the horses."

"Feed him that idea. I dare you." Ian leaned close to her ear, close enough that his breath warmed her earlobe and subtle spice aftershave invaded her senses. "He needs something to rescue him from the northern princess he chained himself to."

"He doesn't want to be rescued." She sniffed to hide the tendrils tingling in her bloodstream. "Besides, he's the one who rescued her, so your interpretation is flawed, Mr. O'Connor."

Ian paused. "The word 'flawed' does not belong in the same sentence as my name. *Ever.*"

The unexpected growl in his voice drew her gaze up, just in time to glimpse his bunched jaw relax, controlled again.

"May I help you?" A man in a red western shirt with a Clancy Stables emblem embroidered at the shoulder ducked out of a stall, a brush in one hand. His gaze flicked to Ian, landed on Gia and lingered with unmistakable masculine interest. Smiling as he approached, he held out his free hand. "I'm Matt."

"Ian O'Connor." Sliding beside Gia, he gave Matt an icy appraisal and ignored the outstretched hand. "My fiancée has a misguided love of horses and insists our wedding won't be complete without her riding up the aisle."

Fiancée? Gia barely hid her surprise behind a bright smile, the one she used to fool people into believing she was ditzy.

"We were informed that, when it comes to horses and riding, Joann Clancy is the best." Ian shackled her fingers and tugged her tight to his side. "My future wife deserves nothing but the best."

Resisting the urge to stomp on the toes of his shiny boots, she went along with his lie and slid her arm around his lean waist. Playing fake fiancée wasn't what she'd signed up for. He could've said they were siblings, friends, cousins, whatever. Instead, he'd used a relationship that required contact to be believable. *Typical Ian.* But she loved her job, and if this case blew up, it would be Ian's fault, not hers. And touching Ian was only a hardship to her mental health.

Matt dropped his hand and hooked his thumb in his belt loop, close to the oversized silver buckle. "Sorry, but Mrs. Clancy isn't here today." He waved the brush vaguely at the stalls behind him. "But if you're looking for riding lessons, our entire staff is qualified. We're required to pass rigorous tests conducted by Mrs. Clancy herself."

Ian shook his head. "No one but Mrs. Clancy will do." He put on his imperious expression, the one that made most other people feel like peons. "When is Mrs. Clancy's next available appointment?"

Matt's smile seemed brittle, but it didn't waver as he pivoted. "Of course. Follow me."

With Matt's back turned, Ian wriggled his eyebrows at Gia and lassoed her hand as he led her past stalls smelling of cedar shavings, hay and —

"Horses!" After a decided struggle, Gia disentangled herself from Ian's grip and rushed to the beautiful black horse poking its head out of the stall's open half-door. "Sweetheart," she crooned, rubbing the horse's forehead as it nickered softly.

An Ian-shaped heat lamp warmed her back. "You can use that sexy voice on me any time."

"Grow a tail and lengthen your muzzle, then we'll talk."

"I've got a tail, of sorts." His breath stirred the hair at her ear. "And it's more fun than a horse's."

Gia smiled as the horse nudged her arm, wanting more attention. She kept her voice at a murmur. "Harassment, O'Connor."

"This is Buttercup." Matt leaned on the gate and rubbed the horse between its ears. "He's Mrs. Clancy's favorite."

Ian tucked a possessive arm around Gia's waist and pulled her back against him. Every point of contact prickled. By some miracle, she resisted the need to run her fingers along the length of his arm. For someone who refused boyfriend status, he knew how to act the part. "He?"

Matt shrugged. "The first thing he ate as a colt was a mouthful of buttercups. The name stuck."

Gia kissed Buttercup's velvet nose. "It's a perfect name."

"I hope I'm a horse in the next life." Matt sighed like an oppressed peasant and gave Buttercup a final pat. "They don't have to do anything to get female attention."

"Because horses naturally deserve affection and only expect sugar lumps or carrots in return." Gia subtly elbowed Ian in the ribs and followed Matt farther into the stables. "Unlike some men I know."

Ian cleared his throat, not quick enough to hide a soft snort.

"The office is a few doors down." Matt's boots thumped softly on shining black tile that looked more suited to an overpriced motel. It was hard to imagine a steaming pile of manure defacing the perfect shine.

Ian grabbed for Gia's hand again and she swatted him away. She danced out of his reach and trailed Matt into what resembled a mini-ski-lodge lounge. A stone fireplace made up one wall, faced by a black leather couch. The oak beams crossing the vaulted ceiling gave the room a rustic edge. Fresh-brewed coffee infused the air. Nestled in one corner, a desk and chair were the only bit of business in a room otherwise meant for relaxing.

Matt leaned over the desk and flipped through an appointment book. Frowning, he turned more pages and thumbed back a few more. "Unfortunately, Mrs. Clancy is scheduled out for over a month." He shrugged an apology. "Her annual trail ride fundraiser for the EQUUS Foundation is coming up next month and has wrangled all her free time. The only possibility is a half-hour session every Monday, Thursday and Friday after feeding time at five a.m. She's open this Thursday."

Gia gasped in horror. She didn't do mornings unless absolutely necessary. No one wanted to endure the consequences of Gia Hellman up before dawn.

"We'll take it." Ian didn't react to the hard pinch Gia gave his arm. "We're always up to see the sunrise, aren't we, love?"

"Only long enough to pull the covers over my head." Gia shamelessly batted her eyelashes at Matt. "Are you sure there's nothing later? I'm incapable of doing anything before eight besides growl. I'd hate to cause a stampede."

A crooked grin lit Matt's otherwise plain face. "I know what you mean. I chose swing shift for the same reason." If he heard Ian's soft snort of disdain, he didn't show it. He shuffled through the planner again and shook his head. "Sorry. There's nothing else open this month."

"Pencil us in," Ian commanded.

Gia slumped.

"Don't look so depressed, love." Ian pressed his lips to her temple in a lingering kiss. "I'll make getting up early worth your while."

Pink tinged Matt's ears as he bent his head, trying to pretend he was absorbed in writing down their appointment instead of overhearing an intimate conversation between apparent lovers, which was a perfect opening for a quick kick to Ian's ankle. He didn't even wince, the jerk. The boots probably offered too much protection. Next time, she'd kick harder and higher...and she had no doubt there'd be a next time.

Matt closed the planner and tugged at his ear. "There's some paperwork to fill out—waivers and a fee agreement—which will take a few minutes to print. Feel free to explore the stables and grounds while you wait. Just don't go into the stalls with the horses. Not all of them are friendly with strangers, and as my grandpa always said, 'the most dangerous parts of a horse are its front and back'." He winked at Gia. "Hard teeth and even harder hooves."

Gia smiled and left the office, sparing Matt the additional discomfort of Ian and his fake fiancée shenanigans.

Alone again with Ian, Gia sniffed as they wandered the line of stalls. "Five a.m., really?" She kept her voice hushed. "Couldn't you have used your super persuasion skills and finagled a humanly decent time, like ten or two?"

He hooked his thumbs in his pockets. "I'll use any available option to see you still in bed." His smirk turned vicious. "Don't be cranky, love. I'll buy you a coffee."

"I don't drug up on coffee" — she smiled, saccharine sweet — "Sugarpop." Gia trailed her fingers along the iron spokes of a stall door. "I'm going to spend the next few moments admiring horses and pretending you're not here damaging the experience."

"You can try," he said agreeably, easily keeping pace. "But I have no intention of letting you forget me."

She whirled on him, fast enough that he bumped into her, and he used the opportunity to wrap his fingers around her arms, holding her close. Wrenching free might raise the eyebrows of anyone who could be watching, so she lowered her voice and kept her smile on tight. "You can't have it both ways, you know."

"I like to think I can." Ian dipped his chin, holding her gaze.

"Not with me." Purposely, she focused on his mouth, so close to hers. While he was clean-shaven, an afternoon shadow darkened his lean jawline, and she almost surrendered to the urge to drag her fingertip along that edge, to test the sensation. "Gia or Ms. Hellman. Choose."

He gave her a bedroom look, hooded eyes, that sinful mouth quirked up at one corner, enough to give the impression he was thinking equally sinful thoughts. With one finger, he teased the tendril of hair near her chin and gently tucked it behind her ear, inching closer. "Every time I flirt with you, every time I touch you," he whispered, "I'm noting the location of cameras, both in open view and potentially hidden." He trailed his finger from her ear to her neck in a track of goosebumps. "I'm working, Ms. Hellman."

"You sly devil." She resisted the need to lean into him. "Roman must be rubbing off on you."

"He's not the one I want rubbing me." His gaze lifted to something behind her, and he stiffened slightly. If he hadn't been touching her, she wouldn't have noticed. He dropped his hands. Beneath his breath, he muttered, "*Chara.*"

Gia's eyebrows rose. *Chara*—Garret's favorite foreign curse word, usually used when crap was about to fly.

Ian pivoted, latched on to her elbow and pulled her relentlessly in the opposite direction.

"Ian?" called a sultry, feminine voice. "You're too close to pretend you didn't see me."

The word he muttered beneath his breath wasn't decipherable, but the nasty tone was more than enough for Gia to get the gist. She pressed her lips together to hide a smirk as he reluctantly turned around. Witnessing Ian O'Connor uncomfortable was a rare event, not to be missed.

A curvy woman in a Clancy Stables shirt, her auburn hair in long braids on each side of her head, strode toward them, a shovel over her shoulder. Her gaze flicked over Gia, instantly dismissing her. The smile she worked on Ian was teasing, the gleam in her green eyes downright dirty. "Are you lost?" She stopped a few feet away and wriggled her hand into the pocket of her tight western jeans. "You do realize this is the boonies and you're surrounded by nature and animals, right? Everyone here has calluses and muscles because we actually work." She swung the shovel off her shoulder and planted the tip on the tile. Her grip slid down the handle suggestively. "You're on the wrong side of town, hon."

Ian wore his wolf's smile. "Hello, Frankie. I had no idea you worked here too. Bartending and barns. Fascinating."

"What? You don't listen to the personal details I share while you slip a hand up some random sorority girl's skirt at Cheshire's?" Her eyes went wide, mocking. "Shocker."

Gia managed not to snort, helped by Ian's tight, almost painful squeeze on her elbow.

"My apologies, but I'm not entirely to blame," he said smoothly. "Your natural country beauty stunned me, as it always does."

"Bartenders are immune to charm. You know that." Frankie twirled her finger around the end of one braid and color crept into her cheeks as if she'd bought the line, but her glittering gaze slid to Gia. "Enjoy him while you can."

Ian cleared his throat and had the grace to at least try to look innocent.

Matt emerged from the office, carrying a clipboard with papers. "All right, we're all set." He handed the clipboard and a pen to Ian. "You and your fiancée need to sign the releases—"

"Fiancée? Congratulations." Frankie's voice was tight and her smile strained fury. "I guess rules don't apply to everyone, do they?" She whirled and marched back the way she'd come.

"Ah, sorry about that." Matt rubbed the back of his neck and gazed after Frankie. "Frankie can be…temperamental."

"No need to explain." Ian skimmed the waiver, his tone cool. "I've faced a feminine storm or two before with no survivor remorse."

Instead of casing the location longer, as Gia expected, after signing the paperwork, Ian grabbed her hand and guided her back to his car in steady silence. When he opened the car door for her—like a gentleman—she knew something was terribly wrong.

She pivoted to face him before getting in. "So, Frankie. Former flame gone bad?"

"I never interact too closely with women who handle my food or drink." He flicked his fingers at her, an impatient gesture for her to stop wasting time with unimportant questions. "That's bad practice. And redheads aren't my preference."

"I didn't realize you had a type." She flounced into the seat and arched an eyebrow at him. "I thought you were an equal female opportunist, so long as she has girlie parts."

"Oh, I certainly have a type, love." His gaze slid slowly over her face, landing on her mouth. Without breaking his stare, he shut the door.

Gia hid a shiver and looked away. He might be pretending to be his usual, confident self, but something was off, and it had everything to do with Frankie. If she wasn't an ex-fling, why was he acting like a fugitive, trying to play it cool while the enemy closed in?

"What is it?" she asked as he slid into his seat and shut the door, sealing them in with the scent of leather, new car and Ian's subtle spice cologne.

He released a barely decipherable breath and calmly said, "Nothing I can't handle."

For some reason she couldn't define, his words sent a jolt through her. Whatever he meant to handle, she suspected it had everything to do with her.

Chapter Three

At the second summons to Mr. Hamilton's office in the same week, Ian forced his shoulders to relax as he knocked on his boss' door. He hadn't been called to Mr. Hamilton's office more than a dozen times during his entire career. Usually, if Hamilton wanted to talk to him, he simply swung by.

In this particular instance, he had a notion of the sticky subject—no doubt spread by one talkative bartender he'd hoped would keep her mouth shut for once. He should've known better. Luck, that finicky shrew, rarely spared a smile for him.

"Come in, O'Connor." Hamilton's rumbling voice carried through the heavy door, the first bad omen. His receptionist had announced Ian's arrival seconds ago, a heads-up that the loyal protégé promptly answered the invitation to face whatever fate awaited.

Striding in with lawyer confidence, Ian shut the door behind him. "What can I do for you, sir?"

Mr. Hamilton lurked behind his monster desk, watching with hawk-sharp eyes. Waiting. Assessing.

"Sit." A command, and not a friendly one. No coffee offering, either.

Chara. Ian obeyed and smoothed his tie. The cushy leather chair did nothing to make him feel at ease.

"I heard the good news." Hamilton's forehead bunched and he set his jaw. Whatever news he'd heard, 'good' probably wasn't the appropriate adjective.

"Fresh maple bars in the breakroom?"

His boss' keen eyes narrowed.

"Right. The university's exciting win last night." Ian kept his smirk in check. "Inspiring game."

"I'm not speaking of soccer, boy." Hamilton remained utterly still, a predator observing while its prey eased deeper into the snare.

"It's technically football, sir."

Hamilton's stare went on long enough that Ian figured another snarky response might get him assigned to the next problem client. Apparently, he was expected to walk willingly into the trap. *Forward ho.* "I know of no other news that fits into the favorable category, but I'm prepared to be enlightened."

"Let's start with your engagement." Hamilton's voice was flat, unamused.

Ian caught his wince just in time. As he expected, luck still hated him. "Judgment call, sir. I felt it was the most believable excuse to be at Clancy Stables with Ms. Hellman without raising any suspicions."

"Yet, two days later, I hear of it"—Hamilton leaned forward—"and not from you."

Gossip ran like wildfire through small towns, which was why he lay low at home and prowled in other, larger cities, far enough to put a buffer between his personal time and his career…usually. Frankie must've passed the rumor along at Cheshire's, one of his hangouts three cities away. Clearly, only three cities away was too close. Running into the mouthy bartender at Clancy Stables had been a giant punch of misfortune.

"If I've heard about it, be assured that everyone else will too, if they haven't already." Hamilton slammed his palms on his desk, an echoing gong of doom. "What were you thinking, Ian? Why didn't you simply say Gia was your sister?"

Ian nearly shuddered. He couldn't think of Gia as his sister. That was *Game of Thrones* messed up. "We look nothing alike."

Hamilton growled. "Cousin or great-aunt or foster sister or occasional cat sitter would have sufficed."

"If anyone researched that claim, sir, they would discover the lie easily enough." He forced his shoulders to relax, settling back into lawyer mode. "A whirlwind engagement is something that can't be readily researched, especially if we haven't made any public announcement. No one wants the problems of an office romance, a simple explanation for keeping it secret."

"Don't play your persuasion tactics on me." Hamilton growled. He pointed a long, bony finger at him. "Do you understand the ramifications?"

Slowly, Ian nodded. It was no longer a matter of pretending to be engaged to Gia for a couple of hours to fool one person or any observers, with the extra benefit of having a valid excuse to touch her. If it got back to Mr. Clancy that they weren't romantically involved, any dunce could put the pieces together — and Joann Clancy would pay the price. "I'll make this right."

"Yes, you will." Thunder entered Hamilton's voice, betraying the controlled storm. "Until we get Joann safely through this, you're officially off the meat market, and if you take advantage of this situation to sully Gia in any way, you'll be on eviction duty for a year."

Horror. Dealing with disgruntled tenants and irascible landlords for months would kill him — almost as surely as behaving himself while portraying the devoted fiancé to Gia. Worse, he'd have to spend more time with her to make their engagement believable, blurring the lines of work and his personal life — letting her closer, deeper.

A strange sensation clenched around his ribs, like a noose readying to hang. No matter which direction he faced, a different sort of danger waited. If he bailed on the assignment, he'd keep Gia at a safe distance…and lose major ground in his bid for the elusive partnership. But if he stayed on, instead of getting Gia out of his system, she'd be a daily infusion. He'd have no escape. His one-night rule would be irreversibly shattered. A sense of panic pushed the noose up around his neck, tight enough to choke.

He forced his hands to relax. He would not allow this unsettling preoccupation with Gia to impact his lifelong goal. The temporary discomfort of pretending to be engaged to the one woman who made him ache on a daily basis was a trial he would win. He could stay in control. Nothing would be lost or jeopardized.

Ian unleashed his shark smile. "Have I ever failed you, Mr. Hamilton?"

"Don't start now." Hamilton's eyes narrowed, glinting. He pointed at the door in dismissal.

Ian left with a dip of his chin. Now, not only did he have the challenge of coming to agreeable terms with Gia, he had to determine how to handle close quarters with her for an undeterminable time without cracking.

* * * *

Perched on a leather chair in Ian's office, Gia couldn't stop studying his unreadable expression. The last time she'd been summoned to his office, months ago, it had entailed a showdown with him that had made her hot in all the right places for all the wrong reasons. So when the call had interrupted her boring paperwork, a dozen different possibilities had skipped through her mind.

Carrying their fake engagement into the real world hadn't been one of them.

"This wasn't part of my ultimate, diabolical scheme, I assure you." Ian planted his butt on the arm of the opposite chair, the casual pose probably meant as some sort of peace offering. "I don't mix work with pleasure. *Ever.* Finding Frankie at the stables simply came back to bite me." He shrugged. "It happens."

"Bite *you*?" She snorted. "What about me? Pretending to be engaged to you for an indefinite amount of time is *not* part of my quest. I don't want a chapter in my new life book titled *Trashy by Association*."

"The suffering will be mutual, Ms. Hellman." He smiled, *the jerk*. "Once our client is in the clear, we call off our engagement and move on with our lives. Easy come, easy go."

"I am not 'easy come, easy go'. If you want me to postpone my personal life mission and sacrifice months to play along with this charade, I have conditions."

His eyes glinted dangerously.

"Since I'll be required to spend my very precious free time with you, everything after five p.m. is overtime." She lifted two fingers, holding his gaze. "While posing as your fiancée, I choose where we go, what we do." Finger number three flicked up. "When the case is over, I get to break up with you—in a really public, creative way."

At his cold look, she batted her eyelashes. Glitter Girl wasn't her only nickname. There was a solid reason her family and friends sometimes referred to her as General Gia, affection not always included. She studied the pink glitter on her acrylic fingernails while he sorted it out.

What had started as the makings of a nightmare had morphed into an unexpected challenge. Resisting Ian's undeniable charms would test the devotion to her decision to wait for love, but with the extra money, she could buy the luscious, overpriced stilettos with the killer bling she drooled over every time she walked by the shoe store next door. She'd be the one girl in town who had managed to win Ian O'Connor's black heart—falsely, but no one else would know—then stomp on it. To every woman who'd hopelessly pined for him, she'd be a hero. But more than that, if pretending she'd fallen for Ian meant helping a woman escape her scumbag abusive husband, she'd do it for free with a huge smile on her face.

Ian didn't need to know the last part.

"I doubt Mr. Hamilton will approve overtime while we pretend to be happily engaged," he said at last. His smooth voice clashed with the fire in his eyes.

"Overtime is nonnegotiable." She folded her arms over her silk blouse. "You didn't consult me before throwing around the F word, so this is all on you."

His mouth tightened, an almost imperceptible move she would have missed if she hadn't been nailing him in place with the Hellman stare-down. "Very well. Overtime."

Gia smiled sweetly.

"But you don't get to choose every detail of our courtship, Ms. Hellman." He straightened from the chair and loomed over her, and her annoying pulse jumped. "This situation, after all, is partially your responsibility."

"Mine? In what possible way?"

"You and your sexy, spun-sugar perfume." He leaned closer, and his eyes held a predatory gleam. "You and your man-killer heels. I couldn't possibly manage to present you as a family member. People would think I'm pervy."

"You *are* pervy." She ignored the heat curling through her. "What I wear is my own business. If you can't handle it, that's your problem"—she smiled again—"Mr. O'Connor."

"Ian," he corrected, easing even closer, his gaze unabashedly fixed to her mouth. "We're engaged now, love."

"I don't recall any proposal on bended knee." She waggled her fingers in his face. "Oh, and look... No ring."

His smile was all bite, his eyes fierce as he smoothly knelt before her and took her hand. "Be my one and only accomplice for the next few months, Gia Hellman." Without breaking her gaze, he pressed his lips to her fingers, a soft disparity to the unyielding grip. "I promise not to ruin your reputation in the process, and I'll concede to a break-up in the manner of your choosing."

"Do you even know *how* to date?" She refused to squirm beneath his intense scrutiny. "We both know you don't do relationships, at least not real ones. To be clear, I'm certainly not going to be paid for any questionable activities, particularly with you."

His right eyebrow twitched. "Questionable activities?"

"Exactly. The stuff real couples do together behind closed doors."

"Like talk and eat dinner?"

"Don't be obtuse, O'Connor." She tried to pull her hand free with zero success. "You know I'm referring to all the things that are constantly slithering around in the gutter that's your mind, all the questionable activities you do in your free time with whatever woman is dumb enough to agree. I'm not that girl." *Anymore.*

"I've never once thought you were dumb, Gia." His voice was matter-of-fact, none of the seductive purr he used when going for the throat.

One truthful compliment wasn't enough to make her melt. "What about PDA?"

"Private time with me isn't part of the negotiations." Oh, he was definitely smirking now. "I believed I made it clear that I never mix business with pleasure."

"*Public* displays, psycho." Gia wrestled her hand free as his smile widened. "How much pawing and slurping in public from you will I have to endure?"

"The bare minimum to make it believable." Leaning over her again, he rested a hand on each armrest, caging her. His tie swung gently between them, a silken noose. "But feel free to paw and slurp me as much as you wish."

She rolled her eyes, even as his clean, spicy cologne invaded her lungs and warmed her blood another degree. "Pretending to be engaged to you is in direct opposition to my personal goals. What if my true love shows up, thinks I'm with you and keeps on going?"

"Then he wasn't yours in the first place." His voice lowered to a husky whisper as his gaze dipped once more to her mouth. "No man deserving of you would surrender without a battle — or at least a siege." An odd expression softened his features, there and gone so fast that she couldn't peg it. He suddenly straightened, all cool courtroom composure. "Do we have an agreement?"

Gia blinked, sure she'd misinterpreted the shocking hint of regard and romance from the unsentimental Ian O'Connor. She sighed, simply to throw him off, and pictured her future sandals — otherwise known as The Shoes — with their sky-high stilettos and dazzling crystals on every strap. For them, she could do this. And picking the perfect way to break up with Ian would get her through the long nights. She'd absolutely be wearing The Shoes while she did it. "Making a deal with the devil... And this week started out so well."

"I suppose you'll need this." Ian reached into his pocket and pulled out a velvet box. He flipped it open. "The salesman at Johannsen Jewelers salivated when I stepped through the door. While the engagement ring selection was limited, he assured me that every gem is of the finest quality, personally selected by the owner during his last jaunt to Belgium."

Something inside her twisted and annoying tears burned her eyes. Her first proposal shouldn't have been like this, even if it was fake and technically didn't count. She'd known Joey had planned to propose eventually, after he'd figured out his music. Life had cut both of their dreams short.

"You're thinking about him, aren't you?" A surprising sympathy entered Ian's voice.

She blinked off any sign of tears and directed her attention out of the window. "Joey's impossible to forget."

With unexpected gentleness, Ian took her hand and slipped the ring onto her finger. It fit perfectly, as if he'd known her ring size, and the diamond was a glimmering rock, far bigger and more expensive than anything Joey could've afforded.

"You must've been confident I'd say yes," she said, the glamour girl in her admiring the ring, no matter the circumstances.

"Accepting the alternative wasn't an option." He turned for the door. "Ready to go?"

"Care to say where?" She stood and smoothed her pencil skirt, not missing how he tracked the slide of her hands over her hips. "This is a partnership, Ian, not a tyranny. I expect my fiancé to share details of our plans." She stopped beside him and leaned close to his ear. "So I can avoid the traps."

He turned his head, his mouth almost grazing hers, thanks to her extra heel-height. "The traps are half the fun. We have further details to discuss and I'm hungry. This can be our first public dinner outing."

Gia refused to retreat. Surrender an inch to Ian O'Connor and he'd take the whole road. "I'm not in any way prepared to act like the appropriate fiancé for the masses."

"Fine, I'll call in dinner and we'll eat at my place."

"The O'Connor Den of Iniquity? I don't think so."

"Very well," he crooned close to her ear. "We'll continue our business discussion with food at your place, Ms. Hellman."

She met his gaze, ignoring the unnerving closeness. "I don't think you should call me Ms. Hellman anymore. What will people think?"

The blue of his eyes deepened, and one corner of his mouth curled up. "One thing you should know about me, love, is that I don't care what the general population thinks of me."

As if she didn't already know that. Gia arched an eyebrow. "And here's one thing you should know about me—every other Wednesday night I eat at the senior center. I'm in charge of the after-dinner dance.

It's fifties night, so grab a cardigan" — she opened the door and smiled over her shoulder — "Love."

Chapter Four

Ian pulled into the senior center parking lot just as Gia shut her car door with a saucy swing of her hips. The full skirts of her red and white polka-dot halter dress rippled in the slight summer breeze, and he had a flashback of Marilyn Monroe.

Sweet, agonizing hell. Marilyn had nothing on Gia Hellman.

One hand planted on her cocked hip, she waited for him on the sidewalk, her ruby-red lips curved in the long-suffering half-smile she usually aimed at him. As he slid from his Porsche, she raised her eyebrows.

"You actually *own* a cardigan?" She looked him up and down, from his loafers to the secondhand monstrosity he'd found after work. "I'm impressed."

"I'm docking the cost of this mothball smelling waste of wool from your overtime." He sneered at the diamond-print design of his find. "It's impossible to look cutthroat in a cardigan. For your sake, there better not be any potential clients here. Seeing me in this won't inspire confidence."

"Don't sell yourself short." Her smile widened, competing with the sunlight gleaming over the patch of lawn flanking the building behind her. "With your natural cockiness, no one will notice what you're wearing. Then again, no one will notice you while I'm around wearing this." She twirled on the sidewalk, showing off her strappy stilettos, a red tulle underskirt and the crimson belt circling her slim waist. He couldn't deny her point. He had no intention of diverting his focus from her. Fake business engagement or not—off-limits or not—he still had all the working male equipment that stiffly informed him that tonight would be miserable.

"How long does this thing last?" He strolled toward the front door of the senior center, wincing at the hint of meatloaf and green bean casserole ruining the fresh summer air. "We have a pre-dawn start tomorrow." He smirked at her as she caught up with him. "And I might show up early, in the hopes of finding you still in bed."

Gia sniffed. "Even if you did find me in bed, you wouldn't be invited to join me."

Heat curled in his gut. "Sounds like a challenge."

"Fact, O'Connor." She slid him a superior look. "You're not what I want."

"Lying to yourself doesn't change the truth," he said, silky-smooth.

In the shadow of the building, she abruptly stopped and faced him. Her golden hair, pulled into a ponytail and still somehow elegant, swung over her shoulder at the sudden movement. "I know exactly what I want and one night isn't it." Her eyes flared, fierce as her unyielding tone. "I want my happily ever after and you want happy-for-you fleeting moments. They aren't the same at all."

"I do my best to make sure everyone's enjoying themselves during my fleeting moments." He flashed an unapologetic smile at her eye roll. "I'm a realist, Gia. Romantic relationships are nothing but an act in a play. Everyone wants the surface-deep diversion, the excitement of the chase and being caught, the pretense of being desired for who they are. But no one lays out all the trash underneath, the full, unadulterated, twisted truth. That would ruin the pretty costume, and once the mask is ripped away, all the thrills go with it, because there can be no more pretending."

"That's the saddest thing I've ever heard." The annoyance drained from her features, replaced by an expression he didn't want to dissect. It looked too close to pity. "What's life without sharing who you are with other people?"

"Uncomplicated and manageable."

"Empty." She studied him, as if seeing him through a different lens, and it was intense enough that he had an unsettling urge to squirm.

He stuffed his hands into his cardigan pockets, standing firm under the scrutiny. He shouldn't have said anything, simply let her believe in fairy tales. She'd learn soon enough that single-night happy endings were far more possible than the 'happily ever after' kind.

She patted his arm — *patted*, not groped or stroked in feminine approval — and resumed walking. "Did you not get enough hugs growing up?"

He ignored his stinging ego. Feigning that he was a child in need of consoling wouldn't change the electricity between them. "Funny that you should bring it up. As a nonnegotiable part of our agreement, I require hugs, lots of them. My mother assured me hugs are necessary for a healthy life, and there's research to prove it."

"Wait, what? You have a mother?" Gia batted her eyelashes. "I always imagined some wilderness traveler discovered you in egg form, nestled in a cranny of some ancient cave that was inhabited only by snakes."

"*Had* a mother. She died years ago."

"Oh. Sorry."

He shrugged, the pain a dim ache, long ago reconciled. "Everyone dies, Princess." He bumped her shoulder with his. "For the record, she would've liked you."

Her teasing grin returned. "My mother would like you too—and I'm not saying that's a good thing. My brothers and sister would make up for it, though. They'd hate you on sight." She gazed at the senior center, her humor fading. "This temporary thing we're doing? Keeping my family out of it is one of my nonnegotiable stipulations. Dealing with our coworkers and Adara will be bad enough."

"Fine with me. Family is overrated." In so many ways, none of which he needed to share with Gia.

"Avoiding a trip home for Thanksgiving and Christmas will be nearly impossible, so I suggest you work your lawyer magic and finish this case before then."

"I'll do my best." And he would. Over a year of Gia invading his thoughts and fantasies had been a trial itself, and that had been at a distance. If he had to spend five months working with her sweet perfume clouding his mind, her curves always within reach, her smile tempting him—and no bedroom action on the side?

Not even the thickest lawyer sharkskin would withstand that siege.

"Quiet time is eight p.m., so I'm sure you'll be home in time for your Grinch recovery slumber." Gia picked up her pace and latched on to his wrist, dragging him along with her. "And now it's time for Ian O'Connor's positive life lesson number one."

"I shudder at the very thought," he said in a bland tone.

"You should." She pulled the glass door open and shoved him through. The woman was stronger than she looked. "When your bubble bursts, no law degrees or smooth charm will save you. I can't wait to introduce you to Emma and Merle. They've been together for over sixty-five years. Love and happily ever after. It happens."

The door clanged shut behind him like a prison-cell gate, with no escape.

Dinner was already being served as Gia led him into a cafeteria with tables lined up along the walls and the center of the room cleared, presumably for old-timer dancing. The choking scent of onions and something he couldn't pinpoint and certainly wouldn't consider edible killed his hunger in one fell strike. He took the tray the kitchen worker offered without grimacing, a true triumph. After enduring this torment, he'd grab sushi on the way home.

A half-hour passed of deflecting unwanted conversation with people who were too nosy for their own good. Cardigan aside, folding his arms and glaring helped, and eventually the Geezer Enquiry Squad left him alone. Gia cheerfully took up the slack. While she chatted with every single person in the room like they were old friends, he watched the clock on the far wall and sipped cloyingly sweet punch. It was barely an hour until eight o'clock. *I can do this.* For Hamilton, for a future partnership at the firm, for a woman who'd silently suffered for years at the hands of a monster —

"Want some gelatin with fruit cocktail?" Gia pushed a bowl of suspicious looking blue goo his way.

He pushed it back at her with one finger. "My delicate sensibilities are already in a kerfuffle with the meatloaf and instant potatoes. I'll pass."

"You're such a food snob." Gia dug her spoon into the wobbling mass and lifted it toward her lovely lips. "There's nothing wrong with eating substances made from ground up hooves." She stuck the spoon into her mouth, grimaced and chugged a follow-up chaser of punch.

Ian smirked. "Regretting my earlier dinner offer at Kaito's?"

"There's no dancing at Kaito's. It's a fair trade off, and at least here I'm guaranteed good company with people who have zero ulterior motives."

"My motives have always been candid." He leaned back in the plastic chair and stared down the old man across the table, who made no effort to hide his ogling of Gia. *Dirty-minded grandpa.* "For the most part."

Gia snorted.

"I'll take his dessert," the leering man said, reaching a mottled claw for Ian's gelatin.

"Back off, gramps." Ian leaned forward, adding more ice to his stare. "Show some courtesy. Maybe one of the ladies wants it."

"Oh, I want it." A blue-hair in a pink sweater with sequins pushed up her wire-framed glasses, but she wasn't eyeing the bowl in front of him. Her gaze slid down Ian's body in a shockingly lewd manner. "Every. Single. Bite."

"Alberta!" Gia widened her eyes at the succubus wearing a grandma disguise, her smile fond. "Ian's shy. You'll embarrass him."

"I'd like to do more than that to him." Alberta winked.

"You can throw some of that sugar my way." The old man turned his leer on Alberta.

It seemed all filters vanished at the age of seventy-six, with no consideration for the growing nausea of others. Ian pushed his entire tray at them. "Take it all. Have fun." At Alberta's approving purr aimed his way, he added, "With each other. You and him." He slung an arm around Gia's shoulders and leaned near her ear. "Enduring sexual harassment by the elderly was not part of our agreement."

"I didn't see any exclusion in the fine print, Sugarpop." She pulled free, her eyes twinkling. "You'll have to survive the bathwaters on your own for the next few minutes. I've got music to set up."

As she deftly slipped away, he scrambled for her hand, her dress, anything to hang on to like a life preserver, but he came up empty. *Dammit.*

"I'd been hoping for some new blood to help me get my groove on." Alberta leaned across the table and latched onto the front of his cardigan. "First dance is mine, sonny."

"My dance card is full. I surrendered it to Gia." Ian wrenched free of her grip and straightened his sweater. "Didn't she show you her ring? I'm off-limits now."

"Experience and treachery will always defeat youth and charm." Alberta winked again. "You're not married yet."

Ian scowled. That sounded suspiciously like something he'd say.

"Alberta, leave the poor boy alone." A woman tottered near, holding on to the arm of a tall man, now stooped with age. She looked like an honest grandmother should — plump, rosy-cheeked, her white hair in a bun. The only sequins were in the silver whiskers of the cat on her shirt. "Merle will dance with you." She patted the old man's arm as he turned Gia's empty chair around for her. With a grimace, she stiffly sank into the chair.

The quick beat of *Why Do Fools Fall in Love?* erupted from the speakers and a transformation came over the cafeteria. Feet started tapping, hands clapping and people Ian could have sworn couldn't do much more than shuffle their feet swung hips, waved arms and danced their slow way into the center of the room.

Alberta ditched Ian for Merle without a struggle, and maybe he should have been insulted, but he gave a sigh of relief and relaxed in his chair.

"I heard you're Gia's young man." Emma patted his wrist with a soft hand, her gaze on the dancing people. "I'm happy you found her. Someone as bright as Miss Gia shouldn't be sad for so long."

No, she shouldn't. Ian turned his chair to face the dance floor too, and a knot formed in his chest. Gia danced with one of her admirers, a flash of gold and red brighter than any sequin vest. No wonder they flocked to her. She was beautiful and carefree and alive. If he was an old lecher, he'd be all over her too.

To be honest, age had nothing to do with it.

"Seventy-five years, and he can still shake it with the best." Her smile wistful, Emma watched Merle perform some sort of hokey-pokey with Alberta, using his cane as a prop. "Merle asked me to go steady for two years before I finally said yes."

"Wore you down, did he?"

Emma laughed, and it was one of the sweetest sounds he'd ever heard, full and open, impossible to ignore. "Like sandpaper." She gave Ian's hand a fond squeeze, exactly as he'd always imagined a grandma would do. "I was only seventeen, not at all ready to settle down. Merle had enlisted in the navy and was set to leave town when he asked me on a date for the last time. For the life of me, I still don't know what possessed me to say yes that night. Merle was too tall, too quiet, too serious, too *everything* for me. But that night..." She sighed, memories sparkling in her dark eyes. "That night was magic. We wrote letters back and forth for four years. When he came back after the war, we got married. I sometimes wonder what life would have been like if I'd said no to him that night too."

"Peaceful?" Ian suggested.

She elbowed him and laughed again. "Boring." Her smile faded at the edges. "Deficient. And missing out on the smoking sexy times?" Emma fanned herself. "That would be a tragedy."

"I could have happily lived the entirety of my life without picturing you and Merle and sexy anything." Ian shuddered and fought the urge to scrape the horrifying taste off his tongue. Emma laughed again, and he pivoted away from her, which put him facing the leering man, only the leer was long gone. Alone, the old man watched the dancers as if he were a shadow longing for the light, wanting to join them as much as he needed to keep apart.

This place is playing with my head.

An hour rolled by of watching dustballs dance to songs better left in the past, and the moment the music ended, Ian swooped in, tucked Gia under his wing and lured her relentlessly out of the senior center into the open air. He dragged in a full breath. It smelled like freedom.

"What? You didn't enjoy yourself?" Gia's smile was all mischief in the twilight, her golden hair stirred by a lazy evening breeze.

"For that torment session, you owe me, love." He snaked an arm around her slender waist, lingering at the soft curve of her hip, their steps quiet on the sidewalk. "Friday after work. Weekly soccer game with the boys. You'll be there."

She quirked an eyebrow in challenge, but the flare in her eyes was something else, something that roused the already-steaming coals in his gut. "I'll have to check my planner."

"You do that." He leaned near her ear, drawn by her sweet perfume and the skin he wanted to taste again. "As you reminded me, this is a partnership. I canceled my plans tonight at your request. Check and balance, Ms. Hellman."

Gia's phone erupted in Aretha Franklin's *Respect* and she scrambled for it in her purse, answering with a breathless, "Hey, Kat—"

The sobbing was loud enough for even Ian to catch. He stopped beside Gia as color drained from her face and tears glistened in her eyes. Her mouth tight, she shook her head at him, turned and wandered across the lawn alone, out of earshot.

He stayed planted on the sidewalk, a knot in his gut that hadn't been there before. Whoever Kat was and whatever had happened on the other end of the phone was slowly wrecking his glamour queen. Her shoulders slumped, followed by a bowed head, and all her gorgeous hair fell over her shoulder, baring her white, vulnerable neck.

That knot inside twisted.

Gia dropped the phone to her side. One by one, she removed her shoes and stood barefoot in the grass, her back to him.

Slowly, he crossed the lawn to her. Without breaking the silence, he eased his arms around her and gently pulled her back against his chest. While most people who knew him understood that he loved women, they didn't get that his affection went beyond the bedroom. He hated to see a woman he respected hurting in any way, which was why he always used utter honesty when it came to hooking up. If a woman was hurt that he didn't want more than one night, at least he couldn't be accused of playing with their emotions. He laid his cheek against her temple as she released a shaky sigh.

"That was my sister, Katerina." She carefully wiped at her eyes, as if afraid she'd smear mascara. "She's getting a divorce."

"Bummer."

Gia looked up at the single-star sky and laughed humorlessly. "Yeah. Bummer. Childhood sweethearts, love eternal, destroyed by short-shorts and thigh-high boots." She tore free of his light hold and whirled on him, fire in her eyes. "What is it with men and cheating?"

"I have no idea. I've never cheated."

"Right." Her voice was somehow both deadpan and accusing. "One of the benefits of keeping it to only one night."

He shrugged, unable to deny her point. But even without the personal policy of short-term romance, he'd never marginalize any woman by cheating. Commitment was a law to be honored. If a man couldn't hack it, he shouldn't take the plunge.

"And don't you dare say it." She pointed an accusing finger in his face. "I don't need to hear your jaded opinion on love and happily ever after right now."

He dropped his chin. Holding her gaze, he said quietly, "I'm sorry about your sister, Gia. Truly." When her bottom lip wobbled, he ruthlessly continued. "She'll get over it."

Making a sound halfway between a growl and a garbled curse, Gia nabbed her shoes and marched past him, barefoot and beautiful.

"Pick you up at a quarter after four, love," he called at her back.

She replied with an impolite hand gesture recognizable in any language and flounced into her car, jerking her full skirt clear of the frame. The door slammed shut and reverberated through the quiet parking lot.

Ian smiled as she revved the engine, backed up at an alarming speed and peeled out of the senior center. He jangled his keys and strolled to his Porsche.

Tomorrow would be categorically engrossing.

Chapter Five

In the sleepy pre-dawn hours, Ian shuddered as he climbed the steps leading to Gia's house. Her place was everything his wasn't. Even dimmed by shadows, tangled flowers in bright colors flanked the sidewalk and the house foundation, a chaotic kaleidoscope. The house siding was painted yellow — not soft and pale, but a shade undoubtedly called Glowworm. *What kind of sick mind paints their home in screaming yellow?*

Shaking his head, he rang the doorbell. A placard in varying shades of pink stained-glass hung beside her house number, claiming the abode as Gia's Castle. He'd always known Gia loved colors — any idiot could figure that out from seeing her day to day — but he'd never expected her glamorous taste to drift into gaudy.

Quick, light footsteps drifted from inside and Gia opened the door. As always, she was a vision of perfection — her hair pinned up, a sparkling pink western shirt clinging to her curves, worn-in jeans and half-boots. Only her smile was missing. She slung her purse over her shoulder like a soldier lugging a pack, slammed the door shut and trudged toward his running Porsche.

Apparently, she hadn't been kidding about not being a morning person.

"If you want to live, there better be a tea waiting for me in your cup holder." A definite growl colored her voice.

"My car doesn't have cup holders, love." As Gia threw her head back and zombie-groaned, he let his grin slide free. "But there may be a Matcha elixir tucked in there somewhere."

She glanced at him for the first time that morning. "Sometimes I think you're almost human."

"Only when I have to be." He opened the door for her and got a blast of her sweet perfume as she ducked inside, all attention on the waiting tea. An image of a different scenario hit his brain, of waking up before dawn with her perfume in his nose, her body pressed close in the tangled sheets, her mouth on his. Heat throbbed through him. Maybe she wouldn't be as grumpy if he woke her up while still in bed. He'd even bring her tea, if she asked nicely...with her hands.

The hour-long drive to the stables passed in silence, and more than once he checked to make sure Gia hadn't fallen back asleep. He didn't mind the quiet. It gave him time to prepare for their first meeting with Joann. He'd researched the Clancy family in the sleepless hours since Hamilton had assigned him this case—whatever personal information he could find online, business names, associated charities, friends and colleagues. The only way he could get Joann safely out of her marriage was to find something tangible that they could use against her husband. He wasn't above nudging the edge of blackmail, but any discovery would have to be done without being caught.

He knew exactly how monsters kept their victims trapped — by fear.

That fear undoubtedly kept Joann from involving the police or from simply walking away. His job was to find enough to undermine that fear, to give her the courage she needed to face her monster and cut the chains herself. No one else could do it for her, another fact he understood firsthand.

As he parked near the stables, Gia finally perked up. "Horses," she mumbled, unbuckling her seatbelt, her tea clutched close. "Only the promise of horses could get me up at this ungodly hour."

"I could think of a different kind of ride that's worth losing sleep over," he drawled, resisting an urge to trail his fingers through the golden locks curled on her shoulder. "And the odds of injury are less."

She paused with her hand on the door handle and looked at him. "I'd be especially happy to use a riding crop on you this morning, O'Connor. Let me know when you're ready to wear a bridle."

"I'll wear whatever you want, whenever you want, Princess." He leaned nearer and couldn't stop his attention from dropping to her full, delicious mouth. "Especially if it's leather."

Her pupils dilated. "I hate leather."

"Don't ever commit a crime and expect to get away with it, Ms. Hellman. You'd never make it past Roman, let alone a jury." He hopped out of the car before she could respond.

Despite being late June, the morning air held a bite, and he was glad for his long-sleeved Henley and jeans. He usually didn't mind the suit and nine-to-five routine, had acclimatized to his chosen prison of ties and four walls, but spending another day surrounded by open country wasn't a disappointment. And he couldn't ask for more stimulating company.

He sidled up to Gia as she shut the car door with her hip. "I believe you forgot my morning hug." At her eyeroll, he added. "Did I not flawlessly perform the doting fiancé role by voluntarily picking up a Matcha for you? With mint?"

She huffed a reluctant sigh, her expression suspicious. "How did you even know I like mint with my Matcha?"

Not ready to answer that, he simply opened his arms in invitation. While it was true his mother had spouted facts about the importance of human touch and demanded a ridiculous number of hugs from both him and his brother, adding hugs to his negotiations with Gia had been an inspired stroke of genius. He had every intention of keeping his emotional distance from her. That didn't mean he wouldn't take advantage of every opportunity to touch her while on display, act the enamored fiancé, claim her publicly as his...keep her close.

There were far worse jobs in the world than pretending to be Gia Hellman's lover.

Grumbling something under her breath, she stepped into his embrace and wrapped her arms around his ribs. A heady blend of her spun-sugar perfume and jasmine shampoo invaded his senses, and her soft warmth against him ignited all the memories from a long-ago winter night—the lemon-lime taste of her lips, the hungry slide of her tongue, her silken hair in his fingers. When she tucked her head under his chin and squeezed him tighter, that uncomfortable corkscrew stirred in his chest, ready to drill a hole in his armor.

One night with her and he could kill this lingering fascination. Maybe once, just once, he had a valid reason to break his rule of no pleasure with business.

"There you go, Sugarpop." She broke free and stepped around him, headed for the barn. "Morning hug quota filled."

He spun and smoothly grabbed her hand, linking their fingers. At her surprised glance, he murmured, "Cameras everywhere, love." He lifted their clasped hands to his mouth and pressed a soft kiss to her knuckles. *Good.* She'd remembered to wear the ring. "We have to be believable."

Gia's responsive smile was so brilliant that his breath almost caught. "I'll do my best to pretend you're Joey."

That corkscrew in his chest became a surgical blade, making a cut so clean and precise he couldn't determine the damage. He hid the pang behind his practiced lawyer mask. "Good plan."

Life filled the stables. Workers hauled hay and grain, brushed horses, led them down the aisle of stalls to the indoor arena or the fields for exercise and freedom. Nickers and the rustle of straw underscored soft, soothing voices and clopping hooves on tile. The scent of alfalfa, horseflesh and leather infused the clean summer air.

Before they reached the office, a slender woman in tall boots and English riding apparel emerged. Ian didn't need the introduction to recognize Joann. He'd seen pictures. Her silver hair brushed her chin in a sleek bob and the way she carried herself spoke of practiced elegance, a woman on constant display. The stone-faced, hulking bodyguard shadowing her merely confirmed his instincts.

Joann's gaze landed on them, and her expression held only polite interest—a teacher meeting her pupils for the first time, not a woman hoping to find a courtroom savior. She approached with one slim hand outstretched. "You must be Ian and Gia. Welcome to Clancy Stables."

"How did you know?" Gia smiled, shaking Joann's hand.

"You can always tell the city slickers from the country bumpkins." She winked and her soft, green eyes gleamed. "No offense."

"I knew I should've worn my cowboy boots." Ian gave the man looming a discreet distance behind Joann a passing look of curiosity as he shook Joann's hand, not lingering on the telltale bulge of a gun at his hip. He was maybe late forties and built like a linebacker, most likely loyal to Clancy, which would make any open discussion difficult. "But not all city boys avoid the rural life, Mrs. Clancy. I'm up for slogging through cow pies and wrangling livestock, boots or not."

Joann's perfectly plucked eyebrow arched, and her eyes sharpened, unnervingly like Hamilton's. "You may call me Joann, and beginners start at the beginning." Even her tone changed to chipped ice. "There will be no wrangling today." She pivoted and headed down the line of stalls. "The first step is becoming acquainted with your main instructors for the duration."

Ignoring the silent bodyguard trailing a few steps behind him, Ian analyzed her curt response to him. It could be that she didn't trust or even like men. Understandable, even if he was here for her. Trust had to be earned, and when it came to those who had given trust and been paid back with betrayal, trust was fragile and stingy. Which meant getting details out of her wouldn't be fast and if she didn't trust them, she wouldn't let them help her. He had no illusions about the courage she'd gathered simply to surreptitiously contact Hamilton. That spark of hope would be easy to crush with any doubt, and she might not try to escape her marriage again.

No matter how bad it got.

"I thought you were going to be our instructor," Gia said, following at Joann's elbow. She frowned an accusation over her shoulder at Ian. "It's why we showed up at this ungodly hour — to be instructed by you."

Joann stopped before a stall and grinned at Gia. "I'll teach you what I know." The horse inside the stall lifted its head and pushed up against the gate, close enough to nuzzle Joann's sleeve. "The rest is learned through firsthand interaction with your hands-on instructors." She faced the horse and fondly rubbed its forehead. "This is Belle. She'll be yours, Gia."

Her eyes shining, Gia caressed Belle's nose. "She's so pretty."

Joann's smile faded as she looked at Ian and crossed to the opposite stall. "You'll have Feathers."

Something smacked the stall gate, hard enough to rattle the iron bars. From the deepest shadows of the stall, out of sight, something snorted.

Ian slid his hands into his pockets and strolled closer, keeping his expression undaunted. *Perfect.* He was being assigned the horse from Hades. The gate rattled again. "Sounds like an enthusiastic animal."

Joann's smile was barbed. "You signed the waiver, I presume?"

"I even read it first." Ian reined in his shark impression with an effort and peered between the iron bars lining the upper half of the stall gate. A death-black horse tossed its head at him and struck the gate once more with a sharp hoof. "Feathers?"

"When he was younger and wilder, he once tore off a groom's down jacket with his teeth and shredded it until there was nothing but feathers." Joann tilted her head. "Don't worry. He's been trained since then." She leaned nearer. "Now he only attacks on cue."

"Whose cue?"

Joann smiled tightly and returned to Gia, who hadn't stopped stroking whatever she could reach of Belle. Eyes half-closed, a blade of straw stuck between its lips, the horse lazily soaked up the attention.

The crack of a hoof on wood pulled Ian back around. Feathers huffed between the iron bars, his breath a hot cloud on Ian's neck. The black forelock hid one eye, but the other gleamed with pooka mischief, as if the horse was already plotting ways to make his life miserable.

"Intimidation doesn't work on me, horse," Ian murmured. He held the beast's stare until it spun around, giving Ian his butt. His black tail swished.

"If you'll join us, Ian?" Joann held a halter and rope and slid into Belle's stall under the bodyguard's watchful eye.

Ten minutes later, after a basic lesson on haltering horses and taking the lead, Joann directed them out of the stables and along a fenced-in trail snaking along the property. Dawn made a bright line on the treetops, the sky clear and promising a perfect summer day. Belle plodded beside Gia like a well-trained dog. Feathers pulled on the lead in Ian's hand, his steps more of a prance, already testing the boundaries of authority. Joann walked between them, ready to take over should the occasion arise. Ian was determined not to let that happen, no matter what the demonic horse had planned.

Gia glanced over her shoulder at the bodyguard following a few feet behind. "Where's *your* horse?" she asked him.

The bodyguard's eyes narrowed slightly. "I'm not here for the horses, miss."

"Don't mind Sean." Wearing a small smile, Joann turned her face toward the first wedge of sunlight rising behind the trees, as if seeking its warmth. "He's my shadow, in case I need backup. When I leave the house, he goes with me."

If Gia was surprised, she didn't show it. Her expression innocent and thoughtful, she looked again at Sean. "Would you like to share Belle with me?" She batted her eyelashes. "It isn't right to be surrounded by horses and not have one."

"I'm good." His gravelly voice softened around the edges, and his gaze flicked to Joann before returning to Gia. "But thank you."

Gia's smile blazed. "Let me know if you change your mind."

Sean nodded once as the granite lines of his face threatened to crack before re-forming. His gaze flicked to Joann, lingering for a half-second too long to be all business. He resumed studying his surroundings, as if a pack of wolves might slink from the distant tree line or a machine-gun-toting mafia squad could suddenly drop from the sky and whisk Joann away.

Ian dismissed the look. As interesting as it was, if Joann trusted Sean, she wouldn't have contacted Hamilton. And if she didn't trust Sean, they couldn't either.

Ignoring the tightness in his chest, Ian battled with Feathers and slowed their pace enough to walk closer to Gia and Joann for a second or two. "Stop flirting, love. I might get jealous."

"Flirting is harmless when I already have the love of my life." Gia's voice was all sugared innocence, so sincere he would have believed her if he didn't know the truth. Her smile turned on him, and for a moment, he could believe that they were engaged, that she was his, that he was the one she needed.

Her smile shifted away and reality returned. Ian wanted to shake some sense into his empty head. Since when did he even think about engagements and belonging to one woman, being needed? Only two days with Gia and she was twisting his very nature.

With her free hand, Gia combed through Belle's glowing chestnut mane. "When do we ride, Joann?"

"Next lesson." For a woman who'd dealt with years of abuse, she hid it well behind a confident, caring mask. Her expression was fond, her voice warm. Of course, that could be the Gia Effect. The Glitter Girl seemed to slide beneath everyone's skin without any effort. "I want you both comfortable with your horses, to get to know each other, earn a bit of trust before moving on. It's important to be able to communicate, to understand your horse—and for your horse to understand you."

"Feathers and I understand each other fine." Ian gave the black horse a sidelong glance as Feathers jerked on the lead in a bid to go faster. He still waited for the devil to make his ultimate move. So far, he hadn't tried to bite or kick. He suspected the horse was simply biding his time, lulling the puny human into believing he was docile so when it came to riding, Ian would be relaxed and unprepared. Falling off on the first day would not happen. "I lead. He tests my authority and I respect that. I'd do the same. But we both know I will ultimately win."

"Should be an interesting match to watch." Joann's voice was quiet and smooth, hiding the true intent of her words. Ian had a feeling she would've added a smirk if she wasn't a prim and proper politician's wife.

"Matt told me you wanted to learn to ride for your wedding. When is the big day?" Completely ignoring Ian, Joann looked directly at Gia, who blinked her gorgeous baby blues in an airhead impression that fooled anyone who didn't know her.

"We haven't set a date yet." Her expression solemn, Gia toyed with the end of the lead. "My older sister Katerina just announced her divorce from her high school sweetheart. No one saw it coming, not even Kat. We thought we'd wait until the timing is better."

"That's kind of you, *cuidiú*. Not everyone would put their happiness on hold for someone else."

Kadoo? Ian's focus sharpened on the conversation, even as he pretended to pay attention to his ongoing battle of control with Feathers. Mr. Hamilton had said he once shared a secret childhood language with Joann, where they'd intersperse Gaelic words with English. Wasting time learning a dead language wasn't on his agenda, so he could have misheard. Or was she trying to communicate the only way she could with a bodyguard hired by Clancy as her constant companion?

"Honestly," Gia continued, quieter, "I can't even think about getting hitched while Kat's marriage is shattering. When it came to marital happiness, she was my role model. My sister's divorce calls into question all my hopes of a happily ever after. If the one couple you thought would last calls it quits, it's hard to believe it could happen for you."

A sharp twist in Ian's heart nearly made him rub his chest. Every word Gia had said rang with truth, and even though he didn't believe in fairytales and happily ever after, hearing her confession made him want to stand guard against the cold world and let her bask in the dream for a little while longer. Reality would break through soon enough.

Instead, he swiped a hand down his face. What was wrong with him, even considering helping her cling to lies?

As if sensing Ian's distraction, Feathers tossed his head, wrenching Ian's arm and ripping the rope free. He danced away, the lead dragging in the grass, a tempting lure for a human bent on domination.

"If you don't show Feathers you're in control, Mr. O'Connor, he'll make your lessons difficult." Joann gave him a firm look, a call to action. "Catch him. Show him you're a capable master, worthy of respect."

A few taunting feet away, Feathers grabbed a mouthful of grass, one dark eye trained on Ian.

"Listen here, horse," Ian crooned as he slowly approached. "I'm the master in this situation. Ever heard the term 'obey and prosper'? Submit and maybe I'll bring you an apple next time." Behind him, Joann and Gia continued their conversation, which was a relief. He didn't want to be the sole focus while he attempted to sweet talk a horse into submission. Matt was wrong about women and horses. Women were easier to persuade.

Feathers pranced a few more feet away, keeping just out of range.

"Oh, so you're more into sugar lumps and carrots?" He managed to keep the growl out of his tone. "How about suffering the consequences of insubordination? Bad horses don't get rewards. They get shipped off to France. Your fine coat won't save you from winding up on the dinner table there. Clearly, cooperation is your only viable choice."

Apparently, the soft voice and promises worked. Still eyeing him warily and stuffing his mouth with grass, Feathers stayed put. A couple more steps...

Ian lunged for the rope and caught the end just as Feathers jerked back. Already off balance, Ian slipped. He crashed to the ground. The lead ripped free from his hold once again, leaving a burn on his palms. He couldn't breathe. White stars sparked over the entire world in blinding, stunning fireworks.

"Do you need some help?" Boots came into view.

Ian's face heated as he dragged in a breath. He had no idea how long he'd been sprawled in the grass, his failure on display to everyone. "No," he snapped, "I don't need any help."

He pushed to his knees, and the second he regained his bearings, he realized his error. Joann had backed up, her arms folded protectively, her expression set on neutral. Sean loomed behind her like a mountain defense.

Ian wanted to punch the nearest fencepost. *What an idiot.* In a moment of mortification, he'd just killed whatever modicum of trust she might have been willing to give him.

Chapter Six

Tucked into a window booth, Gia wrapped her fingers around her cool iced-tea glass and stared at the man across the table from her. Ian had insisted they stop at the mom-and-pop café on their way back to Graywood after the unproductive client conference at the stables. Even though a sign sternly stated that only breakfast was served until ten a.m., he'd persuaded the waitress, who in turn had sweet-talked the cook, to break the rules and make him the biggest, vein-clogging, lard-dripping burger she'd ever seen. He devoured it as if he hadn't eaten in a week.

"What is wrong with you?" She couldn't keep the fascination from her voice.

He at least had the decency to swallow most of his mouthful before responding. "Nuthin'."

"The immaculate Ian O'Connor has grease on his chin, and in case you didn't realize it, that thing in your hand isn't in any way considered healthy or elegant. Your food-snob badge is about to be revoked."

"People change. You said it yourself."

"Yeah, *people*." She snorted. "You're a species all your own."

He swiped at his chin with a paper napkin. "I didn't eat breakfast."

"And being shown up by a headstrong steed made you ravenous?" She didn't bother hiding her grin. Witnessing him out of his element, no control and sprawled helplessly in the grass, had been nothing short of phenomenal.

He narrowed his eyes as he stuffed his mouth full of burger again, adding a chaser of fries.

Gia sipped at her tea to the symphony of sizzling from the kitchen and perking coffee. While it was too early to be sweltering yet, the diner's broken air conditioner would be a customer killer. Simply sitting and inhaling the fat-flavored air made her feel as greasy as the current state of Ian's fingers. She leaned back in the cracked plastic seat, unable to stop studying her temporary fiancé. He'd clearly hated losing control of the situation with Feathers, and instead of laughing it off, he'd gone all grizzly bear. While people dealt with embarrassment in different ways, his brutal reaction had surprised her. He'd lost his cool and cost them precious time with Joann, who'd ended the lesson. Only after some pleading from Gia and a heartfelt apology from Ian had she agreed to schedule two more trial sessions the following week.

She paused, mid-sip. *Oh, wait. That was it.* He was pissed not only that he'd failed, but that he'd bungled before witnesses. Losing control of Feathers so elegantly had started it and not making any progress on Joann's case had undoubtedly amplified the situation. What an interesting discovery from the surface-deep, one-night-only Ian. No matter what he'd said, he cared about how he appeared to the rest of the world, both outwardly and professionally.

Since she suspected sharing the discovery she'd unearthed in the pits of Ian O'Connor wouldn't be well received, she went with the next, most popular current affair spinning in her mind. "What's wrong with people? How could someone want to hurt the ones closest to them?"

"People are monsters," Ian said between fries. "Always have been, always will be."

"Not full-time monsters." She clicked her fingernails on her tea glass. "If that were true, there'd be no kindness, no good in the world."

He held her gaze across the scarred table. "Everyone is a monster, Princess. Some are just better at hiding their nature."

She huffed. "Don't you ever get tired of being cynical?"

"It's not cynicism if it's the truth." He pointed the sad remains of his hamburger at her, and part of a pickle doused in sauce plopped onto the plate. It smelled delicious, but her appetite had stayed behind at the stables, with Joann and her secrets. Lifting his eyebrows, he crammed the last of it into his mouth.

"I hope that all goes to your gut."

He smiled with chipmunk cheeks, chewed and swallowed, somehow without choking. "Me too. Then there'll be more of me to go around."

She rolled her eyes. "There's already too much of you."

"No need to be jealous, love. The offer to you is always open." He gave her his sexy smile, the one that stroked her senses, even through her disgust.

"Anyway," she flicked her straw at him, scattering tiny drops of tea, "it's no wonder nobody suspects Joann is suffering. Her politician's wife disguise is perfect, and with Sean the Boulder always around, no one has a chance to question her."

"Except someone who's searching carefully between the cracks." Ian wiped the grease and ketchup off his hands and dropped the napkin on his empty plate. "Did you notice anything?"

"Absolutely." Gia kept a straight face. "I suspect she won't be signing up for the Ian O'Connor fan club any time soon, which makes me admire her all the more."

"My charm is adjustable. I'll win her over." He gave her a cool look. "Allow me to rephrase. Did you notice anything important to the case?"

She chewed on her straw, deciding. Being hand-picked to help Mr. Hamilton's childhood friend and the heavy responsibility of an unorthodox case — even if it technically belonged to Ian — was an honor. She needed to prove that Mr. Hamilton's faith in her wasn't misguided, so she'd paid attention to every word, facial expression and hint of body language Joann had offered. Sharing her observations with Ian, though... She didn't want him to think she was an idiot by pointing out an insignificant detail. She wanted to be an equal teammate, helpful and valuable.

But beyond the obvious, she didn't have much, and something was better than nothing. She shrugged one shoulder. "Maybe it's inconsequential, but there were a couple times I didn't understand what she said."

His gaze sharpened and he folded his arms, clearly waiting for her to explain further.

"I could've sworn she said 'kabloom' once, which made zero sense."

"Kabloom, as in explosion?"

"Who knows? It didn't fit the subject at the time, which makes me doubt what I heard. And I think she called me 'misha' once. She could've temporarily forgotten my name, but I don't think so. She seems way too sharp for that."

One corner of his mouth curled up. "Mr. Hamilton is right. When Alexander returns from vacation, I may not let him have you back."

Tingles thrummed through her at the approval and she struggled not to smile like an imbecile. If Ian knew how much that compliment meant to her, he'd manipulate it to get what he wanted. "As if you have any say in the matter."

His smile only widened, a dare. "Gaelic. Joann used random Gaelic in her sentences, probably to test us, to make sure we were truly sent by Hamilton. As children, they used Gaelic in secret codes to each other. No one else would know that."

"Get out." She set her tea down before she dropped it. "I'm starting to feel like a spy, not a legal assistant." She leaned forward, her elbows on the table. "So what did she say?"

He grabbed the waiting receipt on the edge of the table and slid out of the booth. "That's what we need to figure out before next week, love."

Gia leaned back in the seat while he went to the register to pay, a thrill coursing in her blood like electric shocks. Hidden abuse, secret languages, a fake engagement with the one man who tempted her to forget love and stick with lust...

Life was about to either get fun or be tipped completely upside down—maybe both—and for the first time in a long while, she couldn't wait to see what happened next.

* * * *

"Let me see the proof." Karen, head accountant at Hamilton & Associates, grabbed Gia's hand in an unrelenting grip and stared at the shiny rock weighing down her ring finger.

On Friday afternoon in the office with her mountains of paperwork, Gia patiently indulged yet another 'congratulations' and imagined wearing The Shoes— sleek, glittering and heels sharp enough to stab with. With her first overtime check, they'd be hers. After their Thursday morning riding lesson disaster, Ian had dropped her off at home to change, beaten her back to work and had wasted no time spreading the latest in the life of the newest Graywood A-list couple, otherwise known as 'Gian'. *The pompous jerk.* He made a terrible fiancé. The entire office was still abuzz with the news, and since Karen had been out sick the previous day, she played catch up.

Slowly, Karen lifted her gaze to Gia's face, her green eyes wide. Resident knower-of-all-things at Hamilton & Associates, she was undoubtedly peeved that she hadn't been the first to catch the newsflash. "Are all your girly parts enchanted or something? How the hell did you bewitch Ian O'Connor into a proposal?"

Gia offered a smile as fake as her engagement. "Never underestimate the power of stilettos and charm, girlfriend."

"I never do. That's why I don't get it."

She let her smile slide into sultry. "And a touch of midnight magic never hurts."

"You sly vixen." Karen perched on the edge of Gia's desk, her plaid skirt a few inches too short to be considered courtroom professional, but she had the legs to pull it off and no one could ever accuse her of looking shabby. "You had everyone fooled. We had a running bet in accounting with variable odds about how long you'd last before falling for his lure, if you'd want more, if *he'd* want more—that was a high-risk bet—but no one, *no one* bothered betting on a marriage proposal."

"Yeah, well, I'm almost as surprised as everyone else." On the way back from the stables, she and Ian had worked out their story. An unplanned run-in at the lake had led to dinner, which had stretched into a weekend and a whirlwind romance neither one could deny. While sudden and unanticipated, their connection was too powerful to doubt, so they'd taken the commitment plunge.

Too powerful to doubt. Like she'd had with Joey. Her heart squeezed.

"I thought we were friends." Karen crossed her ankles and shook her head. "You should've given me a heads-up. I could be rich right now."

"So sorry, Kar." Gia leaned back in her chair. "I didn't realize my *friend* had a running bet on my love life."

"Give me some credit." Karen sniffed. "The bet was only on your level of resistance to the O'Connor one-night-only temptation. I've never even put Ian and love in the same sentence before." She looked a little rattled by the fact that she just had.

"So how much did you make off my ignorance?"

"Three hundred." Karen grinned, all leprechaun mischief with her pixie-short red hair and freckles. "I knew you'd last longer than anyone else."

Except for the interrupted, too-quick tryst at the holiday party… If anyone besides Adara had known about that, the bets would have been completely different. Gia sniffed. "Do tell. I want to know how you recognized my hidden strength?"

Karen's humor faltered, and she fiddled with the pencil stuck behind her ear, self-consciously patting her hair before answering. "Every corner of your heart belonged to Joey. He had a hold on you that not even the unconquerable Ian could penetrate — pun totally intentional — even after…everything." She cleared her throat and fanned her hands near her face, banishing fake tears. "See what love does to me? Pathetic."

"I want you to know that I didn't plan this. It just sort of happened," Gia said carefully, attuned to any flicker in Karen's expression. The entire office knew about the number-cruncher's long-standing crush on Ian. Her motto was Persistence Pays Off. Only with Ian, it never had. "Ian wasn't even on my radar." While technically true in her current quest to wait for true love to find her again, she couldn't deny the physical attraction that had been there for over a year.

"But you've been on his radar since day one." Karen's mouth tightened slightly, and the flash in her eyes belied her carefree tone. She shrugged. "Guess I should've played a different game to win." She straightened and cocked a hip. "Be careful, G. I'd hate to see your heart shattered a second time so soon."

"Don't worry." Gia hole-punched another stack of papers and tapped it on the desk to straighten the edges. "My heart won't be broken by Ian."

"And if it does" — Karen's eyes glinted like poison — "we'll find some creative and evil ways to kick his ass together."

Her smile sincere, Gia grabbed another file. She had time to plot a way to publicly break up with Ian in the future, and it would *absolutely* be creative and evil.

"Are you going out with us tonight?" Karen pivoted and backed toward the door, wriggling her eyebrows. "Or, now that you're engaged, does your fiancé control your schedule?"

Gia snorted. "Fiancé does not mean 'ruler'. He wants me to go to his weekly guy soccer game." He'd ordered her to be at the soccer game. *Ordered*, not invited. On principal alone, she shouldn't go. He didn't own her free time, a straight-up fact he'd learn sooner or later. She lifted her chin. "I haven't decided if I will yet."

"Seriously?" Karen stopped at the doorway. "Watching a bunch of half-naked guys chasing after a ball and jostling each other for free? That's a no-brainer."

An image of Ian running flashed to mind — his perfect hair mussed, his face flushed, his bare chest gleaming from exertion. Her body throbbed in the best spots, and she crossed her legs, biting her lip.

Her smile knowing, Karen waggled her fingers as she turned into the hall. "See you Monday."

Gia mumbled a goodbye and tapped her fingernails on the desk. Then again, showing up at a men-only soccer game could be a perfect demonstration that she had a mind and goals of her own — she couldn't help a smirk — whether or not they aligned with Ian's idea of a fake engagement.

Chapter Seven

Guided by shouts and the *ping* of a hard-kicked ball, Gia strolled across the lonely high school parking lot. Ian's Porsche glared red from the corner, parked at an angle to discourage any company. None of the other vehicles—a beat-up pickup, a family van and several motorcycles—were familiar. Whoever played Friday soccer with Ian didn't work at Hamilton & Associates, which might prove interesting. Despite being fake-engaged to Ian, she still had a future love to find.

Romance randomly ignited in an after-work soccer field? It can happen.

She twisted around the turnstile in the chain-link fence. Turf replaced the concrete, and she congratulated herself on remembering to exchange her heels for sneakers. There was little worse on a girl's attempt to look stylish than sinking into the ground with each step and struggling to break free. The school seemed graveyard-empty, with the students out for the summer. Trailing her finger along the gym's rough brick wall, she smiled at the flurry of obscenities drifting from behind the building, the sources out of sight.

Her brothers played the same way, with bruises and insults—and more than a few times, blood—no matter the game. Competition was its own sport in her family, and survival required learning how to win by any means necessary. Violence, manipulation or craftiness were all allowed.

That familial competition had been part of the reason she'd traveled halfway across the country for her own start. She might not be afraid of competition, but living it day in and day out was exhausting, especially when she had no interest in the games.

Gia reached the end of the gym and stopped, dazzled by the glint of sunlight on slick, male skin only yards away. She leaned one shoulder against the gym wall and slipped her hands into the pockets of her capris, enjoying the view. At least a dozen men, all shirtless, all deliciously fit, ran down the field toward the goalie box. Without any referee to call foul, the elbowing exceeded any aggression normally allowed, but no one seemed to mind.

The tangle of men separated. Ian darted around another player and took control of the ball, moving with supple strength and animal grace.

Her mouth went dry. *Holy snap, crackle, pop, he's beautifully made.* She shouldn't watch him, but it was impossible not to. The expensive suits he usually sported only hinted at all the carnal treasures he hid from most of the world. In nothing but loose nylon shorts and shoes, his lean body flexed freely with each move, exactly as she'd envisioned in her moments of weakness. The man was pure power, from his ridged shoulders to his chiseled chest and abs, all the way to the smooth jut of hipbone and that sexy V leading to...

Gia jerked her gaze away to the tennis courts across the field. Imagining that final frontier would *not* be helpful to her cause. She'd have enough trouble pushing back the sudden, burning urge to lick the sweat off his skin, drop by drop. She counted to ten before returning her attention to the game.

Ian kicked the soccer ball to Roman, a local cop she'd met at Adara's wedding, and a guy she didn't recognize intercepted. The attacker spun, revealing his face, and Gia sighed at the happy distraction. The front was as good as the back. Not as fine as Ian, but enough to hold her captive while she cooled off. He kicked the ball to a teammate.

Said teammate pivoted, ruining her enjoyment with his face. Not that he was physically repellent, but ugliness came in all different forms and Derek had it going on. A fireman, he'd hit on her at a party while she'd clearly been with Joey. *No respect for boundaries.* She didn't mind confidence, but when cockiness became unwanted advances? Automatic turnoff.

She forced her focus from the manly display of flesh to figuring out the teams. Ian was the only one who wasn't law enforcement or fire. His team was Roman and four other badges she'd met—not from being in trouble. She'd only lived in small-time Graywood for three years, but it had been long enough to meet anyone who wasn't a homebody, and despite being involved with Joey most of that time, she wasn't blind or inhuman. A good-looking man would catch her attention, however brief.

Roman made a defensive play for the ball. Derek flung his elbow and Roman went down, clutching his face. Gia gasped, straightening. Everyone stopped, with the exception of Derek. He kicked the ball into the goal and whooped as if he'd just won the World Cup.

Ian's glare at Derek's back was absolute murder. The other guys gathered around their fallen player.

"Nothing's broken." Roman sat up, pinching his nose, blood streaming down his face. He tilted his head back. "I'll be fine."

Derek swaggered to his water bottle and took a swig as he wandered back. "Dude, sorry about that." He grinned. "You shouldn't run your face into my elbow."

Ian pulled Roman up by the hand, his expression set to grim. His friend wobbled and listed to one side, and Ian helped him drop back to the ground. "Better sit this one out, man."

"Team Law forfeits?" Derek wiped the sweat from his brow, smirking. "Leave it to a lawyer to slither out of the game."

"I don't recall mentioning the word *forfeit*, nozzlejockey." Ian's tone was smooth, not even a hint of the snarl Gia suspected twisted inside him.

"You can't keep up with a player short." Derek's eyes glinted a challenge. "No sense denying it."

One off-duty officer grumbled something beneath his breath. A couple more glared. But no one contradicted Derek.

Gia stepped away from the wall. "I'll fill in for Roman."

Every head turned her way, as if they hadn't noticed her there yet. *Insulting.* In her shimmering pink tank top and white capris, she was beyond cute—if she did say so herself.

"Finally decided to show up, Princess?" Ian's smile eased the chill in his expression, but not enough to erase the cutthroat image.

She hid her smile. "My plans changed."

Heat flashed in his eyes.

"Gia..." Derek dumped some water over his head and shook out his blond hair. "Don't tell me you're here for him." He hooked a thumb at Ian. "You can do so much better."

She decided at that moment that she didn't necessarily like *all* firemen, no matter their muscles or importance to the community. "Shut your smokehole, Derek." She smiled sweetly and batted her eyelashes. "I'm filling in for Roman, which is the perfect opportunity to demonstrate exactly how much better I can do than you."

Ian smirked.

Derek's gaze skipped over Gia, as if deciding her worth...which, from the glint in his eyes, mostly included bedroom activities. *What a scumbag.* "It's fine with me if Team Pork agrees not to whine about the handicap when they lose."

Handicap. Gia kept her ditzy smile on tight and slid her hands into her back pockets instead of smacking him upside the head or popping his perfectly straight nose.

The rest of the players turned back to the field, silently accepting Roman's unexpected replacement. And she liked them all a little more because of it. Derek shrugged and followed, leaving her alone with Ian.

"Guess it's pure luck you chose sneakers over stilettos for once." Ian's smirk turned fierce as he held her gaze. "For the record, I prefer the stilettos, especially if there's nothing else."

She ignored the responsive shiver. "Show some respect, Sugarpop." She brushed by him and faced Roman. Even with a T-shirt pressed to his nose and blood spattering his pale skin, he looked ready to take down a criminal at a second's notice. "You're okay with me substituting for you, right?"

"Not even Derek's enough of a dick to elbow a woman in the nose." Roman's voice was nasally, but his dark eyes danced. "Don't let him intimidate you."

"As if he could." She took the field, Ian beside her.

"Have you played soccer before?" he asked, low enough only she could hear.

"I used to watch my brothers' games all the time." She kept her voice light and innocent. "Isn't that pretty much the same?"

"*Chara,*" he muttered, one of Garret's favorite curses, his jaw tight for only a second before smoothing into lawyer calm. Ian O'Connor clearly hated to lose, no matter the game or the stakes.

"Don't discount the underdog." She bumped his arm with her shoulder.

He leaned near her ear, bringing a thrilling blend of summer spice and heated man. "I never do."

The game resumed with a blocked penalty kick and another Derek takeover attempt. He slid between two opposing players and snared the ball for all of two seconds. Amid the jostling and jockeying, Derek hit the ground so fast that Gia wasn't sure what had happened. But she suspected it had something to do with Ian's elbow…or fist.

Derek rolled onto his hands and knees, his head bowed, blood dripping. He lifted his head and smiled through the red flowing from his lip, but the shards in his eyes were icy. "See how easy it is to slip up, counselor?" He rose to his feet, his gaze never leaving Ian's. "Mistakes happen on the field. No hard feelings."

Ian simply smiled and turned away without helping Derek up.

Gia didn't flinch at the blatant payback. Derek had totally earned that one.

Unfortunately, Derek made his penalty kick, and the game resumed full force. Taking Roman's position as defender, Gia hung back, waiting. The ball came her way, driven by Derek, Ian on his heels, straight at her as if he were a freight train and she should move if she wanted to survive.

What a d-bag.

When Derek was close enough that she could make out the sweat on his forehead, instead of dodging out of the way, Gia burst forward. No one ever suspected that a glamour girl could run. She darted in as Derek swerved, too late. Her foot connected with the ball, and she took control. Derek lunged around with a curse, and she elbowed past him. Then Ian was beside her. She raced up the field, waiting for Ian to order her to pass the ball to him like her brothers always did, as if she weren't capable enough. Instead, Ian shielded her from the other team. With every pounding step, every tap of foot to ball, she listened for the signal to let him take control.

It never came. When she drew close to the midfield line, she passed the ball to him by choice and stopped, breathing hard. Ian took it halfway toward the goal and neatly passed it to the teammate waiting undefended by the goal. The ball sailed between the outstretched hands of the goalie.

"Dammit." Derek's tone was more of admiration than annoyance as he stopped beside her. He planted a hand on his hip and looked at her again, dropping the contempt from before. "You're a menace. Playing sweet and saucy, then showing up the guys." He shook his head, his smile crooked.

"That's my girl." Breathless, Ian slung his arm around her shoulders and pulled her close to his side.

The smile slid from Derek's face. "You're together? Seriously? I thought you were joking around."

"I never joke when it comes to women, especially this one." Ian kissed her temple, playing his role perfectly.

"I thought you didn't do the dating game." Derek squinted, as if he couldn't quite believe what he was seeing. He leaned in close, checking Ian's eyes. "I didn't mean to slam into you hard enough to scramble your brain cells."

"You give yourself too much credit," Ian said blandly.

Derek straightened, his expression less friendly. "No more free passes, girl."

"Never asked for one, smokehole." She batted her eyelashes at him.

As Derek jogged away, Ian met her gaze. "I believe I just fell in love with you."

Her heart jerked, a strange little twinge, which made no sense. Ian was a shameless flirt and his words meant nothing. Love was her deal, not his. The heat must be overcooking her senses. She swatted his butt in a total man-sports move, going for casual because, if she didn't, she might stop to analyze why her heart had backfired, and she was sure she didn't want to know the answer. "Soccer is clearly hazardous to your mental health, O'Connor. You just said the L-word, which isn't the same as lust, by the way."

"Bet lust could be close enough." He grinned and tried for a return butt-swat, which she deftly blocked.

She rolled her eyes and trotted back to her position on the field. At least the sport still made sense. Her reaction? Not so much. Ian wasn't love material, true or false or any other kind. No matter how he let her handle the soccer ball or how delectable he looked rumpled and sweaty and breathless. Her tummy tightened. It wasn't difficult to imagine him in another scenario, tangled in sheets, his hair mussed from her hands, his breath coming hard and fast...

Crap. If she kept that thought train going, she'd trash her vow and jump Ian instead, put love on hold. *Again.* She shook out her hands and focused on anything but Ian. *Nope, not going there.*

The game proceeded with less civility and more respect toward Gia. By the end, she was sweaty and gasping and all her hair was out of place. It was the most fun she'd had in a long time. Both teams gathered at the edge of the field.

"You're one of us now, Gia." Talon, the one fireman she hadn't met before and who was one of the nicer players on the field—she hadn't seen him elbow anyone—tossed her an unopened water bottle from his gym bag. "Pizza and beer at Tony's. Losers pay, so you should take advantage of the freebies while you can." He leaned in and lowered his voice. "We won't be so easy on you next time."

Gia laughed and twisted off the bottle cap. "*I* won't be so easy on you fools next time."

"Next time?" Roman gave Talon a friendly shove. The bleeding had stopped, but his nose was red, one eye swollen. "Gia's banned from the soccer field. I don't care how fast she runs or how easily she got inside Derek's guard. I will not be permanently replaced by someone prettier than me." He almost smiled, which was a shocker. The closest she'd seen Roman come to a smile was a mouth twitch. He'd make some lucky girl a fabulous gargoyle.

Derek snorted. "That was the problem. She distracted me." He winked at Gia, easing the arrogance in his excuse. "But don't worry, man. You're still the fairest in the land, even with a shiner."

The only sign that Roman hadn't forgiven Derek was a slight narrowing of his eyes. "As I'm eating my anchovy and garlic pizza tonight, I'll be snuggling up to you, nozzlejockey. Breathing on you."

Ian smirked and stooped for his bag by the bench. "Have fun. Gia and I have plans."

Gia folded her arms and cocked a hip, even as a thrill zipped up her spine. "Plans better than pizza and beer?"

Ian leaned in, close enough for a kiss, and all the other guys nearby, the soccer field and school, faded into nonexistence. His gaze dropped to her mouth, and her lips tingled. "Infinitely better."

She resisted a shiver as he grabbed her hand and guided her toward the parking lot. A few catcalls followed on their heels, and she lifted one finger in the air, a signal that needed no explanation. Hoots of laughter erupted.

"Stop charming the soccer crowd, love."

"Those guys are great." With her free hand, she brushed grass from her shirt. Her capris might have permanent grass stains, but it was a willing sacrifice.

Ian gave her a cool look. "Every one of them would jump you if given the chance."

She smiled sweetly. "So they're like you, then."

"Oh no, Princess." He tightened his grip on her hand. "They're far tamer than me."

"Tame or not, I need a shower before I'm going anywhere." She didn't dare sniff, afraid of what she might smell. Deodorant only went so far.

"You can shower at my place."

She wrenched her hand free. "I don't think so. First off, I'd never be naked within ten feet of you. Second, I'm not showering only to put my sweaty clothes back on and I'm certainly not going to wear any skanky clothes some other woman has left behind in the O'Connor Den of Iniquity."

His lip curled. "Ten feet wouldn't be enough of a buffer zone, love."

Exactly. "I'll freshen up at my own house." She added some steel to her tone in case he thought she was teasing. "Where do you want me to meet you? And there better be dinner involved, because I'm famished."

"I'll feed you, little savage." He hit a button on his keyring and his Porsche beeped. "My place. Fifteen minutes."

His place. She swallowed. Heading into the dragon's lair would require some careful preparation, and she wasn't about to let him know that she needed armor and weapons. "Fine. I'll be there in an hour."

"Half an hour," he said, tossing his bag in the back seat.

She snorted. "You really don't know anything about women, do you? Forty-five minutes, if you're lucky."

His smile was pure shark. "I'm feeling extraordinarily lucky today, Princess. Forty minutes. Don't be late."

Gia stuck out her tongue and trudged to her car. She'd better spend a few of those minutes finding a bazooka and a bulletproof vest.

Chapter Eight

Forty-five minutes after the soccer game—not because Gia needed the extra time, but purely on principle—she parked her hatchback on the dead-end street of Ian's house, turned the motor off and prepared for her imminent destination.

Dark gray siding gave his one-story house an austere edge, and the stand of oak trees looming behind it didn't add anything friendly. Not a single flower, color spot or even a stray dandelion brightened any corner, only shrubs and decorative rocks. The place looked like a neat-freak's dream, not the opulent palace of a womanizer, but it could be a guise, hiding an interior bent on seduction of any female who happened close. The dark stepping-stones through an Irish moss lawn felt more like the trail leading toward a goblin's den than a dragon's—all the danger without the dazzle of bling.

In other words, there was nothing to tempt her beyond the man inside.

She opened the car door, shaking her head. The grim exterior had to be a ruse. Or maybe Ian was so confident in his seduction skills that he didn't rely on props at all. Her attention slid over the red Porsche in the open garage. Then again...maybe not.

Shaking out her skinny jeans — wearing a skirt while alone in Ian's house wasn't happening, no matter the strength of her vows — Gia squared her shoulders and strolled up to the front door. Even the house numbers were severe, black, iron and perfectly straight. Before she could hit the doorbell, the door swung open, releasing a draft of barbecue-scented air.

Ian glowered from the doorway. His dark hair shower-damp, even in jeans and a Henley he held a natural confidence that bordered on arrogance, as if nothing could stop him from ultimately getting whatever he wanted, systematically smashing whatever roadblocks dared to stand in his way. The effect of that confidence alone turned her bones to liquid, and she was beyond grateful he didn't know her weakness. If he ever decided to concentrate that force solely on her, she'd buckle within seconds.

"We agreed on forty minutes." His voice was an accusing purr, as if even annoyed he couldn't help but tempt her. "The cold rice is your responsibility."

"Worth it." She tossed her hair over her shoulder and gave him a brilliant smile, going for a calm confidence of her own. "Looking like this sometimes requires sacrifices, O'Connor." She inhaled and her mouth watered. "Keep your rice and salad. This delicate flower needs real food. Please tell me you cooked steak."

He waved her inside and led her into the living room, where restaurant boxes neatly lined the coffee table with plates, silverware and empty glasses. "I don't cook, Princess." His mouth twitched. "But I suspected you'd want some meat."

She rolled her eyes. "Don't make me sick before dinner."

Ian grinned full-out, and she waved off the sudden buzz in her veins as he grabbed the glasses. The night hadn't even started, and he was already sneaking under her skin. "Want wine? Or"—his gaze drifted to her mouth and his voice dropped an octave—"I can whip up a margarita."

The memory of him pressed hard against her, his hands skilled and seductive on her skin, his lips magic in the dark, made her brain temporarily blank... She blinked fast, shoving it off before she started panting. "Water's great."

Sparks fired electric in his blue eyes, as if he'd experienced the same, sharp memory, but he disappeared into another room and returned moments later with one glass of iced water and a tumbler with whiskey. He handed her the glass and gestured lazily at the waiting food. "Self-service, Princess. Take all the cold rice you want."

"Already planned on it." Gia lifted her water in a snarky salute, halfway tempted to dump it over her head to cool some sense back into her body. Since doing that would tip him off, she grabbed a plate and filled it, mostly with steak, leaving a little room for rice and salad. She settled on the floor cross-legged. Ian hadn't suggested any sitting arrangement and low-key was perfect for her purposes of keeping tonight casual — hands-free, easy to escape.

Following her lead, Ian smoothly sat across from her on the floor. He leaned back against the couch and drew up one knee.

"So, what's your brilliant scheme to quietly make Joann a free woman?" Maybe steering the conversation to business would pull her out of his gravity long enough to survive the black, consuming hole that was Ian. She stuffed a bite of steak into her mouth. It was juicy, delicious and she barely caught a moan in time. Encouraging Ian wouldn't help her cause.

Gazing into the distance, he sipped his whiskey. "Joann doesn't like me."

Gia nearly choked as she swallowed. "Of course she doesn't. She's smart."

"But she likes you." His eyes gleamed.

"I reiterate." She pointed her fork in the air. "Smart woman."

He gave her a cool look. "My point is that Joann won't talk to me until I earn her trust, and we don't have time for that. It will be up to you to gather information."

Sure. Should be easy to dig up delicate personal information one Gaelic word at a time from a woman who was never alone, always surrounded by her husband's employees. "All out of the hearing distance of Sean or anyone else who might be listening."

He lifted his glass. "Exactly."

"If she only feels comfortable using bits of coded Gaelic, getting anywhere fast isn't going to happen, counselor." Gia stabbed another piece of steak with her fork. "Especially since I don't know any Gaelic."

Drumming his fingers on the glass in his hand, he gazed in the distance, clearly plotting how best to go in for the O'Connor kill. "The words Joann used — whatever their true pronunciations may be — had to be her way of testing the waters. She needs to know for certain Hamilton sent us." He slid a coaster near and set his tumbler on the coffee table, a total neat-freak move, and stood. "Once we figure out what she said, we'll find the perfect word you can relay back to her, a confirmation." With that, he strolled into another room, out of sight.

Okay, then. Gia used the alone time to truly enjoy her steak. She took another bite, closed her eyes and released the appropriate, appreciative moan. On a tight budget, she didn't splurge on fine food — after all, shoes were more important and lasted longer — so she'd savor every second.

She opened her eyes and found Ian leaning one shoulder against the wall, a laptop tucked under one arm. He watched her, his gaze smoldering. Heat immediately swept through her face. "Take a picture, pervert. It'll last longer."

"Video would be better," he said, his voice low and husky. "With audio so I could replay your moan over and over." He cocked his head, never breaking his predatory stare. "There's still time to remedy that, Princess."

"In your dirty, dirty dreams, O'Connor." Hers too — more personal information he didn't need to know. If only her insane attraction to Ian had melted away with her vow. Then again, maybe a vow wasn't worthy if it was easy to keep.

Still wearing his annoying, knowing smirk, he strolled across the room and sat beside her. Too close, his knee brushed hers and his spicy cologne drifted near. Steak and Ian made a heady combination. If she could bottle that scent, she wouldn't have to worry about money another second and she'd have an entire walk-in closet dedicated to shoes.

Ian opened his laptop. "Ready for a short Gaelic lesson?" He turned his head, and his gaze flicked from the remainder of her steak to her mouth. "Don't stop eating on my account."

"I didn't intend to." Gia speared her steak with the knife and lifted it to her mouth. She ripped off a chunk with her teeth. Let him see how not-sexy she could be.

Instead of the sophisticated look of disgust she expected, his smirk widened to a grin. Before she could move, he leaned in and licked the corner of her mouth. Her breath caught and she froze, transfixed by his unexpected nearness, his silken tongue on her skin, stirring up more unhelpful memories. He eased back a few inches. "You had some extra steak sauce waiting to drip," he murmured. "I didn't want it to stain your shirt."

"So that's why you didn't give me a napkin." Her voice emerged too breathless and she narrowed her eyes at him, going for irritated. But her mouth tingled, wanting more, clinging to how he'd kissed her before, how she wanted to kiss him again, push the computer off his lap and replace it with her body, slide her hands beneath his shirt, over the hard planes of his lean physique. She gripped her fork in a tight fist, digging her fingernails into her palm.

"We could postpone research until the morning." His voice was rough, his head still close enough to hers that his breath brushed her mouth. "What do you usually do on Friday nights, Princess?"

Find ways not to think about Joey...or you. Gia wavered between leaning in and pressing her mouth to his — what her body screamed at her to do — or following the rational plan of jumping up, hurdling the coffee table and escaping to the safe distance of the chair across the room. No wonder she never resisted much before. Resistance was hard when the temptation was achingly real. But acting on her desires would directly contradict her goal, shove her right back into the corner she'd crawled out of and wind up in another dead-end regret.

She was through with that cycle, no longer a slave to her hormones, despite all the ways Ian brought them to life.

"We're working, O'Connor," she finally choked out. "You're paying me overtime right now, and while I appreciate the steak, no way in hell will you be paying me to tumble into your shenanigans." Hey, at least she remained in control of her speech. *Go, Gia.*

"I don't care what you call it." A throaty growl. "You could clock out. Use personal time for whatever we dream up. I'd feed you all the steak you want in between. No one has to know."

"*I'd* know. Your problem is that you're a slave to your man bits."

"No one has ever complained." His gaze leisurely dipped to her mouth again, and those throbbing pinpricks in her nerves danced faster, harder.

She ripped off another hunk of meat, her best defense to keep her mouth occupied. While she chewed, he watched her mouth like a starving man forced to watch patrons in a restaurant eat. It wasn't her fault he'd chosen whiskey over cold rice. She swallowed and leaned back, out of kissing range.

"For the record, I postponed movie night with Karen. That was my exciting Friday celebrate-the-end-of-the-work-week plan, besides making my weekly stop at

Heelcandy to drool over the shoes I'll be buying with my overtime funds."

He looked at her hand—the hand still gripping the fork like a lifeline—and she immediately dropped it onto the plate. She hadn't fooled him at all.

"It's not too late to cut out and celebrate. I could grab a bottle of wine, lower the lights, turn on some music and we could finish the ditched dance at Garret's wedding." He traced the curve of her cheek with one finger, leaving a trail of electric heat. "You left me hanging, Princess. With spectators. It made people question my reputation."

"Poor thing." She patted his hand like a grandma would a whiny kid, a technique learned from Emma. Time at the senior center was well-spent and a perfect reminder of what she wanted—decades with her true love, not a string of failed tryouts. "Are you questioning your manhood now?"

He once again fixed his gaze unabashedly to her mouth, caught her wrist and drew a slow circle on her pulse with his thumb. "I'm sure a kiss could repair the damage."

The velvet seduction of his low voice slid through her, coaxing all her barriers to relax. Kissing Ian O'Connor wouldn't end with one simple smooch. Her mind played out how it would go. The kiss would start almost sweet with just a kick of wicked. Clothes would slowly come off. The living room would be left behind for the bedroom—or maybe even the kitchen, depending on how she responded. He'd make sure she forgot the case, forgot her goals, forgot everything beyond how he touched her and made her body hum.

Her heart punched faster and her blood awakened with new fire. It would be so easy to play along, to kiss him and finish what they'd started at the holiday party. She could find out if the bolt of yearning still lodged in her chest had been worth keeping.

But no matter what he said, Ian wouldn't treat her the same the next day. She'd be grouped in with all his other one-night women, and even more than sabotaging her goals, she didn't want him to look at her like he did everyone else — like her worth belonged only in the bedroom. The thought splashed ice-cold water on her libido.

"What would *you* normally be doing on a Friday night?" Staring him down, she stuffed the last bite of steak into her mouth.

His smirk returned and he leaned back. "I'm where I want to be, Princess."

Even though she doubted that very much, imagining him wanting to be with her, working on a strange and delicate case, was a nice fantasy.

Apparently surrendering seduction for the time being, he tapped on the keyboard and brought up a website — *Gaelic for Nitwits*. "Where," he asked, frowning at the screen, "did you learn to play soccer like that?"

She grinned and relaxed, reliving the fun from the afternoon. "I have two big, bad brothers. Competition is a way of life in the Hellman household, no matter your size. I may not have their brawn or my sister's WWF moves, but I'm nimble and faster. If they can't catch you, muscles are meaningless."

He paused and smiled at her, a true smile without any underlying motives, and her breath caught. Maybe it was a good thing Ian was brutally honest about not wanting a relationship or any emotional ties. Every time she saw him as a normal person with feelings, she worried about her heart being seduced along with her body. Her chest tightened. Or maybe that was why so many women wanted more, even when he barricaded himself away after their one night with him. If he smiled like that at her more than once, as if she meant something to him, she might be fooled into wanting more too.

Needing something to do, Gia set her plate aside and took a long drink of iced water. The chill eased the steam in her blood. She kept a firm grip on the glass to keep her hands occupied, just in case they got ideas of their own. "Don't you have any brothers or sisters who harassed and annoyed you, shaping you into the shark you are today?"

His smile morphed into his usual style, bland, giving nothing of his true emotions away. "One brother. We don't talk much."

"Oh. Sorry."

"I'm not." He returned his focus to the computer. "He's a prick."

Gia couldn't hold back a surprised laugh. "Too much alike, maybe?"

One corner of his mouth twitched. "Maybe."

He tapped the keyboard. "Repeat Joann's words."

"One sounded like 'kabloom', the other 'misha'" — she shook her head — "but I could be totally off." She twisted around and faced him fully. "Don't you think this whole case, this situation is beyond weird? I'm not saying I mind a little weirdness, but that's usually reserved for my outside life, not my job."

"It's an unconventional method of finding valid reasons for Clancy to grant Joann a quiet, no-hassle divorce." He shrugged, his gaze on the screen. "People have their motives for doing what they do, which isn't our call. But in this particular case, part of our job is finding out why Joann feels she can't walk into our office and hire us to represent her. Filing for divorce is simple. It's getting untangled from another person's life that's the difficult part." Something dark invaded his expression and flickered silver in his eyes, a deep, ancient wound. "Sometimes, the other party doesn't want to let go, and they'll go to any lengths to hold on, to maintain control."

A shiver rolled down her spine. Whatever memories haunted him now, they were bad. She wanted him to say more but didn't dare ask. If he suspected he showed even a pinhole in his armor, she'd never peel away any of his layers. While running on the soccer field beside him, protected and strangely freed by his mere presence, she'd caught a different glimpse of the man beneath the veneer. And while it might be dangerous to all her goals, she wanted more of *that* guy, the one who was real and human.

"Greenville is an extremist, conservative town," he continued, his tone mild, as if he couldn't care less. "Clancy is an advocate of family—the old-fashioned kind where a man rules the household and the woman obeys without question. That's how the majority there rolls, which is part of the reason he's so well respected. If Joann left him, his reputation would be tarnished, and if it came to light that he'd abused her in any way, he'd be ruined. That's enough of an incentive to do whatever is in his power to prevent it."

Whatever is in his power. The shiver sank into her bones. "If it were me, I'd just leave. I'd go to my family, a friend's, a shelter for domestic abuse. There's no way I'd let someone continually abuse me, and if he was publicly ruined in the process, all the better. So why would she stay?"

"Maybe he controls her friends. It's possible she doesn't have any family or loyal friends to help her out. As a prominent politician, he probably has connections in law enforcement, community programs, even abuse shelters. She may have nowhere safe to go." He clenched his jaw and curled his hand on the keyboard into a fist.

"You think he'd do more than..." She swallowed hard, unable to finish the sentence. Abuse was bad enough without taking it further.

"My only concern is seeing this case to a successful conclusion so Mr. Hamilton will have even more reason to name me partner." Ian relaxed his hand and his expression returned to normal, all signs of tension gone. "Prestige and glory, Princess. That's all that matters."

She snorted, grateful for the change in subject. "It's unsurprising that you've got your priorities twisted."

"If we all had the same objectives, were all good and true and noble, the world would be a dull place."

"Or peaceful."

"Or boring. Now that we've got that sorted out, shall we return to our introduction to Gaelic? I'm not disagreeable with keeping you here all night, but you're the one Joann will be communicating with. We need a few helpful words and phrases to start with, such as 'Aye, Ian is smart and sexy'."

"Give me that." She swiped the laptop from him and settled it on the floor in front of her. "I don't want to waste my time on useless phrases in a dead language."

He leaned over her shoulder, his heat seeping through her shirt. If she shifted back at all, they'd be touching. "Irresistible. Look that one up."

"Obnoxious. That's an even better word, one I could use on a daily basis while this case is ongoing."

His chuckle made her pulse flutter. "This may be an eccentric assignment, but I've never had this much fun in the office." He toyed with a lock of her hair. "Just so you know, love."

"Focus, O'Connor."

"I am." His voice, hardly more than a whisper, drove tingles down her back. "Kaboom."

She turned enough to see him. Ian had his phone lifted close to his mouth and his eyes sparkled with mischief.

A soft, lilting voice responded. "Ka-*doo*. Spelled C-U-I-D-I-U with diacritic acute. Definition — *help*."

She went still. *Help*. Ian was right. Joann had been testing them and, luckily, Gia's ears had picked up the word correctly. She twisted halfway around, swiped the phone from his hand and spoke into the microphone. "Misha."

"*Mish*-eh. Spelled M-I-S-E. Definition… *me*."

"Help me." Gia squeezed the phone tight in one hand and fisted Ian's shirt with the other. "Get out."

"I'm sorry," the lilting phone voice said politely. "I did not understand. Please repeat."

Gia turned his phone off and dropped it on the floor so she could anchor herself with both hands. Imagining someone so desperate for help that she resorted to Gaelic code words in the slim chance of someone else noticing completely freaked her out. She couldn't fathom not having the freedom to speak her mind or leave a relationship whenever she chose. And to be stuck with abuse, no one to turn to? She blinked back an unexpected blur of tears.

"It's an unsettling realization, isn't it?" With one fingertip, Ian brushed away escaped moisture from the corner of her eye and studied it as if it were a diamond. "Knowing there are people in this century who are trapped or enslaved? It seems almost medieval."

'Unsettled' was a perfect word for what rolled around inside her, and it wasn't due merely to Joann's confirmation. Without meaning to, she'd pulled Ian close. Her hands and fingers still tangled in his shirt, rested on his firm chest. The heat of him chased away the goosebumps on her arms. She sucked in a slow, unsteady breath, her heart a pounding whip driving her onward. It would be quick and painless to end the space between them. They both wanted it, two consenting, practical adults who could separate romance from business. One night. It could work.

Ian slowly raised his attention from the teardrop on his fingertip, lingering on her mouth before meeting her gaze. Gently, he extricated her hold on his shirt. His teeth flashed in a piranha smile, as if to say she'd waited too long and all prior offers were off the table. "Shall we get back to our Gaelic lesson, Princess?"

Gia managed to nod, unwilling to trust herself with words. She scooted back and slumped against the wall. Whatever this game was between them, he had to know how close she teetered on the edge. How, if he'd kissed her now, the odds of resisting were not in her favor.

But he hadn't pushed against that line, hadn't taken advantage of her weakness. He'd handed her the ball in her own court and stepped back, leaving the next move completely up to her. She wasn't sure how to process that.

Ian set the computer on the coffee table and the night passed with Ian asking questions about everything from her family to shoes while they researched and practiced simple Gaelic words, offering little to nothing about himself. He kept everything low-key business, no touching, no more almost-kisses. She had the strangest feeling that he kept her talking not only to hear her answers, but to simply listen to someone else talk, as if relaxed conversation was a luxury, something to be savored. Once they chose her Gaelic response to Joann and she'd practiced it enough to marginally satisfy him, midnight had come and gone.

"No more Celtic torture." Gia covered a yawn with her hand and stood. "I'm going before I decide crashing on your couch isn't a terrible idea." She grabbed her purse, trudged to the exit and opened the door to a sultry summer night. The porchlight flickered and went out, leaving an outside world softened by darkness. Crickets chirped a distant song and a slice of moon rested on the horizon, the perfect backdrop to a magical moment. She stepped over the threshold before the spell took her.

"You don't have to go." Ian grasped her wrist, stalling her escape. He gently turned her hand over and pressed his lips to her pulse, his gaze holding her entranced. "You're officially off the clock. For the rest of the night, we can be whoever we want. *Do* whatever we want. In the morning, we can go back to being co-workers, if that's what you want."

"What I want?" She tugged free of his loose hold but didn't move away, only the doorjamb separating them. Moonlight reflected silver in his eyes, enchanting. "I don't have a one-night-only policy, O'Connor."

"We're technically engaged, so all policies are temporarily suspended." He leaned on the molding, easing closer. "Besides, my confidence in your Gaelic wouldn't win any awards. We can find other words to practice." His voice dropped, seductive. "Such as 'More'. 'Don't stop'. 'Harder, faster'."

She hid a shiver—barely. "If you're that worried about it, we can work on Gaelic tomorrow."

"It *is* tomorrow."

"At a reasonable hour."

"Can't." His mouth tightened. "I'm busy during reasonable hours tomorrow."

"An engaged man busy on Saturday without his fiancée? That's not suspicious at all. What are you doing?"

"Engaged does not require open sharing." His eyes were hooded as he stuffed his hands into his pockets. "I keep my secrets, love."

Gia fished her keys from her purse. The jangling echoed, too loud, shattering what remained of the spell. "I thought this was a partnership."

"Sunday," he countered.

"Can't." She sniffed and lifted her chin. "I promised to go to church, then see Adara and Garret after. They're back from the honeymoon tomorrow and lying to my best friend about my fake engagement to a man she loathes should be all sorts of fun." Telling Adara about her engagement without giving anything away would be true hell.

"Damn, and I wasn't invited." Ian's grin wasn't at all sorry. The smile faded and an emotion flitted over his features, vanishing as fast as it appeared, back into the void of Ian O'Connor. She'd probably misread the expression, because it had looked a lot like yearning.

Gia turned and skipped down the front steps before she thought on that anomaly too long. "Guess we'll stick to Monday, Sugarpop."

"Quarter after four — a.m." His tone held a smirk.

She zombie-groaned. The simple thought of getting up before dawn flashed its crack to the world made her want to curl up on the sidewalk and get whatever sleep she could.

"Where's my goodnight kiss, Princess?" His voice slid through the shadows, calling her back.

Spinning mid-step, she blew him a kiss and turned back around, afraid she might reconsider. When he didn't say anything, her heart constricted, as if she'd abandoned him to face the dark alone.

Chapter Nine

Hours after Gia had left, Ian shoved off his bed covers and sat up. Trying to sleep was pointless. In only his pajama pants, he slid through the darkness and out of his bedroom. The hardwood floors were cool on his bare feet and he trailed his fingers along the wall, needing the solid reminder more than any guidance in the gloom. He flicked on the light to what had been originally a family room, not a personal gym.

A bench and a rack of weights filled one corner, a treadmill another, and while he used every piece of equipment he had, the heavy bag hanging from the ceiling at the center of the room had by far been his most valuable purchase. He'd repaired the rips so many times that the duct tape made its own protective layer over the damaged vinyl. He jammed on the worn gloves lying neatly on the shelf and faced the bag.

His first punch rocked it, but he didn't wait for it to swing back before launching a kick and another attack...another, no downtime, no hesitation for an enemy to exploit. He continued until a slow burn ached in his shoulders and arms. His shins and thighs throbbed. Sweat dripped off his nose and down his back. Every kick, every strike, every hard-drilled *thud* reverberating through the room was another degree closer to crystallizing his focus, to driving out the silence and suffocation that had receded while Gia had been there.

Gia.

Breathing hard, he hung on to the bag, his shoulders heaving. He could still envision her in his living room, a defiant queen on the floor with her face stuffed with steak. Leaning close with her spun-sugar perfume and pink-ribbon mouth, her summer-sky eyes daring him to break his boundaries.

He dropped his damp forehead to the smooth, slick tape holding the bag together. Wanting Gia in his bed for one night—or two—wasn't comparable to *this*, this driving need to have her with him, holding the shadows back, twisting that empty space in his heart, making him…*want.*

Wanting was the worst, the entire reason he avoided any form of deeper romantic relationship. He couldn't have that relationship, not without cracking and eventually letting her in to his darkness. And that would be a complete disaster with unknown consequences.

Ian slammed his fist into the bag again, over and over until his lungs squeezed and his heart rasped for mercy. The corner shadows seemed to curl, reaching for him. The silence rang in his ears, heavy and hollow. He couldn't catch his breath.

A buzzing cut through the quiet, his phone vibrating in his pajama pocket. He pulled one glove off with his teeth and dropped it to the floor. He was so used to grabbing his phone wherever he went, he hadn't even realized he'd picked it up on his way out of the bedroom. And what idiot would be calling him at two in the morning? He snorted softly. *Probably Garret.*

He grabbed the phone and tapped the screen. *Gia.* His pulse ticked in a strange, not exactly uncomfortable way.

I can't sleep. I can't stop thinking about

The text ended there, as if she hadn't meant to send it, and that tic in his chest doubled. Had she gone home and paced, restless, needing some outlet for the dissatisfaction fizzing in her blood? The words blazed at him, and before he could tell himself how colossally stupid he was being, he typed a return text.

I can't stop thinking about you, either.

His thumb hovered over the Send button, his heart a hammer all the way to his skull. There would be no going back from the truth of that text. While she'd probably assume *thinking* for him meant lewd fantasies about her — and she wouldn't be completely wrong — with Gia, the fantasies went deeper than physical. And that was something he couldn't deny, no matter how much he should.

the case.

The last part of Gia's message covered the text he hadn't yet sent, a technological delay. He released a shuddering breath.

What the words might mean. I'm plotting potential scenarios because I can't sleep and you're the only one I can talk to about it. If you're awake, call me.

His blasted heart ticked off-beat again. He could call her, and they could discuss the case in their different locations, both lounging in their pajamas in the dark, easing the loneliness of night. And the discussion might turn to other, more personal subjects. He might invite her back over and maybe, in a moment of weakness, Gia would say yes. He'd persuade her into his arms again. He might not want to let her go. He raked his fingers through his hair. He *knew* he wouldn't want to let her go, and that was the problem. Even so, he was very, very tempted. Maybe one night would be enough.

Or maybe it would only intensify everything. Allowing her in, subjecting her to his private world would mean he was no better than...

His phone buzzed.

I guess it's a good thing you're getting your Grinch sleep. I'm sure it takes a lot of energy. I'll share my brilliant thoughts with you Monday.

A picture popped up of a monster in pajamas, followed by another one of Professor Snape taking a snooze.

Smiling, Ian neatly stacked his boxing gloves on the shelf and flicked off the light. The shadows had softened, his secrets kept safe. The silence no longer held barbs. Going to sleep wasn't hard and Monday seemed too far away.

* * * *

Sunday afternoon found Gia being held hostage in the Ambrose Gothic mansion beneath the furious gaze of Joey's sister, aka Adara, her best—and most frightening—friend.

"I'm going to destroy him." Adara lunged to her feet, leaving Garret alone on the couch, his dark eyes wide. She stared Gia down. "How, exactly, did this horrible event transpire in the week we were gone on our honeymoon?"

Trapped in the corner of Garret and Adara's gorgeous, only half-filled library, with the door all the way across the room—which would require somehow making it past Adara—Gia had no escape. She planted her hands on the cushioned back of the chair before her, bracing herself, thankful for the barrier between them. She'd made it all the way through church and lunch without saying anything and the pressure was killing her. Explaining her fake engagement to Adara was the one thing she hadn't wanted to even think about. Dar hated Ian. Ian hated Dar. And Gia couldn't tell her best friend the truth, due to case confidentiality.

Before she could make any response, Adara whirled toward Garret like a tank barrel zeroing in on its target, her sleek, dark hair swinging around her face. "Did you know about this?"

"*Chara*, no." Garret lifted both hands, proclaiming his virtue. "I don't have a death wish."

"Ian isn't as terrible as you think." Gia offered her brightest smile. "He has some surprisingly great qualities."

"Like taking advantage of grief-stricken women at work holiday parties?" Dar slowly crossed her arms and leaned in, her gaze sharp. "Did he hypnotize you? Blackmail you in some way? Stun you with sex?"

I wish.

Garret made a choked noise, which sounded suspiciously like a laugh barely caught in time. His expression was all innocence when Adara flashed a glare in his direction.

"Give me some credit, Dar." Gia chose to ignore the way Adara lifted one black eyebrow. Starting a true fight over a fake engagement wasn't what she wanted. "Do you honestly believe I'd get engaged without thinking it through?"

"I don't know what to believe right now. When I left a week ago, you were all about finding fulfillment without a man and letting love find you organically. Ian is the opposite of organic."

Gia rolled her eyes. "Jaded lawyers need love too." She kicked off her sparkly sandals and flopped sideways into the chair. "I appreciate you having my back, but you don't have to protect me from my big bad self anymore. I've got everything under control."

Adara snorted.

"I know Ian isn't Joey —"

"Freakin' right, he isn't Joey." A snarl entered Adara's voice. "Joey is undoubtedly clawing out of his grave right now to get at Ian's brain."

"I *know* Ian isn't Joey." Defensive heat fluttering in her chest, she tossed a throw pillow at Adara, who caught it nimbly with her hands instead of her face. "He's as far away from Joey as a man can possibly get, but, Dar" — she sighed and slumped into the chair — "Ian isn't completely unlike Joey, either."

Adara gasped and pointed a finger at her. "Take that back."

"I know you don't want to hear it, but it's true."

"In what possible way does Ian resemble my brother?" Dar strangled the pillow, her gray eyes razor-bright.

Images of Ian flickered through her mind—on the soccer field, battling with Feathers, learning Gaelic with her and standing in the dark while she drove away. She swallowed, her throat suddenly dry. He might not be perfect, might not really be her fiancé, but he deserved defending. "He's...fiercely protective. Funny, in an offhanded way. Devoted to his beliefs."

"Which includes landing whatever woman he can convince into the sack." Adara tossed the pillow back at her.

Gia shrugged and held the pillow to her chest, which wasn't enough armor to deflect the sting. "I wasn't so different, was I?"

Garret stood and ran his fingers through his shoulder-length hair, looking uncomfortable. He had ridiculously gorgeous hair, like gold-spun summer sunshine. It was an injustice to all womankind that a guy was given locks like that. "This conversation is headed toward a realm where possessing male components might be hazardous." He took Adara's hand and pressed a kiss to her palm, holding her gaze. "Come get me if you need anything, *neshama*."

Adara's expression softened and she watched Garret stroll out of the room until he disappeared from view. Releasing a long breath, she turned back to Gia and perched on the arm of the sofa. "I get it, G. If I lost Garret..." Her throat worked, a hint that her past without him was too fresh, too acute not to remember how empty it had been before he'd relentlessly invaded her privacy. "But you're not like Ian. You want to find what you had with Joey again, and that's not going to happen with Ian."

Tears blurred her vision. Adara was absolutely right, and the worst part of it was that she wouldn't mind at all if Ian could become that someone. More than a few times, she'd forgotten that their engagement was fake. It wasn't hard at all to imagine being a part of Ian's life. When she'd first tangled with him, she hadn't cared about a relationship that wouldn't last beyond one night. Now, if she gave in to him for one night, she'd want more—and he wouldn't. She'd be exactly like all his other conquests, a one-night-only winner. She needed more. *Deserved* more.

"I know what Ian is." She sniffed and blinked the moisture from her eyes. "But he's more than his manipulations, more than what he reveals to the general public. Haven't you ever wondered how a great guy like Garret would stay friends with Ian for years if he was a total scumbag?"

"Garret sees the best in everyone." Adara swiped the air with her hand in dismissal. "And yeah, I've wondered. He always deflects the subject with cryptic answers that hint Ian O'Connor has depths most of the world doesn't see." Her mouth twisted. "I, for one, have no intention of unearthing those contents. There's probably a lot of slimy gunk down there."

"There's no denying Ian's got some gunk going on, but beneath that layer, there's good goo." Gia hugged the pillow tighter and her throat tightened, strangling her next words. "And I'm kinda digging that goo."

"A bit of good goo isn't enough of a reason to get married." Adara lifted her eyebrows and tucked her hair behind her ear. "Ian has the emotional capacity of a rock and doesn't even bother denying it. Don't let his good looks and charm make you forget that."

From another room, the sweet call of a violin drifted into their conversation, Garret practicing, and Gia bit her lip. Memories of Joey sawing the strings danced in the shadows, just out of sight, as if in warning—or encouragement. She'd never find another love like Joey. Still, different didn't necessarily mean inferior.

"Ian makes me feel...significant," she said quietly. The truth of it made her heart squeeze, and maybe she was an idiot, but she couldn't deny that since she'd been spending time with Ian, she hadn't even thought about another guy, hadn't been lonely. Even the constant ache of missing Joey had eased.

It was a sobering realization.

The random violin notes melted into the rhythm of a song, *All I Ask of You* from *The Phantom of the Opera*. Adara's favorite. Whether or not she'd intended to, Dar laid a palm over her heart. Tears brightened her eyes, which was crazy. Adara never cried.

"I might not be your bodyguard anymore, G," she said, equally quiet, "but I'll always be your best friend. You've already had your heart broken once when Joey left us. Be careful with your love. Be sure that the man you give it to is worthy of you." Her smile, more beautiful because it was so rare, warmed the room. "You deserve your own Garret."

Her own smile wobbling, Gia stood and wrapped her arms around Adara. "Garret and I wouldn't work at all. He'd steal my spotlight, and what's a Glitter Girl without attention?"

"It's true." Adara eased back, her expression winsome. "He does love having an audience. it probably has something to do with his amazing hair."

"That's it? You just got back from your honeymoon and that's all you've got to say about your new husband?" Gia shook her head sadly, and Adara jerked away with a scowl.

"There are other parts of Garret that are phenomenal too." She lifted her chin at a haughty angle, her eyes gleaming with mischief. "And absolutely none of your business."

Grateful to be laughing again, Gia slipped her feet into her sandals, ready to make her getaway while Dar basked in honeymoon memories. "Don't forget that you promised to attend the elder abuse prevention charity ball Saturday. Masks required."

Adara's scowl returned. "I'd hoped you'd forgotten about that." She crossed her arms. "Pitiful. Using my moment of gratitude-inspired weakness for helping me win Garret back to blackmail me into attending miserable social gatherings."

"Whatever it takes to drag you out into the open, girl." She batted her eyelashes and backed for the exit as Adara muttered beneath her breath. If she had to run for it, the path to the front door was clear. She'd make it out alive. "And as far as Ian is concerned, trust me, Dar. You don't need to be my keeper anymore. I've got this."

The fact that Adara didn't hiss was impressive, but her eyes flashed with poison. "Just know that if he even cracks your heart, I'll annihilate the scumsucker. His friendship with Garret won't save him." Her smile was absolutely wicked, almost worse than any lecture. "Feel free to pass along the message."

Chapter Ten

Ian clung to the saddle horn and did his best to look regal while bouncing atop the horse from hell, hard enough that he questioned the survival of his manhood during the half-hour lesson. Feathers spun on his hind quarters for the second time and shook his head, snorting. If the fenced-in riding arena didn't restrain the fiend, Ian suspected he'd be on his way to Canada by now…if he managed to stay on that long.

He was starting to get the feeling Joann despised not only most men, but him in particular.

At last, the horse came to a stop near the railing where Joann coolly observed. Smudges underscored her eyes and she absently rubbed her temple, as if a migraine had come on. He certainly could understand why she'd be stressed enough to have a headache.

Making another controlled round over the cedar-chips layering the arena, Gia and Belle ambled by, Sean riding behind her. Gia let go of the pommel long enough to give a smug little wave. She held the reins in her other hand, as if she knew what she was doing. Sean's gaze drifted to Joann and, for a millisecond, his eyes gleamed.

A dart of jealousy twisted in his chest. Sean didn't need to have his hands on Gia's waist. Belle seemed eternally set on the unthreatening speed of plod. It wasn't as if she was in danger of being bucked off.

"Why is it I'm required to tame this beast alone, but my gorgeous fiancée on her easygoing steed requires an escort?" He didn't bother keeping the grumble from his voice.

Joann flicked a glance to Sean and Gia. "Worry about yourself, Mr. O'Connor. Gia is in capable hands."

"I see that."

Sean, who had yet to say more than a few clipped sentences or reveal that he had any other expression beyond stone-faced, lifted his eyebrows. The man must have the hearing of a bat. And the fact that he kept Gia separated from Joann, effectively disrupting any stilted Gaelic communication, made Ian want to grind whatever remained of his molars after the bumpy ride. He turned back to Joann. Then again, maybe it was an opportunity to gain a modicum of his client's trust.

"How long have you been riding, *muinín dúinn*?" *Trust us.* He'd practiced the words so many times with Gia that he didn't question that he'd used the correct pronunciation.

"Forever." Joann's gaze tracked Gia and Sean in their slow circuit around the ring. "Long enough to know one does not learn to ride by talking about it, Mr. O'Connor." Cold, crisp, her tone could numb testicles — which he might appreciate, considering the current state of his own anatomy. But she made no indication that she'd caught his Gaelic attempt and he

Every Breath

had no way of knowing if it was because she hadn't heard or understood.

Or if she had no intention of ever trusting him.

Beyond the treetops, lightning flared far off, one of the area's occasional summer storms that usually flashed to life with hard, fast sheets of rain, only to disappear within moments, leaving a clear blue sky as if nothing had ever happened.

"Did you see that?" Finishing the trek around the arena, Gia effectively drew Belle to a stop and searched the clear sky, her eyes sparkling. "The first lightning storm of the season...the best part of summer."

"A storm chaser, are you?" Joann's question was aimed directly at Gia, as if relieved for the excuse not to interact with Ian any longer than necessary.

"More an admirer than a chaser." Gia swept her hair back from her face, keeping the reins in her other hand. "Lightning is the closest thing to physical magic in this world, wild and electric." She sighed, dreamy. "Completely dazzling."

"Not to mention unpredictable and dangerous," Ian added drily.

Gia met his gaze and held it. "Exciting."

His body tensed, apparently not too abused by riding to react to Gia Hellman. *Exciting.* He could imagine the possibilities, and while they all included Gia in various positions, none of them included lightning—unless it was outside the bedroom window, adding an occasional, brilliant spotlight to her tan skin, free of all clothing.

Thunder boomed, distant but ominous.

Steady, sweet-natured Belle spooked. The horse vaulted one way and Gia went the other—or would have if Sean hadn't lassoed her waist with one brawny arm, keeping her in the saddle. Belle's tail flew behind her as heavy hooves churned a trail of cedar chips.

Joann remained in her relaxed instructor pose on the fence, her eyes bright and focused on the runaway steed, the only reason Ian choked back a shout and resisted leaping from Feather's back to chase after them. He gripped the reins so hard that his hand ached. Blood bellowed in his ears, a demand to do something, anything. If Gia got hurt... His ribs seemed to constrict, a too-close cage around his lungs.

Before Belle reached the far end of the arena, Sean gained control of the reins, brought the horse to a skidding halt and managed to keep Gia astride without breaking a sweat or cracking an expression, like a true western hero.

Yee-haw.

Ian sucked in a breath and released his death-grip on the reins. Through the entire incident, Feathers stood as solid and unmoving as stone, his ears perked, surely another trick. The horse wanted him to forget that it was a demon in equine form. There was no other reason that it would randomly prance about and have a non-reaction to nature's warning or its fellow animal going ballistic.

Gia's sun-kissed face was paler than usual as Sean guided Belle back beside Feathers. Her smile was shaky. "I didn't know Belle could even move that fast."

"It's a great lesson to experience first-hand," Joann said, unhooking her arms from the fence railing and drawing near Belle. "Horses are as unpredictable as humans. Even if you can trust them most of the time, there will be situations that make them dangerous." Her voice lowered and she met Gia's gaze. "Deadly. Never completely relax your guard."

Her eyes huge and solemn, Gia slowly nodded. "Yes, ma'am." She patted Sean's hand, which still rested on her hip as if ready to catch her again, and craned her neck to look at him. "Thanks for not letting me fall."

For a moment, Sean's granite expression shifted, as if trying to form the smallest smile. "It's my job."

"And you're so good at it." She winked, and damn if a bit of color didn't darken Sean's cheekbones.

The woman can thaw icebergs.

Ian contained the growl building in his chest, and he turned away before he did something rash, like sweep Gia from the saddle and Sean, into his arms, and keep her there. He focused on Joann instead.

For a split-second, faster than the lightning that had flashed minutes ago, her expression was pained, her gaze fixed on Sean. The next blink, her calm returned, masking everything. So maybe the feelings between Joann and Sean were mutual. They were doomed—and both probably knew it. Without absolute trust, Joann would never take that next step.

"I'm afraid our time for today's lesson has expired." Joann rubbed Belle's forehead beneath the bridle. "But I have faith that you both can handle removing the tack and brushing your mounts without getting killed. And if you need assistance, Matt is around"—she frowned slightly and glanced at the barn—"somewhere."

"At last," Ian muttered. He swung from the saddle, everything below his waist aching, and steadied himself against Feather's solid withers. He shot Sean a glare. "What's your secret? Balls of steel?"

Sean hopped nimbly off Belle's back and stood by as Gia dismounted, ever the attentive protector. Once Gia's boots hit the cedar chips, he met Ian's stare. "Iron."

Fifteen minutes later, Ian paused in his brushing of Feathers and said to Gia, "I don't trust that guy."

The soft, steady rhythm of bristles on hide stopped, and Gia peeked beneath Belle's neck, her eyes bright and teasing. "What guy?"

"You know who I mean," he muttered, conscious of the cameras subtly hanging from the stable's rafters. Anyone listening would assume he was a jealous fiancé, which was more accurate than was comfortable.

Feathers butted Ian with his nose, a command to continue brushing. The horses were haltered and tied in the corridor outside the stalls while their students brushed them, personal payment for the morning ride. Ian continued the rubdown before Feathers decided to prompt with teeth.

"Why? Because he wrangled me with one hand and stopped a runaway horse with the other, all without changing expression?" Gia's eyes glinted, teasing as she sighed dreamily. "What a man."

Careful to stay out of kicking range, Ian circled Feathers to be closer to Gia. He didn't miss how Feathers watched him from the corner of his eye, undoubtedly hoping he'd forget. "Today was a bust." He held her gaze over Belle's back. "I learned nothing today that I didn't already know."

"You might not have learned anything," she said with a hint of superiority, "but I did."

"Did you now?" During the morning lesson, he hadn't overheard any Gaelic from either Joann or Gia, and since Gia had spent most of her time riding with Sean, there had been few opportunities to communicate with Joann.

Her dimple showed up. "When lightning strikes, hold on tight. *Siúcra*."

Shookra? He lifted his eyebrows.

"You're okay with me calling you 'sugar', aren't you?" she asked, still smiling.

He rested his arms on Belle's back and leaned in, Gia's sweet perfume joining the horse and hay blend. She'd been practicing Gaelic without him, the sexy little sneak. "You can call me whatever you want, Princess, whenever you want."

"I already do, no permission from you necessary." She eased nearer, and when her attention drifted to his mouth and stayed there, his entire body went taut. She slipped her fingers into his hair and pulled his head closer, close enough her lips brushed his ear. "*Muinín dúinn.*"

Before she slid back beyond his reach, he cupped her face with his free hand. "You," he murmured, "are brilliant." To throw any observers off, and because it was as natural as breathing—but mostly because he'd dreamed of her mouth for too many sleepless nights and restless days—he ducked his head and brushed his lips over hers.

Gia stiffened slightly, but whether she realized what it might look like to an outsider or whether she did so out of instinct or mutual desire, she relaxed into the kiss and followed his lead. She tangled her fingers in his hair. If Belle hadn't been a solid barrier between them, he would have pulled her closer, against every aching point in his body, tight enough that she'd have no way of missing the physical evidence of how she affected him.

The silken slide of her soft mouth on his made his breath rough. She tasted of the morning tea he'd bought her for the pre-dawn drive to the stables. Whether flavored with lime and tequila or chai tea, her lips were the sweetest thing he'd ever experienced. Heat shuddered through him, so intense a growl rumbled in his chest.

Ian wrapped his hand around her ponytail and tugged, drawing her head back for access to her slender throat. He nibbled at her ear, not missing the catch of her breath or how she dug her fingernails into his shoulder. No matter how much she clung to her fantasy of forever, she couldn't deny the electricity between them, and since he couldn't—*wouldn't*—be her future, he'd content himself with the present and savor her now. Soft, seductive, he trailed kisses from her ear to her neck and lightly clamped his teeth on her shoulder.

"Holy crap," Gia gasped softly, throwing her head back.

He smiled against her skin. Still so sensitive there, as she'd been so many months ago.

A discreet cough sounded behind them, and they both jolted apart, as if caught mid-crime. Matt stood behind them, his ears bright red. "Ah, sorry." He straightened his shirt, as if needing a distraction. "I told Mrs. Clancy I'd help you finish up before I leave. My shift ended five minutes ago, but"—he cleared his throat again—"I didn't want to interrupt."

"I didn't want you to interrupt, either." Shifting, Ian discreetly adjusted his jeans and glanced at Gia. Her face was flushed, eyes bright, fingers pressed to her mouth.

"Matt, you poor man," Gia said, recovering fast. She assumed a sympathetic face. "Got stuck with the morning shift?"

Before Matt could respond, Frankie popped her head out of a door two stalls down and leaned on a pitchfork. She wiped her forehead with her sleeve, which would have made sense if there was any sign of sweat, which there wasn't. "I can't muck every stall myself."

Ian kept his expression cool. There had been no noise to suggest anyone was cleaning stalls nearby. How much had Frankie heard? It couldn't be a coincidence that she happened to be working at Clancy Stables so early when she usually bartended until the wee morning hours. While he might be vain enough to believe that she took the morning shift knowing he'd be here, there was another possibility. Clancy could have her under his thumb, promised an extra paycheck by keeping tabs on the newcomers — especially since Frankie knew exactly who he was.

Careful. They had to be more careful.

Frankie's sharp gaze went to Gia. "Still here? You must be a record for him."

Gia's smile was nothing but sweet as she resumed brushing Belle. "I'm a world record, sweetie. The unbreakable kind."

Ian smirked. A glamour queen who refused to be brought down by the negative forces swirling around her, even if he was the cause. If a horse hadn't separated them, he'd kiss her again, audience or not.

Snorting, Frankie flipped her auburn braid over her shoulder and disappeared into the depths of the stall. The angry scrape of tines in straw only emphasized the fact that she hadn't been cleaning horse crap earlier.

"Temperamental," Matt muttered to Gia, grinning an apology. His gaze swept over Belle. "She looks good. You get an A-plus on grooming."

Gia wrinkled her nose. "Matt, you should really lay off the breakfast garlic."

"That's not me." Somehow, Matt's ears darkened even more, and he waved a hand at Buttercup's stall behind him. "Joann's been using DMSO on Buttercup for a strained muscle. It can stink like garlic."

"Sorry." Grinning, Gia tucked her hands into her back pockets and rocked on her heels. "I hope the next test has nothing to do with shovels and horse shi—"

"Nope." Matt unhooked the lead rope and clicked his tongue at Belle, guiding her away. "That's what staff is paid for—all the fun stuff. See you next time."

Her tinkling laugh followed Matt, but her gaze found Ian's as he finished brushing Feathers. He didn't need words to know her thoughts matched his.

How much, if anything, had the Clancy Stables staff overheard, and how would it impact Joann?

Chapter Eleven

Gia ascended the front steps of her house as the purr of Ian's Porsche drifted around the corner and faded into the distance. The morning roller-coaster adrenaline still twisted through her — almost falling off Belle, the potential consequences of being overheard and Joann's cryptic Gaelic message of *amárach*, which they'd figured out on the drive home to mean 'tomorrow'. The phantom tingling of her mouth overshadowed it all. Ian had kissed her, and even though it was undoubtedly a cover-up kiss, her body didn't seem to care.

She'd tried to be rational and convince herself that the kiss meant nothing, not to her and certainly not to him. But the electric hum still percolating in her blood screamed another story.

Sighing, she stuck the key in the lock. Falling under Ian's spell was absolutely not conducive to her quest, unhelpful to both her heart and head. Maybe believing she was strong enough to resist him had been a colossal mistake.

She turned the key and the deadbolt didn't click. *Great.* She'd been so zombie-tired this morning she'd forgotten to lock the deadbolt. Her die-hard defensive family would destroy her if they ever found out.

The doorknob twisted easily, already unlocked, and Gia paused. It was possible that she'd completely zoned out locking the door when Ian had picked her up. Getting up before dawn could disrupt any girl's internal clock, and she might have missed one lock. But two? *No way.*

Slowly, she pushed the door open and waited, listening. The quiet seemed to stretch. With no pets or roommate, her house was usually still upon arrival, but the silence felt too deep, almost expectant. Leaving the door open for a quick getaway — and so her neighbors would hear if she screamed — she crept forward, her phone in one hand.

A mug sat on the coffee table. The tiny hairs on her arms prickled. After hitting the snooze button twice, she hadn't had time to drink anything this morning before Ian had picked her up.

A scratching came from the kitchen. Whoever had left the mug was still in her house.

Careful not to make any noise, she hoisted her purse like a weapon and hit the app her brother had forced her to keep on her phone. A deep, booming voice erupted from the phone speaker.

You have made the grave mistake of breaking and entering a Hellman house. Prepare to face the consequences, you sick, sad excuse for a scuzzball!

A high-pitched shriek followed, better than any teakettle or whistle.

A dark head peeked out of the kitchen, and Gia's heart jumped. Instead of the panicked, scrambling escape of some small-time burglar, the brown eyes looking back at her were familiar, the face calm, as if a sudden, threatening shout followed by a siren was completely ordinary.

"Kat," Gia called over the shriek, fumbling to turn off the app.

In the following silence, her sister Katerina wriggled her elegant fingers in greeting. "Hey, G."

Pausing a second for her heart to fall from her throat back to its proper place, Gia studied her sister. In appearance, they were seasonal opposites. Kat had inherited their father's height, olive complexion and coffee-brown eyes. She towered five inches over Gia and could have made it as a runway model if she hadn't preferred pasta over lettuce and boot camp over ballet, much to their mother's distress. When it came to personalities, they were as close as the poles.

Her hands trembling with the adrenaline still rushing through her, Gia dropped her purse to the floor, shut the door and headed for her sister. "What are you doing here?" She wrapped her arms around Katerina for a quick squeeze. "How did you get in?"

"Please…" A hint of annoyance entered Kat's husky voice. "Hellman spare key rules. After checking the third birdfeeder on the right and coming up emptyhanded, I found the spare key in the second siding from the ground on the corner. Pull the fishing line and voila, instant access."

Gia freed herself and frowned at Kat's unapologetic expression. "Knowing the location of the spare key doesn't include an automatic invitation inside, especially when I'm not here, unless you're trying to kill me. But since you weren't hiding in wait, I guess you're not playing an innocent game of family assassin to keep my awareness skills from rusting." She studied her big sister's face. Up close, the lines bracketing her mouth were impossible to miss, the smudges under her eyes stark against her pale skin. She gentled her voice. "What's going on, Kat?"

Flames forked in her sister's dark eyes and her mouth tightened as she straightened. "Can you believe I actually considered producing a spawn with that slimeball?" Without waiting for Gia's answer, she paced to the kitchen sink, tossing her long, wavy hair. "And to make everything so much worse, Cap ordered me to take a leave of absence. *Ordered* me." She whirled and flung her arms. "As if I was the one who had done something wrong. As if I"—she slapped a palm over her heart—"can't handle my emotions or separate my personal life from my profession. All men are idiots, but male cops are on a level all their own." Kat suddenly cocked her head, her eyes narrowing. "Why aren't you at work?"

Work. The world seemed to tilt beneath Gia's feet. *Oh, crap.* While she was sympathetic toward her sister's heartache and pending divorce, having Kat here, in her house, family intersecting her work and Ian—

Crap, crap, crap on a toasted cracker.

"I've been working overtime, so I'm going in late today." She pasted on her best, innocent smile.

Kat's assessing gaze raked over her ponytail, T-shirt and jeans, stopping at her boots. "Is that straw?"

"Straw? Don't be silly." Gia kicked off her boots and shoved them under the barstool with her foot. "Probably just some dried up grass from the lawn." Tucking her hands behind her back, she twisted off the engagement ring as she faced her sister. Having to explain her Ian situation to Kat would be an unnatural disaster. "Why, exactly, did you break into my house?"

"Using the key isn't technically breaking in, sis." Kat hooked her thumbs in her front pockets and leaned one hip on the kitchen counter. She might not have followed their mother's dream of becoming a model or Miss America, but she still looked the part, even in her skinny jeans, Converse and button-down plaid. "Since I'm on a forced leave of absence—and if I run into Vic and his new girlfriend again, I'll probably do something that will make that leave of absence permanent—I thought getting out of town would be a good idea." She shrugged one shoulder. "And what could be better than Graywood with my MIA sister for a couple of weeks?"

"Hawaii?" Gia dragged out a barstool and sat on it before her knees folded. Kat here for more than a day was a catastrophe. "I hear Seattle is great this time of year."

Kat's mouth tightened, then wobbled. She straightened. "Fine. I thought I'd use the unexpected free time to catch up with you, but if you're too busy or disinclined, I'll make other arrangements."

"I'm kidding, Kat. Don't be ridiculous." Gia jumped off the stool and latched on to her sister's wrist as she marched out of the kitchen, her head high. When Kat tried to shake free, Gia held on tight and dug in her heels. If Kat really wanted to leave, she'd have no trouble escaping Gia's hold. "You know you can stay as long as you want. I haven't seen you since Joey—" Her throat unexpectedly closed up. She hadn't seen her sister since Joey's funeral, going on two years. It seemed like she'd been without Joey forever.

As if sensing her grief flashback, Kat stopped struggling, still stubbornly facing the door.

Gia cleared the knot in her throat and pulled her sister back a step. "Kat, seriously. Stay as long as you want. We'll watch movies, eat ice cream, print some Vic pictures for target practice, go dancing, flirt with guys who have zero chance of scoring... It'll be a hoot."

"You know," Kat said, her voice hard, "all this time, I thought you were capricious for never getting married, never committing to one guy very long—with the exception of Joey, of course." She turned from the door and the anger faded for a second. "Joey was great." Her jaw clenched and fury flared anew in her eyes. "But now I get it. Letting a man have any emotional control over you, giving him the power to waste years of your life only to trash it whenever he decides he wants something else, is for idiots."

Gia's stomach twisted. "That's not exactly—"

"Let's do it." Her dark eyes flashed, vicious. "You can teach me how to be single again."

"Hooray." By some miracle, she managed to keep the horror out of her tone. *How the hell am I supposed to juggle all my secrets now?*

* * * *

Ian smirked as he closed the shoe box, hiding the strappy black stilettos with their inordinate amount of glimmering crystals. Figuring out which pair were The Shoes Gia lusted after had been easy. Every employee at Heelcandy knew Gia, and a large tip had ensured the clerk wouldn't tell who had bought The Shoes before Gia returned with her overtime check. Keeping potential manipulation material on hand might prove useful.

The humor faded as he shoved the box back onto its shelf and closed the cupboard. He'd bought them on a whim. She'd earned them, deserved them, but that wasn't the problem. He'd never bought a gift for any woman other than his mother. He rubbed his chin. Giving Gia The Shoes... There'd be no going back from that. Yet, simply imagining the excitement in her eyes when she opened the box...

He growled at himself and returned to the paperwork waiting on his desk. What was he, a twelve-year-old with a crush? *Pathetic.*

Ian's twelve-year-old crushing heart skipped a beat as Gia opened his office door and silently shut it. Dressed in a gray, pin-striped skirt and cream silk blouse, she appeared her usual, glamour-queen self, but the dazzle didn't reach her gaze.

"We have a serious problem." Her customary man-killer heels had replaced the clodhopper boots from the morning and made no sound on the rug as she paced to the line of windows behind his desk overlooking the park. "My sister's here...for I don't know how long."

The chair squeaked as he sat and leaned back, lacing his hands behind his head. "I don't see how that's *my* problem, Princess."

A ghost of her usual playfulness flickered over her lovely mouth. "You haven't met Kat yet." The humor faded and she pivoted, leaning one sexy hip on the windowsill. "Part of our agreement was keeping my family out of it."

"Our agreement was to keep your family out and I held up my end of the deal." He drummed his fingers on his thigh. "I have no control over them entering it on their own."

She pointed at him, accusing. "I had no control over your sleazy weekend doings invading my job, but I rolled with it, for Joann's sake."

"'Sleazy' is an overdramatic description." He crossed his ankles, shifting in his seat. Damn, whenever storms flashed in her eyes, it seemed to have a direct line to his groin. Then again, when she bit her full, lower lip, laughed or even pretended to examine her perfect fingernails while giving him time to determine the wisdom of going along with her plans, his body responded. "And you made the agreement freely." He grinned. "Consider dealing with your sister overtime."

"*That's* already a done deal, O'Connor." She planted a hand on her hip. "But since she's getting divorced after a decade of marriage, Kat's demanding that I show her how to submerge into the single life again."

"Like hell you will." The growl in his voice was unintentional, unadulterated and he didn't care. Without thinking about it, he was out of his chair and looming over her. "You're engaged...to *me*."

Gia's eyes were wide, her lips parted as she blinked up at him. One golden tendril of hair near her chin stirred with his unsteady breath. Clearly, his outburst had surprised her as much as it had him, but this close to her? He couldn't care about that, either.

Slowly, he wrapped the loose strand of silken hair around his finger. It felt almost as decadent as her soft lips, the details burned eternally in his memory. "If it appears to the outside world that we're not engaged," he murmured, mesmerized by the glints of afternoon light in the hair binding his finger, "Clancy will hear of it. After this morning, we can't afford even an ounce of suspicion to cloud our relationship or affect Joann."

"I know," she said, just as softly. Her pulse vibrated in the open-necked collar of her blouse. Her gaze drifted to his mouth, and his lips prickled. "That's why Kat's a problem. If she hears about the engagement, she'll go off the deep end and drag the rest of my family into this. They're like bloodhounds and can sniff out the smallest lie. I think she's currently too overwhelmed by her divorce to pick up on it, but staying for days on end?" She shook her head, pulling the hair from his finger. "She will."

"It's not technically a lie that we're engaged, love." His fingers itched to reclaim the golden strand he'd just lost. "We're engaged to see this case to completion, made promises to see it through together. It's simply a matter of perspective."

Gia huffed, but didn't move away. "Don't use lawyer rationality persuasion tactics on me. Once the truth comes out, no one else will see it that way."

"It doesn't matter how anyone else sees it." His voice was hoarse, his mouth dry with the effort not to pin her against the window and resume the kiss from the stables, make her forget why she'd come into his office and kill all thoughts of resuming any single-life activities, with her sister or not. "A successful resolution to this case is all that matters."

"Is it?" She swallowed, her slender throat working. "All that matters?"

Whatever she asked, it had nothing to do with the case or Joann and he had no inclination to answer honestly. She didn't want the brutal truth when it came to the things that mattered to him. She wouldn't want to know that, no matter how hard he'd tried otherwise, she was on that short list. Or that being on said list was the closest he'd ever allow her to get. Emotionally, anyway. Physically, however...

The curves of her perfect breasts, molded by cream silk, ignited his imagination and were tantalizingly close to his dangling tie. It would be a simple move to snake his arm around her waist and pull her against him. There was no horse-to-bar full-body contact to reunite their skin, laced fingers, tangled tongues. His heart pounded through every extremity in anticipation. Reawakening what they'd brought to life almost two years ago in a dark room, wrapped in muffled holiday tunes and fueled by mutual need, was a living flame in his blood.

And that reawakening had the potential to burn too hot and make him forget—a risk he couldn't, *wouldn't* take, not with anyone, especially Gia.

"Power and prestige, Princess." With a last glance at her lips, he straightened, somehow summoning his reserves of willpower. "All that matters."

Her smile was winsome, her voice soft. "You're such a liar, O'Connor."

Ignoring the hiccup in his heart, he kept his expression cool. Maybe all the Hellmans had inherited a knack for sniffing out untruths. "If you prefer, we can break the good news to your sister together. As you keep reminding me, this is a partnership, not a tyranny." He winked. "I've got your back, Princess."

The winsome edge of her smile didn't budge as she straightened from the windowsill and stepped in, close enough that her silk sleeve brushed his jacket lapel. "The worst part is I can't figure out if you having my back is a good thing or a bad one."

"So bad that it's good." He added a purr to his voice. "And once I get my hands on your backside again, you'll remember why."

She rolled her eyes and circled the desk, drifting slowly away from him. The urge to follow, to pull her back into his gravity, threatened his control. "Not part of my plan, Sugarpop."

"You know what they say about the best laid plans."

"Yep. But I was never good at taking advice." She whirled at the door and stared him down. "For now, I'll handle Kat. In the meantime, you've been warned. My sister's...tough."

Tough people only made him stronger. Nodding, he picked up the case law he'd been studying before Gia's arrival, needing even the illusion of distraction.

"Oh, and O'Connor?" Her hand on the doorknob, she looked over her shoulder at him. "Thanks...for the offer to face my sister with me."

He waited until she'd closed the door behind her before allowing his crooked grin free.

Chapter Twelve

Friday evening after work, Gia was five feet from her getaway car when the voice she'd avoided as much as possible during the week hailed her, too close to pretend she hadn't heard.

"Were you trying to leave without saying good night, love?" Ian slid up and leaned on the car door, effectively blocking her escape. Hands in his pockets, jacket slung over his arm, tie loosened at an angle, he looked ready to play for the weekend. His eyes were hooded, his smirk lazy.

It took all her strength not to pull him down by the tie and nibble that smirk off his sinful, distracting mouth. Since the kiss at the stables on Monday, she'd had trouble focusing on anything else. She'd daydreamed while watching movies and eating ice cream with Kat, enough that even a divorce-consumed sister had noticed and demanded to know what was up. Her nights had been filled with steamy images of Ian that left her achy and restless. Not even a jug of Kat's special green tea had helped her perkiness perk back up.

She'd only caught the Gaelic Joann had filtered in their brief conversations by some miracle, and since they hadn't yet made sense of the words, she'd probably misheard them. At least Joann hadn't seemed worse for wear, other than a migraine and some aches and pains in her legs that she'd laughed off as the consequences of getting older. If Frankie or Matt had reported anything suspicious to Mr. Clancy, there had been no sign.

"I can't go to the soccer game, remember?" Gia adjusted her purse, needing something to do with her hands. The warm air ruffled Ian's dark hair, and the urge to mess it up herself, run her fingers through those strands over and over, formed a hot, electric wire dragging her one way while her brain pulled her another. "I now have a Kat at home to take care of."

Ian cocked his head, studying her, his smirk fading. "How is it you're still managing to keep your sister in the dark? I thought she was a living lie detector."

"Usually, but since she sleeps until noon and stays up until the witching hour devouring sappy movies and ice cream sprinkled with potato chips, her radar's off-line." And as relieved as she was to avoid having to explain the Ian situation to her sister, she hated seeing Kat wallowing. Her sister had always been the solid one, the steely, practical one. She'd never wavered in her career, relationships or decisions, not even when their mother had pressured her toward activities more in tune with modeling. Watching Kat fumble was a kick in the stomach, a reminder that devotion was fragile and could fracture even the strongest person.

Ian lifted his hand, hesitated, then brushed a thumb under her eye, his touch butterfly-soft. "Have you been sleeping at all?"

The fact not only that he'd noticed the signs but acknowledged them, as if concerned, sent hairline cracks along her defenses. She bit her lip instead of pressing her face into his shirt and leaning against his solid frame for a minute...or a million minutes. He'd undoubtedly prey on her momentary weakness and she didn't have the willpower to resist him.

Worse, so much worse, lack of sleep wasn't entirely to blame.

He cupped her cheek. "We still have some Gaelic to decipher, love. You can't blow me off forever." Mischief glittered in his eyes, the usual Ian O'Connor returning. "Actually, I take that back. You can most certainly blow me — "

She smothered his mouth with her hand before he could finish. "On second thought, maybe I'll show up at the soccer game with Kat. If she kills you there — both on and off the field — I won't have to worry about getting bloodstains on my clothes."

He licked her palm, and she jerked her hand away. "Gross."

"If Kat wants to experience the single life, the soccer field is perfect. I'm sure Derek would love to show her his" — his smirk reappeared — "hose."

Gia threw her head back and groaned at the sky. "Save me from insufferable men."

"You don't really want to be saved, Princess." Ian's voice turned husky. "Admit it."

Yes, she did — saved from wondering if she'd ever be loved again like Joey had loved her, saved from those dark, empty moments when she woke up and realized she was alone again, saved from clutching her belief in true love and happily ever after so tight that letting go might destroy her.

"*Gia.*" The low intensity with which he said her name drew her blurry gaze to his. "Damn. Don't cry." Before she even thought to move, his arms were around her, his hand holding her head against his chest, exactly where she did — and didn't — want to be. "I was only... I didn't mean... Damn."

She laugh-sniffled into his shirt, breathing in the spice of his cologne. "I'm not crying."

"The tears wetting my tie say otherwise," he said drily, but his fingers in her hair were gentle, his embrace comforting.

"Your daily hug quota," she said, her arms curling around his back, helpless to resist any longer. "Fulfilled by a sleep-deprived, oversensitive fake fiancée who isn't very good at pretending when she's a hostage in her own home. My castle is crumbling around me."

"Fortunately, you're good at other things" — he brushed a kiss to her temple — "like charming gun-shy clients and their gargoyle bodyguards." Slow and stirring, he rubbed her nape, and she bit back a moan. "Communicating in code." Feather-light, he skimmed a hand along her spine and stopped on her rump. "Stuffing your face with steak."

She pinched his lean waist and he danced away, laughing. *Laughing, the jerk.* Not once in their time together had she witnessed him truly laughing — carefree and uncorrupted — and it altered the rhythm of her heart, made it spin and dip. She swung her purse at him half-heartedly, and he skipped out of reach, his eyes twinkling.

"Missed me." He crooked one finger, challenging her to try again.

Gia paused and narrowed her eyes at him. "You can't stand it, can you?"

"Winning?" He wriggled his eyebrows. "Absolutely."

"Being human and nice for more than two seconds."

Heat warmed his eyes, deeper, stronger than before, and he slid his hands into his pockets again. "I can be nice. For a long," a purr entered his voice, "*long* time, Princess."

"Next time I see Frankie, I'll be sure to ask her about it." She opened her car door before she surrendered to the temptation to experience Ian's version of 'nice'.

He leaned one elbow on the door and gazed down at her, his expression inscrutable. "I'll allow you to neglect your work duties tonight, but don't let your sister keep you up too late. I need your mind sharp. Despite the unorthodox nature of the case, two weeks is too long not to have made any progress. Mr. Hamilton will want an update and I refuse to be emptyhanded." Resting his chin on his arm, the breeze blowing in his hair, he looked younger, boyish, someone she could play with, dance with, live with. "Whatever Joann tried to convey this morning, we need to figure it out this weekend. Tomorrow. Early. I'm not available Saturday night."

Again? She was dying to discover what he did on Saturday nights that was so secret he refused to share, but this Saturday, he had other obligations — fake fiancé obligations.

"You're not going anywhere Saturday night, O'Connor." She leaned in his face, close enough to catch the hitch of his breath. "We have a charity masquerade ball at six for elder abuse prevention at the senior center. I'm in charge of decorating tomorrow morning—which I volunteered to do months ago—so I can't work on the case until Sunday. What would people say if my fiancé didn't join me at such an important event?" She batted her eyelashes and licked her lips, not missing how his gaze tracked her tongue.

"And people say *I'm* a demon," he murmured, his voice hoarse, his attention still unabashedly on her mouth. He straightened from the car door. "You're a siren."

She sniffed. "If you haven't figured out that all women are sirens in their own way, you haven't been paying attention." Unable to deny the urge any longer, she straightened his silk tie, as if they were truly an engaged couple. "Wear your best suit." She patted his chest, the delicious muscles beneath her fingers flexing. "And don't forget a mask."

Before she could pull away, he grasped her wrist. Holding her gaze, he lifted her hand to his mouth and pressed a soft kiss against her palm. "Bad things always happen at masquerades, Princess. Mistaken identities." He turned her hand over and bit her thumb, just enough to sting. "Extra liberties for the sake of anonymity." He licked the small ache away. "Dalliances in the dark."

"Oh, yeah. It's going to be magical." Mesmerized, she couldn't pull her focus away from his mouth near her hand, what he might do next. "With masks and costumes, Alberta will be sure to make a play for you. You probably won't even realize it's her until she's in your arms, slurping on your ear in the garden, cloaked by the night."

He paused and shuddered. "You're going to pay for planting that image in my mind. The only one who will be luring me into the shadowed shrubbery to take advantage of my missing virtue is you." Slow and seductive, he slid her pinkie into his mouth and sucked.

Gia couldn't stop a sharp inhale, and freeing herself of Ian's mouth wasn't even an option. She could barely get the words out. "Don't you ever give up?"

Ian smiled and twirled his tongue once over her fingertip before releasing her. "Give up until I have you, Princess? Never."

"We want the opposite things, remember?" She lifted an eyebrow to throw him off, in case he heard the one-two punch of her heart. "Unless you suddenly think you're my true love, hidden away all this time behind a shark smile and sharp suit, you have a long, dry road ahead to never, Sugarpop."

He kissed her knuckles lightly and turned away. "Look for me at six, love. I'll be the devil wearing a handsome mask."

* * * *

Saturday afternoon, unable to help herself, Gia admired herself in the mirror. Her dress for the charity masquerade was princess-perfect—a soft, shimmering pink confection that clung to her curves just right. Delicate rose appliques and tiny silver beads joined the silk, a dress worthy of any modern-day fairytale. Cap sleeves made it summer-fit, but better than the lace and flash and utter femininity of the dress was the open back. Acres of skin from neck to tailbone lent a sexy edge to an otherwise innocent bit of stitchery, and with her hair up, nothing was in the way. The only piece missing from the perfect ensemble were The Shoes.

She couldn't wait for Ian to see her in it. He'd pop a spring.

"I've seen that smile before." Lounging on the bed with a bag of chips, Kat eyed her suspiciously. "It's the one that says wherever trouble is, that's where you'll be."

"I have no idea what you're talking about." Gia sniffed and erased the smile as she turned from the mirror.

Kat threw a potato chip, missing her hem by half a foot. "That's the second time you've said that today." She sat up and planted her purple Converse on the floor, the chip bag crinkling in her grip. "You're hiding something."

Gia sighed, rolling her eyes for a double effect. "I get that it's pathetic to be excited about attending a charity event with a bunch of senior citizens and yukkity-yuks with spare money to donate, but do you know the last time I had an excuse to get dressed up?" She didn't wait for a response. "Yeah. Me, neither." The hopeful look she gave her sister got the anticipated eyebrows up. "There's still time for you to get ready and tag along."

"Hell, no." Kat snorted, slinging her long ponytail over one shoulder. "Masks are creepy. And stop channeling Mom by pressuring me to change my mind. You're the Barbie doll of the family, not me." A warning snarled in her words. "Lay off."

Exactly why she'd asked Kat to join her tonight. *Again.* Anything to distract her. She'd had too many close calls already today when Kat had surprisingly agreed to join her at the senior center to decorate. Emma and Merle had been there too and as much as she'd tried to monopolize the conversation, Merle had still slipped in a question about Ian. Kat had somehow missed that one while fighting a losing battle with a string of lights. But when Emma had point-blank asked Gia at lunch why her young man wasn't helping, Katerina's punchbag look should have knocked her over. Once Emma tottered away — apparently satisfied by a vague answer that Gia's young man was busy saving the world, and what about those adorable granddaughters? — Gia had drawn her sister off the scent by throwing Emma under the senior dial-a-bus. Dementia, of course. What other reason would an elderly lady ask about a fiancé that didn't exist?

She still felt terrible about it. But not terrible enough to tell Kat the truth.

Gia lifted the plain black mask she'd swiped from the box at the senior center and tossed it on the bed. "Just in case."

"Quit." Kat's tone held a snap, and Gia bit back her smile. Her sister had finally reached the point of true annoyance. Even if she had the smallest inclination to go before, now she'd squash it out of pure stubbornness. And to cement the deal...

"I have a dress that will fit you—"

"I said *no*." Her eyes flashing, Kat jerked to her feet, not bothering to brush the crumbs from her black tank top. "I'm not into bubblegum lip gloss, stupid shoes and useless frippery, G. I thought you, of all people, understood that about me." She flew by in a stomping swirl of darkness. "You're *worse* than Mom." The door slammed behind her.

Gia winced, but not at the sound. She could handle loud noises and arguments, emotions and competitions. But comparing her to their mother?

She pressed a hand to her pounding heart. That...*stung*, especially since Kat knew how much she wasn't like their pushy, prim, socialite mother beyond appearance, no matter how much that had disappointed her entire family. It was as if she was their last chance at adding something soft and sparkling to the family name instead of tough love and violence.

Lifting her chin, she turned back to the mirror. Kat was just lashing out after losing Vic and being put on leave. Anyway, her ploy had worked. Nothing short of murder would get her sister to show up tonight. Another week, maybe two, and Kat would get bored and restless, would go home.

And she wouldn't have to explain Ian to her family at all.

She released a shaky breath, the sting in her heart sharpening to a blade. There were some solid reasons for it—lack of sleep, stress, the pressure of work. Not anything or any*one* else.

Checking her lipstick one last time—a pink precisely three shades darker than her dress—she put on her stilettos and grabbed her mask, a hand-made, white-feather swan replica that covered the upper half of her face. She'd ordered it the same day she'd learned of the event, along with her dress. And yeah, she'd be making payments on the dress with zero regrets until she died.

On the drive to the senior center, a building excitement obliterated any traces of her tiff with Kat, and by the time she pulled into the already-bustling parking lot, she could barely hold still. Men in elegant suits and women sparkling from head to toe strolled toward the center. Through the building windows, tiny silver lights glowed, softer than the falling twilight, adding a hint of magic.

Gia slipped on her fake engagement ring and mask, slid out of her car and glided toward the front door, the material of her dress sighing with every move, silken on her skin. The evening air skimmed her bare back, and a thrill shivered through her. A Glitter Girl handed the opportunity to be glitzy? There was no way she couldn't be pumped. Tonight, she wanted to relax, forget she had any unwanted secrets and pretend that her 'happily ever after' goal wasn't at a standstill, blocked by a man who only wanted 'happily right now'.

After saying hello to the Wednesday night senior dance crew, she paused inside the cafeteria and let the magic she'd worked all day to make flow over her. Tiny, twinkling lights in the rafters gave the entire room a silver glow. Iridescent balloons floated near the ceiling like shimmering, forgotten bubbles, suspended by helium for the night. Old-time photos of residents lined the walls with familiar faces of family and friends, all the reasons for guests with their pocketbooks to feel generous. Expensive perfume laced the air, its source impossible to pinpoint with the flittering people scattered from wall to wall. She found herself searching for any sign of a devil mask. Maybe Ian hadn't arrived yet. Maybe he'd decided to stick to his usual Saturday night secrets.

Maybe she was better off if he didn't show.

Gia turned to begin her social rounds and nearly stumbled into a tall man in an intricate fox mask and pin-striped suit that screamed of money. He grasped her elbows, steadying her, his grip a smidge too tight. He didn't release her.

Dark eyes glittered behind the mask and his teeth gleamed in a sharp smile. "Gia Hellman. My wife Joann has told me so much about you."

She froze as her heart trip-trip-tripped a frantic bird beat. Landon Clancy, mayor of Greenville, Joann's abusive, hopefully soon-to-be-ex-husband...at a charity event in Graywood. *Holy crap. He knows. He has to. Why else would he be here?*

With a calm that clashed with the hurricane storming inside her, she assumed her learned role of Hellman socialite and held out her hand. "If you're Joann's husband, you must be Landon Clancy. It's a pleasure to finally meet you."

As if reluctantly taking up his politician public persona, he released her arms and took her hand in his. He engulfed her hand with his large fingers — and not in the stirring way Ian's did. Clancy's grip was a gesture of power and oppression. "The pleasure is utterly mine."

Managing not to jerk away from his touch, she politely slid her hand free. "Joann is an amazing riding instructor and we're so lucky she was able to fit us into her schedule." She used her ditzy voice, the one that fooled people who didn't know her well. "There's absolutely no way I'm getting married without riding up the aisle on horses. What can I say? I'm a sucker for the fairy tale, and Joann's kindly helping me make my dream come true, even though she's getting the short end of the stick." She forced a giggle, hoping it sounded sincere. "My fiancé and horses don't exactly see eye to eye, and since horses seem to sense even the smallest kernel of evil, it makes for some interesting riding lessons."

"Joann's a treasure." His smile didn't shift, as if his face were ceramic, but the dangerous edge in his tone shot a chill down her back.

"Where is Joann?" Gia used the excuse to break eye contact and scan the room, but not for Joann—for Ian. Or Adara. She'd even be grateful to find Derek. But all the masks, shimmering silks and glittering jewels made a dizzying carnival, impossible to pierce. Her stomach twisted and she fought the need to be sick. "It would be great to see how she cleans up outside the stables. No woman wants to prance around in her riding clothes every day of the week. She needs the occasional gown and a crown to chase away the normal days."

"Unfortunately, Joann wasn't able to accompany me tonight." He leaned down, like a tidal wave cresting over a town, ready to crush. "She wasn't feeling well." His last words were hushed. *A warning.*

A shiver steamrolled through her, followed by prickling goosebumps on her arms.

"You remind me of Joann when she was your age." The darkness in his eyes shimmered. "Naïvely idealistic. She believed she could change the world. She learned soon enough that our world never changes, not really. Take my advice, Ms. Hellman. Focus your efforts on making Ian happy. Accept the status quo. It's the best way to have a long, fruitful life." With a nod of dismissal, he sauntered into the crowd, his politician smile on tight and perfect. A couple in matching harlequin masks immediately engaged him, drawing him away.

Gia could barely breathe and her hands shook. Had he just threatened her or was it her imagination, the secrets she knew about him filling in the blanks?

Before she could retreat to the safety of the hall, Mr. Clancy looked over his shoulder. The fox mask was aimed right at her, and she'd swear the eye holes reflected nothing but black.

Chapter Thirteen

"You have to admit," Ian noted to Roman inside the front doors of the senior center, just as a curvy woman decked out in a glittering gold dress and owl mask sauntered by, "the view here is better than our usual Saturday haunt."

Roman's mouth twitched beneath the edge of his mask. The disguise looked like something a gladiator might wear outside the ring—glossy black with delicate silver whorls. Twin rearing horses flanked each temple and ebony feathers made a sweeping crown. Where he'd found it at the last minute, Ian had no idea.

"I'm not so sure about that, Boy Wonder. Some of the worst dirtbags I've met hide behind fancy clothes." Roman smoothed the lapels of his fancy onyx suit. "Present company excluded."

Ian backhanded his shoulder. "Don't sell yourself short, Baconbits. There's still time to join the dark side."

Grim amusement glittered in Roman's dark eyes. He tilted his chin at the open double doors leading into the waiting chaos of colors and conversation and gave a low whistle. "Who is *that*?"

Following Roman's gaze, Ian went still as his body went on high alert. Even though her back was to them, he had no doubt that the vixen in the wicked-innocent dress was his princess. Gia's golden hair was piled on top of her head, leaving her slender neck exposed. The expanse of sun-kissed skin bared to the world, rolling all the way down to her tailbone, made him want to drop to his knees and worship every inch. Slowly. Thoroughly. Then he'd work his way to what remained behind the screen of shimmering pink.

"I wouldn't mind filling my hands with—"

"Stop eying my fiancée like a slab of salted pork." Ian intended to say the words with his usual cool steel. Instead, a possessive growl carried through, as if his subconscious saw one of his few true friends as a threat. "She's not on the market."

Roman slid his hands into his pockets and rocked back on his heels, his gaze still on Gia. "I'm still waiting for the story on that particular miracle." He finally looked at Ian. "Let's, for the sake of simplification, set aside the fact that you're anti-relationship. Just how the hell did you convince Gia Hellman to agree to *marry* you?"

"That's an insulting question." Ian smirked. "Isn't my charm alone enough? See you later."

His head cocked, Roman snorted but didn't follow as Ian set his sights on Gia and strolled unerringly toward her, as if pulled by a retracting silk string. He stopped right behind her and, somehow resisting the need to slide his fingertips along the length of her bare spine, leaned near her ear.

"I should have known you'd be dressed like an angel," he murmured.

Gia gasped and pivoted. In the same breath, she flung herself at him, her arms tight around his back, her slender body trembling.

"Willingly putting yourself in groping range?" he said against her hair, spreading his hand over the small of her back, her skin warm and soft. "You're scaring me, love."

"Clancy." She breathed the name, as if simply saying it aloud would conjure the man. Easing back just enough to meet his gaze, her slender throat worked. Her eyes within the white swan mask covering her upper face were wide. "He's here. I'm relatively certain he just threatened me."

He curled his fingers around the back of her neck, both possessive and protective as blood pounded, hot and hard. *Clancy. Here.* Threatening someone he... Ian nearly choked on the rage. "What, exactly," he said through clenched teeth, "did he say?"

"I can't quote him verbatim, but anytime the words 'accept the status quo' and 'survive' are said in the same sentence, it's enough to make me question the underlying theme." Gia straightened, as if finding her strength—or preparing for a battle. But she didn't withdraw from the circle of his arms as she lifted her mask.

Not that he had any intention of letting her leave his side. Clancy making an appearance at a charity event in Graywood he could handle, but singling out Gia while he wasn't around and using a coward's intimidation? Every muscle strained with the violence burning in his veins, barely leashed. "Where is he?"

Gia hooked on to his jacket lapels with both hands, anchoring him. "You're not going anywhere near him." Wearing a smile, she murmured the words. "Right now, he can't know for sure that we're working for Joann. If you confront him, it will only confirm whatever suspicions he has. He'll destroy her. Probably you too — not to mention me — and we don't have any solid evidence yet to stop him."

Her firm, steady voice pierced the red haze surrounding him and her logic grounded him. Sucking in a long breath through his nose, he nodded once, curt.

He slid his fingers into her hair and brought his mouth close to her ear, as if sharing some seductive bedroom secret. "Coming to Graywood at all reveals his suspicion and making a point of speaking to you shows he's nervous." His lips brushed the shell of her ear, and the tension stringing his nerves tight loosened a bit. "But if he knew everything, he wouldn't bother with veiled threats or making personal appearances."

She caressed his jaw line at the edge of his mask and whispered back, "Exactly what I thought, which is why I used my ditzy face on him. If anything, he's more confused."

Ian paused, then a bark of laughter escaped him. He wrapped her in his arms and lifted her completely off the floor, high enough that her stilettos went airborne. "You are phenomenal, Princess."

Her surprised laugh huffed against his neck. "As if I didn't already know that."

He set her back on her feet and was instantly aware of the ever-shifting sea of bodies around them, the swirl of sharp suits, shimmering dresses and masks hiding both predator and prey. Keeping his expression casual, he searched the crowd, feigning nothing but idle curiosity. "What is he wearing?"

Gia didn't need specification of the *he*. She looped her arm through his, her heels making her the perfect height to lean her head against his shoulder. "A fox mask with pointed ears and fake fur," she murmured. "Pinstriped suit." Her mouth tightened as she scanned the mob of masks and glitter. "I don't see him."

"I'm not leaving you for a single second." Ian skimmed a hand down her back, her skin beneath his heating his blood despite the threat of Clancy's presence. "As much as I'd prefer to keep you as far from *him* as possible," he said, smiling benignly, "if we don't stay and pretend like nothing is wrong, he'll know his suspicions are right. We can't let that happen."

Gia nodded and released a shaky breath. "Lucky you, spending Saturday night avoiding Alberta. She's already on the hunt. If you see a cat mask, run."

"To be clear, I would have stayed anyway, love." He pivoted and cupped her chin, lifting her gaze to his. "You, in that dress..." His gaze dropped to her pink, perfect mouth. "The devil mask I'm wearing is most appropriate for the thoughts running through my head...of you"—he leaned nearer—"and me peeling you out of that dress, inch by slow, lickable inch."

Her pupils dilated and even as she rolled her eyes, color darkened her cheeks. "You should consider making that mask a permanent part of your wardrobe. It's only right to give innocent people fair warning."

"Where's the fun in that?" He slipped a hand around her waist and guided her against him, the soft press of her curves shooting electric jolts through his veins. "Besides, love"—he dipped his head close to her ear and blew gently, enjoying her shiver — "some people prefer devils over saints."

"Seriously." Adara's voice cut in. "If you're going to make me attend these things and try to stomach your choice in fiancés, at least don't purposefully inspire my need to puke with PDA."

Gia loosened her arms from around his neck and replaced her mask. She gave her best friend an apologetic smile.

Unwilling to allow Miss Crabapple the win, Ian nuzzled Gia's delectable neck and stared rebelliously at Adara. The narrowing of her eyes was enough to satisfy him. Even though Gia had worked her magic and convinced Adara not to interfere between them any longer, he'd never be good enough for her brother's true love — a love severed by death, not choice.

He'd never admit aloud that she was right.

As usual, Adara looked severely Gothic in a black-and-purple fairy mask and gauzy dress. Garret hooked his arm around her slim shoulders. His sparkling gold sun mask matched his neatly pulled-back hair, bohemian at its best. His smile was even brighter.

"Dude…" He held out a fist for Ian to bump.

His smile smug, Ian hit Garret's hand with his own. "Managed to tear yourself away from your musical love nest?"

"Anything for charity." He slid his hand from Adara's shoulder to her waist. "Plus, I get to show off my beautiful wife, so it's a win-win."

Wife. A knot tightened in Ian's heart, and his awareness of Gia beside him turned sword-sharp. Garret was made for marriage, had wanted to find his soul mate ever since they'd been kids. No matter how much Ian had ribbed him about it, Garret had simply shrugged and smiled — unashamed, unwavering. Like Gia, he'd wanted happily ever after and had never doubted he'd find it.

Now that he had, Ian couldn't deny a twist of envy.

Adara suddenly laughed, her focus across the crowded room. She elbowed Garret. "That *has* to be Bob. It's the same medieval get-up he wears for the school carnival. I guess he didn't get the memo that it was a masquerade — not a costume — party."

Roman slid up beside Adara, as if he'd been lurking nearby in the shadows the entire time, and followed her gaze. "We should make sure your new brother-in-law is well aware of his mistake, don't you think?"

Adara grinned up at him, her smile turning sly. "Oh yeah."

Before Ian could protest, Adara let go of Garret and latched on to Gia's arm, dragging her off into the crowd, close on Roman's heels. Gia flashed a look over her shoulder, as if to say 'I won't be alone. I'll be safe'.

Watching her melt into the crowd like a glittering queen among her people, the rock in Ian's stomach tumbled.

"Lay it on me, bro." Garret leaned back against the wall, his hands in his pockets. His mouth flattened in a line that didn't fit on his annoyingly always-happy face. Ian hated that expression, especially when it was aimed at him, *caused* by him.

"It's just work." He kept his tone cool, unconcerned, hoping to throw Garret off.

Garret's dark, knowing eyes narrowed. "The only time that muscle tics in your jaw is when you're five seconds away from thrashing someone who deserves it, and since I just got here, I know it isn't me."

Dammit. Sometimes having old friends who knew too much was a great inconvenience. Ian settled against the wall beside Garret and met his gaze. "It's confidential."

"And has nothing to do with a certain Glitter Girl recently pulled from your clutches?" Garret's stare didn't waver. "I hope you realize the position you've put me in, between the potential fury of my wife and the infamous reputation of my complicated friend. The second Gia sheds a tear, I'm all that stands between you and *'the fiery death of a thousand suns'*. Adara's words, not mine."

One corner of his mouth curled up. He had no doubt Garret would do his best to mediate any brawl between him and Adara.

"Thanks for having my back, but you don't need to worry. I'd never hurt Gia." *Not intentionally.* His throat tightened and he turned his face to the crowd, away from Garret before he read the expression no mask could hide.

"You're not *him,* you know," Garret said with an edge, seeming to read his thoughts. "Blood does not control the man you are."

The noose around his neck clenched tighter. He wished he could believe that someday, that he could detach his past from the present, separate the good memories from the horror—be a man without bloodstains on his hands, do enough, *be* enough to erase those stains.

His usual smirk felt forced. "Saying it enough times doesn't change facts. Not everyone can pop rainbows out of their butt cracks with nothing more than a smile."

"*Chara.*" Garret's white teeth gleamed. "Do you know what I could do with an unlimited supply of rainbows? World peace. Obliterate hunger. Stop global warming."

"*Chara* indeed." Ian pushed away from the wall.

"Create a universal speaker system playing my music every minute," Garret continued, following. "Nothing but smiles and laughter and —"

"Remember that muscle twitching in my jaw?" Ian met Garret's gaze. "It's back...and all yours."

Garret's smile was unrepentant. "All these years, you haven't hit me even once, not like you did that kid picking on me in the fourth grade. I'll never forget his face when you pulled him off my back and punched him to a pulp."

"There's still time to remedy that," he muttered, shouldering his way past a knot of blue-hairs in Victorian masks and sequined shirts. But his smile, this time, felt more natural, and when Gia came into view, surrounded by friends, safe and smiling, a crooked part of him righted and settled into place. It wasn't a big part and certainly not enough to erase the cracks and shadows, but for tonight, it was enough.

Chapter Fourteen

An hour passed by without another glimpse of Clancy. Despite the fact that Gia had no idea how he'd slithered away, with Ian always within reach and as watchful as Roman, the tension in her shoulders eked away with every breath.

She'd tried to stop herself from reaching for his hand too much, from holding his gaze a little too long every time she looked up to find him staring back at her, but she eventually gave that up too. Ian wasn't really hers, at least not in the way she wanted, and yet she couldn't deny the strange sense that she was his. It was only unsettling when she let her rationality take over, so she sipped her sparkling water, smiled and pretended that her heart wasn't warm and fluttering every time he whispered in her ear, pretended that she didn't feel protected with his hand on her hip.

Pretended that she wasn't falling head over heels for a man who didn't want more than one night.

"Are you still worrying about our escape-artist politician?" Ian skimmed his fingers down her spine and goose bumps radiated out from his touch, igniting fire in her veins.

She shook her head. "Not at the moment."

"Hmm." His gaze dropped to her mouth. "So why does it seem you're trying to chew through your lovely lower lip?"

Gia immediately pressed her lips together. Her mother had tried relentlessly to break her of the habit, and even knowing the effects on her lipstick, some addictions never died.

"If you need to be nibbled there — or anywhere else, for that matter — I'll do it." The gleam in his eyes fanned those coals into a roaring, unstoppable inferno. She was painfully tempted to let him, to explore exactly how hot they could burn together, but she had a feeling one night would be enough to scorch her beyond repair or recognition. She might already be permanently seared at the edges.

"Is this thing as dull as it looks?" a husky voice asked behind her, horrifyingly familiar.

Gia whirled and her heart stopped beating altogether. Kat wore the plain, plastic black mask she'd swiped from the senior center earlier. Her glossy hair remained in a simple ponytail. The spaghetti strap baby doll from Gia's closet was far too short for her. She'd compensated by wearing form-fitting white jeans, complete with her Converse, and she was still more glamorous than most of the women there.

Ian steadied her with a possessive arm around her waist, and when Kat's sharp gaze swept over them, it was all Gia could do not to push him away and pretend like he was nothing more than an acquaintance or co-worker...nothing more than the start of a one-night fling.

Crap.

"Kat, you made it!" She made her tone cheerful and subtly moved out of Ian's hold to give her sister a quick squeeze. "What changed your mind?"

She shrugged one shoulder, her unwavering attention still fixed on Ian. "I was bored. Who's this?"

Gia cringed, both at her sister's rudeness and being forced to face the one subject she didn't want to broach, but Ian saved her by extending a hand toward Kat.

"Ian O'Connor. I work at Hamilton & Associates with Gia. If you ever need legal representation, give me a call."

Kat appeared unimpressed by his wink. She stared at his hand a moment, and just when Gia considered shoving her, she took it. "Katerina Hellman. I'm a cop." Her dark eyes glittered dangerously. "If you ever need to be arrested, I'll be there."

Ian's smirk was equally dangerous. "I'm sure you will. Gia, you failed to mention your sister was so charming."

Kat snorted and crossed her arms. "Gia failed to mention you *at all*. Just pass the bar exam?"

Ian's smile didn't fail. "Something like that."

Gia hid a groan and gave Ian a warning look, which he ignored. "Come on, Kat. There's an open bar. I'll buy you a beer."

"Allow me," Ian interjected smoothly. "I know how underpaid cops are."

"I buy my own drinks." Kat gave Ian the Hellman stare-down.

He didn't even blink.

Someone brushed Gia's elbow and she turned to find Merle and Emma smiling behind matching Venetian peacock masks.

"You're not leaving already, are you?" She gave Emma a sad look. "It's barely eight and I know *Supernatural* reruns aren't on until nine."

"I do so hate to miss my Winchester fix, but all that decorating this morning tuckered me out." Emma patted Gia's cheek and faced Kat. "Sweet Katerina, I'm glad to see you decided to enjoy the results of our labor. The lights are glorious."

Her mouth softening, Kat lifted her gaze to the rafters, where the strings of silver lights gleamed, reflecting off the drifting balloons and dancing in every corner.

"And, Ian," Emma said fondly, squeezing his hand, "I'm so glad you found Miss Gia." Not picking up on the sudden tension, she took Gia's hand too, trapping them both. "Don't forget to invite us to the wedding, dears."

Beside her, Kat stiffened. Ian muttered something noncommittal, and Gia waited until Merle and Emma wandered away before looking at her sister.

Kat's expression was carefully blank.

Gia tried to smile. "I'm pretty sure they think Ian is Joey."

It was Ian's turn to go still.

She briefly closed her eyes. She couldn't keep doing this, lying to her sister, pretending she could continue this charade with Ian and still be okay at the end of it. Kat could keep a secret. She'd understand. Ian would too...and would probably find some way to manipulate her feelings for him. Gia opened her eyes just as London and Bob, Garret's sister and brother-in-law, strolled near.

Please, please don't say anything incriminating.

London, five-foot tiny and gymnast-fit, lifted on tiptoes and kissed Ian on the cheek. "You'll be at the barbecue in a couple weeks, right?"

"Burgers, beer and watching Bob dodge cheap fireworks?" Ian smirked at Bob, who frowned. "Wouldn't miss it."

"See you later, kids." London waggled her fingers in farewell and they moved on.

Gia released the breath she'd been holding.

"Oh, wait, I almost forgot." Leaving Bob at the door, London headed back their way. "I need to see the ring."

No. No, no, no.

Helplessly, Gia let London take her hand and *ooh* and *ah* over the sparkling engagement ring. *Don't look at Kat. Don't look at Kat.* She lifted her gaze to her sister.

Fury. Betrayal. And beneath it all, pain.

"Kat—"

"What? They look a bit young for the dementia crap excuse, so try again."

Her heart was pounding, pounding, pounding. "I... We..."

"I asked Gia to marry me," Ian said, saving her. "She said yes. It's a recent development."

London eased away, leaving them to what was clearly a family confrontation. She was one to know, considering the underlying tension still hanging on between her and Adara after Adara had bruised Garret's heart. Sisters didn't always easily forget.

Or forgive.

"I hadn't gotten around to telling family yet," Gia tried, her voice too weak to be convincing.

"And yet everyone here besides me seems to know." Tight, white lines marked Kat's mouth. "I've been at your house for *days*, G. Not once did you mention *him*." She waved a dismissive hand at Ian. "Same old Gia. Running off, having your fun, leaving me to deal with the hard stuff alone."

"Kat, that's not it at all."

That elegant, contemptuous eyebrow went up again, so like their mother's. "Isn't it?" Kat's voice rose, loud enough that heads turned their way. "Do you honestly expect me to believe this isn't another one of your whims? That you won't days or weeks from now figure out you still don't have it right and move across the country? Change your job, buy some new shoes, waste your time and money at the salon, all in a quest to finally fit somewhere?"

A wounded noise rasped in Gia's throat.

"This is a discussion to be held in private." Ian's words were cold, clipped, and Kat's fury turned on him.

"And this is none of your business, suit." She sneered, her beauty turning poisonous.

"Something I can help with?" Roman asked politely, appearing at Ian's elbow, his dark eyes watching Kat. A true protector, he seemed to take stock of the situation's every nuance. He'd probably already prepared for any potential outcome.

Kat's gaze raked him from head to toe and landed on his wrist, where a blue line tattoo peeked from the edge of his cuff. "Great," she muttered. "Go back to the doughnut table."

"No doughnuts, only gelatin. Raspberry. It's not bad." As if calming a victim, Roman's voice was soft and even. "Want some?"

"I'm not staying." Kat pivoted and stalked for the door.

"Kat, wait." Wrenching free of Ian's light hold, Gia hurried after her sister and caught up with her in the hallway, where there were fewer ears and a lot more quiet to amplify voices.

"Why? So you can lie to me some more? Make me feel less important than the senior citizens in your life? Jump on the Kat-can't-take-it bandwagon by keeping your boy-toy a secret?" She ripped off the mask. It dropped from her hand, light and plastic on the tile.

"Enough." Gia's face heated and she clenched her fists at her side. "Ian isn't my boy-toy. He's —" All the true explanations of who Ian was to her were ones she could barely consider and absolutely couldn't say aloud. Not here. Not with an audience. Her silence went on a beat too long.

"That's what I thought." Kat smiled tightly, knowingly and swept out of the door.

Gia slumped and pushed her mask over her head. *Well, that went down swimmingly.*

Roman stepped up beside her, gazing through the door window, where Kat drifted away into the night. He didn't say anything.

"Katerina's going through a divorce," she said, needing to explain why her sister, while always tough, had been a total witch to strangers. As family, she'd expected some backlash, but Ian and Roman didn't deserve Kat's ire.

Roman looked down at her. "That's no excuse to treat people like trash."

True. She glanced over her shoulder, expecting to find Ian, but no one else was in the hall. "Where's Ian?"

"He decided some raspberry gelatin might taste great with a shot of vodka." The corners of Roman's mouth quirked up, a barely-there smile. "I anticipate a betting match on its way. Last time, I won two hundred bucks off the boy wonder."

"Really?" She couldn't imagine Ian losing at anything. "What was the bet?"

"You." He winked, sly. "Thanks for defying the odds and not going home with him the night of Garret's wedding."

Smiling, she shook her head, the knot in her chest, strangely, loosening a notch. "No problem." As he turned away, she added, "But I wouldn't suggest taking any more bets when it comes to me, Roman. I'm clearly a wild card."

"Every king needs his queen"—he bobbed a bow and winked again—"Princess."

As Roman walked away, Gia leaned on the door and gazed into the waning light. Underneath the mean words, her sister had been right. She'd been trying to fit somewhere her entire life, to be someone, to do something that mattered. But not once in the last two weeks had she even thought about it until now.

She was still pondering that anomaly when Ian's spicy cologne scented the air and the man himself spun and leaned back against the wall beside her. He handed her a bowl of red, wobbling gelatin.

"Sadly, the bartender refused to spike it." He studied her face, his expression neutral. "Katerina seemed...friendly."

Gia snorted and pushed the goo around with the plastic spoon. "You always have a unique way of perceiving a situation. I can't wait to get home to my *friendly* sister. I wouldn't be surprised to find out the rest of the Hellman squad is already on the way here to direct me back on the straight and narrow."

"So don't go home." He shrugged at her sharp look. "It's not late. Come over." He lowered his voice. "After who showed up tonight, we need to move."

She narrowed her eyes at him, suspicious. He sounded so matter-of-fact, not a hint of the flirtation he'd used most of the night. "To be clear, we'll be on the clock, right? Nothing...untoward?"

"Untoward?" He looked so innocent she almost laughed. "If I propositioned you, Princess, you'd know it." He pushed from the wall, hands in his pockets. "Meet you there."

Gia watched him walk out of the door and into the night, then tracked him down the sidewalk until he disappeared into the parking lot. With Clancy's unexpected appearance, they needed to make some quick progress on Joann's case, find something they could use. It made sense to start tonight, to not waste any time.

But the fluttering in her heart whispered that maybe, just maybe the suggestion that they work tonight was as much for her as it was for the case.

Chapter Fifteen

Rubbing his grainy eyes, Ian leaned back on the couch and set his laptop aside. For five long, miserable hours he'd researched every possible angle on Landon Clancy, from potential shady business transactions to speeding tickets. Nothing. The entire time he'd dug into the squeaky-clean politician's background, Gia had puzzled out Gaelic in the opposite corner of his couch. The distance didn't make anything less miserable. Every time she shifted at all, her fairytale dress whispered to him, seductive, calling him to bridge the gap between them. Her sweet perfume curled around him, a constant reminder that she was only a stretched arm away. She'd loosened her hair and left it to fall into tempting, golden waves. And the curves of her body, sculpted in shimmering pink, except for the delicious line of her bare back... He swallowed another gulp of whiskey.

Tonight had been the ultimate test of his self-control and he was worn out. If he didn't put more space between them, he might do something stupid and irreparable.

Gia went still. She sucked in a soft breath. "I think I've got it." She uncurled her legs and shifted his way. "Or at least most of it."

He took the laptop she handed him and frowned at the screen. "What am I looking at?"

"The site for Fireside Burial Grounds." She scooted closer and peered over his arm at the screen. "She used *reilig*, the word for graveyard, first. I'm relatively certain the second word was for fireside." Her voice lowered. "*Bás* was the third. Death."

He met her gaze, a chill that hadn't been there a second ago winding through his veins. "Are you sure, Princess?"

Her mouth twisted, apologetic. "No. Not really" — she focused on the screen again, to the simple website of the Fireside Burial Grounds — "especially since the last word doesn't seem to have any connection. *Siar*, which means west." She shifted then dropped her slender shoulders. "I'll try to get confirmation from Joann on Monday." He gave in to the urge to pull her closer, to *keep* her close. "Go get some rest. We have a road trip to Fireside Burial Grounds bright and early tomorrow."

Gia glanced at the computer and scrunched her nose. "Do you mind if I hang out for another twenty minutes? Kat's usually crashed on the couch by three, so it should be safe to sneak in so I can face the storm later."

With the coffee table a barrier between them, he relaxed and smirked. "Staying even later in the den of iniquity? What will the neighbors think?"

"With all the women you usually bring home?" She rolled her eyes. "They'll think everything's normal."

He kept his smirk in place as he turned for the hallway and his bedroom before he backtracked, slung her over his shoulder and dragged her along. "You're under a misapprehension, Princess. I've never brought any other woman here."

Her snort of disbelief followed him into the hall. He stopped at the doorway to his bedroom and pivoted. Her back was to him, only the top of her golden crown visible above the couch back. "You can stay for twenty minutes. No more. And I'm *not* paying you."

At the responsive finger gesture she lifted in the air, he smiled again, slid into his room and pushed the door almost shut with his foot. Ian traded his clothes for his sleeping pants and crawled into bed. Tired as he was, he forced his gaze to the shadowed ceiling. *Twenty minutes.* He'd wait the twenty minutes she requested before going...to...sleep.

The nightmares took him almost immediately.

The dull smack of flesh hitting flesh came from the kitchen — a second later, his mother's sobbing. Ian sprinted into the kitchen and jerked to a stop. His mother — his gentle, beautiful mother — was huddled on the floor, a red welt on her cheek. As Ian hesitated in the doorway, his father drew back his arm and struck her in the face again.

Black danced across his vision. Without another second of hesitation, he leaped onto his father's back.

Lightning flashed and the scene changed.

His father slammed his fist into Ian's nose, followed by a burst of blinding pain. Ian, only eight years old, stumbled into the wall. Squeezing his eyes shut, he covered his head with his arms as the strikes continued, an endless barrage of pain.

Flash.

The fists belonged to Ian. Blood sprayed the floor, the walls, his knuckles and his father's hated features were barely even recognizable beneath the bruising, swelling and broken bones. Yet the rage burned hot, and even though he knew he'd won, he couldn't stop slamming his fist into his father's face, over and over and over.

Flash.

Ian raised his bloody fist for another strike, but the person huddled on the floor, whimpering, wasn't his father or his mother. His stomach revolted.

Gia.

* * * *

A shout ripped Gia from sleep. Her heart hammering, she sat up with a start and fumbled off the couch, scrambling to make sense of where she was. Her legs tangled in her long dress and her knee bumped the coffee table, rattling her phone. She scrubbed at her eyes. *Ian's place.* She'd meant to leave an hour before.

A hoarse sob, muffled by distance and a bedroom door, pushed her pulse into a faster beat. Fisting her skirt, Gia fumbled around furniture and staggered down the hall, led by another strangled noise.

The door was barely ajar, and she pushed it wider. She kept her voice to a whisper. "Ian?"

No response.

Gia stepped in the doorway and paused, adjusting to the dim light. Ian kneeled in the center of the bed, his head bowed, his hands palm up on his knees, his shoulders heaving, as if he couldn't breathe. She was on the bed beside him in two seconds.

Staring down at his trembling hands, he didn't seem to notice her.

She licked her dry lips. If he was sleepwalking, waking him up could be bad, but she couldn't let him stay trapped in whatever nightmare he experienced—and she knew it was a nightmare. She'd had enough of her own to recognize one.

Carefully, she reached out until her fingertips brushed his knee through the black cotton of his pajama pants. "Ian, it's okay. I'm here." She paused. Maybe it would be better to use her name. 'I' could be anyone. "It's Gia. I'm here."

His breath still rough, he slowly swept up his dark eyelashes. His eyes were wild, unfocused just enough that she knew he hadn't yet come up completely from his dream.

"Did you forget me already?" She tried for a small smile, holding his gaze. "I guess I need to step up my game."

He blinked, and the next second he was wrapped around her, his face pressed into her hair as if she was his lifeline to sanity. "Gia." His voice was a broken sob. "Gia."

Something inside her split open and she held him close, the tremors rolling through his big body transferring to her. Finding Ian this way—self-assured, arrogant Ian—completely demolished her reserves. No single, random nightmare could break him so completely. This was something ongoing, deep, secret, unrelenting—and she knew with zero doubt that he'd been facing it alone all this time.

"Sh-h, it's okay," she whispered against his jaw. "I'm here."

He gently raked his large hand through her hair, over and over, as if needing the repetition as an anchor to the present, to draw him back from whatever horror he'd just endured. "Never." The roughness in his whisper scraped her nerves, made her hurt even more for him. "I never want to hurt you."

"You wouldn't." She rubbed slow, soothing circles along his spine, calling him back...back to her. "I know that."

"I will."

She leaned into him, pressing her cheek against his neck, his skin hot and damp against hers. "You won't."

"*He* hurt her, and I'm like him. Violence is in my veins, always right beneath the skin, waiting for someone to pull the trigger." His voice cracked. "He hurt her, and I hurt him."

A chill coursed down her neck and rooted in her heart. "Who, Ian?" she asked quietly, never ceasing the calm circles on his back. "Who got hurt?"

The repetition of his fingers went still, but he kept his face pressed into her hair. "You didn't know?" His voice was gentle in the darkness. "My father hurt my mother, so I hurt him." He eased back and there was nothing but ice in his blue eyes. "Irreparably."

Gia refused to flinch from his gaze or his touch. "Tell me what happened."

Ian slid his hands from her hair and cupped her face. Instead of answering, he pressed his mouth gently to hers, a barely-there kiss that threatened her defenses even more. He nibbled from her mouth to her jawline with more tenderness than she'd ever believed Ian O'Connor was capable of.

"Ian," she said, not really sure if he was truly awake, an advantage she'd take. "Tell me what happened."

He slid his hands around her and pulled her closer against his bare chest. Those magical lips of his waged war on her neck. "I have a better idea," he mumbled against her sensitive skin. "Why don't we both pretend this is just a dream and do what we've wanted to do since that night of the holiday party." He chuckled, low and humorless. "Correction. I don't know what's gone on in your pretty mind, but I've wanted you since the moment you walked into Hamilton & Associates."

She snorted. "That's a given. I have boobs."

His eased back and his gaze dropped to said boobs, tight against her bodice. "Affirmative."

Gia grabbed his hands, which were now roving south, and held him tight. He might try to play his nightmare off as no big deal, but she wasn't about to let it go. Something awful had happened to him, and its claws were still hooked in his back. She gave him her 'General Gia' take-no-prisoners glare. "Stop trying to distract me."

His wolf grin appeared. "That will never happen."

"Don't push me, O'Connor." She tightened her grip on his hands. "Tell me what you were dreaming."

He slowly relaxed and, tick by tick, the humor faded into a dreadful calm, as if he'd decided to pay off the devil by cashing in his heart. "My dream was a reminder that I have to make you stop looking at me the way you're doing now, as if I'm something more than what you see." He took her chin between his finger and thumb, holding her focus hostage. "I'm not."

"It's way too late to retreat, counselor. I've already peeked beyond the surface." She gripped his wrists tight enough to cause bruises, so he'd know that she wasn't playing around. "And if you think I'm that girl who scares easily, you haven't been paying attention."

He broke her grasp and reversed roles, shackling her wrists with unforgiving fingers. He met her gaze, and there wasn't a hint of his slick lawyer personality. His eyes were hard and haunted, a man she hadn't met before. "Whatever you believe you've detected in me, you're mistaken." His voice was as cold as his eyes. Never releasing his grasp, he dragged her off the bed and to the door, where he finally let go. With one finger at her back, he prodded her into the hallway. "Go home. I'll pick you up at eight."

Gia pivoted and faced him. "I'm not letting this go."

He pulled the door mostly shut, leaving just enough of a gap for his face. "How you waste your time is no concern of mine, unless..." His gaze slowly tracked over her body, lingering on all the hills and valleys. "I won't object if you choose to waste the rest of the night with me. I'm half-undressed already."

Leaning one shoulder on the doorjamb, she eased her face closer to his. His breath brushed her forehead. She lowered her voice to a murmur. "I want more than that, Ian."

"That's too bad, Ms. Hellman, because I can't give you anything more." He shut the door, leaving her in the dark.

Her heart thrumming an off-key beat, Gia laid her fingertips on the door and whispered, "Liar."

Chapter Sixteen

The drive to Fireside Burial Ground was a long, curvy bit of business that had been almost fun enough to make Ian forget his nightmares — both the one he'd experienced the previous night and the gorgeous one strolling silently beside him up the weed-choked gravel path. Gia had been uncharacteristically quiet the entire two-hour-plus journey, sipping the jumbo-sized tea he'd brought and gazing out of the window as if the scenery alone was worth contemplating. He should be relieved that she hadn't brought up the interrupted nightmare as she'd promised, but the wait felt more like the calm before a tornado — tense and restless.

Gia stopped at the great iron lichgate leading into the cemetery and looked up, studying the archway, its wording too rusted to read. "This can't be right. Why would Joann send us to a forgotten graveyard?" She shook the padlocked gate, and the rattle echoed in the quiet, a warning clang. "I wasn't on my A-game last week." She glanced at him beneath her eyelashes. "I probably got it wrong."

"I highly doubt that." He shoved his hands into his jeans' pockets and took in the grounds beyond the prison-high chain-link fence. Uneven lines of faded headstones and crumbling markers erupted from the overgrown grass like gnarled fingers grasping for the sky, broken by tangled shrubs and wild trees. Whatever visitors had ventured this way hadn't left any flowers for the dead.

Gia lifted her phone and snapped a picture.

He smirked. "Looking for orbs, Princess?"

"If I wanted pictures of strange phenomena, I'd just take one of you." She pointed her phone at him, took his picture, then another one of the gate. "This feels...important." Slipping her phone into the back pocket of her stylishly faded capris, she grasped one iron bar and peeked into the cemetery beyond. "How do we get in?"

Ian grinned, relieved that she'd slid back into the sassy Glitter Girl he knew and admired. "Leave that to me."

A bent paperclip, a few twists and a delicate prod later, the lock clicked open.

Gia whistled softly, her eyes wide. "Would the real Ian O'Connor please step up."

All humor bled out and he turned away. Thanks to the previous night, she'd already glimpsed more than most, and the only reason she hadn't run was that she didn't understand what she'd seen, not really. Whatever she might be considering about him now, the verdict would change if she knew the entire truth.

He pushed the gate open. The rusty hinges spat and growled, having been set in the same position for too long to go quietly. Together, Ian and Gia stepped into the scraggly grass.

A solemn sort of hush floated among the abandoned graves, stirring leaves and worrying a wind chime hanging in some distant tree. Clusters of identical headstones indicated family burial sites, names long surrendered to the elements. Ian ducked a low-hanging oak branch to avoid stepping on a grave and brushed at the tickle on his face. He looked up. A giant, glimmering web stretched from the trunk to the limb, lustrous in the sunlight. At the farthest edge, higher than his reach, a gray moth struggled in the strands, far too late to escape the spider scuttling its way. He shuddered at the deadly beauty.

"It's so sad," Gia whispered, as though she might disturb someone sleeping and few brown leaves crackled beneath her sandal and that invasive breath of air fluttered her voile blouse, "that they're forgotten."

He trailed a finger over a cracked marble cherub sitting astride a crooked headstone. "Everyone's forgotten, love. Eventually."

She kept quiet after that and he kept his mouth shut too. Every careful step he took carried him deeper into a world where he didn't belong. Wild roses trapped a crumbling cross behind barbed vines, adding a toxic perfume to the air. Tree roots buckled headstones and crawled over monuments long ago erased. They'd trespassed in a place better left alone.

"Ian," Gia breathed his name.

He looked to where she pointed. Near the far edge of the fence, a mausoleum squatted among the gravestones, a dark, watchful presence. Without saying another word, they both turned toward the structure and slowly approached on cautious, silent feet, like ghosts drifting through a timeless space.

A gateless iron picket fence surrounded the mausoleum. Leaves and twigs gathered on the several marble stairs leading up. An abandoned animal nest lay broken in one corner of the narrow porch, leaking feathers and straw.

"That's not creepy at all." Gia lifted her phone for another picture.

"Email those to me," he said softly, studying the steel-plated crypt door. Disjointed faces of iron inlaid the metal, cracked with age. Some were human, others celestial, but the centerpiece of the bizarre embellishment was a mighty angel, eyeless and grim.

"Sorry." Gia frowned at her phone. "No service here."

"Later then." Never taking his gaze from the door, he climbed the steps and entered the shadows created by the slight overhang shielding the narrow stoop. Another padlock kept the door secure, the rust so thick that he couldn't decipher the metal beneath. Above the handle, twined along the angel's grimy harp, was a name.

"Clancy," Gia murmured at his shoulder. She squeezed his forearm and didn't let go. "Use your super-secret lock-picking skills. We need to get in."

Before he could reply, a low growl disturbed the quiet and the hair on Ian's nape prickled. Slowly, they turned, their backs to the mausoleum, observed by an angel with no eyes.

Several yards away, a dog the size of a small pony watched them, its gargantuan head close to the ground, ears pricked. The sunlight played tricks, reflecting fleeting shards of red in its brown eyes. And the *teeth*.

He never knew dogs had that many sharp, curved teeth.

"Nice doggie," Gia murmured. Her voice, undoubtedly meant to be soothing and friendly, shook too much to be believable. "Go home."

Carefully, Ian eased ahead of her, his unrelenting focus on the predator trapping them. The only weapons handy were his keys and phone in his pocket, nothing that could stop a slavering half-wolf for long.

"Cerberus, you infernal mutt," panted a gravelly voice from the other side of the mausoleum, "get back here."

The dog's growling stopped, but it didn't change his attack stance.

Ian didn't relax, either. *Cerberus. Perfect.* He'd always wanted to tangle with the underworld's pet, using only his boots and fists.

A man rushed around the corner of the mausoleum and jerked to a stop. If a scarecrow came to life, he'd probably win in a beauty contest with this guy. Scraggly black hair pulled back in a rattail made a perfect combination with the tobacco-browned teeth. His stained, white wife beater and dirty jeans didn't do anything to hide the skeletal thinness of his frame. Ian was surprised he wasn't carrying a shotgun.

"What are you doing here?" The man's bloodshot eyes narrowed, flicking between them. "This is private property."

"Our apologies." Ian forced the tension from his shoulders, keeping Gia behind him. "We were out driving today and saw the gate from the road. We didn't see any 'no trespassing' signs and the gate wasn't locked, so we thought we'd check it out."

"Bull." The man spat a wad of tobacco on the grass. "That gate hasn't been unlocked for decades."

"So how did you get in?" Gia's voice was innocent, sweet. "Do you live near here?"

He grasped Cerberus' scruff and the dog sat. Ian would've felt better if the monster's tail wagged. "I'm the caretaker."

Ian made a point not to look around at the obviously uncared-for property. Whatever this man did in a cemetery in the middle of nowhere, it had nothing to do with upkeep.

"How long have you been caretaker?" Gia eased from behind Ian, her hands clasped behind her back, her smile bright and sincere. *Feminine manipulation at its finest.* "It must be so interesting to be in charge of such an old graveyard. Do you know the names of everyone who's buried here?"

The caretaker sneered. Maybe he'd been alone too long with his dog to be affected by a beautiful woman. "Private property, private records and none of your business." He jerked his chin toward the front gate. "Now use your fancy shoes to get out before I let Cerberus have a bite of you."

Sunlight or not, the glints of deep red in the dog's intent gaze added some weight to the caretaker's words.

Taking Gia's hand, Ian drew her carefully down the steps and around the again-growling Cerberus and his master. "Once more, we apologize for intruding."

The caretaker flashed brown-stained teeth. "You have five minutes to reach the gate before I let Cerberus go."

They made the front gate in less than three minutes and shut it behind them with a clang. Whether or not the caretaker had unleashed Cerberus as he'd threatened, the dog had yet to appear.

Puffing, Gia lifted one sandaled foot in the air. "Fancy shoes will always get you through the tough times. Known fact."

Ian grinned and leaned over, bracing his hands on his knees. "Never doubted it."

She turned and frowned at the gate and the graveyard beyond. "We're *so* coming back. We need to get into that crypt. I don't know what could be in there that's helpful to Joann's escape, but we need to find it."

"Tonight." Ian straightened and headed for the car parked at the end of the gravel road, Gia close behind. With each step, adrenaline faded and the chasm between them — the undiscussed events of the previous night — vibrated like a plucked wire.

As they reached the car, Ian went to unlock the passenger door and stopped. Enduring the entire drive home without dealing with what she'd witnessed last night would shred him to pieces. He pulled her close and, without intending to, pressed her up against the side of his car. Her soft curves fit against him — too tempting, too perfect.

"Why didn't you leave last night?" he gritted between his teeth.

"I fell asleep." She batted her eyelashes at him, her eyes clear and guileless. "Twenty minutes is a long time to wait when you're tired and on a comfy couch."

"That's not what I mean." His heart rattled hard enough that she had to hear it. "After I told you about..." He couldn't bring himself to say it. "You should have run. You should have locked your door this morning when I showed up. You should ask Mr.

Hamilton to resign from working with me on Monday."

"Actually," she said, trailing her fingers from his shoulder to his chest in a seductive slide, "you're the one who should be doing something." Her palm settled on his racing heart, warm and steady, and she lifted her gaze to his. "You should be telling me what happened."

I have to. Not because he wanted to delve into his past, wanted to talk or even *think* about it, but Gia had to get it through her pretty head that he wasn't some wounded soul in need of nurturing or saving. He was a volcano always on the verge of explosion, and when his control snapped, whatever lay in his path would be destroyed.

"My father was an abusive bastard." Somehow, he managed to keep his tone smooth and calm. "He beat my mother on a regular basis, and when I was old enough to protest, he gave me a taste of it too."

Gia's expression didn't change into sympathy — or, worse, pity. But neither did the jolt of unease he both hoped for and feared make an appearance. She simply watched him, waiting for the rest of the story.

"One day, I walked into the kitchen and found my mom collapsed on the floor, my father leaning over her. The blood —" He swallowed, pushing the memories away. "I'm not sure what happened after that, whether I went into a rage so deep I couldn't think or if I blacked out. When my consciousness reemerged, I was on top of him, my mother and brother screaming at me." Ian forced his gaze to hers. "But I didn't stop. I kept punching him until a cop or a fireman — I don't even know which — dragged me off. My hands and knuckles were so bruised and cut up that they looked like raw steak. I broke three of my fingers."

"No one should ever have to go through that," she said quietly.

"Of course they shouldn't. That's not the point, Princess." He leaned in close to her face and traced her cheekbone with one finger, making his voice warning-soft. "In that moment of darkness, while in the deepest pit of myself, I became *him*, exchanging violence for violence. Our natures are the same, and while I refuse to allow myself to be like him, there is always that niggling awareness that with one word, one act, I will…become him. And I don't know what will trigger that change, when it will happen."

She merely cocked her head, studying him. "I'd say, all things considered, you've turned out pretty great. The only person I've seen you pummel is Derek, and he deserved it." She shrugged. "I don't believe there's anything wrong with standing up for yourself or someone you love, even if it requires violence."

He hissed an annoyed breath. She wasn't getting it at all. "It wasn't simply violence, Gia. It was carnage."

For the first time, worry flashed over her face. "Did you…kill him?"

He shook his head, his throat tight. But it had been close. Oh, so close, and he had no doubt his father wished some days that he hadn't survived. His brother made sure to mention that fact in his scathing, thankfully infrequent calls.

"Okay, then. Thanks for sharing, although I'm a little disappointed that you voluntarily caved. I had diabolical plans to torture the information out of you." Gia's smile was so bright and bewitching that his breath caught. "But I think I'm starting to figure you out now."

He blinked at her and swayed on his feet, dizzy. Revealing a slice of his dark history was supposed to drive a permanent wedge between them, not... *this*. Not this sudden, undeniable warmth in his chest at her steady acceptance, as if she saw the monster inside him and wanted to pet it, make it hers and paint its claws pink.

Gia lifted on tiptoes and pressed her mouth to his in a raindrop-light kiss. "Thanks for telling me, O'Connor."

Before she could move away, he slid his fingers beneath her hair and curled his hand around the back of her head, holding her there. As her soft breath twined with his, he kissed her again. Gia responded in the same irresistible way he remembered from a blurry winter night, open and unrestrained, with a raw sweetness that made it impossible not to reciprocate. The rural stillness seemed to hold them close, the surrounding trees and empty road guardians against invaders. Every part of his body went taut with need, and he pushed his hips against hers, the friction heady torture. When she wrapped her arms around his neck and pulled him closer with surprising strength, he didn't struggle.

There was nothing subtle in the press of his body, the silken slide of his tongue on hers, his hands exploring her curves. Each point of contact burned, awakening all his senses until pleasure and want roared through his veins in hot demand. But beneath the physical sensations tumbling along every nerve, realization threatened to buckle his knees. He drowned in her and still couldn't get enough—would never get enough, and it wasn't simply because she'd haunted him with only a taste for over a year. He wanted her, all of her.

Not only her body for one night, but her smiles and thoughts, her dreams and respect...

Everything.

Every day.

All day.

The raw honesty of it sent a jolt through him and he broke the kiss. He rested his forehead on hers, his breath rasping. Gia's shaky sigh of regret nearly broke him.

Ian briefly closed his eyes, gathering his strength. He met her gaze, held it. "You should have run while you had the chance, Princess."

She smiled and ran her thumb over his bottom lip, removing a trace of pink lipstick that had transferred from her mouth to his. "Princesses don't run, Sugarpop. They fight with tiaras and big diamond rings, whatever assets they happen to possess." Her eyes sparkled like sunlight on water, clear and pure, as she pushed him playfully away and opened the car door. "Come on. We have midnight escapades to plan."

On the drive back to Graywood, their conversation was relaxed and uncomplicated, with not a single mention of nightmares or life-altering kisses. By the time he pulled up to Gia's obnoxious house, they'd hatched a plan to return to the graveyard in the middle of the night, crack open the crypt and discover why Joann had sent them there.

As Gia slowly unbuckled her seatbelt, she stared out of the window at her house, chewing on her bottom lip. He was such a jerk. He should have asked how she was handling her turbulent sister.

"You can go home with me instead." They weren't the words he'd intended to say, but he meant them.

She didn't look at him, probably immune to any shock from his propositions, her gaze still on her house. In the silence between question and answer, Ian waited, teetering on the cusp of a vast canyon, its depths unknown. If she said 'yes', he'd take her home. He'd take her home and keep her there — not for only one night but for as long as he could manage to convince her to stay. And that sent a twisting thrill of both terror and excitement through him.

At last, Gia exhaled and flashed him a tight smile. "I knew there was a knight in rusty armor in there somewhere."

"Right. I forgot to show you the familial suit of armor when you were over." He smirked, keeping his fingers tight on the steering wheel. If he touched her, he'd never let go.

"Or your sword." She lifted one eyebrow. "But whether Kat, my brothers, or — horror of all horrors — my mother are all lurking in there, I need to face my fate."

A tendril of *something* coiled in his chest — relief or disappointment, he wasn't sure.

Squaring her shoulders, she opened the door and got out. She leaned in, her smile gone. "I'll see you at ten." And as she closed the door, he heard her say under her breath, "If I survive."

Chapter Seventeen

As Gia pushed her front door open, the lingering sensation of Ian's lips on hers, his hard, delicious body hitting her in all the right places, echoed in her blood. The murky *thing* between them had changed in that moment, blossomed and stretched into something else, something not yet defined. When he'd suggested she go home with him instead, a barely detectible thread of vulnerability had underscored his voice, both a warning and a promise.

And that one element had hit her harder than his touch, approval or kiss, nearly derailing her goal to wait for love. Only clinging to the car door handle with all her strength had kept her from surrendering.

Then again, maybe she just needed some real sleep. Ian's magic turned her mind and body to mush, and it was more than possible that her heart played tricks on her ears. She was a thread away from being one of the women who took one night in the vain hope that he'd change his mind and want more.

She scrubbed her hair back and shut the door. Only silence met her. Kat could still be sleeping, accompanied by an empty bag of potato chips and her boyfriend-sized body pillow, but the quiet was too deep. A quick jaunt through the house determined that her sister wasn't there. A note lay on the kitchen counter.

Went to the store for more chips. Sorry for last night. I was a jackass. I'm blaming my behavior on an ice cream overdose. When you get back, I want all the details on Ian. And they better be good because my little sister deserves to be deliriously happy, engaged or not.
K
P.S. I didn't play informer to the family. Yet. I'll give you a week.

Gia slumped in relief, dragged herself to her bedroom and flopped face-first on her bed. Thank God for miracles and the magical blend of ice cream and potato chips. *One week.* Maybe, just maybe, she had a shot at surviving the case—and Ian—without getting caught in the crossfire.

* * * *

A few minutes after midnight, Gia tiptoed a step behind Ian along the gravel road leading to the great iron gate of Fireside Burial Ground, guided by the solitary beam of his flashlight. Ian had forgone his bright red Porsche and driven a black truck she hadn't even known that he owned. They'd parked on the road a quarter-mile away to be safe and hoofed it to the gravel road. Wherever the caretaker and his hellhound roosted at night, alerting them wasn't part of the plan.

Ian stopped at the gate and his flashlight shone on the hand-painted *No Trespassing* sign made of scrap wood hanging between two iron spokes. The lock from before was gone, replaced by a shiny, new heavy-duty padlock.

"The caretaker apparently takes his job seriously," Ian whispered. "I can't pick that monstrosity." He guided his flashlight in a brief survey of the chain-link fence and looked at her, his teeth a white glint in the darkness. "Are you up to the challenge of an obstacle course, Princess?"

"That's why I left my gown and crown behind, Sugarpop." Not waiting for him, she curled her fingers in the chain link and hoisted herself up. She climbed as fast as she could, the fence trembling as Ian gave chase. They dropped to the ground at the same time, gasping and grinning like fools.

Then their smiles faded and, side by side, they entered the graveyard, heading for the Clancy crypt and its secrets.

Gia stuffed an escaped curl back inside the depths of her black hood. A strange sort of shiver pirouetted through her as she stepped soundlessly on the unclipped grass, close to Ian. The burial grounds during the day had been undeniably creepy. With only the bobbing orbs created by their flashlights, every shadow held an unseen menace. It was enough to get her adrenaline pumping almost as fast as her heart.

"So this is what it feels like," she whispered.

His hood turned her way, his face hidden in its depths. "What feels like?"

"To be one of the Scooby-Doo gang. Solving mysteries, skulking through graveyards for clues — it was all I ever wanted to do as a kid."

"You're a surprising twist of inconsistencies, love. I'll put a good word in with Roman once this is over."

She snorted softly. Besides her mother, she was the only one in her family who didn't dabble in law enforcement, and since she had no inclination to be like any of her family members, she'd followed her own path, final destination still unknown. "Cop is not in my genetic makeup. Not even the promise of an instant promotion to detective could convince me to sign up for that circus."

"So you turned to the judicial paperwork system instead." Laughter colored his tone. "No clowns there."

"The clowns in court are better behaved, at least on the outside." She sighed as she stepped around a looming angel statue. "My siblings all drank the cop punch. I'm the only one who skipped out on the dance and went for wine instead."

The hood turned her way again and stayed there, as if Ian could read her scowl in the black void of night. "The outcast princess. Interesting."

"Not outcast." She smacked him lightly in the hip with her flashlight. "Glamorously unique." She didn't feel like telling him that her mother was the one who'd recognized the beauty queen inside and dragged her kicking and clawing into the limelight — or that if she hadn't loved all things pink and sparkly, her father would have kept pushing her toward the blue line. "My family's complicated."

"Most families are." He faced forward.

She stepped up her pace until she was right beside him. The clean summer night, joined by a hint of moss, moisture and nearby roses blended with Ian's cologne in a fine, heady scent. Being with him during the day, with people and boundaries and daylight, gave her strength and focus to resist him. Creeping beside him, boxed in by midnight, stars and mystery sent unending trails of prickles along her nerves. The lean line of his silhouette called her to pretend this was a dream, some sort of dark, inevitable magic, and simply surrender to all the times she'd wanted to touch him and breathe him in until she was irreversibly drugged.

She wasn't sure she was already beyond treatment.

"How many cases like this have you handled for Mr. Hamilton?" She frowned into the darkness beyond her flashlight's glow. "I'm miffed he didn't assign me to one before this."

Ian stepped between two headstones and dragged her aside before she knocked her knees into some poor sap's granite epitaph. The heat of his hand on her arm sang through the thin cotton of her hoodie, and she didn't resist the urge to lean into him. "Hamilton and I have an understanding." He slid his fingers down her arm to her lower back, gently guiding. "I'm not afraid to push boundaries." His teeth flashed in the dark. "And I *never* get caught."

"I disagree. Miss Country Bumpkin caught you red-handed at the stables."

"That was merely a stroke of interesting timing, completely manageable, and I wasn't caught doing something I wouldn't have done anyway." He slipped a fingertip between her studded black belt and jeans, a seductive hint of how he'd stroke her skin. "When it comes to wanting you, Princess, I *never* have to pretend."

She snorted to hide the thrill heating her blood. "That's not a compliment. I'm a woman, which makes me automatically on Ian O'Connor's want list."

Ian stopped so suddenly that she almost tripped over his black boot. He pivoted, facing her, and pushed back his hood. In the darkness, his face made a ghostly moon, his eyes glittering silver. "You are *not* every other woman, Gia Hellman." His voice was so low, so rough that she wasn't sure she'd heard him right. He cupped her face and leaned in, close enough that his breath warmed her mouth. "The way I want you is incomparable."

Her heart hitched at his nearness, the heat of his hands on her jaw, the strong line of his body only an inch away. Pulled in by the dream of a magical, midnight kiss, her eyelashes drifted shut.

He skimmed his nose along the rim of her ear and his lips brushed her lobe. "I suggest you stop distracting me, love, before I forget why I'm paying you overtime and instead act out every dark fantasy I've had of you since the moment you stepped into the waiting room of Hamilton & Associates with your pink stilettos, summertime smile and perfect curves." He skimmed her ear with the tip of his tongue.

Gia sucked in a breath as a shiver tumbled down her spine and tingles flared in every secret spot, but instead of making good on his threat, Ian pulled up his hood again and swept onward toward the mausoleum, his flashlight sure and steady.

Right. Prestige and power trumped a woman, any woman. Her hand shook so badly that the beam from her flashlight bobbed and weaved on the grass in a twisted dance as she hurried to catch up.

The mausoleum rose up like a gargoyle in the night, a hulking shade darker than the shifting graveyard shadows. Ian took the steps two at a time and focused his light on the decomposing lock keeping out the living. At least the caretaker hadn't replaced the crypt lock too. Ian pulled something thin and silver from his pocket.

Ian flicked his flashlight off and tucked it into his waistband, setting his attention fully on the rusted padlock. "Hold your light steady, if you please."

"Since you asked so politely." She smirked at his brief scowl and lifted her light to the mausoleum door. While Ian bent over the lock, the metallic clicks and scrapes of his work small and lonely in the silence, Gia couldn't keep her gaze from straying to the unnatural design on the steel-plated door. Graveyards were spooky enough without the enhancements of cracked faces and eyeless angels. The gloom at the edges of her flashlight beam contorted the angels into clawing hunchbacks and added a hellish cast to their eye sockets. A shiver of cold overpowered the heat that had been ignited only seconds ago by Ian.

"Got it." Ian's triumphant whisper made her flinch. The lock *snicked* apart, and he removed it with nimble fingers.

"Were you a burglar before passing the bar exam?" she asked, only half-joking.

"Learning how to escape was a childhood survival tactic. Breaking out is harder than getting in." His expression was cool in the flashlight beam, a well-practiced act. No one recovered so flawlessly from abuse, not even with the best legal education.

Gia resisted stepping close and caressing his face until the mask fell away, until he trusted her enough to be completely real, completely raw. Why he'd shared his family background with her earlier, she wasn't sure, but she wasn't about to break the fragile ribbon he'd tied between them by pressing him for more.

He didn't want more. He'd made that abundantly clear.

With one hand, he pushed the crypt ajar. The ancient door creaked, echoing in the night, a warning to the dead and living alike. They both froze, listening for any response, a bark or running footsteps.

After a minute of nothing but wind and crickets, Ian's smirk gleamed in the shadows. "After you, Daphne." He cocked his head. "Unless you're scared of what awaits you in the dark? If you want, I'll let you cling to my arm—"

Gia poked him in the stomach with her flashlight as she swept past him into the Clancy family crypt. Dust and mildew laced the cold air, tickling her throat. Something light drifted over her face and stuck. A cobweb, which meant—she jerked—spiders. Dropping her flashlight, she swiped frantically at her face, imagining the black, hairy arachnid probably crawling in her hair now.

"Problems, Princess?" Ian's amused drawl didn't help.

She pressed her face into his shoulder and wiped the clinging web remnants on his jacket. A prickle crossed her neck. In less than a second, she ripped her hoodie off and tossed it to the stone floor. Giving him her back, she lifted her hair from her neck. Her skin crawled, amplified by her imagination. "Check me for spiders."

Ian paused long enough that she growled with impatience.

His breath stirred the hairs on her nape, and a light finger caressed her spine to the edge of her scoop-necked tank top. He pulled her shirt away from her body, and the flashlight angle shifted, presumably shining down her back.

"Pink and lacy," he murmured close to her ear. "I should've known."

"More fodder for your twisted fantasies." Her voice was huskier than she'd intended. "Might as well look at my skivvies while you can, since it's the closest you'll get."

He chuckled, low and intimate against her neck. He eased his long fingers around her waist and beneath the hem of her tank top, and it was all she could do to keep from leaning back into his solid strength and offering herself up to his delectable touch until she was lost in nothing but sensation. He skimmed her ribs, stopping just beneath her breast. "Clear so far." His lips grazed her ear and his whisper curled along her nerves. "Want me to continue?"

Every part of her body screamed an absolute 'hell, yes'. It was her annoying mind that played party-pooper, reminding her who he was and how she so didn't need another meaningless fling — no matter how fun it might be while it lasted, and that was the problem. She wouldn't want it to end, and despite the surprising depths she'd discovered in Ian, he belonged permanently on the short-term team. Her heart ached, once, twice, another warning signal to stay true to her vow.

With a surprising show of willpower, she stepped out of his loose hold and stooped for her fallen flashlight. The weak light caught the silver of cobwebs in corners, heavy with dust. Whatever spiders lived here were starving. "Why do you think Joann sent us here?"

"I don't know, but we'll find it." Ian's tone held not an ounce of doubt. He crouched before a coffin that was black with dust and animal droppings. "This crypt doesn't see a lot of visitors. If anyone happened to check, it'll be obvious someone was here. Be careful what you touch."

"You should've been Roman's partner, not a lawyer." Gia couldn't hide the approval in her tone.

"I'd be the star of an unlawful use of force suit within a week," he said absently, frowning at the name on the coffin. "Edmund Clancy, family patriarch. I can't imagine he'd have any clues about his great-great-grandson's nefarious doings."

Gia scanned the wall full of drawers holding Clancy ghosts of the past, wishing she hadn't tossed her hoodie on the floor where any creepy crawlies could scuttle into the folds. The chill in the crypt was more in tune with winter than summer and she rubbed her arms to fight the goosebumps. "What about the other word Joann tossed in, *siar*? West. *Siar* means 'west' in Gaelic."

Ian straightened. In black jeans and hoodie, his dark hair tousled and pale skin, he resembled some wicked fey, returning to haunt his enemy's grave. He pointed his flashlight at the marble wall, presumably the west. Gia had never mastered the art of figuring out which direction was which without the sun. He skirted another coffin that looked like it belonged in a vampire movie and approached the wall.

Following, Gia added her light to his. The black marble was split with creeping veins of silver that gleamed past the thin layer of dust. Unlike the other walls that were filled with names of Clancys long-gone, this one held blanks, waiting for the dead to become. She swallowed. *Except for two.*

"Brianne Clancy." Saying the name aloud sent a shiver down her neck, and the dates marking Brianne's short life made her eyes sting. "Stillborn."

"Logan Clancy." Ian's voice was even softer than hers. "He was only sixteen."

The silence wrapped around them as they stared at the graves of two people whose lives had ended much, much too soon, a sharp reminder of Joey and their life together, lost. Without thinking about it, she tangled her fingers with Ian's. His return grip was firm but gentle, a steadying presence, a reminder that life was warm and something to be treasured. She leaned her head against his shoulder.

"If I had to choose anyone to sneak into a graveyard and break into a crypt with me, it would be you, Princess." He spoke close to her temple, as if he wanted to kiss her there but resisted. "Just so you know."

She laughed softly, grateful for his humor. "I'm honored. What do you make of the cryptic clues, Fred?"

"Cryptic. Nice." She could almost feel his smirk. "And I'd rather be Shaggy than Fred. He never had the poor taste of wearing an ascot."

"Snob."

"Stylish." He pointed his flashlight at Logan's marker. "He has the same birthdate as Joann's husband."

A knot formed in Gia's throat. "Landon Clancy. Logan Clancy. Holy crap." She latched onto Ian's arm. "They were twins."

"I've researched Clancy's family," Ian said slowly. "Parents are deceased, no siblings, aunt, uncle or even a distant cousin. There was no mention of a Logan Clancy."

All the possibilities of that revelation swarmed in Gia's brain. Why and how there was no record of Logan, what had caused him to die so young, why Joann wanted them to know about him... Gia swept her light to Brianne's crypt, and the knot dropped to her stomach. "Landon and Joann would've been married barely even a year. Brianne was their daughter."

"Stillborn." His voice rough as gravel, Ian fisted his hand.

Gia bit her lip to stop the trembling. *Stillborn.* There was more than one reason a child might be stillborn, but her imagination took her to twisted places, to Joann's careful words and perfect persona, what happened behind closed doors, hidden from public eyes. What sort of monster would harm his wife, let alone his unborn child? Even worse, Joann had survived for years in silence, never knowing if or when she'd ever break free.

"We have to get her away from him."

Ian's expression matched the angels on the crypt door, devastating in its ruthlessness. He cocked his head and turned his ear toward the door. He grasped her elbow and relentlessly steered her toward the exit.

"What are you doing?" She jerked free as he shut the crypt.

He fumbled with the rusty lock, replacing it. "Don't you hear that?"

Tensing, Gia tuned into the stillness around them. At first, the only sounds intruding on the silence was their breathing. Then, as though from another realm, a realm of fire and brimstone, a deep, devilish barking. She sucked in a breath. "Cerberus."

Ian straightened. His grin was wild. "Ready to run, Princess?"

She launched off the mausoleum steps, the flashlight gripped tight. Her heart pounded as she raced across the grass, past crumbling gravestones and crooked statues, the barking growing louder with each step. Dogs didn't need light to track their prey, so the midnight hour wouldn't help them, and she had zero doubt that both she and Ian smelled delicious.

Ian's rough breaths and drumming feet played a duet behind her, not loud enough to mask the growls drawing ever closer. The chain-link fence loomed up in the night, and her heart nearly collapsed. Fast and agile as a monkey, Ian jumped onto the fence and climbed. He made the top before Gia made it halfway up.

Deep barks surrounded her as she heaved herself higher, her arms shaking, her hair hanging in her eyes. She curled her hands on the top railing and stalled. Her shoe was lodged in the fence. A hard jerk and twist only wedged it deeper.

A growl rolled behind her. In the gloom, Cerberus streaked between graves, his eyes glowing, luminescent in the dark.

"Ian!" She'd barely said his name before he'd lunged back onto the fence, hurdled to the top and dropped to the ground.

"You idiot," she hissed as he grabbed her shoe and jerked it free. "You could have done that from the other side, where it was safe."

"And miss all the fun?" His teeth slashed a white gleam, feral and reckless.

The hellhound broke free of the graves, a dark, lethal arrow streaking straight at them.

"Go!" Ian's eyes were fierce as he climbed the fence beside her.

Gia straddled the top at the same moment the dog slammed into the fence, shaking it. She gripped the rail with both hands and clenched her thighs to keep from falling.

Ian jerked his boot up as the dog lunged, its teeth snapping, demon snarls rolling from its jaws. It slammed into the fence again, and Gia almost lost her balance.

Swinging his leg over the rail, Ian dropped to the ground. He looked up and extended both arms to her, a silent gesture that he'd catch her.

With the fence shaking beneath her, the dog snarling and snapping for her feet, it didn't matter that Ian was one-night material or that he couldn't promise anything for her future. He was sure and solid, and she had no doubt he'd catch her at this moment—or any other moment while they played this engagement charade.

It made her heart twist in a way she recognized... because she'd felt it all the time with Joey.

Crap.

Gia slung her leg over and dropped into Ian's arms.

He held her longer than necessary, his pulse a hard beat against hers, his breath rough and uneven on her neck. She didn't mind that he twisted his fingers in her hair, as if she was his lifeline.

"You could have wiggled my foot free from this side of the fence and saved yourself all the drama." She lifted her gaze to his. His eyes were still wild and sparked with silver, his smile unworldly.

"If the hounds from hell are on your heels, Princess, I'll be the monster standing in their way if it gives you time to escape." He dipped his head and kissed her once, lightly, nothing more than a whisper, and let her go.

She wobbled on her feet.

"We should vanish before the hound brings his master this way." He glanced at the dog, who still snarled and fought to battle his way through the fence to get at them. "I have no doubt the caretaker keeps a shotgun or two, and I'd prefer to keep my hide free of bullets."

Gia nodded mutely and followed him to his truck. Frankly, she'd forgotten all about the dog and the caretaker.

Chapter Eighteen

After a midnight graveyard raid, Monday morning riding lessons came way too early for Gia. She slept on the drive to Clancy Stables and couldn't stop yawning as she trailed Ian into the barn. Not even the magic scent of hay and horses perked her up.

"Late night, love?" Ian smirked at her.

She zombie-groaned at him, the best verbal response she had at the moment.

"Hey, guys." Matt approached, leading Buttercup, gloves covering his hands. A draft of garlic swept near at his approach. Whether the DMSO was on the horse or his gloves, it stunk. "Sorry, but Joann isn't here this morning."

"Is she okay? Her migraines seem to get worse every time we see her." Gia wanted to wince at the concern in her voice, hoping Matt wouldn't read anything more into it. After Clancy had showed up at the charity masquerade *and* they'd found the mysterious grave of his unknown twin brother, the dark possibilities were too many.

"Queasy stomach. Probably the flu bug or fancy food gone bad." Coming from the other direction, Frankie pushed a wheelbarrow full of manure near. She paused and wiped her gloved hand over her forehead, leaving a smear of grime. "Which means extra shifts for us."

"Extra *morning* shifts," Matt grumbled. "I deserve a raise." Gia solemnly lifted her hand for a high-five. He slipped a glove off and smacked her palm with a little grin, red tinging the tops of his ears.

"And nobody deserves to run into Ian O'Connor so early in the morning." Hefting her wheelbarrow again, Frankie gave them a smile that reminded Gia of a snake, full of fangs and venom. She rolled on by with her manure load. "Happy trails."

Matt scrubbed the back of his neck and murmured, "Extra-temperamental in the mornings." He glanced over his shoulder, as if afraid Frankie might have heard him. "I'd suggest avoiding her."

"Already planned on it," Ian said smoothly, tucking an arm around Gia's shoulders. She didn't mind slumping against his solid strength. "If Joann isn't here, I suppose we'll go."

"Not necessary." Matt tied Buttercup to a railing and pulled a curry comb from his back pocket. "Joann may not be feeling well, but she gave me specific instructions for you."

Ian's arm tensed beneath her cheek, echoing her thoughts. While the flu was a viable excuse, Joann's absence could be the result of much worse, maybe even bad enough that she'd risk sending a message through Matt.

"She wants you to take Feathers and Belle on the easy trail around the property." He ran the comb over the horse's flank with quick strokes, lifting tiny hairs into the air. "She thinks you're ready to try a solo ride."

Gia exchanged a skeptical look with Ian. "We haven't even been on our own in the ring."

"Speak for yourself, love." Ian's eyes glinted darkly. "I've been on my own the entire time, with no Sean to save me."

"There's no Sean today." Matt squatted and checked a front hoof. "But if Joann says you're ready, then you are." He dropped the hoof and straightened, frowning at Buttercup's tangled mane. "Belle and Feathers are as steady as they come and the trail's easy. It loops around the property and the horses know it by heart. Besides, the acreage is completely fenced in, so if anything happens, there's a limited area to search."

"Anything happens?" Ian's icy stare bored into Matt's back. "That's promising—signed waiver or not."

"Where's Sean?" Gia kept her arm looped with Ian's and studied Matt. He was clearly avoiding eye contact. His voice was casual and the red in his ears had spread like twin flames.

"He's never here without Joann." Matt patted Buttercup's rump and grabbed the lead. "You know the routine. The trail starts just behind the barn." He hooked a thumb over his shoulder and strolled away, horse in tow.

Ian looked down at her and rubbed his finger over his lower lip. At last, he lifted his eyebrows. "Well, Princess...cowgirl up."

* * * *

Determined to stay in calm control, Ian forced his grip on the reins to stay loose, his shoulders relaxed. So far, Feathers had obediently followed the trail beside Belle, his gait steady. The horse hadn't even snorted once, the first warning sign. With Joann gone and only a novice rider at his mercy, Feathers would undoubtedly execute his diabolical equine plan when it was most advantageous.

"Do you think Joann's really okay?" Gia glanced at him as she directed Belle through a knee-deep creek. Hooves splashed through the water with no hesitation, not even from Feathers.

"No." Joann's absence was a dagger to his gut. With only a couple hours to sleep, he'd forgone any research on the Clancy genealogy when he'd gotten home the previous night, not that he expected to find anything online. Clancy's appearance in Graywood had been a warning, and Landon Clancy surely knew that Mr. Hamilton was Joann's childhood friend. Any half-decent villain took careful stock of their surroundings, every change or unanticipated arrival. Ian believed Clancy's words to Gia were a test, to gauge whether or not there was any underlying motive for employees from a childhood friend's law firm to make contact with his wife. When Clancy had vanished, he'd thought they'd passed that test.

But deep in his bones, he questioned it. Every lesson with Joann, she'd seemed more distracted, tired and stiff, as if her muscles constantly ached. As slender as she was, beneath her layers of clothes, she appeared to have lost weight. They were all factors that could be blamed on stress. Still, he wondered.

The saddles creaked gently in the heavy quiet and the horses' hooves made a soft, steady beat on the dirt trail.

Feathers flicked his long tail and jerked on the reins, stretching for the leaves of an overhanging branch. Ian jerked right back. He was in no mood to fight for control this morning.

"I don't think she's okay, either," Gia said softly. She turned her head, studying a shack tucked in the trees on the side of the trail. Moss lined the roof and vines hid half its walls, signs the building had stood there, neglected, for years. "I don't trust Matt."

"The wannabe cowboy who blushes every time you bat your eyelashes at him?" Ian snorted. "Hardly spy material, Princess." His mouth tightened. "My money's on Frankie. Her main employment is at a bar. Working until three in the morning there then rushing to the stables before dawn isn't suspicious at all."

"Frankie? Please." Gia waved one hand in dismissal as the trees broke into a long stretch of open grass and sky. "Like everybody else, she clearly has a crush on you."

"Everybody?" He met her gaze, not missing the color in her cheeks.

"I'm not everybody, Sugarpop." Her brilliant smile made his breath catch. When her gaze drifted to his mouth and blatantly stayed there, he shifted in the saddle, adjusting his suddenly strung-taut body.

White-hot light forked overhead, and Ian turned his face to the sky. He held his breath. *Please, no thun—*

Thunder boomed, hard enough that vibrations shuddered through Feathers.

Before Ian could grab for the reins, Belle exploded into a reckless gallop. Gia shrieked, clinging to the pommel with both hands, though she somehow managed to stay in the saddle without Sean.

Dammit! Feathers snorted and pranced in a circle, and Ian gripped the reins, not sure if he should give the horse his head or tighten his hold. As Feathers made another dancing turn, Gia and Belle cut across the meadow ahead, dipping out of sight beyond the hill.

"Stop messing around, horse." Ian put Joann's advice into play. If he remained calm, Feathers would too. Those were the rules, calm and in control. Gritting his teeth, he patted the arched neck as the horse circled again, snorting. "Never follow in a dumbass' footsteps. For the record, I'm referencing your skittish sister Belle, not Gia."

Feathers stopped circling and pulled at the bit.

"We good?" Ian kept his voice steady and soothing. "Because if you make me look even more inept in front of Gia, no carrot. No sugar cube. No apple. Final punishment or reward will be determined at the completion of rescue." He forced his jaw to unclench and turned Feathers in the direction where Gia and Belle had disappeared. "Let's do this."

He dared to urge Feathers into a bumpy trot and hoped Gia would appreciate the sacrifice to his man bits. Gripping the saddle horn with one hand, the reins in the other, he checked the sky again as they broke into the open meadow. Dark clouds rolled in a wall from the east, fast, a deluge on the way. They needed to get back to the stables before that monster hit.

At the top of the meadow, there was no sign of horse or rider. Gia's shriek had ended after the initial banshee wail, but he almost wished she'd scream again so he knew she was okay.

He swallowed hard. Of course, she was okay. Why wouldn't she be okay? Gia had held on with the initial scare. There was no reason she wouldn't still be in the saddle. Belle would calm down. He'd probably find them farther along the trail, in the trees.

Come on, Princess. Make some noise.

Tree limbs closed in overhead, hiding the sky and adding a gloomy sheen to the trail that minutes ago had been tranquil. The air grew heavy, hot and humid, electric-sharp.

Ian wiped moisture from his forehead. Not even the birds made noise, probably because a horse and rider had screamed through moments ago. "Gia!"

Feathers snorted, the only answer he got.

Despite his resolve to stay calm, his heart drummed harder and the reins slipped in his sweaty hands. What if Belle had gone berserk and torn off the trail? He didn't know anything about search and rescue, about horses and trees and wildlife, but he'd heard horror stories of riders being swept off by low branches, ending up with broken necks.

"Gia!" he yelled louder, ignoring Feather's nervous steps.

The trail took another turn over the creek. Across the tumbling water on the opposite bank, white winked in the trees, leaves twisting in the rising wind. If Gia was close, she would've heard him yell. His throat tightened. If she was conscious.

Alive.

He clicked his tongue the way he remembered Joann doing and touched his heels to Feather's sides, pushing him into a trot again. Hooves splashed in the water and cool drops dusted Ian's hands and forearms. Before Feathers crossed the creek, a fat bead of rain landed on Ian's nose, and he lifted his gaze. Black bruised the sky.

Still at a trot, Feathers climbed the bank, following the trail. He nickered.

Another horse whinnied back.

Ian released a breath. Wherever Belle was, Gia would be there too.

Letting Feathers find his wayward companion, Ian held gently to the reins as more drops fell. Lightning flickered blue-white through the trees. The thunder on its heels boomed like a cannon had detonated right beside them. Feathers jerked and sidestepped into the trees, trying to brush him off.

"Don't think so, horse." His teeth clenched, Ian tightened his hold as branches scratched his arms and neck, Feathers refusing to stand still. He pulled on one side of the reins, which made Feathers spin in a circle. "There's only room for one leader here, and it isn't you, future horsehair vest."

The sky burst open, and rain pelted down, stinging. In two seconds flat, even with the protection of leaves, Ian was drenched. He flipped his hair out of his eyes and by some miracle managed to get Feathers back onto the trail. Mud squelched beneath hooves, quickly becoming a mud trap.

"Gia!" He bellowed again over the thundering rain.

Through the trees, off-trail, Belle huddled beneath a fir tree, her saddle empty.

His heart picked up an unhealthy beat and Ian dared to increase his horse's speed. The frightened mare's path wasn't hard to follow. Water quickly filled the deep grooves beyond the oaks, an indication of where Belle had skidded to a stop.

Hardly daring to breathe, Ian urged Feathers to the edge of the steep slope. Gia lay at the bottom, golden hair and pink T-shirt soaked, sweet form still, as if she were a princess sleeping.

Ian leaped out of the saddle to the ground. "Gia!"

She didn't move, and something inside him went feral. He dismissed the danger to himself or the stupidity of jumping down a semi-cliff in a flash flood. Gia was hurt. He slid feet-first down the ninety-degree angle in a shower of mud, grass and rocks and hit the bottom in an unsophisticated sprawl. Groaning, he rolled over and crawled to where Gia lay on her side.

Lightning forked across the sky from one end to the other, brightening her face in eerie white. The thunder hit before the lightning ended, knocking his balance astray. Ian fumbled back onto hands and knees and scrambled back to her.

He set a shaking finger at her throat and nearly collapsed in relief at the steady thrum of her pulse. Carefully, he skimmed his hands over her. As far as he could tell, nothing was broken.

Sheltering her with his body as best he could, he squinted into the rain. Climbing up the cliff with Gia in his arms would be impossible and he'd bet his Porsche that both Feather and Belle had taken off for home after that last thunderclap. He couldn't especially blame them.

The puddles dotting the ground grew larger, wider and deeper, funded by the insane torrent driving down. He considered calling for help and almost immediately discarded the idea. That would only put other people in danger. Yet, they couldn't stay here, on low ground with a potential flash flood.

Gently, he picked Gia up and cradled her against his chest. He knew exactly where to go.

After a grueling walk in the pouring rain and saturated to the bone, covered in mud and shivering, Ian shouldered his way into the shack they'd passed earlier. Dust motes swirled as he stepped across the bare concrete floor, but it was dry, and for now, that was enough. Gia still hadn't regained consciousness.

An old cot rested against one wall and he carefully laid her on it. His black heart constricted. She was so pale and with her hair completely undone and plastered to her head, she looked innocent. Helpless.

His hand shaking, not from cold alone, he stroked the wet hair away from her muddy face. "Come on, love. Open those gorgeous blue eyes. Ream me out for manhandling you and taking advantage of your unfortunate riding incident. I at least grazed the side of your boob."

He gritted his teeth, her non-response rattling through him. "You look like a disaster." He'd never thought that about her and he didn't now, but if anything could rouse Gia from the depths of her mind, it would be a jab about her appearance. "Wake up or I'll take a picture of you and post it online."

Gia didn't stir and that squeeze on his heart became a vise.

He gripped her cold, limp hand between his, and for the first time in a year and a half, he imagined what life would be without Gia Hellman on the outskirts. He wouldn't have a reason to wander past her desk to get a cheap coffee from the break room, even when he already had one waiting in his office. He wouldn't hope to catch a glimpse of her walking out to her car after work in those inordinately sexy heels she loved to wear and he loved to ogle. He wouldn't have any chance of running into her at office parties or weddings, smell her sweet perfume, see her open smile or make a passing, snarky remark to rile her up.

While it was pathetic and something he'd never admit to anyone, not even Garret, in the year and a half before they'd been assigned to work together, those moments had been the highlights of his existence. Without Gia and her sparkling stripes of color in his life, there'd be nothing but the nightmares and shadows fueled by the past.

Clenching his teeth to hold in the knot of emotions clawing up his throat, he gently stroked her hand and rested his forehead on hers. "Please wake up, Gia." His voice cracked. "I need you."

Chapter Nineteen

Someone was playing drums on her head. Gia didn't move, knowing that the second she did it was going to hurt. Everything already hurt — her neck, her ribs — and whoever was currently using her head for a drum was going to die. *After* she got warm and dry.

Why am I wet?

She squinted her eyes open and tried to make sense of her surroundings. The light was minimal, and the air smelled of dust and ozone. The surface beneath her was bare and hard. Her chest tightened. Had she broken her margarita limit, fallen off the no-date wagon and wound up in some dude's cellar? *Wonderful.*

"Gia?" Ian's handsome face suddenly filled her view and for a few heartbeats, she forgot all about being cold, wet and hurting. Mud streaked his nose and forehead. His dark hair was alarmingly disheveled, as if he'd been running his fingers through it. The wildness in his eyes wasn't even remotely the slick, calm and composed Ian O'Connor that she knew.

"Are you okay?" She struggled to sit up and winced at the jackhammer in her skull.

"Am *I* okay?" His laugh edged on insane. "You've been out cold for almost half an hour and you're asking me if *I'm* okay?" Fisting both hands in his hair, he paced across the small room. He came back her way and paused, jabbing his finger at her. "No, I'm not okay." He heaved a breath. "Thanks for asking."

"You're welcome?" She had a nearly undeniable urge to shrink back at the fever in his gaze. Instead, she settled for leaning against the wall for support. With all the mud and grass stains already on her jeans and shirt, a little extra dust wouldn't matter.

"I found you, Gia" — his voice was raw, the same tone he'd used when she'd interrupted his nightmare — "lying on the ground as if you were dead. You wouldn't wake up. The horses ran off, a flash flood is going on outside and my knowledge of outdoors and medical procedures are limited." He loomed over her, his eyes flashing. "I'm so far beyond okay that I can't even give you a correct definition of the word right now."

"And I thought that drumming was in my head, not rain on the roof." She smiled weakly as his expression turned scary. "I'm awake now." She gingerly stretched her body, testing for injuries. Everything throbbed, but the parts all moved like they were supposed to. "Bruised, but not broken."

Ian sank to his haunches and buried his face in his hands, muffling a stream of creative curses her brothers would appreciate.

Gia would've laughed if her skull didn't feel like a spike was being driven through it. She carefully touched the back of her head. The tender goose egg there was almost as big as her fist, and the surrounding hair was wet and matted. She drew her hand back. Red gleamed on her fingertips.

Finally done with his rant, Ian lifted his head. His gaze landed on her fingertips, and he went still. His color faded to a white paler than the remaining clean spot on his muddy, pinstriped shirt. Ian's eyes rolled up in his head. Before she could move, he'd toppled to the concrete floor.

Gia peeked over the edge of the cot. At least he'd been squatting and hadn't had far to fall. Considering what little he'd told her of his past, it wasn't surprising that he had a problem with blood. But Roman's bloody nose at the soccer game hadn't seemed to faze him. Neither had splitting Derek's lip with a well-placed elbow. She went completely still.

He'd freaked out because it was *her* blood.

A strange sense of wonder stitched across her heart and she took the unexpected moment to drink him in. Even when splattered with mud, out cold and unceremoniously sprawled on grimy concrete, he was a masterpiece of masculine beauty, every plane and angle of his body lean and strong. With his customary sarcastic edge softened by unawareness, it wasn't hard to see the man beneath the surface. Whenever he forgot himself and smiled at her, really *smiled*, another shard of her heart swept into his gravity, beyond her control. She was losing a siege that he didn't even know about and the only casualty of war would be her.

Ian stirred and his eyelashes fluttered. Moaning, he rolled flat on his back. He threw an arm across his forehead and stared at the low ceiling.

"Feeling okay now, Sugarpop?" Gia couldn't hold back a smirk.

He blinked at her several times. His eyes went wide, and he scrambled up, ripping off his shirt without unbuttoning it. Metal buttons clattered and plinked against the floor and walls, muffled by the hammering rain overhead. His black undershirt stretched over his biceps as he rolled up his shirt and reached for her, his gaze fiercely determined.

Gia leaned back until her shoulder blades hit the wall. "What are you doing?"

"You're bleeding," he said through clenched teeth. "That's not good." He frowned. "It's...bad."

"You're the strangest man I've ever met." Gia couldn't keep the laugh from her voice. "And I've met a lot."

"Now's not the time to torture me with your past conquests." He paused and his frown deepened, not enough to hide how shaky it was. "Or any time, for that matter. I don't want to know who else has enjoyed what I want."

The sudden warmth curling around her heart killed the laugh bubbling up. It was clear he was barely holding it together, and that made her all gooey inside. This man, who rarely shared his true emotions, was falling apart because she'd been bucked off and bumped her head, and didn't that just make him all sorts of adorable?

"Don't move," he said, sounding gruff as he stretched his buttonless shirt to its full length and slowly reached behind her, as if the blood in her hair would leap off her skull and lick him.

Gia bit her lip to keep her smile inside, but as he leaned in to her and oh-so-gently went about tying his ridiculously expensive and still very wet and muddy shirt around her head, that gooey deliciousness spread.

The T-shirt he still wore was as soaked as the rest of him, and it clung to his torso, accentuating every muscle and ridge beneath. Sparks ignited, surging more intensely than the aches in her bruised body and tingling in the best places.

More than she'd ever admit, his sheer physical attractiveness lured her—which wasn't usually the main ingredient she noticed first in a man. She, maybe more than most, understood the minimal value of the outward façade. But catching glimpses of the man within, that real and vulnerable person beneath the nearly impenetrable surface, made him so much harder to resist.

No matter what vows she'd made.

Done tying the improvised bandage around her head, Ian sat back on his heels and met her gaze. The wildness in his eyes had calmed some, but not enough to erase the worry lines peeking through the dark hair tumbling over his forehead.

Gia twirled the loose shirt sleeve hanging near her ear. "Never thought the hippie vibe was a good look on me."

"You look gorgeous in anything." His voice was low, without a single hint of mockery or suggestiveness. "Show up at this office like this, and you'd start a drowned-rat fashion craze." His throat worked as he swallowed. "I do have some bad news, though."

"Besides being stuck in a hovel an hour's walk away and possibly being caught in a flood?" She pulled one knee up and wrapped her arms around it, shivering again. "Do tell."

"Your headband was lost somewhere between thunder roll number one and the pitch and ditch that cut the unstoppable Ms. Hellman down. Good luck getting the grass stains out of your shirt."

His grin was so cute and boyish that she kissed him without thinking.

The cool, soft contact of her mouth against his plunged a stake through her heart. She wanted a man she could give everything to, and no matter how much she wished otherwise, every time she thought of that man, Ian's face plastered her brain like a movie poster. That stake twisted, making it hard to breathe.

Before she gave in to a mortifying bout of tears, she eased back and rested her chin on her knee. "That was just a thank-you kiss, in case you were wondering."

"Was it?" His voice was husky, his gaze unabashedly attached to her mouth. "I should rescue you more often. What are you doing tomorrow? If we're not confined to the enclosed ring after today, we can go for another solo ride. We clearly need more practice and I need more of your mouth on mine." He shrugged. "Or any body part. I'm not picky."

And as quick as that, any true emotions slid behind the 'shameless flirt' disguise. She bit her lower lip to keep from laughing. Or crying. Maybe both. "You're incorrigible. You'd let me climb on a horse in the hopes that I'd get bucked off again, merely for a chance to maybe feel me up?"

"I already did that when I carried you here." The old Ian smirk back in place, his eyes gleamed. "Nice, round and soft, a perfect fit for my hands." He suggestively cupped the air with both hands.

"You just had to ruin the moment, didn't you?"

"What?" He looked between his hands, as if bewildered. "You have two boobs and I have two hands. It seems an obvious equation."

"You also have two testicles, so I suggest you focus on those instead."

He wriggled his eyebrows. "Variety is the spice of life, love."

She sighed and leaned back against the wall. Her head hurt too much to banter. "If I had to choose anyone to be rescued by—manhandled or not—it would be you, Sugarpop. Just so you know."

Heat lit his eyes for a heartbeat, there and gone like a candle snuffed between two fingers. He suddenly stood and turned for the door. "Now that I'm sure your death won't in any way be accountable to me, I'll make sure the creek is still crossable." He glanced over his shoulder. "Don't go to sleep, Princess. I know that much about concussions."

Gia sighed as the door shut softly behind him. He might pretend to the world, but she wasn't about to let him pretend with her. Even if the consequences cost another part of her heart.

* * * *

The hour-long walk back to the stables was a cold, wet, muddy trek through hell, and by the time Gia stumbled into the warm barn—where Belle and Feathers calmly munched grain, the worthless beasts—she wanted to curl up in the straw and die. Instead, Frankie tucked both her and Ian into thick, hairy horse blankets, offered heavenly hot drinks and fussed over Ian before he growled that they had to go. Apparently, taking Gia to the emergency room to ensure she was truly okay wasn't one of Frankie's worries.

Gia knew Ian wasn't truly okay either, since he didn't even suggest that she strip off her muddy clothes before getting into his Porsche, and it took all her charm and pleading to convince him that she wasn't going to die any time soon and to take her to the Graywood hospital rather than the closest medical clinic.

Rain pelted the roof the entire drive, so when he pulled beneath the emergency room awning and parked, the sudden quiet seemed loud, Ian's exhale even louder.

"Odds are you're going to survive," he said coolly, gazing past her toward the double doors of the ER, "but it's too soon to tell the amount of brain damage."

"Glad to see you've got your sense of humor back, O'Connor." Gia opened the car door, only then noticing he hadn't turned the car off. "Don't tell me you're afraid someone might see you looking less than pristine?"

He met her gaze, his expression solemn. His fingers gripping the steering wheel were white. "I don't do hospitals."

The ghosts in his eyes were enough of an explanation. She lifted her chin and slid out of the car, the horse blanket still around her shoulders. "This particular princess can handle a doctor visit without any prince holding her hand, Sugarpop." She flashed him a smile. "Even if I do look like a drowned rat sporting the latest fashion in mud accessories."

"You're always beautiful, Gia," he said, his tone soft and serious. "Text me when you're done."

She shut the door and turned away before he could see the tears pricking her eyes. There went another slice of her heart, forever lost to a man who didn't want forever.

Chapter Twenty

Ian straightened his collar and smoothed his clean, damp hair, but none of that could erase the chill lingering beneath his skin. He couldn't stop the images replaying in his mind of Gia lying on the ground, lifeless — her blood, red and glistening on her slender fingers, the pure joy in her face before she kissed him, the understanding and regret in her summer sky eyes as he'd abandoned her at the hospital.

Leaning his hands on the marble bathroom sink, he closed his eyes. He didn't want this, not the sledgehammer beat of his heart, the shaking in his hands or the empty pit that had opened in his stomach. When the emergency room double doors had closed behind Gia, it was as if she'd walked out on him. He didn't want that, either.

Over an hour had passed with no text from her, no assurance that she was okay. A bomb had been chained to his chest, and it was only a matter of time before it exploded, demolishing everything.

Focus. He had to focus on the goal that had kept him going all these years — become skilled enough that the most prestigious attorney in town would add his name to the firm, respected enough that no one would question his quality. *Be* enough to deserve it.

That was all he'd wanted, all that mattered...until a Glitter Girl had walked into his life and impaled his heart with her killer heels, infected him with tequila-laced lips, then proceeded to revise his rules, one saucy step at a time. He glared at his reflection in the mirror. And if he botched Joann's case, none of it mattered.

Leaving the bathroom, he pulled his phone from his jacket pocket. Still no text from Gia. At the hard rap on his front door, he smirked. *Roman, punctual as always.* He swung the door open.

"This better be good," Roman grumbled as he slouched inside, his hair dark with rain. "It's my day off. I had plans."

"Listening to your police scanner and hoping for some major crime to happen so you have an excuse to go back to work isn't what I'd call plans, Baconbits." Ian shut out the cool draft of the summer storm. "Are you still on good terms with that human services clerk in the capitol?"

Roman sprawled on Ian's couch, moisture glinting silver on his black jacket. "Before I answer that, why do you want to know?"

"I need a death certificate, fast. Like yesterday."

Rubbing his chin, Roman's eyes narrowed. "Why aren't you at work?"

"Special assignment." Ian stuffed his hands into his pockets and planted his butt on the edge of the recliner. "Can you help or not?"

"That depends."

"On what?"

Roman steepled his fingers, his innocent expression not at all convincing. "On where you're taking me to lunch."

A drive to the state capital, steak, pie and a pitcher of beer later, Roman slid into the passenger seat of Ian's Porsche and handed him a manila envelope. Raindrops left fat, dark smears on the paper.

"What took so long?" Ian lifted the envelope flap, his fingers cold and fumbling.

Roman gave him a patient look. "Charming clerks into a rush job is not a quick or simple process, Boy Wonder. It requires finesse, careful maneuvering and promises of private shooting lessons. You owe me."

Ian paused. "I just forked out over a hundred dollars for your lunch alone, and even after your second piece of pie, I refrained from mentioning the word 'pig'. That's a sacrifice right there."

"Ian O'Connor, the epitome of gracious." Roman nodded, solemn and mocking.

Exhaling slowly, Ian freed the death certificate. Logan Demetrius Clancy — same dates of birth and death as in the crypt, same parents as Landon Clancy. Cause of death — heart attack.

"How many sixteen-year-olds have you heard about dying from a heart attack?" He lifted his eyebrows at Roman.

Roman studied him for a long moment, then his mouth twisted, a calculating tell. "You want me to find out if there's a coroner's report, don't you?" He snatched the paper from Ian's hand. "A coroner's report from fifty years ago?" Glee filled his voice. "If it exists — and that's a jumbo-sized *if* — I might be able to finagle a way to expedite it. Of course, this is my day off and I *am* super-busy, not to mention that you bailed on me Saturday."

"I'm not paying for your dinner, cheapskate," Ian growled. "You live for this kind of crap, so just do it." He punched Roman in the arm.

Roman retaliated with a headlock, and after a brief scuffle and tap-out, released Ian with a tiny, triumphant grin. "I suppose I could squeeze it into my schedule, but if there is a coroner's report, I can't promise I'll be able to get it today. My power has limits." The humor faded and his expression flipped back into the usual grim. "You're not in any kind of trouble, are you?"

Only if I can't help Joann safely out of her situation. Having a client so unreachable in every way twisted everything, made every step frustratingly small and exceedingly difficult. Joann had been in trouble from the beginning, and if he didn't handle the situation carefully, that trouble could take an even nastier turn. The old scar in his chest twisted. He refused to fail another abused woman who needed help.

"This case is the one that will put my name beside Hamilton's." Ian turned the key in the ignition and backed out of the parking space in a screech of tires. "*If I'm successful.*"

"Dude." Roman snapped on his seatbelt and relaxed in the seat, big hands splayed on each knee. "Unless it's a bet you make with me, you never lose."

Ian tightened his grip on the steering wheel. *And I don't want to start losing now.*

* * * *

236

Seeing Kat's SUV pull beneath the emergency room awning almost brought Gia to tears. Three hours of hanging out in the ER looking like a vagrant was enough to deflate any Glitter Girl. She trudged across the sidewalk and yanked the car door open. "Thanks for getting here so fast."

"You look like you were dragged through the mud for a mile." Kat scowled as Gia buckled herself in. "Why didn't you text me right away?"

Gia laid her head back in the seat. "My stupid cell isn't working right...again. I had to use the hospital phone to call you to come get me."

"What happened?" She pulled her auto away from the curb and the rain rattled on the roof, the storm still going strong.

"I took a tumble, bumped my head." She sighed. "No big deal."

"Big enough to be taken to the hospital." Frowning out of the windshield, Kat's eyes narrowed. "Why isn't your fiancé with you?"

Thinking about Ian made her even more tired, achier. Going into the hospital alone, waiting alone, had been the best possible reminder of everything Ian wasn't, everything she wanted and he didn't. "I don't want to talk about Ian."

For a few miles, Kat kept silent. The rhythm of the rain made a lullaby, and Gia's eyes drooped. The doctor had said it was okay to sleep and she had no intention of going anywhere but her bed.

"Mom and Dad got divorced," Kat blurted, her gaze fixed to the road. "They wanted to wait to tell you during the holidays, face-to-face."

"What?" Gia blinked at her sister. No way had she heard right.

"It was finalized a couple months ago." Sadness lined Kat's face, in her eyes, around her mouth. "They just realized they were living different lives, so." She shrugged. "They're still friends. It was all very…amicable."

"Friends? What do you mean *friends*? Did I wind up in a Twilight Zone episode when I bumped my head? Mom and Dad aren't friends. They're—"

"Divorced, G." Kat parked in the driveway, turned off the motor and shifted in Gia's direction. "This is why no one wanted to tell you, especially after you lost Joey. We knew you'd freak out."

"Freak out?" Gia forced herself to smile, even though she felt like she was free-falling down an endless hole. "I'm not freaking out. I'm fine. Totally fine."

Kat crossed her arms. "You look like you belong in the next psycho movie."

Gia kept her smile on tight. Her parents—divorced. Katerina—almost divorced. Joey—gone. Ian—not really hers. Maybe happily ever after was a fairy tale only granted to certain people like Emma and Merle, Adara and Garret. Maybe she wasn't meant for the kind of true love that changed lives, touched souls and lasted forever.

"I'm going for a walk." Ignoring Kat's response, she ducked out into the rain and walked away. She wandered around the corner, to the park at the end of the street, and kicked off her boots and socks. Slumping, the grass cool and wet beneath her bare feet, she let the rain destroy every last trace of her outward persona.

Minutes—maybe hours, she wasn't sure—later, footsteps fell soft on the lawn behind her. Gia didn't bother turning. Rain plastered her hair to her head. Her

T-shirt and jeans clung to her, darkened by the streams running over her neck and back. She had zero doubt that her waterproof mascara had lost the battle and streaked black down her face. For once, she just didn't care what she looked like or who might witness her fall from glamour.

"You didn't text me." At Ian's disgruntled voice, she briefly closed her eyes. His warm hands settled on her shoulders, his heat against her back far too familiar. "I've been looking for you."

She lifted her face to the rain and grimaced. "You didn't need to."

"I know," he whispered against her temple. "I wanted to." Gently, he turned her to face him. "Are you okay?"

Gia hiccupped, a half-laugh, half-sob. "I haven't been okay for a long time." She closed her eyes as he brushed a thumb over her cheek. It was too painful to imagine that he wanted anything more from her than the benefits of their false engagement and maybe a congratulatory tumble after Joann was safe and free. She'd wanted to find love organically, not lose her heart again tragically.

Sighing, she opened her eyes. "I wouldn't call myself a religious person by any means and I've messed up so many times that I'll never reach sainthood, but ever since I was old enough to appreciate pretty dresses and makeup, I prayed — every day — for my prince, because I knew he was out there. And I kissed a lot of frogs before Joey found me."

Ian went still, warily holding her gaze.

"I believed my prayers were finally answered. I found someone who loved me not just for my appearance or my body, but for *me*. Even at my worst, even when I had no clue as to where I belonged in the world, what I wanted to do, who I wanted to be...Joey loved me." Her throat tightened. "When he died, my faith in love died too. I went back to the pond and all those gigantic toads...until Adara found Garret. At their wedding, somehow, my hope reignited." Fresh tears joined the rain. "But I'm doubting the fairy tale right now. Big time." She knuckled her eyes. "Some princess I am, huh?"

Ian's breath warmed her mouth. "You're perfect, Princess."

His tone was low enough, odd enough that she paused. Rain soaked through his shirt, sculpting the material to his skin. His dark hair hung in his eyes, dripping, and rivulets of raindrops coursed down his face and fell off the tip of his chin. His eyes held not a hint of the mask he usually wore, and the unexpected openness made her knees wobble.

She forced herself to continue with the truth, needing to confess everything she'd kept stored deep beneath her sunshine tank. "More times than I care to admit, I second guess everything—who I am, what I'm doing, where I'm supposed to be, what I even want my future to look like. Maybe Kat's right, that I pretend everything's fine and fill in the gaps with sparkles and salons. And maybe you're right too, that fairy tales are an illusion."

"When have you ever listened to me?" One side of Ian's mouth crooked up at the corner, and she glared at him through the rain. He cupped her face between both hands. "If anyone deserves a happily ever after, it's you."

"But happily ever after doesn't matter if it's not real." A sob caught in her throat. "And maybe praying for two loves in one lifetime is asking too much for someone who can't even figure out where she belongs."

"I hate to repeat myself," Ian said softly, lifting her chin with a finger, "but you're perfect, Gia Hellman, no matter where you are or what you're doing."

"Perfect." She choked on the word and pushed his hands away. "Right. I'm perfect if all you want are these." She palmed her boobs, enjoying the shock in his eyes, hating herself that she also enjoyed the follow-up flare of heated longing. "Or this." She trailed a hand down her body, a silent dare to deny it. "You've made that clear enough."

He took her jaw in one hand and squeezed, every ounce of gentleness gone. "I have always wanted you," he rasped. "I'll never deny that, but don't fool yourself into believing that I don't want to own every part of you." He brought his face close to hers and his eyes flared, deepening a shade. "I'd lie, kill, sell my black soul to the highest bidder if it meant I could share every breath of this life with you." He paused and his throat worked. "And I'm every bit as appalled by that admission as you probably are."

Somewhere along the way, she'd started shaking and couldn't stop. Her heart thrummed in her fingertips, her chest, a giant gong in her head. Ian's gravity paralyzed her, sucking the breath from her lungs.

"I've tried to do the right thing for both our sakes, but every attempt I've made, you destroyed." He snaked one arm around her waist and hauled her close against his firm warmth. "I tried to tell myself that one night with you would cure this raging need that's been driving me slowly insane since you showed up at Hamilton's." He dragged in a long breath. "But even then, I recognized the lie. I knew one night would never be enough, even as I tried to make you understand why I'm the last person you need."

He eased his hold on her jaw and brushed the backs of his fingers along her cheek, gentle again. "I'm done, Princess. Done denying that you don't already own me. Done offering excuses. Done pretending to be halfway decent or deserving of you just so you'll smile at me again. Maybe you're not perfect for everyone, but you're my damn definition of perfect."

Gia blinked away the crystalline drops from her eyelashes, lifted on her tiptoes and pressed her mouth to his. His lips were wet with rain and tasted like summer, and she kissed him with every ounce of yearning she'd stored up since the ill-fated holiday party over a year before, as if she could erase every bad date, choice and emotion she'd endured since Joey had left her. She knotted her fingers in his damp hair and clung to him.

He tightened his hold, lifting her bare feet completely off the grass and dragging her toes up his drenched jeans. His response was hungry, fierce, with tongue and teeth and an unrelenting grip on her that screamed possessive. Maybe it was a warning sign that she should heed, but the thrill coursing through her blood only sparked a desire for this man who protected her only when she needed it, who made her feel worthy and wanted and *more*.

Still holding her against him, never breaking the kiss, Ian carried her to the wooden picnic table close to the river, beneath an oak tree that provided some shelter from the rain. not that she cared about the rain or the solid surface now beneath her butt. Ian slid his fingers up her knees and slipped between her legs.

Gripping his collar, she pulled him closer. Gia locked her legs around his hips, in case he changed his mind. A low moan hummed in his throat, and when he squeezed her hips, she didn't even feel the rain. Dizzying warmth swept through her, intense and intoxicating, as his words settled over her heart and branded it with his name.

Ian. Ian, Ian, Ian.

"What the hell are you two doing?" The voice pierced the haze of pleasure clouding Gia's brain and she managed to drag her mouth away from Ian's. Roman stood behind them, glowering, his dark hair shining with rain.

"That's a stupid question." One arm still locked around Gia's hips, Ian glanced over his shoulder at his friend, annoyance tight in his features.

"It isn't when I overhear a radio call about a suspicious man at a public park and before I even make it here, there's another one reporting public indecency."

"Only my feet are bare. What's indecent about that?" Gia looked down at herself and her cheeks caught aflame. *Oh. Right. Wet T-shirt contestant number one.*

Ian pivoted and faced Roman, blocking Gia mostly from view. "We're the only ones here — at least we were until you showed up. Feel free to leave at any time."

"Don't be a punk." Neither Roman's tone nor expression changed. "Take it inside before an on-duty cop shows up. And you owe me two beers — one for saving you from a citation and another for forcing me to ruin my hairstyle." He craned his neck, as if trying to get a better peek at Gia. "Make it three for getting me all hot and bothered." With a dismissive wave of his hand, he stalked back to his parked car.

Giggle-snorting, Gia looped her arms around Ian's neck and laid her forehead on his wet shoulder. "I adore that guy."

"Yeah, he's a limited edition." Ian's voice held an edge of fond annoyance.

She jumped off the picnic table and gathered her socks and boots, suddenly feeling shy and awkward. On one hand, she didn't want to break whatever spell that had made Ian confess he wanted more from her than a one-night fling. More than that, she needed to know he wasn't setting her up only to let her fall.

"I'd take you home with me, but…" Ian swiped his hands through his hair and fisted them, as if needing to keep them still. "I need to make sure the bump on your noggin isn't messing with your emotions or making you do things you wouldn't normally do." He gave her a superior look. "I don't want to be accused later of taking advantage of a woman with a head wound — and I'd most definitely take advantage of you."

"Ian." She clutched her boots and socks tight to her heart, the only available protection. "I'm not the only one who was out cold today." She studied him, the relaxed lines of his face, the unusual softness in his eyes. "Are you sure you're completely rational right now?"

One corner of his mouth curled up. "Are you questioning my integrity, love?"

"Maybe just a little." Gia pinched the air.

His smile faded. "I wasn't expecting you," he said softly. "I didn't want this. One by one, I've revised and broken all my laws for you, and now the statutes are erased, leaving me with no guidelines to follow." He stepped near and looked at her, keeping his hands still. "I'm arrogant, stubborn, selfish and a dozen other negative qualities, but if I say I'll catch you when you fall, Princess, I will."

"I think," she said slowly, her heart fluttering, "I've already fallen."

He uncurled his fingers and guided her into a walk. "True." He smiled benignly. "I'm the one who found you on the ground."

Chapter Twenty-One

The ring was perfect, an inordinately expensive, strikingly pink diamond set in rose gold worthy of any Glitter Girl, but the detail that pushed Ian over the edge to click the Buy button was the meteorite lining the band inlay. A meteor was as close as he could get to lightning in a ring.

He slumped back on the couch, his heart a raging beast inside his chest. Perhaps it was too cocky, too reckless, too soon, but besides the unrelenting awareness that his life path was to walk with justice in some manner, he'd never been so soul-deep certain of anything in his life.

He belonged with Gia and she belonged with him.

He rubbed his lower lip, that fine line between terror and excitement making him reel. Yesterday had been a cyclone that had picked him up and spun him around until he wasn't sure where he was, what to do, where to go. When he'd finally been released from its grip, outside Gia's obnoxious front door after he'd seen her home from the park, the crooked pieces inside him had shifted another degree, some of them snapping into place.

The fairy-tale-spiked punch had finally gone to his head and he didn't care about the unlikeliness of happy endings anymore. As long as Gia was with him, he'd move worlds and strip endless layers of masks to give her the happily ever after she wanted.

He stood and headed for the front door, nabbing his keys along the way. Even with the terrible fall the morning before, Gia had insisted on keeping their riding lesson with Joann this morning. She refused to postpone making sure their client was okay. He didn't bother telling her that he'd already planned to keep the appointment, with or without her, nor did he try to dissuade her from coming along. He preferred to have her beside him — preferably not on horseback, but he'd take what he could get.

First stopping for a chai tea, Ian drove to Gia's house and parked. Instead of texting her upon his arrival like he usually did, he took the front steps in one lunge and hit the doorbell. After a minute, the door opened and his pulse skipped. It seemed like days, not hours, since he'd seen her, had her in his arms.

But Kat, not Gia, stood in the doorway, squinting in the dim light, her long hair sleep-fuzzed. She must have crashed on the couch.

He assumed his wolf smile. "Good morning, Katerina."

"Why are you here so early?" Even her voice was rough, the words croaking.

"Gia and I have plans."

She gazed blearily past him to the gray world beyond. The sun had yet to rise and a dreamy quiet hung in the atmosphere, the cusp between waking and sleep. He deciphered clearly in her expression that she thought he was an idiot, not only for being up so early, but also for forcing her to get up too.

Must be another universal Hellman quality.

"If I'd have known I'd disturb you, I would have brought you a chai tea too."

She eyed the cup in his hand with disdain. "I don't drink that crap." Angling her head, she yelled, "Gia! Your suit is here." Her dark eyes narrowed, glaring at him. "If she comes home battered and bruised again, I don't care how she feels about you. You'll wish you'd never seen my face."

"As lovely as your face is, I have already wished that I could forget it." His smile didn't budge at the fireworks erupting in her eyes. "I suspect our low regard for each other is mutual, but I'll make one fact very clear. There are only a handful of people in this world who are important to me and Gia is one of them." A growl underscored his tone. "I'll be damned before hurting her."

Gia appeared in the doorway behind her sister, her smile unusual considering the time. She elbowed past Katerina and swiped the cup from Ian's hand. "Go back to bed, Kat." She prodded Kat back into the house. "And you don't need to threaten Ian. I've got this."

With one last glare for Ian, Kat muttered something under her breath, scowling, and shut the door.

Before Ian could comment, Gia wrapped her arms around his ribs for an impromptu, unexpected hug. Her sweet perfume curled around him and the pressure of her small body against him made his heart trip again, while the rest of him coiled tight and needy. He held her close and breathed her in.

"I thought I'd start on the hug quota early." Her voice was muffled by his shirt, and she squeezed him so hard that he laughed.

"Rough night, love?"

She groaned against his chest. "I should have rejected your unusually noble offer yesterday and demanded to go home with you. Instead, I signed up for a family torture session, which was awesome with a killer headache." Gia lifted on tip-toes and kissed him once, light and sweet. He let it go, because if he kissed her like he wanted to, they'd never make it to the stables. "I'll tell you all about it on the way."

On the drive to Clancy stables, Ian listened to Gia explain about her parents' divorce and another almost-altercation with Kat about her injury, including a lecture on the merits of staying single. When she was through, he told her about the odd death certificate for Logan Clancy and that he'd convinced Roman to order the coroner's report. While he wasn't sure what to expect from the report, he suspected some telling detail would show. No one died at such a young age from a heart attack without even an obituary in the newspaper archives.

As he pulled into the stable's parking lot, Gia's smile faded, her gaze on the barn. "I hope she's here, that she's okay."

"Joann has survived this long in her marriage. I'm sure she's managed worse suspicions than an attorney and his fiancée taking riding lessons." He took her hand and pressed a kiss to her palm. "We're close. I can feel it. Roman thinks the coroner's report will arrive today. Whatever it contains will pay Joann's ransom."

"How can you know that?" Her fingers curled around his, trusting.

"Lawyer's intuition." He winked. "Now, let's go see how our noble steeds are faring after yesterday's excitement."

Hand in hand, they strolled into the barn's front door just as Joann and Sean emerged from the office. Ian's blood went cold. Joann's face was haggard, pale and strained. A rash stained her cheek above the bony line of her jaw, and a Clancy Stables scarf was wrapped around her slender throat in a thick, red ribbon. Her white, linen shirt was long-sleeved, hiding her arms. While she wore her usual riding pants and boots, she couldn't hide her slight limp. When her gaze met his, the dull gleam in her green eyes told him everything.

He'd seen that same look in his mother's eyes every time she'd been beaten by his father. It was the look of hopelessness…of surrender.

Gia released his hand and immediately embraced Joann. Sean stiffened and he set his hand on the pistol at his belt, but he remained behind Joann.

"Are you feeling better today?" Gia eased back, studying the other woman. "We really missed you yesterday. And when I say really, I mean *really*. Did Matt tell you what happened?"

The warmth Joann usually demonstrated for Gia didn't reappear. "Frankie informed me of everything." Her voice was clipped, her expression cold. "I'm sorry, but I must terminate our agreement."

Gia's arms dropped to her sides. "Why?"

"The health and treatment of my horses are my utmost concern, as well as the safety of any guests at my stables. Using my absence to your advantage endangered my horses and demonstrated a reckless and inconsiderate nature that I cannot abide. There will be no further lessons."

Ian kept his features calm. Joann's explanation was an excuse, an intentional misunderstanding to save herself.

Gia shook her head. "But we —"

"Ms. Hellman"—Sean shifted around Joann protectively. His expression was stony as always, but there seemed to be a glint of regret in his eyes—"the topic is not up for discussion." His focus switched to Ian. "Do you need my assistance in immediately departing the premises?"

"We can manage." Ian grasped Gia's hand and gave it a warning squeeze. "It was never our intention to breach any rules or bring any harm to Belle or Feathers, Mrs. Clancy. We simply overestimated our riding skills, and in our excitement, we erred. Our deepest apologies." He held Joann's gaze steadily, a silent encouragement and understanding. "Should you change your mind about giving us a second chance, please contact me any time."

"I appreciate the apology, Mr. O'Connor, but there will be no further contact." Without a goodbye, Joann strode purposefully away, Sean a solid barrier behind her.

Squeezing Gia's hand again, he hustled her out of the barn and to his Porsche. Once they were both inside, doors shut, she turned on him.

"Did you see her limp? How horrible she looked?" Gia flung her hands, her eyes wide and worried. "And that scarf... I have zero doubt there's evidence of abuse behind her scarf. Do you know how much I wanted to rip that thing off and expose Clancy's dirty secret to the world?"

Ian calmly waited for the outburst to end. "And how do you think that would have panned out, Princess?" He kept his voice smooth and soft. "Sean is Mr. Clancy's man. Matt is probably on Clancy's payroll, too, and with Frankie's version of yesterday's escapade, there can be no question who her loyalty belongs to." He shifted, facing her. "Joann is surrounded by enemies. Her only defense is to hide. Clancy knows exactly how to control her — through fear and pain. Canceling our lessons was her way of backing out." *Of surviving.*

Tears filled Gia's eyes. "We *can't* back out." She grabbed both of his hands and held tight. "We *can't.*"

"We won't." He leaned forward and kissed her. "She doesn't know that we went to the crypt or that we're following her lead in checking out Logan Clancy's death. She has nothing hopeful to cling to, but once we get the coroner's report, that could change." He cupped her face and stroked her cheekbone with his thumb. "Sometimes, courage only needs a spark of hope to set it on fire. We'll do our best to fan that spark into a damn inferno and watch Clancy burn."

As Gia smiled back at him, fiercely adoring, and despite the danger Joann now faced alone and the very real possibility that Hamilton might learn Ian had essentially been fired before he could salvage the case, Ian had never felt so free.

Chapter Twenty-Two

"Got the coroner's report," Roman said into the phone before Ian could even say hello. "And an unexpected toxicology report." An edge of excitement made his voice rougher than usual. "The coroner's report lists cause of death as heart failure. The toxicology report—a private test performed at the request of the decedent's mother prior to cremation—lists traces of thallium." His pause nearly vibrated with tension. "Dude, your guy might have had a heart attack, but it wasn't from natural causes."

Ian jumped up from his office swivel chair, unable to sit still. "Are you absolutely certain?"

"Of course. What makes it even more interesting is that the toxicology report wasn't entered in the electronic data system. You can thank me later for requesting to see the actual paper report. Anything before the last half-century is considered historic and kept in storage. Jenny, the assistant I now have to take on a ride-along—you owe me—had to search for the file. It wasn't where it was supposed to be, misfiled, so it took some extra time. We found the toxicology report tucked in the back. It was almost as if someone hoped it would be eventually found—but not quickly."

Pacing the length of his office window, Ian couldn't contain his sudden energy. His pulse raced, pounding in his chest. This was it, the break he'd been hoping for.

"That's only the start of it." Roman's voice lowered to a gravelly whisper. "Attached to the report were some old high school newspaper clippings starring your guy. He'd won some chemistry contest using DMSO."

Ian stopped, his feet cemented to the floor. "DMSO? That's a solvent used on horses, right? To soothe sore muscles?"

"How the hell should I know? I don't even own a cowboy hat. All I know about it is that a football buddy of mine used to put it on after practice, and his breath would always reek like garlic afterward. Once coach found out, he banned it, said it was the same as taking every germ of every team member, wiping them on your skin and sucking them into your blood. That was enough of a deterrent for me."

"Damn. Are you saying that if someone used DMSO on, let's say, their hands, anything they touch after that would be absorbed into their skin?"

"According to Jenny, yeah. Hey, do you want me to bring my copies over? Jenny wouldn't give me the originals. My charm only goes so far."

DMSO. Joann, feeling sick. Logan, dying of thallium poisoning, something that could have been absorbed through his skin from touching anything after applying DMSO...such as the daily use of a saddle, bridle or curry comb.

His blood went cold.

"Dude? You still there?"

"Thanks, Baconbits. I owe you."

"Say that again so I can record it."

"Hang on to the copies for now. I need to figure something out." Ian hung up and resumed pacing. Joann's sickness could be caused by a variety of factors, but with the evidence found in Logan Clancy's file, he had a sinking suspicion that the same poison was slowly killing Joann.

The common denominator was Landon Clancy.

He texted Gia.

I've got news.

Her response flashed in less than five seconds.

I'll be at your office in a minute.

If Logan's mother had requested a toxicology report, she had to have been suspicious. Maybe she simply wanted to put any fears to rest — or perhaps she needed her fears confirmed. Cremating the body made it impossible to exhume later and confirm foul play. She had to have known, and maybe she wanted someone to find out after she was gone. Maybe she knew and, having lost one son, she didn't want to lose the other. And if Joann had guided them there, she had to have somehow known that Logan's death hadn't been natural. She certainly couldn't conduct her own investigation.

Ian paused at the wall of windows overlooking a school playground, the swings and monkey bars empty of children. If he moved fast and careful, it might be enough to free Joann before Clancy did something irreparable. Sometimes the mere threat of a scandal was enough to sway a politician.

His email inbox pinged, and he returned to his desk. At the name on the screen, he froze.

Landon Clancy.

A breath of dread skittered across the back of his neck. Never mind that only a handful of people knew his personal email address, but even if he'd blasted his contact numbers across the Internet, that particular name in his inbox, today of all days, would have given him pause.

Ian hesitated, his fingers on the keyboard. Whatever the message contained would impact the case, his next move, *everything*. He felt it to his very bones. But going in blind was a risk he couldn't take. Whatever game Clancy had initiated, Ian needed to know what it was. His shoulders tight, he opened the message with a sharp tap.

Charged with Attempted Murder as a juvenile. I understand how Hamilton might overlook that, given the circumstances. What about the three years in the Youth Asylum for Boys? Does Hamilton know about that part of your mental history too? Or does the lovely Miss Hellman?

All the blood drained from Ian's head. He planted his hands on the desk as the room tipped, dizzying. That part of his stained record — his flawed, ugly, left-behind life — had been sealed, court-ordered as part of the plea agreement upon successful completion of rehabilitation. No one should have access to it. No one in Graywood even suspected.

Another email pinged, from Clancy.

I believe you understand how to maintain the privacy of your sensitive history.

A bitter laugh built in his chest, choking. All this time, he'd been hunting for viable reasons to persuade Clancy to let Joann go quietly while Clancy had been doing his own subtle investigation. He'd been an idiot not to suspect a crooked politician wouldn't come from this angle. So personal. So poisonous.

Ian dropped his elbows on the desk and fisted his hair. If people discovered he'd spent three years battling his demons and nightmares in a psychiatric institute, he'd be ruined. Everything he'd worked so diligently for, all the years of dedication and single-minded ambition, destroyed. Moving out of the area wouldn't matter, not with the wide spotlight of social media. Hamilton would never name a former psych-ward patient as partner, no matter his winning courtroom record. Branching out on his own would be pointless. No one in their right mind would hire him without the backing of Hamilton. And Gia…

Needle-sharp ice splinters filled his stomach, twisting. She deserved far, far better than to deal with the bottomless pit of his past.

All his dreams trickled through his fingers, gone. There was only one possible way to patch the sudden, gaping hole in his path, to salvage any of the wreckage and keep Gia out of the crossfire.

The knock on his door sounded muffled, as if it came from another world away, a world where he hadn't just lost the future he'd only tasted.

The future he wanted, only recently found and now eternally lost, opened the door and peeked inside, her smile heartbreakingly unaware of the hairpin corner and cliff coming up. "I got here as fast as I could. What's the news?"

Motioning her in, Ian pushed aside the nails driving through his gut and waited for Gia to sit. He forced his expression to reveal nothing, made his voice smooth and steady. "I'm closing Joann's case."

Gia's smile froze. "But it's not done. Joann's still a hostage in her own home."

Putting on the lawyer mantel he'd perfected so well, he leaned back in his chair and gave her a cool look. "As far as we're concerned, it's done. You heard her this morning. She's chosen not to seek our assistance anymore."

A line appeared between Gia's fair eyebrows, a line that didn't belong there. She scooted to the edge of the chair, studying him, seeing too much. "That's a complete one-eighty from this morning. What changed?"

"Reality." Holding her gaze without flinching took all his strength. "There's nothing we can legally do for her."

"The *reality* is that she's scared." She stood and planted her palms on his desk, and he tried to ignore how her golden hair caught the sunlight, how her blue eyes saw into his soul. He tried to forget how perfect she'd felt in his arms, pressed against his heart, the tiny mole on her collarbone and the sweet, secret smile she gave him whenever he flirted with her. No matter the length of time, he'd never forget the smallest detail about her, a personal hell brought on by his own weakness. "Don't pretend you don't understand that, Ian. Don't pretend that we can walk away from someone who has no one else to turn to."

"It's not walking away, Princess." He smiled benignly, but it cost him. "It's called being fired."

"What about the coroner's report?" She watched him with a detective's focus, gauging every move, searching for any tell. "What did it say?"

"That Logan Clancy perished at the tender age of sixteen from a heart attack." He spread his empty hands and it took all his considerable lawyer acting skills not to crack. "A dead end."

Her chin lifted, obstinate. "I don't care what Joann said." She pointed an accusing finger at him. "We need to help her."

"We're not doing *anything*," he said, his words purposefully iced and clipped. He held her gaze, unblinking. If he didn't, if she sensed any weakness, it was over. He had to be the cold-hearted bastard she had once believed him to be, no matter how it killed him. "I, perhaps more than most, understand that you can't help someone who refuses to help themselves. I watched my mother be beaten down. She never once tried to leave — *not once* —" His jaw clenched. "Joann is beyond our help now."

Gia's eyes flashed, fireworks exploding. "That's crap."

"It's truth."

Her mouth tightened and when she spoke again, her voice shook. "You know what it's like to be helpless in the hands of a monster. You risked your life for your mother. *That's* truth."

"That's different. Personal." All this was personal, every word a razor to his heart.

She looked at him as if she'd never seen him before, as if he was a repugnant stranger, and he knew he'd won...even as he lost everything. "Joann has no one to protect her, no one to jump into the fray on her behalf. How can you turn your back on her? This is personal too."

"*This* is business. End of discussion. And if you can't accept it, our agreement is at an end as well. I'll make sure the overtime is included in your next check."

At his stony words, Gia recoiled, and he felt it like a fissure slicing across his heart. A chasm erupted between them, unbridgeable, and the sudden emptiness threatened to pull him under. He'd expected it, braced for it, but the hurt in her eyes struck him worse than a blow from his father's fist.

"I guess I'm not so different from the others, after all," she said quietly, her voice steely. "I honestly believed you wanted more. That you *were* more."

He wanted to say something flippant, some shallow phrase to stay true to his image, but his numb mind was useless. Only one phrase repeated in his mind.

I've lost her, I've lost her, I've lost her.

She removed the engagement ring and set it silently on his desk. Without another word, she turned and walked stiffly to the door.

The growing distance between them was a hungry void sucking his soul dry. Something inside him collapsed, crushing the breath from his lungs. He wanted to leap over the desk and drag her back into his arms, to kiss her until every memory of abuse or failures or lost loves fell into the abyss of nothingness and only they remained. Instead, he remained fixed in his chair, chained to his past, crippled by his failures.

She opened the door.

"Gia." Her name whispered from his lips, unintended and cracked, the irrepressible part of himself that belonged to her, that he'd never been very good at controlling.

Whether or not she'd heard him, she opened the door and swept through. She didn't look back.

Chapter Twenty-Three

Blurry-eyed, Gia stared through the window of Heelcandy at the empty spot where The Shoes had once been and gulped for breath, the summer air ineffective on her cold skin. She wasn't sure how long she'd been there, her head filled with the boom and clap of her heart cracking beat by beat.

What an idiot she'd been, believing Ian had feelings for anyone else besides himself, wanted anything beyond his own needs. And now The Shoes were gone, the final stomp on her dignity.

Turning from the window, she stalked to her hatchback in the parking lot behind the buildings. She violently kicked off her sandals, and they bounced on the pavement, sparkling wildly in the sunshine before landing with a dead thump against the tire of someone else's car. He'd admitted from the start that happily ever after was a lie, and yet she'd chosen to forget that little snippet, chosen to believe — like the naïve dreamer he knew she was — that his mind would change.

For her.

She wrapped her arms around herself, trying to keep her heart pinned together. He'd known all along what he was doing. He'd known the end of the case would be their end too and had probably hoped he could coax her into his bed before that happened. Joann had beat him to the punch by firing him, but that didn't gloss over the fact that she would have given him everything. Ian had manipulated her in the worst possible way, through her weak heart and sparkly rainbow dreams.

A laugh caught in her throat, bitter. Well, at least she'd managed to squeak out of being added to Ian's list of physical conquests. He probably didn't believe broken hearts were worthy of keeping track. She pressed a hand to her stomach, needing to do something to ease the yawning pit there as tears of rage, of pain, pricked her eyes. She wanted to rip him apart, force him to admit he was wrong, shed his lawyer skin and, for once, be human and vulnerable. Had he honestly felt nothing for her the entire time? Played his part so well she'd forgotten his true nature?

A terrifying knot gathered in her chest and her breath hitched. She couldn't do this again, couldn't be the girl who one-hundred-percent believed she'd found true love, only to lose it once more. She couldn't be controlled by emotions that would slowly erode her identity until all that remained was numb and empty, hiding in a shell of glamor and glitter.

Slowly, like a robot set on autopilot, Gia collected her shoes and clutched them to her aching heart. Maybe Ian was partially right and not all princesses found their own fairy tale, but no one could steal her crown unless she let them. She needed backup, needed the rational guidance of someone who'd shut herself off from love and somehow managed to find it again. She wouldn't find that at home, with Kat. With a shuddering sigh, she fished her phone from her pocket and texted Dar.

I'm collecting on your promise to Joey. Meet me at Flaming Nails?

Maybe she should feel a little guilty for using the coercion of Joey's deathbed influence, but she needed her friend and the magic only a pedicure could bring. Besides, Adara had the rest of her life with Garret.

The reply pinged right back.

Be there in twenty.

Gia made it to Flaming Nails in five. Except for Sally, her favorite nail technician because she never pressed Gia to talk, the salon was mostly empty. An hour or so past lunch was a slow time there, which suited her fine. She requested a chair in the back, and Sally set up the water before disappearing for Gia's usual lime spritzer.

Gia sat in the salon chair, removed her shoes, dipped her feet in the warm, soothing soak and laid her head back against the leather headrest. Lavender infused the air with a mild perfume. If only the scented water could be a balm to her heart too. She closed her eyes. How was she supposed to go to work every day with Ian there as a constant reminder, a daily dose of her dreams being ground to dust beneath his expensive heel? She couldn't avoid him. Her jaw clenched and tears formed behind her eyelids. *Wouldn't* avoid him. He could be as fake as he wanted, but she wouldn't allow him the power to push her into diminishing who and what she was, even if it meant an unhappily ever after for now.

Crap. She could really use some liquid strength, more than a lime spritzer possessed.

"Afternoon law break?" Roman's gravelly voice threaded through her thoughts, so quiet she thought she might be hallucinating.

Gia opened her eyes and blinked away the blur of tears. Roman stood beside her chair, decked out in his black uniform, silver badge and duty belt. The radio at his shoulder crackled.

"You do know there aren't any doughnuts here, right?" Somehow, her voice didn't even catch.

One corner of his mouth twitched, and he lifted the paper coffee cup in his hand. "I'm still trying to talk Sally into serving pastries, but she resists — not sanitary or whatever. Lame excuse." He sat in the chair next to her, set his coffee on the table between them and began loosening his boot laces. "Every man needs to keep his feet pretty. Don't judge what I choose to do on my break."

"Only if you let me pick your color." She managed a weak smirk. "Your toenails definitely need Kiss You Pink."

"It's bruise purple or nothing." He looked up from untying his boot, his dark eyes seeing too much. "You look like hell. Anything I can do? I owe you — one for filling in for me at the soccer game and another for kicking Derek's ass in the process."

"I didn't realize I was earning Roman points."

"I like to keep score." He shrugged and his duty belt creaked.

"Appreciate the offer, but I need a woman's perspective for this one." She dug for a compact in her purse. Ian had thrown her so off, she hadn't even checked her reflection. "Adara's on her way."

His eyes widened slightly. "If Ian is involved, I don't want to know, especially if you're planning to discuss it with Adara. That's one battle I will steer clear of at all costs."

Gia paused, the mirror in her hand as Sally appeared and silently filled Roman's foot bath. Telling Adara what had happened... Roman was right to be wary. Adara's tolerance of Ian didn't mean she'd forgiven him for what she believed was a deplorable transgression on her best friend's grief. But no matter how many margaritas were involved, Gia had never revealed that her holiday party indiscretion with Ian had everything to do with actually feeling something after Joey's absence, something wild and raw and wholly alive.

And now those feelings were wrecking her.

Once Sally left, Roman sloshed his bare feet into the tub, studying her. "Damn, it *is* Ian, isn't it?" He shook his head. "While I suspected foul play — after all, you're so far beyond his emotional league that, despite his skills of persuasion, I can't comprehend how he convinced you to marry him. I actually thought he'd finally let himself be happy." He swiped his fingers over his short hair. "My bubble will be irreparably burst if you two don't make it."

Tears stung her eyes again. So he wouldn't see her on the verge of crying, she nabbed Roman's cup, took a sip of his coffee and nearly coughed. What sort of monster destroyed a perfectly good coffee with hazelnut creamer? At least now he'd assume her watering eyes were from his terrible brew.

Gia cleared her throat and met his gaze. "Will you answer something for me?"

Frowning, he swiped his coffee back and held it protectively close. "Then I'll only owe you one," he said seriously. "Just so you know the price."

She smiled, the pain in her heart easing the tiniest bit. "Sounds fair. Where do you and Ian usually go on Saturday nights?"

A gleam of suspicion lit in his midnight eyes. "The capital."

Expecting more, she waited until it became apparent he wasn't going to expound. "And?"

"And what?"

"What do you do there?"

"The answer will cost you my second favor." He cocked his head. "Are you sure you want to waste it on Ian?"

She laughed. "You're a treasure. Did you know that?"

"Of course." He looked offended.

"I'll spend my last, priceless Roman favor on knowing what you and Ian do at the capital on Saturday nights." It wasn't like knowing Ian's dirty weekend deeds could hurt her heart any more than it already did.

He hunched over the arm of his chair, a conspirator ready to tell a secret, and she couldn't help but lean toward him. He dropped his voice to a whisper. "No one else knows, so you must make a vow of silence first."

She rolled her eyes. "I promise I won't tell anyone."

He nodded, solemn. "We search for missing and runaway kids. We scour the streets, connect with the homeless population—who can be very helpful once their trust is earned. More than once their tips have led us to someone we never would've found otherwise." He sipped his coffee. "It's something to do on Saturday nights."

She might have accused him of lying, of making up a noble pastime to cover his buddy's back if his expression wasn't so grave. She'd imagined all sorts of underground clubs and dark betting rings, always with nameless women out for a good time. Not once had she considered Ian might sacrifice his Saturday nights doing something...decent.

"There have been nights we've been out until dawn looking for someone we can't find, and I've had to drag Ian away." A voice on his radio rattled off numbers and a message Gia couldn't understand other than 'request for backup'. Roman cursed and mumbled something into the radio. He dragged his feet out of the water. "O'Connor doesn't know when to give up. It's both a sickness and a gift. Right now," he said, hastily toweling off his feet, "I'd consider it a gift to have a few more minutes without a call. How is a guy supposed to get a proper pedicure?"

O'Connor doesn't know when to give up.

A suspicion curled in her gut, tremulous and fragile. Ian had counted on winning Joann's case, had counted on the victory inspiring Mr. Hamilton to name him partner. That factor alone should have been enough for Ian to have stayed invested in the case. *Why would he backpedal now?* Even if the coroner's report contained nothing solid, their encounter with Joann this morning was proof enough that she needed help, no matter what she'd said to their faces before witnesses loyal to her husband. Would a man who usually spent his Saturday nights hunting for missing kids turn his back on an abused woman, especially a man whose own mother had been abused? *No, he wouldn't*, but something had changed, and whatever that change happened to be...

Her pulse fluttered like a trapped and dying moth, frantic. Ian hadn't trusted her enough to confide in her. No matter how much she loved him or the depths of his feelings for her, even if he had a perfectly valid reason for cutting her out, they'd never stood a shot. A couple without mutual trust held zero future. That betrayal hurt almost as bad as her cracked heart.

"Roman." Adara eyed them both as Roman finished retying his boots, his scowl still in place at the injustice of crime interrupting his pedicure. "What are you doing here?"

"Harassing innocent citizens, obviously." With a coffee cup salute, he stood and strolled away.

Adara gave her a questioning look.

Gia lifted her hands in a gesture of innocence. "I didn't invite him."

"So you didn't call me for a bail out or alibi? I guess that's good." Adara settled into the other chair beside Gia. She wore a flouncy, red, sleeveless top with a flower-print skirt. It was so bright and colorful and unlike stay-back Gothic Adara that Gia blinked twice, completely forgetting about her Ian issues for a second.

"Are you feeling okay?" Gia leaned over and laid her palm on Adara's forehead. "You're not wearing a stitch of black."

She shoved Gia's hand away, but that didn't hide the flush in her pale cheeks. "Garret likes red and I like to make him happy."

"Red reminds him of that killer dress I helped you find to seduce him back into your darkness, doesn't it?" Gia smiled sweetly, even as her chest ached. It might be nice if Ian tried to seduce her back into his darkness, whether or not they had a future together. At least it would show he hadn't given up completely. "You're welcome."

Dar lifted her chin, which didn't hide her deepening blush. "My love for black remains unchanged."

"Good to know some things in the world remain sane." Gia leaned back in her seat as Sally emptied the bath and began gently scrubbing her feet. "I hope I didn't ruin any violinist-teacher love games. I have to know that at least one of us is getting the goods."

"You've blocked Ian?" Adara grinned evilly. "That's frickin' *hilarious*."

Initially, she'd intended to tell Adara everything—that she wasn't truly engaged to Ian, that their fake engagement had led to something more only to fizzle. But after Roman's reveal, the ground beneath her feet felt even shakier. She wasn't sure about anything anymore.

"I'm trying out the Garret celibacy route, since it worked so well for the two of you. I'm worth the wait, right?" Her voice wobbled and she made a face. "And since true love is forever, I'll have time to make up for it."

Jaw tight, Dar studied her. "You know I suck at getting all emotional, but I'm always here for you. And you should never doubt that you're worth the wait. Talk to me, G."

Gia slumped in the seat. "Was Joey a nice person?" Why she'd brought up Joey she couldn't say, but once the words were out, she couldn't stop. "Or maybe I've completely martyrized his memory, because I can't remember him being anything but a fierce, beautiful saint who loved us."

Adara's gray eyes went soft and her jaw relaxed. "Joey was my brother and I loved him unconditionally, but he wasn't always a nice guy. He was selfish and angsty and sometimes forgot everything and everyone else beyond his music. He could be sweet when he wanted something, and since one of those somethings happened to be you, he was his best person while he was with you."

Tears burned Gia's eyes and she smiled through the emotions bottling her throat. She didn't think she could speak. She missed Joey so much sometimes that it killed her, and yet with Ian, the loneliness had faded. With Ian, she'd felt...important. Protected. Supported, like she could do anything, *be* anything, and Ian would be behind her every step.

Until the door-slam today.

"The two of you together were like some sort of magic," Adara continued, "bringing out the best in each other." She tucked her hair behind her ear and huffed. "You shouldn't settle for anything less than what you had with Joey, someone who naturally brings out the best and worst and the fire in you. If that person turns out to be Ian, I'll learn to live with it." She grimaced as if she'd just swallowed a bug. "But I'll keep my knife sharp for when he screws up."

Gia reached between their chairs and clasped Adara's hand until she could talk normally. She needed the right words to lay out the thought that had come on the heels of Adara's practical insight. "Do you love me, Dar?"

Suspicion immediately filled her best friend's eyes. "That's a rhetorical question. Whatever you're about to hit me with, just do it. I'll then decide who I need to kill." She turned toward Sally. "I've changed my mind on the pedicure. Do you have a red polish for me? A color close to blood?"

Sally grinned and rushed to the wall filled with racks of bottles, as if she knew something hardcore was going down and only the right polish would keep the peace. She was right. Adara was already thinking about killing someone and Gia hadn't yet mentioned Ian's name.

Gia used her best dazzling smile, even knowing it was useless against Adara. "The last month, I've been working on a hush-hush, high profile case assigned by

Mr. Hamilton." She washed the sawdust in her throat down with a drink of her spritzer and squared her shoulders. "With Ian."

Adara jerked her hand free, and her gray eyes were as icy as Ian's could be. "Your point?"

"You brought up the subject of fire." Gia traced the rim of her glass with one finger and forced herself to say the words out loud, not only for herself but for Ian's sake. "That night at the holiday party" — she ignored Adara's growl — "had everything to do with fire and nothing to do with too many drinks or a slick lawyer preying on a grief-stricken victim." She lifted her gaze to Adara's. "I needed to feel *something*. After Joey's death, I was so tired of feeling numb and lost and hopeless of finding someone who'd make me feel the way I felt with him again."

Dar's eyes warmed, and Gia continued before that changed.

"Joey was the best thing that had ever happened to me. Ever. I didn't understand how I could resume the life I had when the life I wanted had been ripped away. Watching you fall in love with Garret, at first, reminded me of everything I'd lost, not that I'm anything but happy for you."

Adara watched her, letting her talk.

"But at your wedding reception, I went off for some alone time to put myself back together, and I had an epiphany. I was going about everything all wrong. I wasn't looking for love when Joey found me, and I knew hunting for it would only make me crazy. My happiness doesn't hinge on any other person. You and Joey taught me that, and it took me a long time to believe it, but I believe it now. I like who I became after being sifted through Joey, and even though Joey isn't here for the benefits of who I am now, I think he'd be happy that he left such an impact on me."

"I know he is." A telling sheen brightened Adara's eyes. She blinked and it vanished. Crying in public was never her thing. "He'd be so proud of you."

Gia smiled. Now for the bomb. "One of the things Joey taught me was to never judge people on surface level only. Of course, anyone who wants to judge me by my heels is more than welcome to."

Adara rolled her eyes. They'd never shared the same sense of style or love for shopping and all things glittery. Adara wearing color was a miracle in itself. Garret was a good influence on her.

Sally returned with a selection of colors for Adara and vanished again, giving her a few minutes to decide. Gia paused before continuing, giving the polish time to dazzle her friend. She never underestimated the power of sparkles and color.

"As I said, I've been working with Ian this month."

A bottle in each hand, Adara arched an eyebrow in her 'please tell me you haven't done something stupid' expression.

"I tried not to fall for him, told myself he wasn't an option, that we didn't even want the same things, but he showed me sides of him I never knew existed. No matter how I resisted, my heart chose him."

Adara maintained her expression, not surrendering any ground.

"When you shut Garret out, pushed him away, initially, you thought you were doing the best thing for the both of you, right?"

Slowly, Adara set the fingernail polish bottles on the side table, never breaking her stare. "What's your point, G?"

"My engagement with Ian is off."

Relief flooded Adara's face and she slouched in the chair. "Thank God."

"But Ian hates to lose," Gia said slowly, Roman's previous words catching fire in her brain. "He doesn't give up." Especially if it cost him the partnership he'd spent years working for—among other, more important things like Joann's welfare. She released a shaky breath. Ian had never confirmed his feelings with any confession of love, didn't trust her enough with the truth, and even though there was no hope for a future with him, she couldn't believe he'd abandon Joann. She had to give him that much, and since Joann's case was as much hers as it was his...

"Don't say it," Adara warned. "Don't say his name again unless it's combined with jerk-face and ex."

Gia wriggled her toes as her heart sealed up the cracks for a temporary fix. "My business with Ian isn't done quite yet."

Chapter Twenty-Four

Ian reclined in the wooden patio lounger and propped his shoes on the porch rail. Nothing but country met his gaze, an endless line of trees and grass. The faintest breeze caressed his neck. Even the air at his mother's cabin was different—fresh and fragrant, not an ounce of pollution or perfume or the kaleidoscope of scents that manifested even in a small town like Graywood. It smelled of home.

And the emptiness made him want to curl in on himself like a wounded animal.

Gia's sweet scent still clung to his shirt and her taste lingered on his lips, the phantom touch of her mouth on his a tormenting memory. He'd never forget how, for a few perfect, wonderful, terrible days, she'd made him believe the impossible, that he could forge through his past without fear of repercussions.

He absently rubbed his bottom lip. He'd never been in love before, and his only prior experience with affection in any capacity was for his mother, Garret, Roman—maybe even some for Mr. Hamilton. But that was a different sort of love—a boy's devotion to his mother, a man's respect for his friends, admiration for a mentor. What he felt for Gia was more like a gnawing hunger that he couldn't satisfy with any substitute, so intense and powerful that it made his senses reel and his rationality crack. He wasn't sure how he'd fought it off for so long.

Or how he'd live without her.

Gia. She made him so weary of the cold, polished façade he maintained. He'd thought he'd resigned himself to everything he couldn't have because of his violent past, but she'd smiled her way through his barriers and dazzled him beyond repair by accepting his darkness as if it were nothing more than a feisty kitten in need of being cuddled. And that darkness adored her for it.

The tangled knot of emotions he'd managed to keep chained in the corner of his soul while at the office tightened, painful, and he clenched his jaw, choking back the pitiful noise coming from his throat. He jerked his tie loose. A long breath hissed through his teeth. None of it mattered. Cutting Gia loose before she got sucked into any fallout was the best gift he could give her. She deserved a life without his stain and all the trash that went with it. He'd resort to admiring her from afar again and content himself with the memories and one-night stands with women who would never affect him.

His heart throbbed raggedly at the empty picture he'd painted for himself. He blinked hard. *Control yourself, idiot. Gia's over. Deal with it.*

The soft rumble of a motor preceded gravel crunching beneath tires. Ian clasped his hands behind his neck and watched the sun making its way behind the trees.

He didn't look up as a car door slammed and a solitary set of footsteps creaked on the porch stairs.

Garret sat in the unoccupied chair beside his and handed him a cold bottle of beer.

Ian met his gaze. "Dude, you always know just what to say."

Flashing his sunshine smile, the one that made it impossible to dislike him, Garret clinked their bottles and joined him in companionable silence until the sun melted into shadows.

"Speak, my son, and I will hear you." The fact Garret said those words with a straight face only demonstrated that once a geek, always a geek.

"Nothing to talk about." Ian felt his friend's gaze on him, but he didn't break.

"Let me guess, then." Garret twisted in his seat, facing him, probably so he could decipher any hint of emotion that might mistakenly slip into his expression. "You've met a woman you can't live without, and now you're without her."

"Bz-z-z. Wrong." Ian didn't dare look at him. "Try door number two."

"And it scares the hell out of you," Garret said in a soft, knowing voice. "Don't do me the discourtesy of denying it. Besides, Gia tells Adara everything." At Ian's glance his way, he nodded solemnly. "Everything."

Ian scowled. "What happened to not kissing and telling?"

"Those rules don't apply to women."

"But your ice princess told you."

Garret's smile was sly and a little goofy, enough to make Ian's heart squeeze with envy. "My princess loves me. That's the difference."

Ian snorted and waved his fingers in dismissal. "You're just as bad as the women."

"Lies. I haven't told anyone." Garret nudged Ian's knee with his boot. "Talk to me, Goose."

Taking a long swig of his beer and letting the sour taste darken his already sour mood, Ian closed his eyes. "I'm not a touchy-feely guy like you." He ignored the amused noise from Garret. "I can't be that guy. It's not who I am. I can't even pretend to be that guy, not even for her — especially not for her."

Garret, surprisingly, said nothing.

With his eyes closed and the silence surrounding them, it was easier to speak his fears. He started with the oldest, deepest scar. "I'm afraid I'll become like him." The confession was soft, matter-of-fact and agonizingly true. "I'm afraid that somewhere down the road, when I'm not expecting it, the part of him that resides in my blood and in my head will surface. That I'll lose control, become him and hurt her."

Garret released a soft sigh into the twilight. "You're not your father. The blood that pumps in your veins, that steely trap inside your head, is all Ian O'Connor. How can you not see that?"

Ian opened his eyes and met his friend's dark gaze. "Because every time I look in the mirror, I see him. I see the blood on my face, my shirt, my hands. I went into a fury so deep that I can't even recall the details. How am I supposed to let someone else, someone I care about, close enough to risk that?"

"Because the other half of you, the more dominant one, is colored by your mother." Garret folded his arms over his black T-shirt, hiding the cartoon picture of an armored violin attacking a guitar with its bow. "When I look at you, I see her."

Ian turned his attention to the trees. It was the best way to hide the sudden burn in his eyes. If Garret noticed, he'd never hear the end of it.

"Your love for her is what drove you that night, not your hate." Garret drummed his fingers on the beer bottle, his silver rings clinking on glass. "That's the biggest difference between you and your father. I've never seen you reflect him."

"What about when I pulled Billy off your back in grade school and beat him to a bloody pulp?" Tears safely subdued, Ian resumed a bland expression.

"That was just the beginning of our beautiful bromance." Garret held out his fist and waited for Ian to bump it with his own.

He did, after a marked hesitation to demonstrate his reluctance. "I want Gia to be safe, and I…" He swallowed hard. "I'm afraid, if she's too close, I'll infect her."

"Dude, you're not a cancer." Garret gave him a steady look.

Ian took another drink to wash down the lump in his throat. "I don't want to hurt her."

Garret leaned forward and tapped Ian's knee with his fist. "So don't."

One of the ties that kept them bound as friends was Garret's uncanny way of seeing things as they were and not judging. He always made everything sound so simple, even when Ian had disappeared for three years, admitted to the psychiatric hospital. When he'd returned home, Garret had embraced him with open arms — no questions, only welcoming acceptance — and their friendship had continued where they'd left it, as if Ian had never been away at all.

A sudden need to tell Garret the truth hit him hard, and before he thought about it for too long, he went with it. "Did you never wonder where I was? After what happened with my bastard of a father?"

Garret shrugged, absently wiping the bottle condensation on his jeans. "I figured you'd tell me if you wanted to." His dark eyes were calm, filled with nothing but affection. "Some secrets need time to heal before coming out into the light."

"A psychiatric unit for boys." His throat was so tight, the words were nearly indecipherable. "Three years." He couldn't even look at his oldest friend, afraid of what he might see.

A silence followed, broken only by crickets chirping near the creek and a faint stirring of leaves. At last, Garret chuckled. It was the last thing he ever expected from the most compassionate person he knew.

"Dude. Did you not hear me right? I was in a psychiatric unit for *three years*."

"I heard you. So many things are clicking into place." Garret's teeth flashed in a teasing smile. "Your insane taste in food. Your crazy sense of style. Your demented need to win. Click, click and click. Everything is so clear now."

"You're a prick, Ambrose." But at Garret's laugh, a lightness eased the shadows he'd carried for so long, simply from sharing a secret he'd believed no one in their right mind would embrace so easily. "And a bit unhinged yourself."

"A violinist rocker slipping off his rocker." He wriggled his eyebrows. "I own it."

"Yeah, not everyone else would be so understanding." Ian tapped the beer bottle in an uneven beat, and Garret joined in with a perfect counter-rhythm of his own. "Hamilton never would have hired me if he'd known."

"Why not?" Garret's beat stopped. His forehead creased, as if he truly didn't get it.

Ian exhaled noisily. "The most prestigious law firm in the area won't risk its reputation on a kid from the loony bin, no matter how long ago it was. With my juvenile record, it was a miracle he gave me a chance at all. If my mother hadn't gone behind my back and met with Hamilton to spill her sob story and beg him on my behalf, I'd be working in fast food right now." He shuddered. "All that grease and pink goo... I'd be a completely different person."

And now that Mr. Clancy knew—a chill rolled through him—that could become his reality. *Flawed. Failed. Forever.*

"Fast food workers are the best. Smile at them, treat them with respect and they give you extra fries." Garret leaned forward, resting his elbows on his thighs. "The only parts of your past that define your future are the ones you empower. Do you know why you're a great lawyer?"

"Easy. My sharp suit and power tie."

"Those are merely the trappings. Beneath that, you care about the cause, even when it's easier not to. You fight as hard as you can when smaller men would settle for less. You put your heart and soul into every case, whatever the payout. It doesn't matter where you've come from, only where you're going, and you don't need someone else's name or blood or image to take you there."

"You're just full of wisdom tonight." Ian took a swig of beer, needing time to collect himself. His throat was too tight, his heart too bruised. "I screwed up and Gia walked out on me — as she should have."

Garret pursed his lips. "Yeah. Heard about that too. So what are you going to do about it?"

Even as the word *nothing* formed on his tongue, the question curled around him, echoing in his head. He had another horrifying, revealing option. He could expose his secret to Gia, give her the power to destroy him first. But if he did that, he'd have to tell her about Clancy's message. She'd expect him to do the right thing and sacrifice his dream and reputation to save Joann, and none of it guaranteed Gia would love him in the aftermath.

And the other option was to cement an existence absent of the one woman he couldn't live without, an existence with the constant fear of exposure, an existence with the shame of knowing he could have helped a desperate woman who'd come to him for help and he'd chosen not to, an existence where he never had a chance to tell Gia that he'd been in love with her since the day she'd walked into Hamilton & Associates and bewildered him with her smile and stilettos.

The knots in his stomach tightened. *My partner.* That was Gia — not just a woman he worked with and burned endlessly for, or a girl who made him question the delusion of happily ever after. She'd somehow managed to temper his darkness. She was more than a person he respected and admired, more than a friend or potential lover. With Gia, he wanted to play, fight, laugh, and conquer the world. Together. Gia was the one who made him believe that maybe, possibly, he could reveal his deepest flaws and still be wanted. Worthy. *Enough.*

"It's terrifying to need someone else, isn't it?" Garret said, as if reading his mind. "But to never love, to miss out on all those inspiring and heart-pounding moments that break you apart and sew you back up again? *That's* where the tragedy lies. Don't compromise the best part of life for the sake of fear. The fear will always be there, no matter what you do."

"I know that." His hand trembled and he fisted the beer bottle to stop the shaking. He'd never been a coward. He'd always had a soft spot for the underdog, the weak and helpless. Not folding to tyranny, even at the cost of his own safety and freedom, was what had brought him to this very choice.

If he had to trade in his dream of partnership for a chance at keeping Gia in his life…

Instead of the horror he expected, a surprising peace rolled through him. Ian drained his beer, handed the empty bottle to Garret and sprang to his feet. "I have a curse to break, a dragon to kill and a princess to win back."

"*Chara*, I knew I should've brought my violin." Garret's dark eyes sparkled as he stood too. "I could have sent you off with a battle song."

"Next time." He leaped off the deck and ran for his Porsche. "Thanks for the beer." On a whim, he raced back and gave Garret a manly hug with a hard pat on the back. "And for being friends with a closet lunatic."

Garret laughed as Ian released him and took off again. "I should bring you beer more often." He added, louder, "Dude, don't forget to grovel."

Ian flashed his wolf smile over his shoulder. "Already planned on it."

* * * *

Her car parked, Gia got out and walked the familiar pathway to Clancy Stables. It felt strange to cross the cobblestones in stilettos, not boots. Since riding wasn't on the agenda tonight, she'd left her jeans behind too. Her summer dress fluttered around her bare legs, kissed by the warm July breeze.

The pond glinted with silver shards in the light of the twin lampposts, its depths murky and mysterious beneath the trees. The gentle chatter of running water massaged at the edges of her tension, calling her to relax. After her talk with Adara, she still felt off-balance, not ready yet to confront Ian and demand the hard truth. If he'd abandon a woman in need without a smidge of conscience, the caulking on her heart wouldn't bear the pressure. If that was his choice, it was a hurdle she wasn't sure she could leap, whether he refused to trust her or not.

She blew out a breath. In her short time at Clancy Stables, she'd found that simply brushing Belle calmed her, made everything in the world seem at peace. Joann hadn't specifically banned her from the stables, and whoever tended the horses at this hour — hopefully, not Frankie — might let her visit. If she could finagle her way into even petting Belle, maybe the off-kilter sense that her next step would send her tumbling off a cliff would leave.

Pausing at the gleaming oak door leading into the stables, Gia ran her fingers along the Clancy Stables emblem. She traced the iron horse, following the line of its striking foreleg, aimed at some enemy only it could see. Had Joann chosen that emblem on purpose, a silent plea for someone to hear her, to look beyond the finery and see the horror happening underneath the surface? Her stomach churned. Even if Ian turned his back and

Joann gave up, somehow, some way, she'd figure out how to help Joann escape her abusive marriage.

As she pushed open the door, soft classical music drifted out, serenading the night. The familiar stir of hooves in straw and a muffled snort joined the melody as the sweet, unique scent of equines filled the air. Gia drew a long breath, her shoulders relaxing. No matter what the future held, a horse was nonnegotiable.

Her heels clicked on the black tile lining the walkway between stalls, and as she passed the office doorway, she glanced inside. It was empty — no one to ask permission, no one to tell her not to enter Belle's stall for a quick visit. The cameras mounted at every stall would record her and if anyone manned the surveillance computer, they'd know she was there. The swing-shift employee would surely show up soon, and if that employee happened to be Frankie, Gia's superpowers of batting eyelashes and smiling sweetly would be rendered ineffective. She had to make the most of her time.

Gia removed her stiletto sandals and padded silently down the aisle. She resisted petting each nose that poked out as she passed, and every welcoming whinny tempted her to stop and rub between perked ears or stroke velvet-soft muzzles. She got why Joann had opened a stable, creating a tiny haven for herself in an otherwise unsteady and unhealthy world. Horses had a magic all their own, soothing cares away.

"Hey, sweetheart," Gia whispered as Belle stretched her nose from the split door of her stall and whickered a greeting. She grabbed the brush hanging beside the door, careful not to make any noise, and slipped into the stall. When Belle nuzzled her neck, she couldn't stop a soft laugh.

"I missed you too. Has it only been a day?" She rubbed Belle's soft forehead, keeping her voice quiet. "And no worries about the lightning storm. It wasn't your fault, and without your help, I doubt Ian would have ever admitted that he's somewhat human." She looped her arms around Belle's neck and leaned against her solid frame with a contented sigh. "I should have brought you a treat. Some friend I am."

Belle lipped at her dress, apparently forgiving the slight.

From the stall next door, Buttercup thumped the wall, and Gia smiled. He'd have to wait his turn. Another thump followed, hard enough to shake the entire structure, and Belle tossed her head, breaking her loose hold.

Gia sighed. If Buttercup caused a commotion, he'd draw attention and her visit could be at an end. Giving him some attention might assuage the horse's demand. "Be back soon," she promised Belle with a parting scratch beneath her chin.

Carrying her shoes by the straps, she tiptoed to the stall next door. Buttercup wasn't straining out of the open door as she'd expected, vying for attention. His tail was aimed at the door, and his head was lowered to the straw-covered floor. Gia leaned on the door. An upside-down saddle sprawled on the straw, and beside it a slender form wearing tall boots and English riding pants. A glimpse of silver hair...

Joann.

Forgoing any stealth, Gia flung open the stall door and crouched beside the horse nuzzling Joann's hair, as if telling her to wake up. Sweat beaded on Joann's forehead and her skin was waxy, too pale.

"Joann!" Gia shook the woman's frail shoulder with her free hand.

Moaning, Joann's eyes flickered and opened, unfocused. Her breath wheezed, an awful, rattling sound.

"I'll call nine-one-one." Her hand trembling, Gia pulled her phone from her dress pocket. The screen was black, blank. She hit a button, then another. Nothing. "No. No, no, no." Her phone had officially kicked it.

Joann blinked rapidly. "Gia —"

Gia forced herself not to react to the weak, broken crack of Joann's voice. She gently squeezed Joann's arm. "I'll get help. I'll be right back, I promise."

Joann's eyes widened and she flailed weakly in the straw, as if trying to get up.

Before Gia straightened, wiry arms banded around her, holding a foul-smelling rag over her mouth and nose. On the outskirts of her consciousness, she was vaguely aware of Buttercup jerking away, of Joann fumbling in the straw and falling again. She clawed at the arms around her, at the face behind her, raking skin. Her shoes were another weapon, and she blindly struck behind her, over and over.

The responsive grunts of pain barely penetrated her panic. Darkness edged her vision and drifted over her senses, weakening her limbs, slowly stealing her strength. The grip covering her nose and mouth held fast. Her last thought as the flame was finally snuffed out was one of regret. She wouldn't get to see Ian one last time.

Chapter Twenty-Five

Gia jerked into bleary awareness, thanks to being dumped onto a death-cold, bone-hard, gritty floor. Dust kicked up, itching her nose, and she coughed, rolling to her side. A blinding light kicked on directly in her face. She shielded her eyes, smacking herself in the head with what felt to be shoes, their straps still tangled in her fingers.

The heavy slam of a door killed the light. A metallic clank made the finale, leaving her in silence and shadows.

Her skull throbbed, as if overstuffed with cotton. She swallowed, her throat dry, her tongue swollen and tasting of chemicals. Easing to a sitting position with the darkness spinning around her, Gia clutched her head in her hands. Everything flooded back — her impromptu trek to the stables, finding Joann collapsed in the stall, the arms locked around her and the awful-smelling, suffocating cloth.

Oh—her breath snagged—*crap.* She'd been shanghaied and confined somewhere out of the way. She groped along the floor for any clues. Grit rolled beneath her fingers and palms. Dirt, maybe, but the surface beneath was hard, smooth and cool. From the layer of grime, she'd guess no one came here very often. Her elbow bumped something solid, and she fumbled along the edges of a smooth, oblong shape easily as long as she was tall. It rose a few feet off the ground.

Helplessness constricted her ribcage as she inched forward, feeling by touch alone. Her hand met a wall. A metal handle, flush with the wall. The shape of a drawer and another beside it, above it, below it. A chill scampered down her scalp to her back.

She'd been locked in a crypt, and she'd bet her enviable shoe collection that it belonged to the Clancy family.

Frantic, she felt along the wall, ignoring the warning caress of spider webs as best she could until she came to the door. She jerked on the handle. It was locked, of course. And it would be stupid to make any noise yet, not when whoever had stuffed her in the crypt could still be nearby. Other than kidnappers, only Cerberus would be in the cemetery at night. When the hellhound discovered she was there, he'd bark loud enough to raise the dead, including his master. But she'd take her chances with the shady groundskeeper and his watchdog.

With her back to the door, she sank to sit and held back a sob. Considering her abductor had successfully tagged and bagged her, she couldn't imagine Joann's fate had been any better. The image of Joann on the stall floor, pale and fumbling, brought another chill. That weakness hadn't been the cause of any natural illness and, combined with the attack at the stables, she could guess what it meant. Mr. Clancy had finally decided to get rid of his wife.

Gia swiped a shaking hand over her eyes. Even though she'd interrupted Clancy's dirty deed, she'd ultimately failed right along with Ian. And as horrified as she was about Joann, if she didn't do something, she'd share Joann's fate. She had no intention of fading quietly into the night.

A low groan came from somewhere in the crypt, and all the hair on her arms and neck stirred. Gia couldn't breathe, her heart a living drum in her ears. She wasn't like Dar with her love for horror movies and Gothic darkness, because she believed in *things* – like spirits, the other side of the veil, eternity with good and evil choices. Being trapped in a mausoleum with the vengeful spirit of Logan Clancy wasn't her idea of fun, and coming face-to-face with a phantom wasn't the last drop in her bucket list, either.

She curled in on herself, shaking, and squeezed her eyes shut. Even though it was dark, there was no way was she going to see something that would remain forever burned in her memory.

"Hello?" A woman's voice, frail but familiar, threaded through the darkness. "Is somebody there?"

Her eyes popped open. "Joann?"

A pause. "Gia?"

Gia fumbled on her hands and knees toward Joann's voice. "Keep talking so I can find you."

"Where are we?" Joann shifted in the darkness, her clothes scraping softly on the cement as Gia inched closer. "I don't feel right. I think I'm going to be sick."

"Don't puke." Gia fumbled and met material, a bony knee, an icy hand. She grasped Joann's fingers. "We'd be stuck with the smell and I may be able to take a lot, but not that." Wrapping her arms around Joann's shivering body, she held the older woman close. "I think we're in the Clancy family crypt."

"Matt." Joann spat the name. "Of all the people I suspected to be on Landon's payroll, he wasn't one. When he put that cloth on your face…" She squeezed Gia's fingers. "You shouldn't have come back."

"Never trust a man whose belt buckle bling outshines your own." Gia sighed. As much as she hated that Joann was stuck along with her, both the company and the fact Joann hadn't been killed were a relief. She forced her voice to be strong and steady. "Don't worry. Nothing gets by the cemetery groundkeeper's watchdog. He'll sense we're here and bring his master."

"The groundskeeper is loyal to Landon." Joann gasped, trembling. "Something's wrong with me."

Gia wasn't sure whether to hold Joann tighter or let her go. No one knew where to find them. No help was on the way. They were at the mercy of a man who abused his wife, bought people willing to look the other way and wasn't afraid to throw innocent women into the family crypt. "Did he beat you again? Where does it hurt?"

"No beating." She wilted against Gia, her voice reedy.

"What did he do to you?"

"Nothing." Her breath wheezed across Gia's shoulder. "I'd had one of my migraines all day, which isn't out of the ordinary. I was following my usual routine, rubbing down Buttercup after my evening ride, and my palms and feet went numb. I got so dizzy that I grabbed onto his mane for balance. That's all I remember until you woke me up and Matt took you. I must have blacked out again, because I woke up here with a splitting headache and what feels like a knife carving out my stomach."

"*Matt*," Gia growled. "What a worm."

A strained laugh came from Joann. "And all this time I thought Sean was the main inside enemy to watch."

"Oh, Joann." Gia tsked, trying for a lightness she didn't feel. "Sean was the best distraction ever. He's totally into you."

"Sean is not into anything with me." Joann shivered and straightened. "Landon hired him to keep me under his thumb, that's all."

"Maybe that's how it started out. But now? No way." Gia made careful, comforting circles on Joann's thin back, horrified at the distinct knobs of her spine. She was hardly more than skin and bones. "You might have missed all those furtive looks, but I didn't. He's a tortured man, longing for the woman he can't have." She went still. Would Sean suspect something when Joann didn't show up? Or would Clancy feed him a line that he'd believe until it was too late?

"Don't put your romance with Ian on the nonexistent relationship between me and Sean." Joann took a breath and pushed away from Gia's support. "That boy is so in love with you he can't see straight."

"I wish." Gia scooted back against the wall and laid her head against the cool marble, her ribcage squeezing. "I'm afraid the only goal Ian can truly see is the title of partner with Hamilton & Associates. I want mutual trust, undying love, forever. Happily ever after isn't possible with someone who's only about being in the moment." She rubbed the wetness from her eyes. "Maybe I'm better off keeping my fantasies to myself."

"Never regret standing up for your dreams with everything you are, even if it means being vulnerable or losing someone." Joann's cold hand wrapped around hers. "Pretending will only bring pain in the end. If I had stood up to Landon in the beginning, left him after that first strike, before he gained any power or prestige, we wouldn't be here. By pretending everything was fine, I failed the community, you and my daughter Brianne." Her voice broke. "It's better to be isolated with dreams than to be trapped with someone who makes you feel helpless and alone."

The quiet stretched between them and Gia exhaled softly. "Do you think some people are fated to go solo, Joann?"

Joann paused and said slowly, "I think that some people choose to stay single for reasons only they fully understand. It's okay to be lonely. But if you want someone to share your life, don't give up hope that you'll find the one meant for you when the time is right." She leaned her head against Gia's, so much like Kat used to do when they were girls sharing secrets that new tears welled up. "I need to believe that there's hope for others to have the life I missed out on because of my mistakes."

"It's so much easier to talk to you without any Gaelic code."

A pained huff came from Joann. "I was never entirely sure you understood me. Your Gaelic is atrocious."

"Hey, I practiced." Gia sniffed. "And don't sell yourself short, lady. You're not exactly out to pasture. There's still time for your happy ending. It's not over."

"Isn't it?" Joann's laugh was more of a sob. "Landon confessed to me that he poisoned his own brother — whether to frighten me or because he needed to tell someone else, I'm not sure. Ever since he told me, I've been very careful, but with my headaches and declining health, I suspect he might be slowly poisoning me too. He said he did it because Logan wouldn't do what he wanted. That *monster*—" her voice cracked. "That monster is all about control, and he'll do whatever he wants to get it." A long, wheezing breath followed, a sign that Joann was collecting her composure. "I sent you and Ian here in the hopes that you'd find something, anything. If he killed his twin with no remorse, he won't blink about doing the same to you or me."

She wasn't about to express the fear tumbling through her veins, that no one would find them until it was too late, that Landon would get away with it, that she'd never see Ian's sly smirk again, never touch the scar just beneath his mouth, never hear him call her 'love' or 'princess' or any of the other meaningless terms of affection that he enjoyed tossing her way in the hopes of getting a reaction.

Would he even miss her for longer than an occasional, fleeting moment, when bored at the office or when he caught sight of some killer heels that reminded him of her?

Gia lifted her chin. "It's not over. It *can't* be over. The bad guy doesn't win. Everyone knows that."

"Tell that to Logan." Joann's voice caught. "To Brianne." She leaned away and retched violently.

Holding Joann's hair, Gia rubbed her back until she was through being sick. *Brianne.* A child, killed in the womb by her father. She deserved justice and Gia preferred to be there—alive and kicking—when justice was served.

"It's always number three that takes them out, Joann. Hang on. Don't give up. Clancy is *so* going down." As Joann slumped against the wall, her breathing ragged, Gia stood and felt her way to the door. But first, she had to figure out how to escape a locked family crypt.

* * * *

Ian barged into the senior center and searched for a familiar face, one of the geriatric dancers who adored Gia. The maze of old-timers hobbling on canes, inching along the hallway with walkers or gathered to gab made it hard to navigate. Managing not to knock anyone over along the way, he paused in the doorway of the cafeteria, assaulted by a nasal blast of onions and dust.

Gia wasn't answering her phone, not that he expected her to after dumping him so elegantly. He'd already been to her house and found it dark and empty of all Glitter Girls and Kats. He doubted she was with Katerina, since both of their cars were gone. Karen hadn't heard from her since that afternoon. Adara had grudgingly told Garret that she hadn't talked to Gia after meeting up with her at a salon. The senior center was his next hunting ground.

In the cafeteria corner, the geezer who'd ogled Gia at the dance and had tried to steal his gelatin sat alone. *Finally, someone I recognize.* As he headed for the man, each step came slower than the next. The old man slouched in his chair, his leer absent, looking at something in the distance with such naked longing that a stab of pity echoed in Ian's chest.

Ian tracked his gaze. At the opposite end of the cafeteria, Emma and Merle gathered with what had to be their grandchildren, talking and laughing.

That stab in Ian's chest became an open, gaping wound, stealing his breath. *He* could become that leering man one day, alone with only his thoughts to keep him company, staring through a window at the life he'd rejected in exchange for his secrets. No matter how many single nights he shared with beautiful women, they left only links in a broken chain, memories that blurred together, worthless. No matter how many cases he won, what title his name bore or how perfect his appearance to the outside world, none of it would save him from one day sitting alone and yearning to be a part of someone else, important to someone else. Important to Gia.

Sucking in a breath, his heart beating too fast, he changed course toward Emma and Merle.

Emma looked up at his approach and her smile brightened. She sported yet another sequined sweatshirt, complete with flowers and birds. "Ian, we're celebrating with our grandkids. Come join us."

Several innocent faces turned his way, bright eyes taking him in, mouths and cheeks smeared with chocolate and whipped cream. Devils disguised as tiny humans.

"I appreciate the invitation, but I can't." He clasped his shaking hands behind his back. "I'd hoped to find Gia here."

"Sorry, dear. Miss Gia hasn't been here since the fundraiser." Emma's smile faded as she studied him. "Is everything okay?"

Ian forced himself to smile. "If she happens to show up, would you ask her to call me? It's nothing to be worried about. Just work."

"Are you sure you don't want to stay for cake?" In typical grandma fashion, Emma had already sliced a piece, put it on a plate and shoved it his way. "We have plenty and you're too skinny. Miss Gia needs a man she can hold on to." Merle nodded dutifully, patting his own slight paunch.

"Gia won't have to worry about that." He eased beyond reach, backtracking toward the door. "I have no intention of letting her go."

Ian ran his fingers through his hair as he escaped from the senior center, back into the night. Not at home, not with Karen or Adara, not hanging with her old-timers. *Where are you, Princess?*

Lightning forked across the sky in a streak of silver as he strode along the sidewalk.

Thunder grumbled in the distance, a memory of the last, disastrous ride on Feathers.

The stables. It seemed a long shot, considering the events of the morning. After Joann had essentially trespassed them, showing up again might wind up in being arrested. But spending time with Belle and the solace of the stables might be exactly what Gia would go for, especially with Katerina marching around, looking for things to rip apart.

Flipping his keys, he ran back to his car. Driving time wouldn't be much of a loss, considering his failed search so far. At the least, if she'd been to the stables and subsequently sent away, someone there would know.

An hour later, Ian sprinted across the stables parking lot, ducking his head against the downpour. Lightning burned the sky behind the barn, illuminating everything in electric white, and the almost immediate crash of thunder made the ground shake. He ducked beneath the barn porch and spun, wiping rain from his eyes.

Besides his car and another pickup, the parking lot was empty. He clenched his jaw. Another dead end. But since he'd made the trip, he might as well ask if Gia had been here at any point.

He pushed his drenched hair from his eyes, wiped the wetness from his face, and entered the stable. Despite the classical music flowing from the speakers, horses nickered nervously, probably from the storm at their doorstep. The crack of hooves on wood imitated small thunderclaps. At the far end of the corridor, a woman with red braids backed out with a wheelbarrow in tow.

What is Frankie doing here again? Whatever the reason, he highly doubted she'd tell him if Gia had been there. Before she caught sight of him, he ducked into the stable office and quietly shut the door. Blowing out a breath, Ian turned.

Matt stood beside the desk, a shovel in one hand and a paper in the other, his eyebrows high.

Ian grimaced. "I didn't want Frankie to see me," he confessed, stuffing his hands into his pockets, his jeans damp from the sprint to the barn. "She's not my biggest fan."

Matt slowly laid the paper on the desk. Red marks razed his cheek, as if a cat had just royally kicked his ass. "*Did* Frankie see you?"

Thunder boomed, and the lights blinked before settling back into steady.

"I don't think so."

"What are you doing here?" Matt kept a firm grip on the shovel and none of the friendliness he always showed Gia made it into his expression. "I heard Joann canceled your lessons."

Discussing the truth of how he couldn't find his fake fiancée wasn't a topic he wished to share with Matt, but he didn't want to endanger Joann more. "Gia and I had a lover's tiff, and she's icing me out." He shrugged. "I thought maybe she came here. You know how it is with women and horses. Have you seen her?"

A dark gleam entered Matt's eyes, and maybe it was the electricity in the air, but the tiny hairs on Ian's nape stirred.

Another blast of thunder shook the building and the lights flickered completely off. The music died mid-note. Horses whinnied in the stables beyond. As darkness settled and quiet descended, the scuff of boots approached Ian.

"Doesn't this place have a generator?" Ian planted his hand on the wall, a landmark in the gloom. The windowless office made the blackness complete.

"Should kick on in a minute if the power doesn't come back on." Matt's voice was closer. "I've got a flashlight." A blinding beam glared in Ian's face and he shielded his eyes just as something hard — presumably the flat side of Matt's shovel — slammed into his temple. Pain exploded in Ian's skull and white stars filled the darkness.

Thunder trembled overhead and vibrated in his blood, a familiar burn of violence. Ian dropped to the tile and rolled.

Chapter Twenty-Six

The lock to the crypt rattled in the dark, and Gia's pulse skyrocketed. She scrambled behind the Clancy patriarch's coffin and slipped out of her heels. A stiletto gripped tight in each hand, she forced her breathing to stay steady. Anyone who scoffed at heels didn't understand their true value—an impromptu weapon in plain sight, hard and sharp enough to take out an eye. Kat had taught her that.

A strange calm settled over her as the door squeaked open with a wash of fresh night air. The beam of a single flashlight panned across the crypt floor, searching. It landed on the corner where Joann still huddled, unconscious for the last half hour. A breath hissed from the intruder, followed by quick steps.

One. The rustle of clothing drew near. *Two.* Steps drilled beside the coffin she hid behind. *Three!*

Gia leaped up from her hiding spot and flung one shoe at the invader's head. "Die, scumsucker!"

The creep ducked, and the first stiletto sailed overhead, missing by an inch. The second shoe struck him square in the forehead with a thud. He staggered back with a curse.

Gia charged, fists flying.

"Princess!" He hissed and spun away as she nailed him in the chin. "It's me!"

Ian! It was too late to stop the other fist from landing a solid blow to his stomach. He doubled over, wheezing.

"Crap!" She leaned over him. "I didn't know it was you."

He lifted his head and met her gaze. "Sure about that?"

"I didn't say I was sorry, only that I didn't think it was you." She gave him a small smile, but as he straightened, rubbing his stomach, she flung herself at him. As he caught her, she clung to him, his spicy cologne the best thing she'd ever inhaled. "But I'm so glad it's you. You found us." She sobbed into his neck. "You found us."

His arms tightened around her and for a moment she let everything else go—that Ian would never truly belong to her, that Joann lay unconscious in the corner, that Clancy knew everything. For a moment, nothing mattered beyond the circle of his embrace.

"Princess," he muttered against her hair, "what's wrong with Joann?"

Reluctantly, she released her fantasy and let Ian go, turning toward Joann. She'd done all she could to help, which consisted of pillowing Joann's head with her sweater and holding her hair both times she'd puked, nowhere near enough. "I'm not sure, but we suspect she's been poisoned. She complained about her legs and stomach hurting. We need to get her to a doctor." Her pulse jumped to a presto beat and she grabbed Ian's arm. "We need to get out of here before Matt comes back."

"Matt." Ian growled the name. The flashlight gave his face a ghoulish cast as he picked up her shoes and handed them to her. Smudges striped his face and shirt with shadows. His dark hair was mussed, one side matted with blood. Red coated his ear.

She gasped. "Ian, you're bleeding. My stiletto got you good."

He brushed his fingers over his skull and winced. "As great as your throw was, love, that blood is a result of a shovel to the head, courtesy of Matt."

"*Matt.*" She fisted her hands. "I'm going to kick his cowboy ass out of his clodhopper boots."

"No need. After he so kindly introduced me to the flat side of his shovel when the power cut out and it was dark—which was most unsportsmanlike, by the way— I demonstrated the benefits of knowing how it feels to be hit. Unluckily enough for him, I'm practiced at it. He's not." He flashed a wicked grin. "When the generator kicked back on, I found an interesting key on the desk. Rusty iron, sitting beside a shiny new key that looked like it might fit a padlock strong enough to keep a cemetery gate secure. I followed a hunch." His gaze met hers, and he said softly, "I couldn't find you."

Her heart fluttered. "You're..." The tangled knot of emotions made it impossible to pick only one adjective. *I love you* emerged as the winner, but her tongue locked up.

"Amazing. Irresistibly sexy. So I've heard." Ian waved a dismissive hand, his eyes gleaming. "And since I prefer to remain among the living, let's take this discussion somewhere less surrounded by Clancys and beyond the reach of Cerberus."

She tucked her feet into her shoes. "Best plan you've come up with yet."

Gia tracked his light as it landed on Joann. Their client curled against the wall beneath Brianne's name, so small and frail in the shadows.

"She's been out for at least half an hour. She complained of her stomach cramping then she just…" Gia shook her head and bit her lip.

"She's definitely been poisoned." He shoved the flashlight at her. "Hold this while I pick her up."

A chill sliced through her at the sight of Joann's frail form cradled in Ian's arms. Her usually immaculate hair clung to her forehead. Sweat dotted her nose and upper lip and her skin was pale enough for any ghost. She shook, as if she were afraid, even in her oblivion.

"I'll explain as we go." His jaw set, Ian carried Joann out of the crypt.

Gia followed him down the steps. She breathed in the fresh air and almost sobbed in relief.

"I believe Landon used DMSO to slowly poison Joann with thallium," Ian said as they hurried through the unkempt grass, following the bobbing beam of the flashlight. "Getting even a hint of DMSO on her fingers when she's tending Buttercup would be enough, especially if there are traces of thallium on the saddle, bridle or brush."

"Matt." Gia strangled the flashlight.

"Or Sean."

Arguing right now about Sean's potential feelings for Joann wouldn't be productive. She skirted a cracked gravestone that reared into the flashlight's glow. "While Joann was conscious, she told me Landon had

302

once confessed that he'd killed his brother, poisoned him. She wasn't entirely sure he didn't say it just to scare her."

"The best way to scare someone is with the truth." Ian shouldered past a tree branch and glanced at her. "I've been keeping secrets, too, love. The toxicology report contained damning evidence. Logan Clancy died of a heart attack, but the underlying cause was thallium. I should have told you."

"Why didn't you?" She nearly choked on the words.

Pausing in the splintered shadows beneath the spidery branches of an oak tree, he caught her gaze, his eyes glinting silver. "I have another secret." He drew a long breath and exhaled slowly, watching her. "The situation with my father…afterward, as part of plea negotiations, I spent three years in a psychiatric unit."

Without intending to, she reached up and lightly squeezed his arm, something deep down inside recognizing he needed her touch to steady him. The clenched line of his jaw and tension in his stance made it clear he expected her to run screaming into the night—or clobber him with her shoe again.

"Besides Garret, you're the only person I've told," he continued, his voice steady and sharp as steel. "Not even Hamilton knows. If he did, I wouldn't be a part of his—or anyone else's—law firm." Ian adjusted Joann in his arms, still watching her.

"And you're telling me this now, why?" Gia wasn't sure what he'd expected her to say or do. Everyone had a past, and the fact that his had been tragic and violent didn't change who he was now.

He stared at her, his eyes hard. "That's all you have to say about it?"

Whatever had made him believe she'd judge him for what he went through made her heart hurt and she was absolutely sure he wouldn't want to hear that. She went for flippant instead. "At the moment, I have bigger concerns than determining how I might use your past to torment you later, O'Connor."

He was suddenly in her face, so close his breath skated over her mouth. "I'm telling you now, Princess, because Clancy knows about my stint in the psych ward. Exposing that part of my past to the public will affect *everything*. He banked on it, but his blackmail pushed me into a corner and forced me to make some hard decisions long overdue." He briefly closed his eyes, and the night seemed to close in, listening. "I don't want to be that old geezer at the senior center."

"You've completely lost me." Maybe Ian was more bonkers than she'd thought. He wasn't making any sense. "What old geezer?"

He shook his head and started walking again. "I shouldn't have let you leave today without a fight."

Gia followed, her tight throat making it hard to speak. "Fight for what, Ian? A fake engagement?"

"I meant every word I said before." His voice was soft but firm, unapologetic. "I have no practice at romantic relationships. You deserve a man a million times better than me, a man who isn't flawed by violence or a past that will impact you negatively. I'm terrified that I might snap one day and become my father, but I discovered something that terrifies me even more, something I'll trade my secrets and reputation merely for a single shot at possessing it." He glanced at her, his eyes deep and unyielding. "I don't want *us* to end. I'm renegotiating the terms. Permanently."

Her heart squeezed and she almost stumbled, the ache of longing stealing her breath. When it came to relationships, Ian was the most honest person she knew, but she couldn't bear it if he decided the only way to have her was to pretend or string her along. It had taken every ounce of willpower to give his ring back, to turn away and keep walking when he'd whispered her name like a broken prayer.

"I'm not willing to compromise what I want, all those things you *don't* want such as true love, rainbows and sparkles, happily ever after." Her voice trembled. "Don't play games with me, Ian."

"I just confessed my deepest fears, my darkest secret, and you question my honesty?" His voice was ice, so frozen it threatened to split. "Don't play games with *me*, Gia. If you don't want to try with me anymore, simply say so. But don't be so gullible as to believe that I'll let you strut away again or that I'll suffer in silence. I pick my battles very carefully and once I've set a goal, I don't give up. *Ever.*" His smile was all shark. "Do your worst, love. I'm not going anywhere."

Something inside her snapped, so fast and fierce that Ian had to hear it. She grabbed his sleeve and pulled him to a stop at the open cemetery gate. "Swear it." She didn't know when the tears had started and didn't care. "Swear you'll fight through whatever stands in the way of a happily ever after with me."

His stony expression softened. "On my mother's grave. For you, I'll add happily ever after to my goals." The velvet of his voice changed into clipped business. "But it's a reciprocal term of our contract." He continued walking, gravel crunching beneath his boots. At the end of the drive, his gleaming red Porsche shone through the trees, a beacon guiding them from the nightmare. "I promise there will be moments of regret. Gird your loins. Forever with me won't be easy."

A motor rumbled from the road and headlights swept over Ian's car. A pickup barreled into the tiny parking lot and skidded to a stop. Matt leaped out, aiming a hunting rifle at them. Dried blood flaked on his upper lip and his nose was swollen, the bridge black and blue. "Stay right there."

With Ian carrying Joann and any protection the gravestones might offer too far behind them, there was nothing to do but obey.

Gia's pulse beat in every extremity, blood a waterfall roar in her head. All this time, Matt had seemed mild-mannered, incapable of violence, despite being guilty of working for Clancy. With bruises staining his face, her claw marks on his cheekbone and his eyes gleaming like a feral animal's, she realized how wrong she'd been. He'd attacked her, hit Ian with a shovel and had probably been the one to put Joann in the crypt. He was as much of a monster as Clancy.

"Don't be rash, Matthew," Ian said, calm and lawyer smooth. "All you have to do is let us go. Clancy will suspect we were the ones to find Joann, to take her out. You don't even have to tell him we were at the stables."

Matt sneered and he looked nothing like the friendly stable hand from earlier days. "Clancy already knows everything. He'll be here any second."

"Alternative number two." Gia cleared her throat, her hands shaking. Matt had always responded better to her than Ian. "We were already gone by the time you got here. He'll never hear otherwise from us. Come on, Matt." She added a coax to her voice, and the softening in his features gave her hope. "Don't do this. Don't do Clancy's dirty work. We have families, friends, people who won't stop searching for us. Clancy's practiced at his act, but do you think you won't crack beneath the pressure? It will ruin your life…if Clancy doesn't ruin you first."

"I'm sorry that you're mixed up in this, Gia." True regret flashed in his eyes, but the rifle didn't lower. "You weren't supposed to be there tonight. Neither of you. This was all supposed to be easy, uncomplicated. No one was supposed to get hurt."

"Except for Joann." Ian's voice was all the sharper for its softness.

Matt's mouth tightened.

Another set of headlights stretched across the parking lot and a nondescript sedan pulled in beside Matt's truck. Politician polished in a suit and tie, Clancy stepped out, a pistol equipped with a silencer in his hand.

Gia's heart dropped into her stomach. No silky-smooth words or persuasive arguments could win their escape now.

"Set my wife down, if you please." Clancy's request would've been polite if he didn't have the threat of a gun in his hand.

Ian paused. Clancy looked like a lawyer, sounded like a lawyer, but any lawyer scruples he might've possessed had long ago melted away beneath politician motives, power and personal greed.

"Don't make me ask again, Mr. O'Connor." The warning didn't even change the timbre of Clancy's voice, yet it held enough authority to imply the threat was real. "You have something of mine." His gaze flicked to Gia. "Don't make me take something of yours."

At the mere implication of harming Gia, violence ignited in his chest and rose to a simmer. While Gia hadn't made him any promises, he hadn't dredged up his past and decided to give happily ever after a chance only to lose. But Clancy was the one with the gun, the one with the power.

Reluctantly, Ian settled Joann on the cool cemetery grass. Pale, her face shining with perspiration, she looked like a fairy wilting with the approaching dawn.

"You may go, Matt," Clancy said, not even looking at the other man. "I won't forget your assistance."

Matt lowered the rifle, his brow wrinkled. His gaze darted to Gia, then back to his employer. "I can stay."

"Not necessary. Go." Clancy made an impatient gesture. "Wait for me at the stables."

Matt hesitated. "What are you doing to do with them?"

Clancy's expression hardened. "What I do with them is none of your concern, Matthew. You've done your part and your young sister will receive the medical care she needs, as I promised. What happens from here on out is my responsibility, not yours."

Swiping his fingers through his hair, Matt's throat worked, and Ian's gut tightened. Matt might be backstabbing vermin, but he wasn't inhuman. He'd been manipulated, had betrayed them all in exchange for promises made by Clancy. Matt was smart enough to suspect what would happen once he left, and he probably didn't even know that Clancy was a man who regularly abused his wife, had murdered his own twin brother and had caused the death of his unborn child. Taking out an interfering lawyer and his partner was nothing to a monster in human form.

"What are you waiting for, Matthew?" A hint of steel entered Clancy's voice.

Without another word or look back at the people he was sentencing to a grim end, Matt jumped into his truck. He eased past Clancy's sedan and pulled out of the cemetery parking lot, leaving them behind with the corpses of the past.

For the first time, Clancy smiled.

A chill fought with the frustrated blaze boiling beneath Ian's skin. He hated it when someone else had the upper hand...and had always considered it a challenge to overcome. He pulled on his training like a powdered wig and robe. He'd settled hundreds of cases through negotiation. Setting aside the fact that Clancy possessed a gun and lives were on the line instead of money or property, this situation was no different.

"Let's not pretend this will end well for you, Mr. Clancy." An eerie calm settled over Ian. "Controlling the circumstances and evidence of one death might be possible, but three?" He shook his head, ignoring how Gia stiffened beside him. "Even you aren't that powerful."

"For the moment, I'll overlook that you're underestimating me," Clancy said, studying him. "Believe what you wish, but I prefer other alternatives to inspire cooperation from those around me. Death is simply a last resort, one avenue rarely used."

"Forgive me for being skeptical. May I point out that you could have simply let Joann go rather than poison her."

Clancy sighed, as if resigned. "I tried so many different methods to convince Joann to fulfill the vows she'd made on our wedding day to be an obedient and faithful wife. You understand, surely, why I couldn't allow her to break our marriage bond. It would undermine my public image, put into question everything I stand for. But enough with unpleasantries… Let's discuss the future."

Gia eased closer to him, close enough that he could feel her trembling.

"On the drive here, I prepared a settlement that I believe will be agreeable to everyone concerned. First, my proposal for Ian. What do you think of O'Connor and Associates? A respected firm of your own, solidly supported and personally approved by me. Your juvenile record would be erased from existence, not simply sealed. No one would ever question you about anything. You could do whatever you want, have whatever, *whoever* you want."

As Gia sniffed a soft disapproval beside him, Ian paused, and he hated himself for that simple pause, for being tempted for even a second by the dream of being forever untouchable. But even if Clancy followed through — which was highly questionable — and his record was somehow forever destroyed, even if he rose to damn attorney general with Clancy's influence, it would be meaningless. The flaws would still be beneath the surface. He'd still wonder if someone from his past would show up and ruin everything. He'd still be looking over his shoulder.

All details he didn't need to reveal to Clancy.

"If it's choosing between working for you and dying, well" — Ian shrugged, ignoring Gia's wide-eyed stare, hoping she knew him well enough to understand he was simply buying them time — "It's an easy choice. I'm rather fond of staying alive."

Clancy's teeth gleamed in the gloom and he lowered the gun. "Excellent." His predator's gaze turned on Gia. "And you, Ms. Hellman? What is it that *you* want?"

Ian forced the tension from his shoulders, kept his expression smooth and empty. *Please play along, Princess.* His pulse made a dull gong in his ears.

"There are a lot of things I want that you have zero power to provide." She didn't hide the sneer in her tone, and Ian forced his body to stay relaxed and ready for whatever Clancy might do in retaliation. He'd get Clancy to shoot him first, maybe give Gia time to run, to escape. "I hate what you've done to Joann," she continued, "and that I couldn't help her. Most of all, I hate that you'll probably get away with it."

Clancy's eyes gleamed in the night, cold and calculating. "Careful, Ms. Hellman. I know you understand how vulnerable a woman is on her own, especially a newly divorced, middle-aged woman...such as your mother. From what I've seen, she is quite charming—a perfect politician's wife, whether or not her youngest daughter remains alive to witness her rise on the social ladder."

Gia sucked in a breath. "Leave my mother out of this."

"I believe you already know the price for that request," Clancy said, a gentle warning.

She released a long, trembling breath. "Fine. Leave my family alone and I'll stay quiet."

"Good girl." Clancy's smile was even worse when filled with ultimate victory, sharp and bright as a murderer's blade.

"Wait. There's something else I want." Gia removed her stilettos and lifted them by the straps. She twirled one lazily on her finger. The silver crystals reflected a flickering, hypnotic rhythm and the lump on Ian's head throbbed at the memory of being clobbered. "I have an unhealthy obsession with shoes."

"Done. Unlimited credit to whatever store you choose." Stepping forward, gun barrel angled at the ground, Clancy gave them each a fatherly smile of approval. "Do you now understand how matters only have to be unpleasant if one side is completely inflexible? It could have been the same for Joann if she'd simply been submissive."

The glints from Gia's shoe whirred faster.

Ian dared a glance at her face. Her eyes were blue fire, her lovely mouth set and nothing in her expression marked surrender. *Holy hell.* She was set to attack.

As he lunged forward, one shoe rocketed through the air. The pointed heel struck Clancy straight between the eyes with a dull thud. The second shoe hit his wrist, right above the gun in his hand.

The mayor staggered on a grunt and clasped his free hand to his forehead. The gun slipped, not enough to fall from his fingers. Clancy recovered his balance, too fast to offer any advantage.

Pointing his gun at Gia, he fired.

Chapter Twenty-Seven

The suppressed gunshot *ping* split the air. The next moment passed in splintering, blinding fragments of time. Ian's boyhood nightmare re-formed before his eyes, breathed to life by an abusive man leaning over a woman rendered helpless by savagery—a woman he loved. As if no years had passed and history stood still, fear and rage blended in a conquering storm of red.

Driven by the beast unleashed, Ian launched at the one who so callously harmed someone precious, attacking with quick, hard, practiced strikes. The gun still in Clancy's hand and how badly everything could end faded into nothingness. Black and blood painted the night and violence-laced adrenaline consumed every ounce of his rationality.

They fell to the ground. The thud of flesh beneath Ian's fists made a dull drum beneath the pulse roaring in his skull. He struck for all the times he'd been hit, for all the times his mother had cowered in the corner, shielding her head with her arms, for all the times he'd found her bruised and broken in the darkness and for all the times he'd been helpless to fight back, to protect her, to save her.

To save himself.

A hard object slammed into his temple and white lights filled his vision. The next blow knocked him to his back. He peered through a fountain of blood, up at his father looming over him, a sneer twisting his features into a brutal, uncaring mask. The barrel of his gun pointed at Ian's head.

He blinked as the rage dimmed—not his father. Clancy.

Bruises already bloomed, destroying the politician's disguise, and red dribbled from his swollen lip. His eyes glinted black, merciless.

Details from the present filtered in, cruelly cutting through the haze. The night was still, watchful and waiting. Icy fingers touched his hand, and he turned his head, daring to take his gaze away from the death coming for him.

Gia. His chest collapsed. She lay in an expanding pool of her own blood. Her beautiful face was etched with pain, her eyes, always so alive, glazed. One hand was pressed against her stomach, unable to staunch the flow of ebbing life. The other hand eased into his, weakly holding on. He wasn't even sure if she truly saw him…or Joey, as if she gazed beyond the veil of the living to the dead.

Don't go, Princess.

"A tragic Romeo and Juliet tale," Clancy said, his breath ragged. "So easy to see how it happened. Famed attorney Ian O'Connor's past came back for him and he snapped. His lovely fiancée tried to fend him off, but he was too far gone. She had a gun. Before she could shoot him, he wrestled the gun free and shot her instead. Realizing what he did, he dropped the gun and she picked it up, shot him in the head." He bared red-stained teeth. "Such a shame. She could've been saved if she'd only made it to the hospital in time."

Ian returned his focus to Gia, to what was important. He held her dimming gaze. "Hold on, Princess. Don't go anywhere. Don't go to Joey." His voice cracked. "Stay with me."

Her lovely mouth twitched, as if she wanted to smile and didn't have the strength. Her eyes drifted closed, and he gripped her hand, hard enough to make bones creak. "Gia!"

"Before I kill you," Clancy said, crouching close, forcing Ian's attention to him, "let's take a moment to reflect on what just happened. Gia will die and the blame ultimately lies on you. You couldn't protect her, just like you couldn't protect your mother or Joann." He waved the gun nonchalantly. "How does it feel to die, knowing what an ultimate failure and disappointment you are? Your mother didn't want you to live a life of violence and yet, here you are, dying from an act of violence, right beside your lady love, who will die with the image of you in a mindless rage."

The anger boiling beneath the cold broke free and Ian snarled. "I'll be waiting in hell for you, Clancy. Every minute I spend there will be preparing for all the different and creative ways I plan to torture you when you arrive." His voice shook with fury, ice rolling through him in a numbing wave. Gia was dying or dead, and he'd never forgive himself, not what remained in this ruined lifetime or the next. "I'll see you there."

Clancy straightened to his full height and shook his head. "What a waste. We could have been an unstoppable team." Sighing as if pained by regret, he pointed the gun at Ian's head again. His finger hooked the trigger.

Rebelliously holding Clancy's pitiless gaze, Ian refused to wince, refused to cower to another monster.

A dull *pop* rippled the night as the gun went off. Instead of the pain Ian expected, a hole appeared in Clancy's forehead and a thin stream of blood shot out. Slowly, like an elephant stunned by a drugged dart, the tall man toppled. He dropped to his knees and landed on his face in the grass inches from Ian.

The rhythm of running feet spurred Ian to grapple for the gun still clutched in Clancy's twitching hand. Whoever had shot Clancy wouldn't want witnesses and he had no intention of screwing up this second chance at getting Gia to a hospital in time.

"No need for the gun, Ian." Sean approached at a cautious speed, hands up and empty. His black T-shirt and jeans blended with the night, the moon of his face a pale gleam, his light hair covered in a black beanie. The stony expression was exactly the same. "I'm here to help you."

Sitting up, Ian pointed Clancy's gun at him anyway. "Sorry if I'm slow to believe you. I have my reasons."

"Understandable." Sean's gaze flicked to Joann, who was curled up on the ground behind them, still unconscious.

Ian refused to look at Gia, at the blood, refused to watch her fade away from him. Refused to believe it. "If you want to help, call nine-one-one."

"Did it the second Clancy pointed a gun at you."

A wave of relief slid through Ian, but he kept the gun aimed at Sean. He could be lying.

"It's my fault Mr. Clancy acted against you," Sean said. "I was born in Scotland, lived there until I was ten before coming to the states. I know Gaelic too. I didn't trust you, and since it's my job to protect Joann while I'm with her, I told Mr. Clancy what I'd heard in Gia's fumbling attempts at Gaelic."

"I didn't trust you, either." Never taking his gaze from Sean, Ian stood. "Still don't."

Sean's mouth thinned. "Every time Mr. Clancy gave me the night off," he said quietly, "Joann wouldn't be the same in the morning. It didn't take long to notice how, after my nights away, she'd wear long sleeves, scarves, turtlenecks. Whenever I gently inquired, she'd clam up, refuse to speak to me for days. So I let it go. I figured if it was bad enough, she'd tell me. I hated it, but with only suspicions and her refusal to talk, I was powerless to help her."

Ian refused to wince at the echo of the story he'd told Gia to convince her that Joann couldn't be helped.

"Then she started getting sick and I knew I had to do something." As Sean spoke, he drew closer, his hands still up and in clear sight. "Tonight, when Mr. Clancy told me to go, I left the estate and holed up in the woods between the street and the house, beyond the fence." He shrugged. "I'm not sure what I was expecting to see, if anything. Security kept me from getting too close, and the trees blocked my binoculars, but I needed to *know* what happened while I was away." His gaze flicked to where Joann still laid on the grass. "I'd barely been watching ten minutes when his car came down the drive, both of them in it, so I followed.

"When Joann was dropped off at the stables, I had to decide which of them to follow. I chose Landon, which brought me here." Sean was only a few steps away now. "It's true that Clancy hired me to watch Joann, to do more than protect her from outside forces. I was instructed to report any unusual details. When I reported you and Gia to him, I never anticipated any of this." His throat bobbed, the first crack in his composure. "I…care about Joann a great deal." His face twisted with guilt. "I should have acted sooner."

Ian lowered the gun. "You and me both."

"I'm going to her now." Sean's voice, while gentle, held an unyielding warning, and he slid past Ian toward Joann.

Ian tossed the gun aside and kneeled beside Gia, careful not to jostle her. He ripped off his shirt, shoved it into a ball and pressed it to her stomach, dimly acknowledging the amount of blood. For the second time in his life he prayed, but as the distant wail of sirens broke into the cemetery quiet, he wasn't sure if it sounded more like salvation or the toll of funeral bells.

* * * *

Someone landed a heavy hand on Ian's shoulder and he jerked awake. The hospital room glared white at him, the antiseptic a constant, familiar burn in his sinuses. The steady, mechanical bleep of the machines had even invaded his nightmares, a black, beeping monster chasing him, inescapable. He looked up at the owner of the hand still on his shoulder.

Roman's black eyes shone with sympathy. "Any news?"

Ian stood from the plastic chair parked beside Gia's bed and stretched, everything aching, inside and out. He shook his head and rubbed his grainy eyes.

His friend's gaze settled on Gia, so still and small beneath the hospital blankets, the tubes adding to her frailty. "You need a break, Boy Wonder."

He shook his head. Playing the fiancé card to the hilt, he'd planted his ass by Gia's bed and refused to leave. Even Adara had eventually let him be, after a long tirade he'd ignored, his attention fixed solely on Gia. He'd only left the room when nature called or to answer questions from law enforcement. While conveying what had happened, he'd remained by the tiny door window looking in on Gia. What if she woke up and he wasn't there?

He'd argued that point constantly with himself, wondering which would be worse, staying or leaving. The last memory she had of him would be of him losing to his darkness, going into a rage and beating Clancy to a pulp, exactly the man he'd warned her he was afraid he'd become. He couldn't bear to see any contempt in her eyes when she looked at him.

"Dude" — Roman settled his hands on each of Ian's shoulders and held his gaze — "I'll stay with her. Forty-eight hours is too long to be in this room, suffering Katerina's wrath and enduring her family's accusing looks."

Honestly, he'd barely registered Gia's family entering the room, hovering. Introductions had been made — he was relatively certain about that — and none of it mattered to him. He didn't care what Gia's family thought of him. He cared only about her.

Roman shook him, not ungently, regaining his full attention. "It's not your fault. Clancy is the villain in this tale, not you."

What a lie. Any step in a different direction might have spared Gia being shot. If he'd swallowed his fears and tracked her down sooner, if he hadn't been so stubborn, if he'd told her everything—

"Boy Wonder..." Roman assumed his cop glower. Being under its intensity wasn't a pleasant place to be. "Go home. You won't be any help to her looking like GQ death and smelling like you haven't showered for two days." He lifted his eyebrows. "Oh, right. You *haven't* showered in two days. I tried to be nice, but apparently you don't respond to polite. You're stinking up the place. Take care of it."

He focused blearily on Gia. Maybe Roman was right, Gia's family too. If he hadn't been with Gia, she wouldn't be in the hospital now, her brightness dimmed. He nodded.

"The doctor said she'll be fine. The surgery was a success. You hanging around won't help her rest any better." Roman clapped him on the back. "If she wakes up before you get back, I'll call you."

Not bothering with an answer, Ian forced his feet to move away from Gia and out of the room. It felt like struggling through water. Slouching through the hall with his head down, he nearly collided into Katerina.

"At last," she said, the sneer in her husky voice unshielded, "you're leaving."

The contrast in sisters still surprised him. Where Gia was sunlight, Katerina was the deep darkness. Yet similarities declared them sisters—the slender nose and full lips, graceful stature, the strength beneath the shine.

It took some effort to slide into his lawyer skin and take up the hammer. "I'll be back."

"Don't bother." Her mouth thinned. Her eyes flared in challenge, so similar to Gia's that the dagger permanently embedded in his heart twisted. "When she wakes up, your face will be the last one she'll want to see. Trust me on that."

He forced a bland smile. "I'll let Gia make that decision. Maybe you could channel the woman-scorned energy into being there for your sister."

Kat bristled. If she had been a porcupine, he had no doubt he'd be filled with quills. Before she answered, the door to Gia's room swung open. Roman stood in the doorway, feet apart in a battle stance. His black eyes flashed, and every ounce of that ire was aimed at Katerina.

"Hellman, this is a hospital, not a street." Even his voice held a river of ice, momentarily freezing the Death Star that was Kat. "Take your hostility elsewhere and leave Ian in peace."

"Peace?" She hissed the word. "He's the one who got her into this mess. He doesn't deserve peace. He deserves a jail cell."

Ian walked away, putting distance between himself and the rest of the hushed conversation. None of what Katerina said was new. He'd told himself the same thing a thousand times in the last two days. He should be the one in the hospital bed. He should be the one suffering.

Never Gia.

As he emerged from the hospital doors, the sun on his head lacked any warmth and the air carried a weight to it, dead of any breeze.

Chapter Twenty-Eight

A whispered argument threaded through the darkness of her mind, and Gia clutched on to that string with all her strength, letting it drag her up from an ocean of nothingness into pain and light.

"I told Ian I'd stay," a man's voice rasped. *Roman.* "So I'm staying, even if it means suffering a sentence with a shrew."

"Call me that one more time, and —"

"Let me guess. You'll kick my testicles into my throat."

Kat's familiar snort followed, trailed by a silence cut only by a steady, mechanical beat.

With an effort, Gia forced her eyes open. A television hung on the white wall in front of her, its screen black. Vases of colorful flowers filled the stand beneath it, joined by a couple of shiny balloons floating above. *Get well soon. Hugs and kisses. We love you.* A yellow smiley face.

Her gaze followed the hideous blue polka-dot blanket covering her from the waist down. The nightgown she wore was enough to make her shudder, old-lady pink flowers on white. Not even the pink could save it. A tube was taped to her wrist, leading to a bag dripping fluid.

Hospital. She blinked slowly. She was in a hospital…and being tube-fed something that made her feel like her head floated above her body like the bunch of balloons.

"Gia!" Kat's lovely face filled her vision, relief in her dark eyes. "You're back!"

Roman smiled grimly at her from the side of the bed and dug his phone from his pocket. "Ian will want to know you're awake."

"No." Gia weakly pawed at his wrist, dragging all her tubes. "Don't. I don't want him here."

Roman's mouth tightened, making his austere features even more solemn.

Gia swallowed, her mouth dry, the drugs in her system dulling all her senses. "Just…tell him not to come here, that it's not what he thinks. He's okay, isn't he?"

"Alive and stubborn as ever." After a marked hesitation, Roman put the phone away.

Kat tossed her dark hair and glared at Roman. "You should go, officer." She sneered the last word, as if she wasn't sure Roman would catch her contemptuous tone. "Family only."

Ignoring her, Roman nodded at Gia. "Glad you're back with the living" — he winked and headed for the exit — "Princess."

Once the door had shut behind him, Gia focused blearily on Kat. "What happened?"

"I only know what the local blue chose to share." Crossing her arms, she narrowed her eyes. "Your *boyfriend* is as worthless as the investigators around here, and the only reason—"

"Don't have the energy for rants." Gia hit the pain button. "Is Joann Clancy okay?"

"She was released yesterday after being treated for thallium poisoning." Kat's expression softened. "Nice lady. She asked about you several times."

"And her husband?"

Kat's mouth set in a firm, thin line. "Dead."

The fist clenching her heart relaxed. They were safe. Clancy would never hurt anyone again. "How?"

"Shot to the head, all Roman would say." She rolled her eyes. "The whole family is here, currently in the cafeteria. Thought I'd let you know, to prepare before I text them that you're awake."

Gia hit the pain button again. She'd need the extra drug kick to deal with her family. "Thanks for the warning."

Awkwardly, Kat took her hand between hers and tears shone in her dark eyes. "I was really, really worried, G. I know I'm not the easiest person to deal with, but I'll always be your big sister. I'll always worry about you."

"I love you, Kat, even when you're a jackass." Gia was still smiling as darkness again folded around her like a blanket and tucked her in.

* * * *

The heavy silence in Ian's house threatened to strangle him. He flicked on a soccer game to make some noise, to ease the emptiness, and dragged himself into the shower. He lifted his face to the pounding water and let it sluice off his skin. It did nothing to remove the layers of guilt, the aching sense of loss.

Whether or not Gia recovered, he couldn't combat the sense that he'd lost her. Either she wouldn't get past being shot, connecting that pain and trauma forever to him, or his last display of uncontrolled rage would make her realize exactly how much he wasn't what she'd *thought* she wanted. She'd find a graceful way to dance free, as she should have from the start. No matter his vehement promise in the cemetery — if she wanted to be released, he had to let her go. For her sake, not his own.

Bowing his head, he planted his hands on the shower wall and let the water punish him for a few more minutes before walking free. He'd barely toweled off when the soccer game cut out and a local news update blared.

The Graywood police public information officer reported that an autopsy confirms that Landon Clancy, Mayor of Greenville, was killed by a gunshot wound to the head. From the information gathered so far, local attorney Ian O'Connor of the Hamilton & Associates law firm was assisting Landon Clancy's wife, Joann, in filing for divorce, but no further details have been made available to the public. The investigation is active and ongoing —

Ian snapped the television off. He didn't need to relive the event that had cracked the foundations of his world. He pulled on some jeans and a sweater and hoped the extra layer would ease the relentless cold in his bones.

The doorbell rang and he cursed beneath his breath. Barefoot and weary, he trudged to the door and opened it. Hamilton stood on the doorstep. Ian's guts twisted even more. Never, not once during his years at Hamilton & Associates, had his boss made a house call.

"Ian." Hamilton looked strange in his suit, standing on his doorstep. Was it Monday already? Or Tuesday? His mentor had stopped by the hospital after the shooting. That appearance seemed like a dull memory from a different time, unimportant. This particular visit was the opposite, too clear and intense to be anything but important.

Hamilton glanced past him purposefully to the house interior. "Going to invite me in?"

Ian opened the door wider. "I don't have any coffee made."

"I knew I should've stopped to grab some."

"I've got bourbon."

Hamilton waved a hand in dismissal as he passed by. "Never mind. I'll survive."

Not waiting for Mr. Hamilton to sit, Ian shut the door and slumped onto the couch. "Whatever it is, don't sugarcoat it for me, sir."

"Apparently, you've forgotten who I am. I don't do sweet." Hamilton perched on the edge of a chair and leaned forward, elbows planted on his knees, hands clasped, his piercing gaze on Ian. "I am faced with a problem, and I'm not sure how to handle it."

"Me. I'm your problem." Ian smiled without humor.

Hamilton nodded. "I spoke to Joann, of course."

Ian had thought he was too numb to feel anything else, but new ice splinters cut through his bloodstream and dropped his temperature another degree.

"She asked me to thank you." Hamilton's stare never wavered. "When I asked you to handle her case, I knew you were the only one at our firm capable of doing it, because you don't mind stepping beyond the bounds of courtroom convention. You don't care what other people think of you. You'll do whatever it takes to win and still be within the law."

"And that's the problem?"

"Partly." Hamilton angled his head to the side, just enough of a shift to be noticeable. "Have you seen the news?"

Ian raked his fingers through his still damp hair. "Unfortunately."

"The firm's reputation is at stake, and whether or not you are exonerated, the public might not be so generous. Clancy was well-respected in the community. He might have been a bastard to Joann and a criminal, but people believe what they want to believe."

"And you have to care about that," he said around the knot in his throat. "I get it."

"I asked you to handle this case off the grid, out of the public eye." Hamilton leaned back and folded his arms. "This is about as *in* the public eye as you can get, and I'm not blaming you for that. You can't control what other people do, which is also part of the problem. Two clients have already dropped us."

"Their loss."

"True, but we're nothing without clients." Hamilton tapped his long fingers on his forearm. "You earned Joann's appreciation, her loyalty. She's free of that scum. That is a great win, O'Connor."

Ian nodded. He was happy for Joann, truly. Every person deserved to live without oppression and torment. But the cold waves rolling through him felt more like a crushing defeat than a victory.

"I've never regretted hiring you."

A lump grew in Ian's throat, one he didn't swallow, and it made his voice croak. "But?"

"For now, a leave of absence is the best action." Hamilton's eyes glittered with something that could be either sympathy or pity. Neither emotion was welcome. "I can't guarantee what the future may hold for you at the firm. If it comes to needing a reference —"

"I'll be fine." Ian stood abruptly, his heart thudding hard, muffled beneath the frozen layers of skin and blood. "You don't have to concern yourself with my welfare, Mr. Hamilton. I'll always be fine." Everything Clancy had threatened was coming true, haunting him from the grave.

Hamilton's expression hardened as he stood. "You don't dictate what my concerns are, boy. If I choose to be concerned about you, I sure as hell will be. Letting you go isn't what I want."

Ian drew a long breath and lifted his chin. "You gave a chance to a rebellious kid who had no resources, referrals or experience. You helped me achieve my goals when no one else would have. I will always be grateful for that, but I know my mother didn't fully explain to you where I had come from."

Hamilton's eyebrows rose, but he remained silent, expectant.

"For three years, I was in the psychiatric unit for boys." For some reason, his voice wasn't trembling. It should be. Hamilton had maimed his dream for partnership, and now Ian himself was murdering it. "I know my mother explained I had an assault on my record, but I doubt she told you that I beat my father so badly — with only my fists — that he nearly died. He lost an eye, has to use a cane, needs assistance to go anywhere. And you should know that I'd do it all again in a heartbeat without a single regret, which was probably why I was committed."

There. He released a long breath. It was done, any hope of partnership with the most prestigious law firm in the area gone. Once word got out, he probably wouldn't be able to eke out a living in his chosen profession. He'd find himself in a state-funded senior center, alone, staring at the life he'd never had and only recently discovered he wanted.

For a long moment, Hamilton studied him, his expression unreadable. When he spoke, his voice was quiet thunder. "I suspect your father got what he deserved. It was never about where you came from or who you'd been, O'Connor. When I first met with your mother, she was already proud of you. She already believed in you. She'd be damn proud of what you did for Joann, risking your career and life for a woman in desperate need of being rescued. No session in the funny farm can change that." He spun on his heel and headed for the door. "I'll be in touch. Until then, lie low."

The click of the door shutting behind Hamilton rang in the sudden silence. Ian couldn't move, his feet frozen to the floor, his blurry gaze on the door. As much as his boss' words were meant to comfort, he couldn't find any solace in them. When he'd decided to break the chains of the past, he'd understood the risks. He'd jeopardized everything by revealing the darkness still coiling inside, even after three years in the psychiatric unit and fifteen years under the bridge. One of those casualties now included his partnership at Hamilton &

Associates, no matter what Hamilton had or hadn't said. With the Clancy scandal attached to his name, his past was only another hook binding that dream permanently to the ground. It was a twisted sort of freedom, exposing one's past, equally liberating and hollow.

His phone buzzed in his pocket, breaking his thoughts apart, and he fished it out. A text from Roman flashed across the screen.

Gia's awake. Doesn't want you to come. Said it's not what you think, whatever that means. I'll keep you updated.

His pulse leaped and dropped in the same second. Gia didn't want him to come, and whatever her reasons, something inside him caved, knocking the breath from him. He slowly sank onto the couch. Even though he'd expected it, knew the rejection was coming and didn't blame her in any way…damn.

Losing Gia destroyed him.

Chapter Twenty-Nine

A week after having been released from the hospital — one hundred and seventy-two hours, thirty-three minutes and thirteen seconds of quiet time and letting her injury heal — had been a hell all its own. Gia sipped her tea and gingerly leaned against the kitchen counter. She'd managed to pry free of her family, except for Kat, with promises of a trip home to explain everything once she was fully recovered. The latest update from Roman said Matt had been apprehended, thanks to a tip from Frankie. Joann was feeling better, with Sean as her constant companion. There was only one loose end left.

Ian.

He hadn't texted her or dropped by even once, and she supposed that was his way of letting her forget that fateful night, their fake engagement and any trauma-induced confessions — like forgetting him was even possible.

Her heart squeezed and squirmed. An entire week without seeing Ian, talking to him, touching him.... While avoiding him had seemed like a good plan at the time, it was putting her imagination on overdrive. All her old impressions of Ian returned, pushing at the man she had come to know, the real, amazing man behind the suit and sneer. What if it had all been in her head?

The doorbell rang, and before Gia could set her mug aside, Katerina marched to the door. She swung it open, as if expecting to scare whoever was on the other side. Snapping a rude response under her breath, she snatched a box from the person on the doorstep, slammed the door and stomped back to Gia.

"Delivery." She studied the box with narrowed eyes, turning it over and inspecting the tape securing it. "No return address... I'd better check it. That Clancy dirtbag probably has lowlife friends."

Gia grabbed the box from her sister's hands, wincing at the jolt of pain in her stomach. "My house, Kat. Hands off."

"Gia." Kat's voice held a warning. "You have to be careful."

"I don't have to be anything." Gia clutched the box to her heart and stared her sister down. "This is my life, my choices to make, my path to walk." She refused to back down at the combative flash in Kat's eyes. Strength came in more forms than being in law enforcement or the manipulative power of a beautiful socialite. Knowing who she was and wasn't formed a shield that wouldn't break unless she let it. "I appreciate that you worry about me, Kat—that you all worry about me—but I'm not a bomb set on self-destruction. I don't have to fit the typical Hellman mold to be capable."

Kat's eyebrows shot up and she dropped her arms to her sides. "I've never thought you were incapable, G. Just..." After a moment, she shrugged. "You wander into places you don't fit and get lost sometimes. That's all."

Her heart made a strange kick and ticked fast. Tucking the box beneath one arm, Gia stood and slung the other arm around her sister's neck. Kat stiffened, then relaxed and hugged her back.

"You don't have to puzzle out my life for me. I've got the most necessary details ironed out in my own glamorous way." *Maybe.* Hopefully, and she couldn't wait any longer to finish up the blueprints. "Good accomplices are hard to find and sometimes require searching in sketchy places." She cocked a hip. "To be clear, I don't *need* a partner. I can do it on my own. My worth isn't defined by anyone else but me, and anyone who disagrees can suck it."

A smile slowly spread until it lit up Kat's entire face, bringing a glow to her natural beauty. "I don't think getting involved with shady politicians and attorneys then letting a sludgesack shoot you is a solid game plan, sis. When you're back to one hundred percent, we're going to the range. Daily. You're going to be the next local firearms expert. If anyone does the shooting, it's going to be you."

Gia laughed. "Not unless you buy me a pink, sparkly gun."

Kat looked horrified by the idea.

Using a kitchen knife, Gia sliced the packaging tape from the box while Kat hovered at her elbow. A white shoebox tied with a silver ribbon rested inside. She exchanged a look with Kat, untied the silver ribbon and cautiously opened the lid. Nestled in pink tissue paper were shoes. *The Shoes*, the ones she'd admired every time she passed them by in the store window. The ones she'd planned to buy with the extra money from working with Ian on Joann's case—ridiculously expensive, completely impractical, uselessly beautiful.

Shaking even more, she lifted the stilettos from the box. A pristine white card rested beneath them, so small that she almost missed it. She set The Shoes on the counter and opened the card.

Because beautiful does not always mean pointless…and every Glitter Queen needs her bling.

Ian's neat handwriting and the fact he'd twisted Joey's special name for her brought tears to her eyes. She clutched the card to her heart. How Ian had known that she loved those particular shoes, that she didn't need the glitter or glamour to be happy or that beauty was a happiness… It all affirmed what her heart already knew.

"That's from O'Connor, isn't it?" Kat leaned her elbows on the counter. "I still blame him for everything, and I doubt I'll ever like him." A breath hissed between her teeth. "But no one voluntarily sits beside the hospital bed of someone he doesn't care about." She paused, frowning. "Unless he's driven by extreme guilt. Never mind. That's probably why he was there."

"Thanks, Kat." Gia rolled her eyes. She plucked The Shoes from the tissue paper and slipped them on. "I have to go."

"Where?" Kat followed her to the door.

"To put the first phase of my life plan into place." Gia grinned over her shoulder and carefully descended the front steps. Phase two would be entirely up to Ian.

* * * *

Sprawled on his bed, Ian stared at the tiny, threatening velvet box that had been delivered an hour before. He didn't want to open it, didn't want to see the solid symbol of everything he'd risked and lost. The blame lay entirely on him. If he'd been smart enough to own up to his past, Clancy never would have had any ammunition against him, and Gia...

His chest ached, hollow. Damn, he missed her — missed her smile, her sparkle, the sweet and snarky way she called him 'Sugarpop'. His one-night rule had backfired and turned into a life sentence, a prison he had no idea how to escape.

He poked the box with one finger and snorted at his cowardice. Opening it wouldn't change anything. He popped the lid. The ring he'd ordered on a whim gleamed back at him — pink diamond, silver meteorite, white gold. Perfect for a princess who loved lightning.

The image of it on Gia's slender finger sliced through him, enough to shred his breath, and he sat up, fast. *What the hell am I doing?* He'd spent years, long, torturous *years* battling his demons, fighting on a daily basis to overcome his past, struggling to be the best at whatever he chose to do, going after what he wanted without fear. And now he was going to sit here and wallow at a setback? Sure, he'd been rocked by a major blow, but he'd faced worse — *survived* worse and thrived because of it. No matter that his mother wasn't alive to witness his actions. He'd be damned before disappointing her.

He stood and paced the room, needing some channel for the sudden, fierce energy burning in his veins. Failure had never stopped him before. He wasn't dead yet. Lifelong goals could still be accomplished. And as for Gia...

His pulse thundered, a vibrating cord all the way to his fingertips. He refused to give her up. If she wanted a life without him, she'd have to tell him to his face. Then he'd dedicate every miserable breath to winning her back. No method would be too low or too shady. He'd use whatever worked—schemes and seduction, too many margaritas and mistletoe, rainbow glitter and an entire department store of shoes.

Five minutes later, dressed in jeans and a pin-striped button-down, his face washed and shaved, teeth brushed, hair combed, Ian stalked toward the door and flung it open.

The beauty standing on his doorstep, her hand raised to knock, froze his feet to the floor. Gia gazed up at him, her sunshine hair loose, the blue sky reflected in her eyes, picture perfect in a halter-top summer dress.

Brutal joy and savage doubt warred inside him, making his heart throb too hard and his blood rage through his veins. She was here. His Princess. Her spun-sugar perfume called to him with a sweet sigh of *at last. Home.*

Her gaze slid over him, down his chest, along the lines of his legs to his deck shoes and back up, snagging briefly at his body's stiff and obvious reaction to her. Prickling heat rushed along every inch of his skin, throbbing at the simple sight of her. Instead of falling to his knees at her feet, he leaned one shoulder against the door and silently dared her to look again.

She did. Nothing more than a fleeting glance, but...she did. He told himself it probably meant nothing, that it was a normal, healthy feminine reaction to any semi-attractive, sharp-dressed man. But his hope stirred like the rest of him. He didn't bother trying to shut it down. When it came to Gia, he was completely out of control.

"Are you going to let me in, O'Connor?" She planted a hand on her cocked hip, impatient and sassy, which did nothing to help his own cocked situation.

He shouldn't let her in. It wouldn't end well, her showing up unexpectedly on his turf. Putting other people off-balance was one of his tried and true ploys, and he did it because it usually worked. It had undeniably worked on him. Choking back a growl, Ian opened the door wider and stepped aside. As she passed by, her perfume wrapped around him, amplifying her magical lure. The door shutting behind him deepened the silence into awkward.

Gia pivoted, facing him. "You look terrible."

"You look gorgeous," he said truthfully.

"Couch potato sessions are my new beauty regimen. I was thinking about filing for a patent and selling it as a program, but some customers might balk at the initial step of getting shot." Her tone was playful, teasing, not at all the demeanor of a woman cutting him out of her life. And he had a lot of experience with being walked away from, even if half of those women had hoped he'd chase them, despite a one-night agreement.

Or maybe his hope was playing tricks on his ears and this was payback. He'd always been heartless when it came to the morning after. He'd thought he was off the hook because he'd been honest, that it was a woman's own problem if she felt things she shouldn't. Now he'd been sidelined by a woman he couldn't live without, and she could clearly live without him, no problem. *Karma at its best.*

He cleared his throat. "What can I do for you, Princess?"

Her smile faded, chilling his blood. "I wanted to thank you."

"For?" His voice was hardly more than a croak, his efforts to portray calm and uncaring completely failing.

"For helping me figure out how to leave my mark on the world." She perched on the couch arm and folded her hands in her lap. "Joann's case was out of the box in every way—unconventional and weird, dangerous and potentially fatal."

Ian braced himself. Here it came like a bulldozer, the logical and undeniable reason she'd use to put a permanent wall between them. She deserved a prince, someone good, someone who didn't have so much darkness to work through, darkness he'd probably always be fighting.

But not fighting to keep her felt all wrong.

"The thing is," Gia continued, "dangerous and potentially fatal are the everyday lives for women in abusive relationships. It's something I'd never thought about before. If we hadn't agreed to help Joann, hadn't put our own lives in danger, she would have been the dead one instead of Clancy." She squared her shoulders and held his gaze steadily, as if expecting a battle. "I'm going back to college for my law degree so I can help other women who face domestic abuse and feel hopeless, helpless and alone."

That wasn't what at all what he'd expected her to tell him. He sank into the chair facing her. "You'll make a great attorney and advocate for abused women." He meant every word. "And you'll brighten up a courtroom with your unstoppable sparkle."

Her smile broke free and full-on, as if she'd been waiting for his approval, which didn't make sense. She didn't want or need his approval for anything.

"Maybe I can be your assistant." His mouth struggled to tick up, to make some sort of a cynical gesture, but the wound was too raw to offer enough power. "Hamilton put me on leave. I don't expect an invitation back."

Gia's face fell. "Seriously? You put your life on the line for a case he personally asked you to take and that's how he repays you?" Blue flames ignited in her eyes. "My respect level for Mr. Hamilton just bottomed out."

The way she defended him despite everything he'd put her through infused him with a sliver of warmth. "He's only doing what he believes is best for the firm, and he doesn't owe me anything. Without him, I probably would have been on the other side, employed by Clancy."

Gia rolled her eyes. "No, you wouldn't."

"Why are you still defending me, Princess?" he asked, the words choked.

She lifted her eyebrows and looked at him as if he was an idiot. "Because I know you, O'Connor." She cocked her head, her gaze piercing, a fierce imitation of Hamilton on a quest for the truth. She'd have no trouble being an attorney. "Don't I?"

His heart battered his ribs, a demand to accept her challenge with utter honesty, no matter how much it might hurt later. Ian nodded and forced his hands not to tremble where they rested on his thighs. He exhaled, long and slow. "I didn't want you to know me. Letting you in makes this all the harder."

"This?" she echoed.

The darkness inside him snapped, and somehow, without meaning to, he was on his feet, looming in her face, so close her startled breath brushed his mouth. "*This*," he hissed. "You. Me. Being with you then…not. Letting you see *me*, all of me, and destroying this unexplainable, devastating, unexpected *thing* between us."

"You came to the hospital, even though you don't do hospitals," she whispered, not backing down. Tears glimmered in her eyes. "Then The Shoes were delivered today."

She lifted one foot, showing off the sexy, strappy shoes he'd bought from Heelcandy before she could. It seemed a lifetime ago that he'd stashed them in his office. Torn between his desire to make her happy and the need to keep his distance, he'd waffled, stored the box and the carefully worded note in a cupboard. He wasn't sure if he should thank Hamilton for shipping them to Gia or seek revenge on his mentor later.

"I might've gotten the wrong idea, but I need to know for sure." She bit her bottom lip. "Did I? Get the wrong idea?"

"Princess, I'm not even sure what your question is right now." His heart was beating so hard that he could barely hear himself think. "Roman gave me your message, that you asked me not to show up at the hospital, and I respected that. I hated it, but—"

"And the other part of that message?" Gia stood and fisted her hands in his shirt, as if he might run. "Roman told you the rest, didn't he?"

"That it's not what I think." He held her gaze. "I've had some very dark thoughts, love, and every day without any hint from you made them even darker."

"I knew you'd blame yourself. I knew you'd think I'd want miles of space after witnessing what you did to Clancy." Her expression softened. "Which was badass, by the way."

He was shaking. *Why am I shaking?*

"I didn't want you to see me as a victim," she continued. "I didn't want you to look at me and think of personal failure or be reminded of violence. I wanted you to look at me and see a triumph over evil — and me lying in a hospital bed wearing that horrifying, open-backed gown wasn't it."

His throat was too dry to speak. All this time, she'd been worried about how *he'd* perceive *her*. She truly was a princess, an angel who'd stashed her halo.

She took his right hand and lifted it. Scabs and bruises still made a grisly map across his knuckles. Nothing had been broken, but they still ached every so often. Gently, she brushed her thumb over the injured ridges. "When I see this, it's not the ugliness of violence that comes to mind. It's the beauty of protection."

Good God... Gia was a slice of something pure and untouchable, mistakenly left behind on this earth. He was so blown away that he could barely breathe.

She lifted her gaze to his. "I know it will take me a few years to get through law school." She worried her bottom lip with her teeth and when she spoke, a shyness he'd rarely witnessed in her showed up. "But I was hoping, when the time comes, that you might consider, maybe...partnering with me?"

Since he couldn't speak anyway, he kept his stare on full speed.

"I thought we made a great team, working Joann's case," she rushed on, apparently taking his silence for something else. "And I know it would be a huge pay cut, not the prestigious career you envisioned, but it would be a good cause, worth sacrificing expensive shoes and stature for." She dropped her gaze to his knuckles again, her long eyelashes shadowing her cheeks. "I know it's a lot to ask and I wouldn't be able to contribute much, at first. I could be your assistant until I passed the bar. Be a law clerk. Whatever."

"You want *me* to be *your* business partner?" His voice was low and rough, didn't even sound like his own. "Is that all you want me for?" He hadn't meant to say the words, wasn't sure he wanted the answer. But he needed to know. Somewhere along the way, charmed by glitter and smiles, he'd rewritten his laws and traded restrictions for risky ventures.

Slowly, her eyelashes swept up. Unsmiling, she held his gaze. "I guess that depends."

"On what?" The words were nothing more than rasps.

"What *you* want *me* for."

Hardly daring to believe he'd heard her right, he gently pulled his hand free from hers and cupped her chin. "Everything." He swallowed hard. "I want it all, Princess. Only with you. I'm so in love with you that my brain rebooted. I can't even produce a half-decent comeback."

"I knew you could be reasonable, O'Connor." Her smile dazzled him. "I love you too…more than shoes." Gia rose onto her tiptoes and brushed a barely-there kiss against his cheek. "More than gowns and crowns." She pressed her mouth to his, then, "More than senior center dances and gelatin."

A small, soft laugh left him, and all the weight he'd been carrying seemed to leave with it. "That's an auspicious beginning."

"It's *our* beginning." Taking his face between her hands, she held his gaze, promises and the future shining in her eyes. "Ready to fight for happily ever after, Sugarpop?"

The dam of restraint inside him broke, and he lassoed her slender waist, pulling her against him. He delved his free hand into her silken hair and cupped the back of her head. "With you, Princess, forever."

Ian fisted the back of her dress, giving her no avenue of escape, and caressed her lips with his. He kept the kiss light and lazy, savoring her sweetness, the heat and friction of her mouth and tongue as she opened to him.

Moaning and leaning in to him, Gia slid her slender fingers into his hair, over his neck, along the ridges of his shoulders and back in a restless path, as if she couldn't stop touching him, as if memorizing every slope and plane to recall later, exactly as she had during their night interrupted months and months ago.

Even if hell opened a portal in his living room, there'd be no stopping him now.

Picking her up without breaking the kiss, he carried her, step by slow step, to the bedroom. He pushed the door open with his foot and set her down, smiling at her muffled protest. His fingers at the hook of her dress, he backed Gia toward the bed, not caring that the sheets were rumpled from a week-long mope or that his heart raged like a beast in his chest. Gia was here, in his arms.

Mine. Forever.

The backs of Gia's knees hit the mattress and she toppled with a hiss, not of pleasure, but of pain.

Ian paused, looming halfway over her, ashamed at his loss of control. So quickly, he'd forgotten she'd been shot only days ago, lying in a hospital bed. He scanned her dress as if he could see the wound beneath. "I'd give anything to have traded places with you, to be the one Clancy shot."

"And give up my killer war wound?" Her eyes glittered as she fumbled with the bottom button of his shirt. "Not even. I plan to show it off. The only non-law enforcement sibling shot in the line of duty. It's poetic justice."

He forced himself to stay still, to not give in to the demanding heat tumbling through his body. Instead, he smirked. "An epic tale to tell our kids."

"Kids?" She stopped at the next button, her eyes wide and worried.

"Isn't that what you want, Princess? The fairy tale, the happily ever after, love eternal? A prince in tarnished armor wielding a black sword, coming to your rescue should your stilettos fail to dazzle?" He cocked his head. "Or put an eye out with a well-aimed throw of a killer shoe?"

She relaxed and slid her hands beneath his shirt, warm against his skin, making him shudder with restraint. "You can rescue me any time you want, but I have law classes to take. Any fairy tale of mine questions the inclusion of children."

"This is your fantasy, love. I'm merely a hapless bystander drawn willingly into your magical web." He closed his eyes as she slipped her fingers into his waistband. As much as he wanted her — right now, yesterday, tomorrow — he didn't want to hurt her.

"And all this time I thought you weren't romantic."

"I'm not." He barely resisted a growl.

"Then what about these shoes?" She kicked out a foot, revealing the sexy straps of her sandals. "You listened to me, even when the subject was shoes. You took the time to figure out what I love and shopped for me." She sighed. "Completely romantic."

"Completely manipulative." He managed not to groan as she kicked off her stilettos and ran her foot up his thigh.

"And how many other girls have you bought shoes for?"

"Only one." As her eyes narrowed, he added with a smirk, "My mother."

"You're saying I remind you of your mother?" Her foot went still.

"Very well, if you must know the truth, I bought them in the hopes you'd give up your quest for true love and settle for me instead."

"You didn't need the shoes, O'Connor." She smiled up at him and fisted his shirt, pulling him down to her. "But I'm not giving them back."

Ian braced himself above her, nearly exploding as she nibbled on his neck. "Gia, your injury—"

"I'll deal." She found his mouth with hers again, and her kiss, hungry, hot, and demanding, netted his very being and drew him in.

He couldn't bring himself to deny her. The best he could do was try his damnedest to be gentle. With a press of his hips, he eased her to the bed, careful not to put any pressure near her wound.

Gia's response was anything but gentle. She hauled him on top of her, scrabbling through the last of his shirt buttons and working at his jeans. She pushed his T-shirt up his back, sliding her hands over his skin, a desperate bid for more.

"Ian." Her breath was uneven in his ear as he settled over her, adjusting his weight while slowly exploring the sweet, smooth length of her neck. "You're wearing too many clothes."

"That *is* a problem." He shucked his shirt and kissed her, a long, deep, claiming connection, pouring out every ounce of his dark heart, his hopes and promises. It was a vow of his own, that he'd fight for her, for them. Forever.

She moaned into his mouth as he trailed a hand up her thigh, rucking her dress up to expose the smooth expanse of her lovely legs. When he slowly traced up her hip, she writhed beneath him with a growl.

"This," she snarled, "is not the time to be slow or gentle." She reached between them and wrapped a hand around him, making everything ache and burn at her stroking touch. Blue flames surrounded her dilated pupils. "I've waited much, much too long for you, Ian."

He drew a deep breath as his heart squeezed with longing, joy…love. The sensation was both frightening and freeing, but that didn't matter. This woman who accepted him, all his layers and shadows and rust, he'd give her anything she asked.

Ian dropped his pants and dragged off her dress without another word. He only paused when every inch of her lovely body was stretched bare on his bed, the sight stealing his breath. Not even the patch of gauze still taped close to her perfect belly button stopped his pulse from throbbing and dancing through every extremity in a torturous beat. He eased his body over hers, the drag of her silken skin on his excruciating. Somehow, he managed to resist touching the curves of her breasts, the slopes of her hips, the secret spot waiting between her thighs.

"Just one more thing," he rasped, ignoring her protest, and reached for the velvet box still open and tangled in the sheet near her head. The fact that she hadn't noticed the ring demonstrated the utter depth of her distraction and gave him a shot of masculine smugness. Gia was more attracted to him than she was to jewelry. He dangled the ring in front of her. "Marry me? For real this time."

Tears brightened her eyes and her smile stole his breath anew. She pulled him down for a long, drugging kiss. "Yes." Flinging her arms around his neck and her legs around his hips, she laughed into his neck. "Yes."

"Forever, Princess," he whispered as he slipped the ring onto her finger. Kissing her, he slid into her at last, full and deep. Pleasure rolled through him, and when she moaned into his mouth, the last, disjointed piece of him aligned with a soft pulse that echoed in his soul. As they moved together, as their hearts beat in unity and the world shattered around them and slowly reformed, he finally understood why Gia relentlessly chased happily ever after.

Belonging to someone else made everything sparkle.

Epilogue

"It's so…big." Gia's voice echoed eerily in the empty building as she turned in a slow circle, taking in the bare white walls and sand-colored tile. The distinct lack of color made her shudder.

"The exact words you said last night." Ian smirked at her, his hands stuffed into the front pockets of his ridiculously sexy jeans. Even on a Saturday, he'd gone for classy in a blue button-down and shiny shoes. "I believe they were moaned in between the 'don't you dare stop' and 'Ian, you're blowing my mind'."

"Your memory's a little off." She stepped close and slipped her arms around his waist, leaning against his heat and strength. The way his eyes flared shot a thrill through her, and when he pulled her even closer with a soft growl, a series of tingles awakened all the best parts of her body. *Ding, ding, and ding.* "My actual words were 'don't you dare bring me sushi instead of steak' and 'Ian, you're'…" She pretended to think about it and grinned. "Oh, wait. I *did* say that one."

"Along with other" — he kissed her nose — "most suggestive" — her cheek — "and thoroughly stimulating words." He pressed his lips beneath her ear, and she shivered as he slid the tip of his tongue over her skin and sent ripples of molten fire through her veins. "Who knew a princess could have such a potty mouth?"

"That's your own fault for stereotyping me, Sugarpop." She wriggled free of his embrace before he distracted her again. A week of being honestly engaged to him had proven that when it came to Ian O'Connor, she had almost zero resistance. "When you said you wanted to look at office buildings, I was picturing something more modest. Affordable." She arched an eyebrow at him. "Next month, I'll be a starving college student living on yogurt and tea and whatever spare change I find between the couch cushions. I can't —"

"Yes, you can," he said with smooth lawyer confidence. "I'll provide the funds, you provide the charm and I freely admit I'm getting the better end of the bargain." His eyes gleamed. "The sparkles you create will be worth more than the building."

Her heart squeezed and, right there, she melted into a gooey puddle at his feet. She'd found this man who valued every nuance of who she was as a whole person, not just a Glitter Girl who'd finally found her purpose. How could she not love him madly?

"Besides, I'll keep you properly fed, purely for self-protection purposes." Ian strolled to the window of the sizeable office space and gazed out. "You get a little snarly when you're hungry, love."

"True, but Kat's staying longer and has agreed to pay rent. I'll be able to buy my chai tea, so you're relatively safe, not that I'd ever turn down your…meat." She wriggled her eyebrows.

One side of his mouth kicked up. "It seems I've corrupted you beyond redemption. And I'm sorry about the prolonged Kat situation."

Gia shrugged one shoulder. "Not as sorry as Roman's going to be. She agreed to take the temporary firearms instructor position at the police department while she's on leave."

Ian's low chuckle was nothing short of devilish. "I believe I'll let Baconbits discover that unwelcome development when the time comes. I don't want to ruin the good week he's having with all the Clancy investigations."

She joined him at the window. The view wasn't as good as his office at Hamilton & Associates. There was nothing but a narrow strip of shrubs and flowers that separated the space between them and the solid brick wall of the building next door. Gia spun and perched her butt on the windowsill so she could read his expression. "So how did your meeting go with Mr. Hamilton?"

Ian's expression revealed nothing as he kept his gaze aimed outside. She waited for a tic in his jaw or the small smile that he used in the courtroom when he didn't want to show his cards, her pulse stuttering. Giving up his lifelong goal of being named partner couldn't be easy, and she prayed he wouldn't someday look back and resent his choices or the part she'd played in Joann's case and the resulting layoff. Or regret her.

Finally, he looked at her and his smirk was all genuine Ian. "He offered me the partnership."

She sucked in a breath.

"I turned it down."

"What?" She stared, sure she'd misheard. "Why?"

His expression softer, more open than at any other time she could recall, Ian traced a thumb along her jaw, as if memorizing every inch he touched. He took her hand in his, pressed a kiss to her palm and held it against his heart. The steady rhythm vibrated into her bones, calling her to sway to its beat.

"I believed that power and prestige would be enough, would make *me* enough," he said quietly. "But somewhere along the way, a Glitter Girl infected me with glamour. I've never quite been the same." He brushed his fingertip over her ring and her heart expanded, so full that she thought she might float away. "Creating your happily ever after is a challenge I have no intention of failing, and if I'm going to form a partnership, well" — he trailed his hand down her back in a suggestive slide — "I want a partner who understands that while money is useful, helping people who need it is somewhat more important. And I undeniably prefer a particular princess, even if I'm not the Prince Charming you envisioned at the beginning of your noble quest."

"I think you always were that prince." Gia blinked off the sudden burn of tears and touched her mouth to his, softly, tenderly, pouring all her emotions into the kiss. When she pulled back, they were both breathing hard. "You were just waiting for the right fairy dust to break the one-night rule spell."

"Gia, love, the one-night rule never applied to you." He lowered his lashes and tucked her hair behind her ear, not fast enough to hide the moist glint in his eyes. "One night would never have been enough."

"I always suspected you were as smart as your fashion sense, O'Connor." She gave him her best smile and jumped into his arms, wrapping her arms and legs around him. And as he spun her around, laughing, she could have sworn the distant strains of a violin drifted on the air, playing *Glitter Girl* for the final time, a celebration of the final chapter in a cherished book, now closed.

Want to see more like this?
Here's a taster for you to enjoy!

Single in Seattle: Reeling in Love
Gloria Herrmann

Excerpt

"I think we got it," Molly said confidently to the almost naked man standing in the corner, wearing nothing but a stark white towel draped across his tan waist.

"You sure?"

Molly nodded as she scrutinized her work. "Yeah, the lighting was brilliant. I don't think we could have done any better."

"If you say so. You're the expert with that thing." The model pointed at the large camera Molly cradled in her hands, the screen displaying the digital shots from the day of working with him.

Molly loved her job as a professional photographer. Her friends were insanely jealous. What woman wouldn't be? She spent her days in her studio behind the lens of her trusty camera, capturing sexy images of some of the most gorgeous men from all over the world. Either she was paid to travel to them or they flew to Seattle to have her work her magic. Authors in the romance industry adored her photos. Her attention to detail had won her awards over the years, but what she loved the most was bringing the characters from books alive. Sure, it didn't hurt to look at well-defined muscles and sculpted abs that begged to be touched and to know what was hidden beneath the scrap of cloth that usually covered these men, but that wasn't how the business worked. Her friends would argue it was just because Molly didn't throw herself at these scantily clad men that she was missing out on these valuable opportunities.

If they only knew how nervous most of these men were, their fragile egos stripped down for her. It took Molly the first half of the shoot to calm them, easing them out of their shells, getting them just to loosen up enough for the right shot. It was more like babysitting rather than staring at a buffet, despite what her best friends thought. Not all the models lacked self-confidence, however. There were some who would stroll in, look directly into the camera and own it. But, for the most part, a lot of the guys were unsure and needed coaxing. Molly often felt more like a counselor than the world-famous photographer that she was.

Today, the Seattle sun was shielded behind soft, white clouds, filtering its rays into her studio that overlooked the Puget Sound. Her tall, glass windows provided the most stunning views of the shimmering water and the bustling city. Molly had worked hard for this view. It hadn't come easy or cheap — or without her busting her ass to make her name known in the photography industry. She had the scars — mostly emotional, but scars, nonetheless — to prove the struggles she'd endured, climbing to the top. Now she was one of the most sought-after photographers. Models from all over the globe wanted her to shoot them. *New York Times* and *USA Today* bestselling authors and publishers almost begged for her to shoot their covers. They wanted the best and…well, Molly was. Her skills proved that she had something special and everyone knew it.

Not bothering to sit down at her desk — bending over, instead — to focus on the images she was uploading to her laptop to edit, she almost forgot to say goodbye to the model she had just worked with. It wasn't until he was standing close to her, now fully dressed, that she realized he was still in her studio. Having him near her like that shifted the atmosphere in the room. His dominating presence was invading her space, creating nervous waves in her stomach. She inhaled his expensive aftershave, looked up from her screen and smiled.

Molly managed to say, "Great shoot today. Thanks again."

Remember to breathe, Molly.

"Yeah, it was amazing. You're amazing." The man paused, running his fingers along his day-old beard, the perfect blend of refined and unkempt sexy. His voice was silky and oozed well-practiced enticement. Molly watched him stand still, contemplating his next move. She was tempted to grab her camera and snap another shot. The light was hitting him just right and his pose was thoughtful and natural. This man was gorgeous.

He turned his mesmerizing gaze toward her and asked, "Do you want to grab a drink?"

Molly swallowed. It wasn't the first time she had been asked out by a model after a shoot. Sometimes it was the result of having bonded over their frail vulnerabilities. Sometimes they figured she was as good a lay as any while they were in town — another stamp in their romantic passport, so to speak. Molly wasn't so sure about this one. He wasn't overly emotional or guarded about his body, nor did he seem to really desire her. *So, what is he after?* She watched him scan the large studio. There was her answer. This type of square footage didn't come cheap and he knew that.

"You know, maybe another time. I'm really excited to get this edited." Molly pointed at her sleek silver laptop, delivering a fake smile in hopes it would put him off.

He nodded and thanked her again as he saw himself out. *The nerve.* Molly rolled her eyes and released the air she had been holding in her lungs. While she was in mid sigh, her cell phone chirped.

"Hello," she answered, a little more gruffly than she'd intended.

"Wow, so what's with the 'tude, lady? Bad day?"

It was one of her best friends, Tiffany.

"Just got done working with a model."

"Well, then why do you sound all cranky? Was he awful? So good-looking that you couldn't handle it?" Tiffany teased, causing Molly to laugh and her mood to lighten.

"You know the type. He wanted to go out for drinks—"

Tiffany cut her off quickly. "And you said, yes, right? Because if you didn't, you honestly need to have your head examined."

"I'd have to say he was more interested in my real estate than me." Molly frowned.

"Like real estate, as in the prime location between your legs? You know, it's all about location, location, location, baby."

"I wish." Molly huffed in frustration. "No, more like the prime location of my studio."

"That sucks."

"Tell me about it. He was gorgeous and he smelled divine. He was totally your type—tall, dark and devilishly handsome."

She heard Tiffany's disappointment through the phone. "Really? Oh, I just don't know how you do it, Molly. I have to give it to you. I would simply come undone working with those gorgeous men and not taking advantage of them every chance I got."

Tiffany always acted like she was some aggressive sex kitten, but they knew the truth. She was actually quite timid, which was a huge reason why she was single. All three of them were single and not dating anyone special. It didn't usually work that they were unattached all at the same time, but they were now. Their other best friend, Mackenzie, was the mother hen of the group. Well, more like the bossy one—completely overbearing, but with an absolute heart of gold. She, too, teased Molly about her line of work, but Mackenzie loved being a teacher, as it helped fill her maternal void. They had biological clocks that had gone haywire over the last couple of years, but everyone had warned them as they entered the dirty thirties that baby fever would hit soon after, and it had for Tiffany and Mackenzie. Every time they passed a stroller, neither could resist the temptation of peering in to catch a glimpse of some infant swaddled in fuzzy pink or blue blankets. Molly? She had her moments. They were brief and passed quickly when she heard the wail of a newborn or the shrill sound of a tantrum from a toddler. That didn't tempt her to want to rent out her womb for nine months.

She looked at her spotless, chic studio. Her smile went deep into her soul, masking the want for a baby. Her space sparkled and gleamed with the afternoon

Seattle sunlight, illuminating sleek lines and utterly contemporary taste.

If she were being completely honest with herself, yes, she did indeed want a child, eventually. But Molly also realized she was missing a very important part of the equation—a man. She didn't want just a sperm donor, though she and her friends had discussed that over far too much wine and Chinese food one night, considering it as a last resort. That had left them laughing for hours. No, Molly wanted the real deal. They all did. They wanted a man—a sexy, successful and simply wonderful man. *Is that really asking for too much?*

Being single, especially in Seattle, came with its challenges. Molly thought the enormous Emerald City should be plentiful with eligible bachelors, but Molly assumed that, as with any place, being single was a mixture of bad luck and an overly detailed list of the personality traits she wanted in a boyfriend. As time passed, her list had grown a lot shorter. She'd crossed off quite a few of her must-haves and was looking to review her available options. Now she figured it was mainly the bad luck that was keeping her single. Molly had been unattached the longest out of her friends, who were more like her sisters. Tiffany had been on a dating spree recently, but Mackenzie and Molly had known that none of the guys were Mr. Right for their friend. Mackenzie also had a pretty extensive list of requirements for her ideal mate, and she was even more stubborn than Molly when it came to sacrificing the qualities she was willing to live with, so she dated very little.

"Well, since you didn't want drinks with that sexy model, how about meeting up with us?" Tiffany asked.

Molly smiled. Yes, a drink with her best pals she could do. "That sounds lovely, actually." She could use some cheering up. The best cure for her bruised ego was some quality time with her besties.

"Great. I'll pick up Mac and we'll swing by the studio and grab ya. Sound good?"

"Perfect. I have some edits I want to go through, so just buzz when you guys get here."

Molly said goodbye and hung up. She stared at the monitor in front of her, the images of the model in various poses looking back her.

* * * *

Lost in her work tweaking the images with an array of filters, Molly was so engrossed that she almost didn't hear the loud buzzing that echoed off the large studio walls. She got up quickly from her desk and jogged to the massive double doors to let her friends in.

"Jeesh, what were you doing? I have been ringing that dang buzzer for, like, *forever*," Tiffany complained as she slipped past Molly into the studio. Mackenzie frowned and hugged Molly.

"We've only been standing outside the door for a minute," Mackenzie assured her.

Tiffany walked over to one of the large windows facing the Puget Sound. The sun was setting, casting a tangerine hue over the haze of the city. "God, do you ever get tired of this magnificent view?"

Molly shook her head as she joined her, staring out at the glittery lights in the surrounding buildings that seemed to stretch up toward the sky. "Nope."

"Yeah, I didn't think so." Tiffany laughed as she faced Molly. Her dark hair was loose on her thin shoulders. Tiffany's large eyes were a soulful brown and she had the best cheekbones. Tiffany was gorgeous in a unique and completely unexpected way. Molly's brain acted as a camera, capturing shots of her friend's delicate features as the sunset cast a shadowy light on her face. Tiffany sensed what Molly was doing and threw her a pouty look.

Mackenzie stood next them. The willowy blonde towered over Molly, making her feel short and stubby. Mackenzie had the figure of a teenager, slim and athletic. Her sun-kissed hair was cut in a sleek bob, framing the sharp angles of her face. She was another beautiful woman. Molly couldn't help but snap mental pictures of Mackenzie, too. She searched Molly curiously with soft mocha eyes. They all had brown eyes in varied shades of the common color, but resembling their different tastes in coffee. Tiffany had the espresso, dark and bold. Mackenzie was more of an iced mocha with an extra shot. Molly's resembled the instant crap coffee variety that no one really liked. Molly hated her eyes. They were plain. Her friends had tried to convince her otherwise, but they both had spectacular depth and richness in theirs. Molly thought hers looked like a muddy puddle after a typical downpour in Seattle — watery, with a sad, muted tone. Nothing special.

"What's going on with you?" Mackenzie reached for Molly, concern swimming in her eyes and worry creasing her otherwise wrinkle-free face, the result of fabulous genetics.

Molly sighed. *Is there anything going on with me?* They usually accused her of being moody, but she was an artist. *Isn't that sort of the job description? Acting the part of the tortured soul?* They sure never let her play that role for very long.

Tiffany stared at her hard and added, "Yeah, you seemed cranky on the phone. So what's up?"

"I don't know. I mean..." Molly really couldn't explain how she felt. She had a blessed life. Granted, she had worked for it, but, regardless, she knew she was lucky. Happy? Well, that was a different ball of wax.

"Drinks. That's what we need." Tiffany perked up, her hand on her hip, taking a sassy stance. She reached for the oversized purse that was slung over her shoulder. A Louis Vuitton knock-off, but it looked as real as they came. It was their little secret. Tiffany dug around and retrieved a bottle of Prosecco, holding it up for them to all gaze at her prize.

"You were carrying that in there? Oh dear. Seriously, Tiffany," Mackenzie scolded.

Tiffany winked and answered with a wicked grin.

"I, for one, am thrilled our friend is lugging around a bottle. You never know when you may need it." Molly grinned happily at Tiffany. "It does make you look a little like a wino, but you're my favorite drunk."

"No, you have me mistaken. I'm fun, not a drunk." Tiffany defended as she moved toward a long table that was against the wall opposite the windows. "Besides, at least I bring the good stuff."

"I have an idea. Let's stay in. Want to order some food?" Mackenzie suggested.

"Yes, let's do that. Molly's got one of the best views in all of Seattle. Let's just hang out here," Tiffany replied while she peeled the label away to get to the cork.

"Chinese?" Mackenzie whipped out her cell phone and started to dial their favorite takeout.

"Hell, yes," Molly and Tiffany answered in unison.

These were her girls. It didn't matter if they stayed in or went out on the town. As long as they were together, they were guaranteed to have fun.

Shortly, they were seated around a large glass table that Molly normally used to lay out prints from shoots. They dined on their fill of chow mein, pork fried rice and more Kung Pao shrimp than any woman should ever eat. White cartons, soy sauce packets and chopsticks were littered around them as they chatted about everything—mostly about the lack of sex or romance in their lives. Biting into a crispy fortune cookie—her favorite—Molly surveyed her beautiful friends. She couldn't understand why any of them were single. Tiffany was gorgeous, sweet and sassy… What was there not to love about her? Mackenzie was stunning, witty and full of love… She had so much to offer. Then there was her. She knew she might not be the sexiest thing on the planet, but she was successful, caring and everyone constantly complimented her on how pleasant she was, even telling her she was sort of hot, especially when she wore her glasses. *So how is it that I haven't landed the perfect guy yet?* Cracking open another cookie, she read the thin slip of white paper. Bold red font stared back at her, reading, *'There is nothing truer than the company of friends.' How right is that fortune?*

More wine flowed and, to keep the mood light, Molly blasted the radio. She and her two best friends danced barefoot in the empty studio, singing their hearts out and putting on a drunken performance that could rival the best pop star's. Tiffany swayed her hips to the song. Mackenzie took a while to loosen up, but then started to bop to the beat. Molly busted out some goofy moves that reminded her of middle school dances, her favorite being the 'running man'. They laughed hard, clutching their sides when Tiffany took a spill on the slippery wood floor. In their feeble attempt at helping her up, they all ended up on the floor somehow, spread-eagled, staring up at the vaulted ceilings. Music continued to play, filling the wide and open space, but the mood had shifted. That was when the laughter died and the deep realness of their friendship was exposed.

"I love you, guys," Tiffany whispered, her dark tresses fanned out against the honey-colored bamboo floor.

"Me too," Mackenzie added softly.

Molly tried to swallow the lump that was forming in her throat, feeling tears starting to surface. "I love you both. Thank you for tonight."

They all stayed on the floor, listening to several more songs before Tiffany said, "God, this floor is killing my back. I feel old."

Mackenzie and Molly both laughed.

"And for the record, we *are* old," Mackenzie replied.

"I wanted to say the same thing, but figured I would tough it out until one of you cracked." Molly started to get up.

Mackenzie and Tiffany groaned as they eased themselves off the floor. Working quietly as a team, they cleaned up the remnants of their dinner.

"I would totally live here, Molly," Mackenzie commented as she tossed several cartons into a waste basket.

Tiffany was wiping up some sticky Kung Pao sauce. "Seriously. This studio is so fabulous. You need to let me move in here."

"I do love this place." Molly looked around at her kingdom. An enormous clear-glass shelf that held her many awards was against one of the walls. Expensive frames that contained some of her best work were hung precisely in the perfect locations. Various shades, light fixtures and tons of other photography gear were set up in one corner. The room celebrated her. It showcased all of her efforts but, more importantly, it proudly displayed her passion for this form of art.

After every last morsel was cleaned and the work space was back to being immaculate, they made their way back to the window. The sun had long since disappeared, leaving the city lights to twinkle silently as the three of them stared out at the busy traffic below.

"Thank you again, guys. I really needed this tonight."

Mackenzie and Tiffany linked their arms through hers as she stood in the middle.

She would be lost without them. They knew all her secrets and her fears. They had supported her during her moments of crippling self-doubt. They'd loved her when she was at her worst. They'd dried her tears when critics had given her harsh reviews. They were her cheerleaders. They'd pushed her to continue to pursue her dream so many times when she'd just wanted to give up. They had been the first to celebrate when she finally did become successful and had told her countless times how much she deserved it.

These women were more than just friends. They were her tribe, her sisters. They were Molly's everything.

Home of Erotic Romance

Sign up for our newsletter and find out about all our romance book releases, eBook sales and promotions, sneak peeks and FREE romance books!

About the Author

C.J. Burright is a native Oregonian and refuses to leave. A member of Romance Writers of America and the Fantasy, Futuristic & Paranormal special interest chapter, while she has worked for years in a law office, she chooses to avoid writing legal thrillers (for now) and instead invades the world of paranormal romance, fantasy, and contemporary romance. C.J. also has her 4th Dan Black Belt in Tae Kwon Do and believes a story isn't complete without at least one fight scene. Her meager spare time is spent working out, refueling with mochas, gardening, gorging on Assassin's Creed, and rooting on the Seattle Mariners…always with music. She shares life with her husband, daughter, and a devoted cat herd.

C.J. loves to hear from readers. You can find her contact information, website details and author profile page at https://www.totallybound.com